TELL ME THE TRUTH ABOUT LOVE

Also by Erik Tarloff

NOVELS

Face-Time
The Man Who Wrote the Book
All Our Yesterdays
The Woman in Black

PLAYS

Something to Hide
Another Weekend in the Country
Cedars

TELL ME THE TRUTH ABOUT LOVE

A NOVEL BY

ERIK TARLOFF

RARE BIRD
LOS ANGELES, CALIF.

THIS IS A GENUINE RARE BIRD BOOK

Rare Bird Books
6044 North Figueroa Street
Los Angeles, CA 90042
rarebirdbooks.com

For more information, address:
Rare Bird Books Subsidiary Rights Department
6044 North Figueroa Street
Los Angeles, CA 90042

Set in Minion
Printed in the United States

FIRST HARDCOVER EDITION ISBN-13: 9781644283110

10 9 8 7 6 5 4 3 2 1

Library of Congress Cataloging-in-Publication Data available upon request

For Treva Silverman
Esteemed colleague, great friend, ideal reader

Will it come like a change in the weather?
Will its greeting be courteous or rough?
Will it alter my life altogether?
O tell me the truth about love.

—W. H. Auden

PART ONE

1

THE LYFT HAD ALMOST reached the Four Seasons when Toby's cell phone rang.

"Toby dear...I'm running late." It was Magda. No mistaking that dusky contralto. "I'm stuck here. The bastards are making me reedit a segment for eleven o'clock."

"How bad?" Toby asked.

"Not terrible. I'll need an extra half-hour."

A quick calculation. "Listen, I can't afford to be late tonight. I have to be ready to pounce."

"Of course. Go in without me. I'll be there as quick as I can."

"You're a stand-up guy, Magda."

She laughed at that. And then, with an exaggerated, humorous whine, "But *why* did I say yes to this? It's going to be ghastly, isn't it?"

"Of course. But it's an opportunity to see me abasing myself. That's a plus, surely."

"Ah yes, fair point. I do find the spectacle arousing."

"I'm glad there's something."

"That would be it."

"Plus, there'll be a herd of gazillionaires in attendance."

"Not a draw in itself. Although one of them *is* rather attractive. Bradley Solomon. The guest of honor. He's quite sexy."

"You fancy Bradley Solomon?"

"'Fancy' may be too strong. He does have a certain something, though."

"So you know him?"

"I've met him."

"He's old enough to be your father."

"Mm, part of his appeal. I always fancied my father. Spent hours on the couch talking about it."

"You mustn't crowd him, now. Leave me room. I'm the one doing the hustling tonight."

"I won't make my move till you have a promissory note in your pocket."

"And you won't humiliate me?"

"Dear boy. Absolutely not. This is a night where you humiliate *yourself*. All I ask for is an unimpeded view."

~

ONCE INSIDE THE HOTEL, Toby took an escalator down to banquet level and approached a table outside the designated banquet room. It was presided over by a couple of elegantly dressed young women, the sort of well-bred volunteers found at such affairs.

"Toby Lindeman," he announced.

One of the women ran her finger down a list. "Could that be *Tobias* Lindeman?"

"I imagine so."

She handed him a name tag, told him the number of his table, and welcomed him to the dinner. Pinning the tag to his lapel, he pushed through double doors into the ballroom. The room was large and tastefully decorated, with lavender-and-gray carpeting and purple drapery on the tables. It was already quite crowded, although nobody was seated yet; things were still at the pointless milling-about stage. Toby snatched a glass of white wine from a passing waiter and scanned the room for Bradley Solomon, the only reason he was here. Solomon hadn't exactly *promised* a big contribution, but he'd definitely hinted he was amenable to the idea. It was Toby's job to seal the deal.

No sign of him, just lots of people considerably older than Toby, all looking eminently respectable, eminently prosperous. In any city besides San Francisco one would assume them to be WASP Republicans. Here most of them were probably Democrats, likely either Jewish or Italian, but in some fundamental way the characterization remained just:

They occupied a comparable social stratum and performed a comparable role. They were the people who ran things.

At one side of the room was a head table on a dais, which was ominous, presaging speechifying after the meal. On the wall behind the head table was a banner welcoming guests to the annual dinner of the Save the Redwoods Association. Toby had forgotten the nature of the event till he saw the banner. It was irrelevant to his mission. Still, it was nice to know it was for a reasonable cause.

Since there was no one to talk to, and because he felt conspicuously solitary, he decided to head to his assigned table and wait for Magda. Circling the room, he eventually located his place—which, given its remote position, was obviously a charity banquet Siberia—and as he approached it, stepping carefully among tables to avoid dislodging silverware and crockery, he heard a woman's voice say, "Looking for the nearest exit?"

Was she addressing him? He stopped and turned. Facing him a few feet away was a woman several years younger than he, probably on the enviable side of forty. He took her in quickly and without being crass about it; thirty years of practice had trained him to camouflage the vulgarity of overt sexual assessment even if the assessment itself was habitual and automatic. She was petite, probably five foot four or so, slightly built, and not exactly pretty, but with a pleasant, attractively open face and a merry, intelligent smile. Her black dress was unpretentious and demure, flattering her trim figure. Chestnut hair—possibly colored—done simply, back and down. Little makeup beyond lipstick.

"Me?" His eyes met hers; hers were big and brown and sparkling, and seemed bottomless. He had to force himself not to look away. They made him feel transparent.

"Uh-huh," she said. "You have a sort of fish-out-of-water aura, if you don't mind my saying so."

"Despite my tux?" A Hardy Amies shawl-collared number, beyond his budget but, given his profession, a defensible investment.

She waved his question away. "An elegant fish out of water. A tropical fish out of water. So what's the deal? Are you some sort of tree-hugger? You have a thing for redwoods?"

"Nah. I mean, I don't have anything against them. I wish them nothing but the best, but I can't say they occupy a prominent position in my consciousness."

She smiled. "So you're not a donor?"

"Bull's-eye."

"No? Well, let's see…no, don't tell me, I'll get this. Are you, like, a professional escort? Hired to squire a biddy? With God knows what's expected of you at the end of the evening?"

"It's that obvious? Damn."

For one startled moment, she looked abashed. Her eyes widened, her hand went to her mouth. Then she lowered it, revealing a mischievous frown. "Wait. You're shitting me, right?"

"Well…yes. But I'm flattered you thought it was possible."

She smiled. "God, you actually had me going for a sec. I was about to start apologizing. Groveling. While pretending to be blasé."

"Sorry to have missed that."

"Although I liked the idea too. You don't run into many male hustlers at these events. Except metaphorically." She moved in close to squint myopically at his name tag, taking his silk-lined lapel between her fingers. "Tobias Lindeman. Should I have heard of you?"

"Nope."

"Are you the donut guy?"

"That's Entenmann."

"Oh right." She released his lapel and extended her hand. "Anyway. My name's Amy Baldwin. Pleasure to meet you, Tobias."

He shook her hand. "People call me Toby." And then, "How come you're not wearing a name tag?"

"I don't like poking holes in my dress. Are you here with a date?"

"Yes. Well, that is, I'm meeting someone."

If she had a reaction to that, she didn't show it. "Female?"

"Uh-huh."

"Can't be sure in this day and age."

"Absolutely."

"But it isn't a business transaction? At least as the term is commonly understood?"

"Right."

"So if you're not a donor, not a gigolo, and don't have the baked goods concession—"

"What *am* I doing here? Is that your question? I'm working. I'm a fundraiser. Not for myself, to be clear. And not for redwoods, either. For a worthy cultural entity, let's call it. I'm cadging cash. Panning for gold."

"Any stream in particular?"

"The mighty Mississippi." She looked puzzled, so he explained, "Tonight's guest of honor. The Solomon guy."

There was a brief pause. Then she said, "It's a worthy cause?"

"Does it matter? The causes are usually worthy. But these pirates… what they do with their money is their business, they can squander it on Milk Duds if they like. But they're all such assholes, that's what gets you after a while. I've never met one who didn't make you bleed copiously for whatever you get. And from what I've heard, Solomon's among the worst."

"Is that what you've heard?"

"That's his rep. I'll find out first-hand soon enough. But what brings *you* here? Are huge conifers a passion? Are you a donor yourself? Or maybe someone's date?"

"Those aren't mutually exclusive. I *am* a donor, as it happens."

"That's impressive."

"Depends on the size of the donation, doesn't it?"

"I thought size doesn't matter."

"That's one theory," she said.

"I've been misled?"

"You're the escort. You tell me."

Out of the corner of his eye, he suddenly noticed Magda across the room, waving at him. And was surprised to feel disappointed. He wasn't quite ready to disengage.

"Listen," he said, "this has been great, Amy, but—"

"Let me guess. You've spotted your biddy. Or she's spotted you."

"Exactly. I mean, not the biddy part, can't let that pass without protest—"

"Whatever. Go do your duty. Maybe we'll have a chance to talk later."

"I'd enjoy that."

"Yes." She elongated the final consonant, which made her sound oddly ruminative.

~

MAGDA WAS THE FIRST woman Toby had slept with when his marriage ended. They actually began before the split was official but after Jessie let him know she was in love with someone else. There was a brief interval when he was ostensibly trying to salvage things, although deep down he doubted it was possible, or even desirable. Everything was confused during that awful time. He was wounded, fragile, steeped in misery and self-doubt. He met Magda at a gallery opening—having gone only because his friend Jonas, a former lover of the artist, insisted—and after an hour of brittle banter in front of the ugly, angry paintings— many of them distorted, impressively endowed nude male bodies— and too many plastic cups of bad white wine, she'd taken him back to her place. He remained incredulous throughout the entire experience. Years previously, he had relinquished any hopes of ever enjoying such an adventure again. And such an adventure! This wasn't a garden-variety hookup. Magda was beautiful and stylish; she was accomplished; she was the Sarah Lawrence–educated, socially polished daughter of a Hungarian diplomat, who had served for years in London before being assigned the San Francisco consulate. She retained an odd sort of Mittel-European accent, Magyar with a dash of British, that lent her an almost Cold War aura, a Natasha Fatale-like glamor. And she was currently the arts editor on KQED, the local PBS affiliate. She was a figure on the scene, a personage.

After he awoke the next morning, he lay immobile beside her sleeping form for several minutes, barely daring to breathe, his incredulity unassuaged, feeling needlessly guilty (he knew Jessica had spent the night with her lover), and anxiously ignorant of the proper etiquette: Was he supposed to shake Magda awake and bid her a cheery good morning? Pad into the kitchen and make coffee for them both? Discreetly tiptoe out of her apartment, out of her life, and forget the whole thing had ever happened? It had been more than a decade since he'd slept with any woman other than Jessie; for whatever reason—probably only to occupy the moral high ground—

he'd consistently resisted temptation, of which he'd had his share. So he was out of practice; he no longer knew the rules. Besides, it seemed likely that as soon as Magda awoke, she would turn over, take one horrified look at him, curse her weakness, and swear off white wine for the rest of her life.

But that isn't what happened. After a few interminable minutes, she stirred, muttered something unintelligible, rolled over toward him, nuzzled against his neck, and unceremoniously grabbed his cock. In a matter of seconds, they were at it again.

As his friend Jonas would say, go figure.

For a few weeks, he believed he must be in love. His existence had been so joyless for so long, and she was the nicest thing to have happened to him in years. She was gorgeous, she led a glamorous life, and she even liked fucking him. What more could a fellow ask? But when, after a month or so, he suggested they consider living together, she burst out laughing. "Darling, that's very sweet. But so, so stupid."

He was willing to be instructed. "It is? How come?"

"Because that's not what this is about." When he started to protest, she continued insistently, "Look, we enjoy each other's company, and the horizontal part is fabulous. Why complicate things?"

"So we're...*fuck buddies*?"

"You say that like it's a negative. Listen, dear boy, your life's just been turned inside out, and you don't have a clue what you're worth on the open market, and you can't believe something nice has happened. Well, this *is* nice, but you're in no shape for love, and frankly, I doubt even in the best of times you're wired for it. You don't seem to realize it yet, but you're actually a very cool customer. Detached. Smooth as glass, nothing to hold onto. So let's just have fun, okay? Avowals could ruin everything."

At the time he'd thought she was being sophisticated and European in the worst senses of both words, but now he realized she'd been wise. He'd been desperate for a safe haven because his life had slipped its moorings, but she understood how lost he was, and at the same time how unready for anything beyond grief and personal reassessment. And unruly sex. She helped him through it all, but she also refused to consider herself his girlfriend. And in the five busy years since, he was never again tempted to get serious, not with her and not with any of the many other women he dated.

And now he and Magda were pals more than anything, and convenient companions for events where the deportment of one's date mattered. They were pals, even if at times a late night extended into the following morning. Their lovemaking, when it occurred, was reliably satisfactory but no longer passionate, as friendly and almost as casual as a peck on the cheek. He didn't mind hearing about her troubles with other men when she chose to confide, and he often turned to her for advice about the women he was dating, along with the problems he might be having with his daughter or ex-wife. She was a useful second opinion, yin to his friend Jonas's yang.

And those youthful years she'd spent as the daughter of a diplomat stationed in a couple of prestigious posts made her a perfect date on evenings like this one. Sitting at this dreadful table with predictably uninteresting strangers, she was able to produce an effortless flow of appropriate questions and alert responses that gave every appearance of genuine engagement. And just as importantly, she occasionally met Toby's eye and raised her own eyes skyward to ensure he understood she too considered the experience an ordeal, she wasn't *really* interested in the vacuous palaver.

"We're stuck for the speeches, aren't we?" he whispered to her during a lull in the astonishing conversation that had just occurred, about the discomforts of catheterization. Toby hadn't had much to contribute but appeared to be unique at their table in that regard. Even Magda produced a touching reminiscence.

Her look of amused disapproval served to confirm what he already knew. "Of course we are. You can't be surprised. You've been to a million of these things."

He grimaced. "I thought we'd be at Solomon's table, I'd be able to chat with him about the weather and exchange macho bullshit about the NCAA, and then, when the moment was right, casually slip in how nice it'd be if he forked up five million bucks. And then out the fucking door."

She patted his hand sympathetically. "Hang in there," she said. "Try not to nod off."

The speeches started after the ice cream was served but before it was fully consumed. Somebody introduced some Save the Redwoods honcho, the honcho reported how much money the dinner had raised—lots of applause—and then he introduced some expert who assessed the progress being made with regard to redwood preservation, after which she introduced Bradley Solomon as the Association's Person of the Year.

Solomon rose and sauntered over to the rostrum. Shorter than average—five-seven or eight, was Toby's estimate—and burly, with broad shoulders and a barrel chest. Probably about sixty, although someone so vigorous might be ten years older without looking it. Silver hair and a rich tan—he'd probably come to this dinner straight from the last good skiing of the season in Vail or Jackson Hole or one of those places the filthy rich went—and a vivid presence that commanded attention. With a voice to match, deep and resonant. Toby guessed he'd had coaching. That kind of diaphragmatic sound production rarely happens by itself.

He talked briefly about the humbling beauty of redwoods, about how being among them gave him a sense of peace, about communing with them during his visits to Bohemian Grove. It was an effective performance. He knew not to drone on too long, he was a casual master of the space he occupied, and he occupied more space than his size warranted.

"He's pretty good," Toby whispered to Magda. "Better than I expected."

"Your expectations were unrealistically low."

She was right. For some reason he'd never bothered to examine closely, it was easier to hustle people when he didn't feel much respect for them. Respect was a distraction. Which was odd, since he wasn't selling aluminum siding or some dubious cryptocurrency; he was straightforwardly soliciting support for a worthy, even noble, enterprise. Nevertheless, without being fully conscious of the process, he usually tried to work up some resentment, or even scorn, before he went into his spiel. It fueled his zeal, made him more persuasive.

When Solomon finished speaking, and the audience rose for the obligatory standing ovation, Toby moved his head close to Magda's and whispered, "Tora tora tora."

"You *are* going to abase yourself, right? You did promise."

"You have my word."

"If you let me down, you're going to have to fuck me later. So the evening won't be a total loss."

"You drive a hard bargain, I'll say that."

Toby offered Magda his hand and the two of them started threading their way among the tightly packed tables in the direction of the dais. Toby knew they had to be quick.

They weren't quick enough. An elderly couple got there ahead of them. Toby and Magda waited while the couple shook Solomon's hand and exchanged a few words with him. It seemed to Toby that Solomon endured these well-wishers with minimal grace; he wasn't overtly rude, but he responded to their questions and observations in a flat tone that closed off conversational avenues rather than encouraging further discussion. It didn't do him much good; the well-wishers were intent on prattling on for a while, and nothing short of physical intervention was going to stop them.

While waiting, and conscious of the number of people who were assembling behind him and Magda, Toby was surprised to notice the woman with whom he'd spoken earlier—what was her name? Amy something?—approaching Solomon from the dais itself, slipping up behind him and putting a hand on his shoulder. In response to her touch, Solomon glanced up, saw her, and then turned away from the couple who were talking to him in order to pull her down and give her a quick hug and a buss on the cheek. Shit. She should have warned him before he'd put his foot in it. How badly had he trashed the guy when they'd been talking?

Solomon patted the woman's arm, turned back to the couple, said something Toby couldn't hear—evidently *not* an introduction to Amy what's-her-name—and after another quick set of handshakes, they walked away. The couple looked crestfallen, as if they'd been treated with less respect than they'd anticipated and then been peremptorily dismissed.

Troubling. But the prospective encounter had been prearranged between Solomon and Toby's boss, Doris Raskov, so he wasn't too worried. Still, he wished this Amy person wasn't a witness; he wasn't sure why, but he didn't want her observing him in a precative role.

He approached the table, guiding Magda along with him. "Mr. Solomon?" It was awkward to be on the other side of a raised table, an inferior position physically as well as socially. This was the way Mussolini had arranged his office, with his desk on an elevated platform. Not the most reassuring of precedents.

Solomon looked down at him and all too visibly sighed. "Yes?"

At the same time, Amy, standing behind the seated Solomon, vouchsafed Toby a playful smile of recognition. "Well, hi there," she said. "Long time no see."

"Yes, hi," said Toby.

Solomon looked at Amy and back at Toby. "You know each other?"

She said, "We met tonight."

"Chatted briefly before dinner," Toby added. Then he said, "Mr. Solomon, my name's Toby Lindeman." He extended his hand across the table. "And this is—"

"Hello, Magda," Solomon interrupted. "Good to see you."

"Hi, Brad," said Magda.

Brad? That sounded a tad familiar to Toby. But Magda usually calibrated these nuances nicely. She'd spent her whole life at it. Solomon looked directly at Toby again, and then—but only after a rather ostentatious show of reluctance—reached across the table and took the hand Toby was proffering. "How do you do."

"I believe Doris Raskov mentioned I'd be here tonight," Toby said. Doris and her husband were social friends of Solomon and his wife.

"No, I don't believe so," Solomon answered, frowning.

At this extremely unwelcome and unexpected—not to say bewildering—turn of events, Amy suddenly cut in with, "Listen, I should run. Brad, I just wanted to tell you your speech was excellent. Toby, delighted to have met you. Good luck with all your endeavors." And with that little barb, and after nodding pleasantly to Magda, she turned and strode off the dais.

Toby watched her go, then turned back to Solomon. "I'm sorry?" was all he could come up with. "You were saying—?"

"I was saying, I don't know what you're talking about."

19

"Toby Lindeman?"

"Yes, I caught your name."

"About the opera?" Toby prompted. He couldn't believe what he was hearing. In over a decade of fundraising, during which there had been plenty of mishaps, he'd never encountered *this* problem before. It was why you prepared the ground, to avoid such embarrassments.

"What about it?"

"She told me she'd approached you about, about…perhaps helping us."

"Helping you?"

"With a contribution."

"To the opera?" Solomon still looked blank.

"To fund a new piece. To celebrate the city. You know, after all we've—"

"Now see here," Solomon interrupted sharply, "this is obviously the wrong time for this. Jesus Christ." He gestured in a way that seemed to encompass the entire room, as if the setting by itself explained his mounting indignation. "Call my office if you want an appointment. Don't just *spring* something on me. That's chickenshit stuff." And then he looked past Toby, toward whoever was standing behind him in the press of people. The interview was over.

Toby glanced at Magda as they stepped away. She raised her eyebrows but waited until they were out of earshot before saying, "I guess you don't have to fuck me after all."

~

BUT HE DID ANYWAY. When the cab reached her place, after they'd ridden in pained silence for several minutes, she invited him up for a drink, and maybe it was the promise of hard liquor, or maybe it was just an urge to vent, but he accepted readily. Both of them knew that if he entered her apartment at this hour it was unlikely he'd schlep home before morning. As Rubicon crossings go, this wasn't especially momentous. It happened several times a year.

"What an asshole," Toby said, as, without asking, she handed him a snifter of cognac. His jacket was folded over the back of a chair, his collar open, his bow tie hanging loose around his neck. He'd collapsed onto one of her sofas, staring exhaustedly at the ceiling. "What a thoroughgoing irredeemable asshole." He leaned forward to take the glass from her and brought it to his lips. Ahh. The way it burned down his esophagus was pure balm.

"Any chance there was a genuine mix-up?" Magda asked.

"Nah. Doris told me this morning she'd talked to him. She isn't a flake."

"He forgot?"

"Did you see the look in his eye? Pure malice."

"Why would he bother?"

Toby shrugged. "For your benefit? That other woman's? Because he can? What difference does it make? He was a total prick."

"I guess that's a perk when you're Brad Solomon."

"But why would you want such a perk? Where's the pleasure in it?" He shook his head disgustedly.

"Are you going to call his office? Will you pursue this?"

"I'm such a slut," he sighed, granting her a twisted smile. "I'll talk to Doris first, of course, but…hell, they always make you crawl one way or another. If we get the money, it's worth it. Not to me, I'd be happy to let him burn in hell and his money along with him. But to the company."

"You have to regard your pride as expendable. You're a foot soldier in the culture wars."

"Veritable cannon fodder."

"It was a nice novelty, though, seeing you squirm. You're not normally a squirmer."

"Glad you enjoyed it."

After a few seconds, without any overt transition, she said, "Bring your brandy to the bedroom."

Once they were in bed, as he began handling her body, tracing its familiar contours, and she began responding in familiar ways, he whispered, "I just wish you'd say you agree with me." It had been bothering him since they'd left the banquet.

"I'll say whatever you want," she answered. "You have me at your mercy."

"I'm serious," he said. Not letting this seriousness interfere with what he was doing.

"So am I. You've always had great hands, Toby."

He wasn't conscious of doing so, but he must have made some sound of annoyance, some sort of grunt, because she took hold of his hand, stopping him. And then she put one of her hands against his shoulder and pushed him back, kept pushing until he was supine, and then began kissing her way down his chest, murmuring as she did, "He was a bastard, okay? No two ways about it. It was as plain as...as *this*." She had reached his abdomen, and now gave his cock a couple of playful laps, watching his involuntary responses closely, with smiling attention.

"But you think he's sexy," Toby pointed out.

"For God's sake, Toby...*while I'm giving you head*?"

"But do you? Still think he's sexy?"

"It doesn't mean I approve."

"So...what? Assholery adds to his allure?"

She looked up at him—he raised his head to meet her glance—and said, "In a sick sort of way. That's just evolution. Psychobiology. We girls are wired for it. It isn't a moral choice." She sucked him into her mouth and neither said anything for a few seconds. Then she slipped off him, still expertly working him with her hand, and said, "Look, part of me was offended, part of me thought it was kind of hot."

"But—"

"Just shut up." She slid up his body until they were eye-to-eye, kissed him, meanwhile firmly pushing his shoulders down with her open palms, and then drew her knees up so she was straddling him. A second later, he was lodged inside her. As he arched his hips up, hers began an intricate series of circling movements.

"You're sexy too," she said. "And you don't even throw your weight around."

"No weight to throw."

"You make a virtue of necessity."

"But it's galling...what's sexy about a strutting bully?"

"It's a display of power, isn't it?" She leaned over him, so her heavy breasts were against his chest. "Dominance behavior. Makes our little primate hearts go pit-a-pat."

"Your little primate hearts have caused me nothing but grief," he said. "Since the seventh grade."

"I'd say you're managing pretty well at the moment."

He shifted his hips slightly. There was an angle that, if he managed it just right, always seemed to do the trick for her.

"And besides," she said, "you're not so pure, you display your coxcomb too. Quite a nice one. Different from Brad's, but just because you hide your alpha light under a beta bushel doesn't mean...wait... hold on a sec." She adjusted her weight, ground down hard against him, once, twice, a third time, and then came with a heaving shudder. And then, without breaking their connection, she collapsed, burying her face in his neck.

He knew her well enough to remain still. She would signal when it was time to resume. After perhaps half a minute, she began to move again, rocking gently back and forth.

"Anyway," she whispered, as if there had been no interruption at all, "you chaps aren't immune to psychobiology either. When you see a girl you like, well, let's just say it's obvious to any objective observer. You go into your little song and dance."

"Is that what Solomon was doing? A little song and dance?"

"Well, he's probably a bastard even when the ladies aren't watching, but I'm sure Amy and I were a spur. A gallery to play to."

"The cheap seats."

She gave him a playful swat.

Toby said, "You called her 'Amy.' You know her?"

"To say hello to. I know *everybody*, Toby." She quickened her pace.

"What's her full name again?"

"Amy Baldwin."

"And who is she?"

"Owns some sort of internet business. Doing rather well, I understand."

"Yeah, but...who *is* she?"

"Oh. I see what you mean. I thought you knew. It's kind of an open secret. She's Solomon's girlfriend." And then, five seconds later, "Hey, what's the matter?"

Toby had lost his erection.

2

H E DIDN'T!" SAID JONAS, genuinely shocked. It was the next morning, and Toby and Jonas were having a quick breakfast before crossing the street to the Opera House, Jonas to a rehearsal, Toby to the administrative offices. "He pretended to have no idea who you were or what was going on?"

"That's about the size of it."

"You're sure Doris had prepped him?"

"Yep."

"Christ," said Jonas. And then, "Well, maybe I'm not one hundred percent surprised. Solomon's got a reputation. Supposed to be a son of a bitch."

"I've heard that too."

"An unregenerate cocksucker. And not the fun kind."

Toby smiled. Jonas being Jonas. "No, definitely not the fun kind."

For several years Jonas hadn't been much more than a friendly work acquaintance in Toby's mind, someone he nodded to in the halls and with whom he played the occasional game of racquetball or shared a post-show drink. They had enjoyed each other's company, but their worlds seemed too different for a really close relationship: Jonas gay—and if not at all swish, still aggressively, proudly out—and a violist in the pit orchestra; and Toby straight, and a "suit," the sort of bureaucrat traditionally deeply distrusted by the artistic side of the house. For a long time their conversation, even their banter, was guarded, careful, circumscribed by clear privacy lines neither would dream of transgressing.

It was only when Toby's marriage began to fall apart that Jonas proved to be a much better friend than mere politesse required.

Especially during that awful first month, when Toby first discovered Jessica's affair and had to move out of his house and didn't have a clue what had hit him, when many of his friends acted as if one night with him was all the charity they were required, or able, to extend. During that time Jonas had been a brick. "Come over and talk if you want, or look out the window and don't say a word. Or stare at the TV and drink until you pass out on the couch. No judgment. We've all been there, brother."

He had offered advice that felt useless at the time, but later, struck Toby as potentially helpful, as the cloud of despondency over Toby gradually began to lift and as he began to recognize it was actually a relief to be out of a marriage that brought far more pain than joy. "The truth about love is, it's just self-hypnosis. We do it to ourselves. The other person's incidental, like the corpse at a funeral, indispensable but ultimately irrelevant. And the proof is how you feel after you're finally over it. You can't remember—you can't *imagine*—what all the fuss was about. Nice person, cute trick, maybe even a great lay. But your soul mate? The one person on earth made for you? Not so much."

Toby wasn't entirely convinced, but Jonas had the receipts, he couldn't be dismissed out of hand.

It may have been a result of Toby's misery at the time, but he and Jonas developed a new mutual candor during those awful first months, a new closeness. It was an odd friendship the two slowly developed, but it turned into a very close friendship. Indeed, at a time when so many of Toby's relationships had fallen by the wayside, or were assessed strictly on the basis of utility or convenience, Jonas was someone he spent time with primarily because he really liked the guy.

And the friendship incidentally granted Toby entrée—honorary entrée—into a sexual Freemasonry from which he would otherwise have been excluded, a culture interesting in itself and vital for him to be able to navigate smoothly. After all, almost every man he dealt with professionally was gay. At the opera, it was Toby who, statistically speaking, was queer. No doubt his closeness to Jonas, the frequency with which they were seen together, added fuel to the rumors that Toby himself was gay. Which was fine. Rumors to that effect probably made his professional life marginally easier, and besides...what the hell. Keep 'em guessing.

And Jonas had been wry about that aspect of things. "Listen, pal, you may be the luckiest straight guy in the world. You're...I mean, except for the unfortunate fact you like women, you might as well be gay. You've got all the gay virtues. Women love that stuff. You're suave and well turned-out, and you know which restaurants to go to and what wine goes with what and when to tip the captains. All the *savoir faire* shit. Women are suckers for it. Or so I'm told."

And now, just before Jonas took a last bite out of his bran muffin, he asked, "Does Doris know what happened with Solomon last night?"

"If she reads her email she does."

Jonas raised his eyebrows. "This could turn into an interesting day."

~

DORIS RASKOV WORE CLEAR plastic glasses secured by a thin gold chain around her neck, kept her gray hair pulled back in a bun, favored frilly blouses and frumpy suits. A fit, handsome middle-aged woman who chose to present herself as an old lady, a rich man's second wife who refused to look like a trophy. That was one of many reasons Toby liked her. It obviously was a deliberate choice. Why she'd made it remained a mystery. And always would. You don't ask someone about something like that.

She was behind her desk, and Toby was seated in a chair facing her. "Just one second," she murmured. She was reading a piece of email on her computer. When she finished, she removed her glasses, letting them hang down on her breast, and swiveled to face Toby.

"Okay," she said. "Brad Solomon. He was a naughty boy last night."

"Well, yes."

"And I told him so."

"You talked to him?"

"We texted. He apologized."

"To you or to me?"

She smiled. Toby understood the significance of the smile: She found the question shrewd. "To me, of course. He said it was a mix-up, and he was sorry."

"Which it certainly wasn't. And which he probably isn't." Of course the apology was made to Doris. This system in which they functioned was virtually feudal, and the general manager, along with the donors and volunteers—the people who weren't engaged in it as a trade—were at the apex of the feudal structure. A vassal like Toby didn't merit an apology. He wouldn't even be considered the injured party.

"Brad's..." Doris stopped, searching for a way to continue, and then went on, "Brad's Brad. He has his quirks. Which I don't defend. But he's a friend, and he has many good qualities. With which you, of course, need not concern yourself. I'm not asking you to like him."

Toby started to answer, but she rode over him: "And don't forget, he has more money than God, and he says he's prepared to give us some of it. That's the overriding consideration if Brian's going to get his new opera. If *we* are going to get a new opera. So the only question is, can you make nice with him? If you can't, I'll handle it myself, or let Angie over in Major Gifts deal with him. By rights, it's her baby anyway."

It was Toby's turn to nod. Doris knew how to play him, another thing he admired about her. Only ten years or so older than he, she still enjoyed a sort of maternal power over him. But she deployed it sparingly, and only when she felt the ends she was pursuing justified its use.

"No," Toby assured her, "I'm fine. Solomon and I don't have to be *pals*."

"Good. I appreciate your professionalism. Now listen. He suggested you come to his office this afternoon. Three o'clock."

Toby considered this. "Will I have to sit there cooling my heels for a couple of hours before he deigns to see me?"

"If that happens, I'll murder him personally, okay? With my own bare hands. But it won't. I get the impression he's a little abashed about last night."

"You could tell that from a text?"

"Don't underestimate me, Toby."

"Never." Only a fool would underestimate Doris. "Okay, let's see how it plays out."

"And Toby...you be punctual too, all right? No games. This isn't about payback."

Damn she was good. Almost a mind reader.

THE DAY WAS COLD enough—overcast, with a cutting wind from the bay—that the walk from the Opera House to the financial district was bracing. Toby welcomed it. It sharpened his mind, helping him to prepare himself for the prospective encounter. The primary challenge was to find a way to use his annoyance to fuel his pitch. And not feel intimidated. This last was crucial, and, he reluctantly admitted to himself, far from a given. Toby wasn't easily intimidated, but there was something about Solomon...It wasn't his money and it wasn't his position, Toby was pretty sure about that. So what was it? Had he secured an advantage through that earlier display of disregard?

Or was it the woman, Amy?

What Toby hadn't let himself realize until this moment, as he quick-stepped down Van Ness, was how impressed he was that Solomon was with a woman like Amy. She wasn't at all the type Toby would have figured on: Someone younger, prettier, blonder, more elaborately turned-out, more voluptuous. Mistress material.

Solomon obviously could have arranged that had it been his preference, arranged it effortlessly. There were no serious impediments to *anything* for a man in Solomon's position. And voluptuous mistresses weren't such a rare commodity...Hell, plenty of women have been in training for the role their whole lives. Were virtually bred for it.

It said something interesting about Brad Solomon that he hadn't chosen a woman of that sort. Arm candy. Bed candy. Whereas Amy seemed like a serious personage. This conclusion was based solely on one short conversation, but it had made an impression. A big impression. She was quick. She'd made him laugh. He liked her attitude. He liked her face.

The idea that Solomon possessed good enough taste to choose Amy Baldwin over the sort of woman ninety-nine out of a hundred gazillionaires would unhesitatingly have gone for said something unsettling to Toby. Not to mention that Solomon was capable of attracting such a woman, one who, Toby guessed, might be immune to cruder varieties of blandishment. This was intimidating data. They suggested Bradley Solomon was more than the sum of his parts, more than the sum of his connections. His parts and his connections didn't intimidate Toby, but if, in addition, he had a *soul*...well, that could make a fellow feel seriously diminished.

In a matter of twenty minutes he reached the office building where Solomon had his headquarters. A massive newish building down near the Embarcadero, all smoked glass and concrete, likely built and owned by Solomon himself. Toby climbed some steps and traversed the broad front plaza, dominated by a huge Calderesque sculpture painted deep maroon, and then entered the cavernous lobby. After a moment for his eyes to adjust to the gloom, he crossed the lobby to the marble wall that contained the building directory. Solomon Enterprises occupied the entire penthouse level.

Acting on a hunch, Toby peered a little lower. Sure enough, there she was, Amy Baldwin, suite 425. She probably got a deal on the rent.

There were different banks of elevators reserved for different floor levels. He found the set that reached the penthouse, put his thumb on the PH button till it glowed pink, and stepped through the doors that opened to admit him. The ride up was so rapid as to be nauseating. When the doors opened again, he stepped directly into a luxurious reception area. He approached a big marble desk presided over by a drop-dead gorgeous young Asian woman who seemed just the type Solomon *should* have chosen to share his recreational hours. A bimbo transmogrified, elevated to the level of aristocratic elegance.

Toby gave his name, and added, "I have an appointment with Mr. Solomon." And waited for a tense few seconds. What would happen now?

She was checking something on the computer in front of her. "Oh, yes," she said. "Please have a seat, Mr. Lindeman. Would you like something to drink?"

"Oh, boy, would I ever," is what he didn't say. Instead, he declined politely. There was a sunken waiting area to his right, with leather sofas and chairs grouped around a mahogany coffee table. Several potted plants. He strolled over, unbuttoned his suit jacket, and sat down, still wondering what he was in for. Without his willing it, part of him was hoping he'd be ill-treated. It would spare him the necessity of being polite to that fuck-head Solomon. And Doris had promised vengeance if Solomon pulled anything. It would be fun to see those two go toe-to-toe.

But his wait proved brief. Within five minutes, another *Vogue* model—a busty blond WASP this time—approached him. "Mr. Lindeman? Come this way, please."

Jesus, Solomon commanded a fucking seraglio.

Toby rose, rebuttoned his jacket, and followed the woman through the reception area and down a long corridor. At the end, he saw Solomon in an open doorway. Jacket off, tie loosened, collar button unbuttoned, cuffs rolled up thick hairy forearms.

"Toby!" he boomed. "Good to see you again. Thanks for coming by."

"Mr. Solomon," Toby said. When he was within reach, he grasped and shook Solomon's extended hand. No hesitating. He was conscious of being four or five inches taller than Solomon, and conscious too that it seemed to confer no advantage.

"Call me Brad. They offer you something to drink?"

"Yes, they did. I'm fine, thanks."

"Good, good. Come on in. Alice, bring me a Perrier. And hold my calls." Ushering Toby through the doorway into his magnificent office, Solomon said, "About last night. An unfortunate mix-up. No hard feelings, I hope. Now, have a seat and tell me about this opera thing." His voice was different from the previous night, rougher, gruffer, his accent redolent of the street.

Toby took an unobtrusive glance around. Solomon's office was vast, could easily have housed, had it been subdivided into cubicles, an entire good-sized business. One entire wall consisted of a picture window with a breathtaking view of the financial district, the bay, and the East Bay hills beyond.

At a gesture from Solomon, Toby seated himself on one of the sofas. Solomon claimed an easy chair catty-cornered to it. He rested his feet on a rung just below the surface of the coffee table. The black alligator loafers he was wearing had an incredible shine and silly little tassels.

"Okay," said Solomon, "you have my undivided attention. Make your case."

Toby cleared his throat, at which point Alice entered with a small bottle of Perrier and a glass containing a lime wedge. She padded toward them and placed her burden on the table in front of Solomon, who said, "Thanks, Alice. Toby, you want to reconsider?"

"I'm good."

Alice glided out, and Solomon said, "No more interruptions, that's a promise. And once again, I'm really sorry about the little misunderstanding last night."

As Solomon started to pour Perrier into the glass, Toby was surprised to hear himself say, with palpable irritation, "Oh, please." Solomon looked up sharply. Toby went on, "I mean, calling it a misunderstanding is kind of disingenuous." Evidently, some part of him was more affronted than he'd realized. There was an instinct, or an impulse, that let the first of Solomon's bland apologies pass by, but when the second came, that evidently exceeded its tolerance.

Solomon stopped pouring, even though his glass was only about a quarter full. "I beg your pardon?" he said. His eyes had hardened, and they were staring right into Toby's.

Toby met the stare. He was in too deep to retreat. "You obviously knew what you were doing. It was something you *chose* to do. Not a misunderstanding, not a mix-up. I'm perfectly willing to forget it and move on, and, of course, I recognize you have all the power in this interaction, I'm here hat in hand. But still, you mustn't assume my willingness to put up with bullshit is limitless." He was pleased to note his voice remained steady throughout this little speech, and its volume at ordinary conversational level. "I'll bow because that's the convention, but I'll be damned if I'm gonna kiss your boot. You see the distinction, I'm sure."

There was a very long pause. Solomon reached for his glass, brought it half-way to his lips, then put it back on the table. All the while, Toby was thinking, Doris will murder me for this, and Brian'll be livid. To have indulged his own personal pique with an opera commission at stake…It was a firing offense.

Solomon was staring at him steadily. The seconds ticked away, ten, twenty. Time had never inched by so slowly. And then something unexpected happened. Solomon began to smile. At first he seemed to be fighting it, but it gradually took control of his face, and soon he was grinning broadly. Then he laughed out loud, a harsh bark of grudging amusement. "Okay," he said, "point taken. Now. You gonna tell me about this opera of yours or what?"

Toby exhaled, more loudly than he would have preferred. "Sure," he agreed. "With pleasure. But first, if it isn't too late, can I change my mind about that Perrier?"

"Mouth a little dry?"

"Something like that."

"Yeah, I'll bet." Solomon chuckled. "You've got balls, Lindeman."

~

LATER, AS TOBY CROSSED the lobby again, heading toward the smoked glass front doors, he was uncomfortably aware his body had treated this meeting with Solomon as a species of fight-or-flight ordeal. His heart was still pounding from the sustained rush of adrenaline, and his shirt felt wrinkled and clammy, adhering to his back even in this chilly weather. Pity. It had just come back from the cleaners, and now it was destined straight for the hamper. And he was conscious of an acrid odor coming from his armpits, and could only hope it wasn't evident to anyone else in his vicinity.

As he pushed against the big door, he almost literally bumped into Amy Baldwin coming the other way, her nose and cheeks bright pink from the cold. She noticed him first. "Well hi there," she said.

His self-consciousness about his body odor ratcheted up several notches. He made a point of keeping his distance from her as he stepped backward into the lobby and returned her greeting. And felt a renewed surge of adrenaline. Just what he didn't need.

Her eyes were twinkling, and she was smiling the same amused, knowing smile he'd found so attractive and so unsettling the previous night. In his present state, that wasn't a good thing. It felt like a provocation. Almost an insult. Let Solomon keep his buildings and his vacation houses and his art collection and his private jet. Why should he also have someone like this? Aside from the injustice of the arrangement, it was such an obscene *waste*. Toby, on no evidence at all, was convinced of it. Like giving a bottle of Château Lafite to some teenager who just wants to get shit-faced.

"Saw Brad?" she asked. When he nodded, she said, "How'd it go?"

He shrugged. It wasn't something he cared to talk about, or even knew *how* to talk about. Magda had characterized Amy's relationship with Solomon as an open secret, which suggested that, however open it might be, it was still ostensibly a secret. The subject was a minefield.

"I'm reconsidering the escort business," he said. "It's getting more appealing all the time." While he spoke, she was looking at him closely, seemed to be studying his face. It was disconcerting. "What?" he asked.

"Oh. Nothing. Listen…"

But whatever she was going to say was interrupted. A woman's voice yelled, "Amy!" They both turned. A well-dressed, youngish woman was approaching them. Bearing down on them, it seemed to Toby.

Amy sighed. "Aw shit," she said under her breath. "I don't like this woman."

She said it so artlessly, with such unaffected, winsome mournfulness, that Toby, even in his sour mood, had to laugh. But his laughter immediately triggered another pang. Everything about her was appealing. "I should go," he said. "I have to get back to the office, report on my meeting with…" He didn't bother to finish. "Anyway, it was nice to see you."

"Yes, very nice." She gave him her hand. When he took it, he again had the impression she was searching his face. But it was all over in a second, and he quickly turned and went out the door into the chill afternoon.

A FEW HOURS LATER, Toby showed up at Jonas's apartment with a plastic bag holding several cartons of take-out sushi. The door was opened to him by Brian Hughes, in jeans and a rust-colored cashmere sweater, barefoot. "Jonas is in the kitchen," Brian said. "He'll be right out."

Brian was the opera's handsome young music director, a golden boy who had been appointed only two seasons before. A daring and somewhat controversial appointment. Brian wasn't yet forty, from the San Joaquin Valley, Oberlin-trained. He'd done some well-received work in Charleston and Houston, and two recordings, of *Albert Herring* and *L'Incoronazione di Poppea*, both of which, although not released on a major label, got respectful notices. The board took a gamble on him because other candidates presented more immediate difficulties, and, just possibly, because of the aura of glamour around him. After two seasons, his tenure was judged promising but not quite stellar. The deal somehow still had to be sealed.

Under ordinary circumstances, he would have functioned on a plane so far above Toby their paths would have crossed only on official occasions and their relations characterized by professional formality. But because Jonas and Brian were a couple, Toby frequently met Brian on the neutral terrain of Jonas's apartment, where a spirit of equality governed. "The leveling power of buggery," was how Jonas put it.

It was disorienting, the first few times Toby found Brian there, to see him sprawled on Jonas's couch, drinking wine, gossiping, making dirty jokes, talking sports or politics, his shoes off and his feet up, just a guy. Quite a personable guy. Brian was a dignified, imposing figure in public settings; you wouldn't have thought informality was in his repertoire. But then, he'd recorded both *Albert Herring* and *L'Incoronazione di Poppea*—he commanded a broad repertoire.

It was Toby's impression that Brian was drawn to Jonas partly for this very reason, because Jonas was so casual and his humor so irreverent you really couldn't put on airs in his company. The times Brian and Jonas were alone, or alone with privileged friends, may have been the only times Brian didn't feel himself onstage, didn't feel obliged to play the role of Herr Kapellmeister. And could be damned sure if he tried it he'd be subjected to merciless teasing.

The leveling power of buggery was operative, but also its protective cloak. Brian was still, at least officially, in the closet, and there was no one in his intimate social circle whose discretion couldn't be relied on. For a while, Toby, the only straight guy in that circle, seemed to make Brian uneasy, seemed to inhibit him. But those days were in the past. Toby had since become, as Jonas put it, "an honorary fag."

Toby had been privy to the beginnings of the romance at second hand, from Jonas's excited next-day reports. It was a romantic tale. Brian didn't play the piano in public, hadn't since his teenage prodigy days, but he was an accomplished pianist, and he sometimes invited members of the pit orchestra to his place for evenings of chamber music. This was no doubt sound politics in addition to being a pleasure in itself, a way to form alliances with the musicians who played under him. One night he and Jonas were sight-reading their way through Shostakovich's viola sonata, the composer's bleak last work, and somewhere during the long final movement, Brian looked up, perhaps to alert Jonas to a tempo change, and their eyes met, and, as Jonas reported by phone the next day, "That was it. We knew."

Did anyone else notice?" Toby had asked.

"I don't think so," Jonas had said. "It was just a glance. But...who knows? When something like that happens, it feels so huge you're surprised it isn't on the eleven o'clock news." Jonas had waited out the other players, hoping he wasn't being too obvious about it, clearing wine glasses and plates from the living room, and then, back in the kitchen, putting Saran Wrap around leftovers. Finally, when no other guests were left, Brian shut the door firmly, turned to face Jonas, and said, "You're staying?"

That was almost a year ago. The two men were still discreet about their relationship, and the press, mercifully, chose not to go near it, but it was no longer a deep dark secret. And since Jonas had been first chair before the romance began, there were no grumblings about favoritism.

Tonight, the three of them sat on the floor around Jonas's living room coffee table eating the sushi Toby had brought and drinking Brian's Puligny-Montrachet. Toby was recounting the details of his meeting with Solomon, trying to imbue the tale with the brutal dramatic values of a Sergio Leone western. The only way to deal with his nagging unhappiness over the business was to treat it as a comically epic misadventure.

Brian grumbled, "I ought to strangle you." It wasn't clear he was joking.

Toby shrugged. "Doris said the same thing when I got back to the office. But what's the problem? My strategy worked like a charm."

"Your *strategy*?" Jonas harrumphed. "A hissy fit is not a strategy."

"I knew what I was doing."

"The fuck."

"Well...what if we call it a calculated risk? Work with me here."

"Holy Christ," said Brian, "do you have any idea what I've got riding on this?"

"You're not the only one who's got something riding on it." Toby knew Brian hoped to be named artistic director someday and assumed the opera commission was part of his grand scheme. But Toby didn't feel himself to be solely, or even primarily, a foot soldier in service to Brian's career aspirations. Their agendas might overlap, but they weren't identical. "The whole city's supposed to benefit."

"Right, right."

"Besides, my ass was on the line too." A useful little dig; Brian's proclivity to solipsism shouldn't be indulged. "Anyway," Toby continued, "we should celebrate. Solomon said he might pledge the full five mil. That ain't peanuts."

"No," Brian conceded, "it ain't."

"Believe me, if I'd started off like a beggar, he would have haggled."

"Jewed you down," proposed Jonas, the only one in the room who could get away with it.

"But he didn't blink. Said it sounded doable. No, wait, first he called me a...a *gonif*, I think was the word he used. What's a *gonif*?" He looked over at Jonas.

"A thief."

"Coming from Solomon, that's probably a compliment. So this thing is moving along very satisfactorily. A little show of appreciation might be in order."

"You make a convincing case," Jonas said. "Don't you agree, Bri?" He raised his glass. "Let's drink to Toby."

"And to the new opera," Toby said. "May it not stink up the joint."

"I should call Jeremy," Brian said.

Jonas frowned. "No, let's drink the toast first. And eat the food and enjoy the evening. That's what we're here for. There's plenty of time to call Jeremy."

A brief, oddly tense moment ensued. Perhaps Brian wasn't used to be being contradicted by one of his players, even one he happened to be sleeping with; he knit his brows and looked down at the table, displeased. But then he looked up again, smiled, raised his glass, and said, "All right then, to Toby and the opera—may it not stink up the joint—and, and—"

"And to a triumphant premiere and long tenure for the future artistic director," Jonas proclaimed, doing his part to dissipate the tension.

THE NEXT DAY, TOBY was in his office, writing an email to Doris. A delicate task. He knew—as almost no one else did—that Brian had settled on a composer and tentatively approved the subject of a libretto. Official approval by the general manager was probably largely a formality, and, although Solomon had indicated he'd want to know more about the project before he transferred any funds, it was unimaginable this could present much of a stumbling block; he wasn't an opera buff, it was unlikely he had strong views on the subject. Still, Brian and the composer he favored, Jeremy Metcalfe, were treating the commission as a *fait accompli*, and there were still hurdles to clear, not all of them low. The high-handed way Brian managed things could itself raise eyebrows; there was no denying he'd jumped the gun. Besides, the subject he'd chosen, while certainly a testament to San Francisco's colorful past and abrasive vitality, could prove controversial.

At the end of the previous evening, after the sushi and wine had been consumed and Toby was heading for the door, Brian gave Jonas a quick nervous glance and pulled Toby aside. He quietly asked Toby if he might act as intermediary with Doris, and, by the way, could he please use all the discretion at his disposal when he did so? He even hinted that it might be best to shade the truth a little, to keep secret how far things had progressed, and instead frame the whole business as merely a proposal, albeit one the music director's enthusiastically supported. Once Doris concurred, the irregular way things had been arranged would no longer matter.

In a funny way, the conversation was reassuring. It at least suggested Brian knew he'd transgressed. So Toby reluctantly agreed. On the plus side, the commission shouldn't really present a problem. Not that this was Toby's bailiwick, but the elements seemed plausible, politically shrewd, and best of all, artistically promising. A talented young Black composer, Juilliard-trained but with roots in popular music, was a definite plus, and the controversial subject would make everybody involved feel adventurous and virtuous without, God willing, any important feathers being ruffled in the process. Not that it was risk-free—it could even be said to bristle with hazards—but it did promise a project that would generate buzz. Brian's instincts as an impresario were sound even if his tactics dubious.

But those dubious tactics put Toby in an awkward position. He wasn't used to dissimulating with Doris. It seemed unworthy of their working relationship, which was normally open and candid. Besides, she was perspicacious enough that even in the medium of email, anything less than full candor made him feel exposed. Brian had been foolish as well as reckless, making a gratuitous end run. If he'd been willing to trust her, she could have been a useful ally; her loyalties were with the artists.

Toby was staring at his computer screen, struggling to find the right words and the right tone, not to mention the least misleading account he could devise. So when the phone on his desk rang, he reached for it, grateful for the interruption. "Yes?"

He heard the voice of Daniel, his assistant, saying, "There's an Amy Baldwin on the line. Should I put her through?"

"Yes, absolutely." This was unexpected. He felt a flush of adrenaline.

There was a click, and then her voice. "Hello? Is this where I call for the escorts? Or do I have the wrong number?"

Only then did Daniel click off. Oh shit. Oh well. No real harm done. "No," he said, "you don't have the wrong number. We offer solutions for all your pesky escort needs."

"I'm looking for ten guys in top hats and tails who can sing 'Puttin' on the Ritz.'"

"Our specialty."

He could practically hear her smiling. He was emboldened to add, "Unless you'd prefer 'Once in Love with Amy.'" And then, quickly, before she had time to respond, "We run a kind of gigolo karaoke operation around here."

"You've certainly found a marketing niche, I'll give you that." Then, when neither of them could think of what to say next, she added, "Hi there."

"Hi." Another pause. He wondered if he should ask why she was calling. That might sound too businesslike, less than welcoming. But she wasn't volunteering an explanation, so anything personal might be premature. "I'm glad you called," is what he finally settled on.

"Yeah? Why's that?"

Putting *him* on the spot. Bitch. "So anyway, what can I do for you?" Spiking the ball back into her fucking court.

"Yes, okay. See, what I've been thinking is, maybe it's time I made a contribution to the opera. To diversify my eleemosynary portfolio, so to speak."

"Always a good idea. Whatever you just said."

"So it's a good thing we met the other night, don't you think?"

"Yes indeed. I couldn't be more pleased. Are you a big opera fan?"

Another silence. Then, "Not really." Then, "I kind of hate it, to be completely honest. But...you know, I *respect* it."

"Well, that's the main thing."

"That's what I figured."

"So here's what you need to know. You should make the check out to me personally, that'll expedite the process."

"No, listen, I'm serious."

"You are?"

"Mmm."

"You want to have lunch and discuss this in depth?" Go for it, boyo; you may never get another chance. She wouldn't have called if there wasn't some sort of interest. He had sensed it right away, and his instincts in that department, normally sound, were unlikely to have gone *completely* haywire.

"Or dinner," she countered. That upped the ante, rather. And then she upped it further: "Are you free tonight?"

He glanced at his calendar, not that he had to. "I'm seeing my daughter. We have dinner on Thursdays." Not to mention a tentative date with a woman named Christine afterward. He and Christine had been out, casually, a couple of times; her invitation to drop by after dinner suggested she regarded tonight as the turning point. No need to share *that* information, however.

"That's sweet. You two are close?"

"I wouldn't say *close*. I try to keep the current flowing." No need to get into that can of worms. "How about tomorrow?"

"I'm going out of town tomorrow. For several days." She added, "On business."

"That's too bad."

"I feel the same way."

What was going on here? He felt an inexplicable urgency, distinct from the avidity with which he normally pursued a sexual prospect. It felt different enough that he made a split-second decision: The deal with Christine could wait. A quick call would take care of it. He said, "Listen, if this is completely inappropriate, I'm sure you'll tell me, but… Cathy and I eat early. She's in high school; I have to get her back to her mother at a reasonable hour. Otherwise I get yelled at, and, you know, why bother getting divorced if you're still gonna get yelled at? So how about meeting up after? I can, you know, watch you eat, or we can have a drink. Or some permutation of that."

"That works."

It was almost too easy. "I won't have to sing 'Puttin' on the Ritz,' will I?"

"Not if you know 'Once in Love with Amy.'"

They agreed on a place and time. Toby's head was spinning.

IT WAS ALWAYS ODD to pick up Cathy at the little house in Cow Hollow she shared with Jessica. It used to be his house too. Jessie and he bought it together, the year before they got married. Once a symbol of hope, it was now impossible to see it as anything but a symbol of failure.

Especially since Jessica had bought out his share of the house as part of the divorce settlement. He'd been in no position to argue since at the time he needed the money.

Jessie opened the door to him, gave him a quick, uncomfortable kiss on the cheek. "You're looking well," she said.

"You too," he said. It was true enough; Jessica was an attractive woman. But she suddenly frowned. It was so pronounced a response that he asked, "What?"

She shook her head. "Nothing. Cathy'll be right down. She's fixing herself up."

Toby sighed. "I wish she wouldn't."

Which got a laugh from Jessie. "Yeah, her fashion sense is…let's say it's nascent."

"Have you tried talking to her?"

"I can't talk to her about much of *anything* these days."

He nodded. "We knew the teen years were coming, but there's no preparing for them, is there?"

"And it's harder for the mother. I don't know why. I mean, it's not just a question of custody, although I'm sure that makes it worse."

So far, given the potential contentiousness of the topic, they were handling things pretty well, Toby thought. No implicit recrimination from either side. "It's a stage," he said fatuously. "We just have to wait it out and look forward to her emergence on the other side."

"I hope so."

"How's she doing at school?"

"Her grades are okay." She lowered her voice. "But something's bothering her. I don't know what it is. When I ask, she bites my head off. Maybe you can talk to her."

"I can try. She won't tell me either."

"Don't tell her I mentioned it, it'll get her back up."

"No, I—" They both heard Cathy's step on the landing above. "Don't worry, I'll pump the bejesus out of her," he whispered, which won a small smile from Jessie.

"Hi, Daddy!" Cathy called, looming above them on the stairs. "You two kids getting acquainted?"

Toby watched her descend. Denim overalls with suspenders, a plaid flannel shirt, plum-colored lipstick, Buddy Holly glasses. All of it so intrinsically unflattering only the naturally beautiful could get away with it. Was it fashion, or a sneaky conspiracy of the attractive against the rest of the world? He felt a hopeless, distant sort of tenderness for her, along with despair at how much of her life he was missing, and at how graceless her adolescence was proving to be.

"Hi, honey," he said. After she came to him and accepted his kiss, he added, "You're going to need a jacket."

"I'm fine."

"Get a jacket," Jessie said flatly.

Cathy rolled her eyes, but she didn't make a big production out of it. When she went to the closet to fetch a parka, it was Jessica's turn to roll her eyes. Toby responded with a good-natured shrug, trying to convey that this wasn't so bad, that maybe too many of these battles had put

Jessica on edge herself, that the girl's behavior was within acceptable teenage bounds.

"I'll have her back nice and early, Mrs. Lindeman," he said.

"I'm Ms. Galfand now. As you well know."

The only borderline-hostile moment in the whole interaction.

~

WATCHING CATHY TUCK INTO her burger and fries, Toby wondered why she wasn't more self-conscious about diet. Friends of his sometimes complained their daughters were aggressively, obnoxiously health-conscious, chastising their parents for too much gluten, too much sugar, too much animal protein. That didn't seem like anything to complain about.

"So, can I tell you something?" she asked after an interval that hadn't been quite long enough to be uncomfortable, but was getting close. "I mean, without you getting upset?"

"I can't promise that in advance. But you can say anything that's on your mind." Could the problem Jessie suspected just tumble out without prompting? Hardly seemed likely.

"See, the thing is, Mom *really* needs a boyfriend."

Toby laughed, out of surprise rather than amusement.

"I mean it. She is *such* a pill. Worse than usual, if you can imagine. I know you have to take her side, that's the divorced parents' code, but… every trivial nothing is World War Three."

He sighed. Refereeing their battles was a hopeless task. "It's natural you're getting on each other's nerves nowadays. She's your mom, and you, you want to be independent, you're almost an adult, and—"

"Yes!" Cathy interrupted. "Exactly! See, you get that."

"I wasn't quite finished," he said. "You're still living in her house and—"

It was Cathy's turn to sigh.

"—and you're *not* an adult yet, Cath. You want to push against the limits, that's natural. But the limits are there for a reason, they're not arbitrary or unreasonable."

"You don't know that. You don't know what sort of limits Mom imposes."

"She isn't an unreasonable person."

"You say that now. You were singing a different tune before you made your escape." She picked up three French fries, dipped them in a little pool of ketchup on her plate, and put them in her mouth.

"Are her rules stricter than the ones your friends have?"

She swallowed, and then said, "Yes! She has all these frustrations, and she takes them out on me. If she was seeing somebody she'd be much nicer. It's way past time she got herself a boyfriend. Don't you think?"

He knew she didn't expect an answer. "How's *your* life?" he asked. It was interesting, though, if she was right that Jessica didn't have a man in her life. The affair that broke up the marriage was long over, ending with a nasty whimper rather than a bang, and Jessie was a good-looking, accomplished, self-sufficient woman. Someone plausible should have grabbed her up by now.

"I'm fine."

"I'm not just making chitchat, honey. You have no idea what it's like, being out of your life. Divorce is awful in every way, but a lot of the bad stuff fades after a while. Not the parenting part, though. I need to feel connected to you. I need to know what's happening."

"Well, it's senior year, so a lot of what's happening is just waiting for the year to be over. Senioritis, we call it."

"We called it that too."

"But otherwise things are okay. Except for the shit with Mom, better than okay."

"You've got friends?"

"No, Daddy, I'm a total recluse," she said disdainfully. "Of *course* I have friends."

"Are any of your classes interesting? Does school engage you at all? Or are you just waiting for it to end and that's the whole story?"

"No, that's not the whole story. I'm in drama club this year, and I love it." She became more animated. "I may even major in theater in college. Hank, that's the drama coach, Mr. Ortega, he thinks I have talent. I'm in the school play this semester. I hope you'll come, it's in June. We're doing *All My Sons*."

"That's great." Not the majoring-in-theater part, of course, but it was great she was excited about something, even if it meant he had to attend a school play. "A good part?"

"There are no small parts," she proclaimed sententiously, "only small actors." And then laughed, to let him know she was joking. "A very good part. The lead, sort of. The female lead, anyway. Kate Keller. The mother."

"Honey, that's terrific."

"Will you come?"

"Of course."

"Mom thinks I'm spending too much time on it. Letting my other classes go."

"Are you?"

"Probably. But colleges don't care about your last semester. No one cares but Mom."

"I care."

"Sure, right." And then, quickly, "Anyway, Hank insists on lots of rehearsals and improvs and acting exercises and stuff. He's a slave driver. Weekends and shit. But it's worth it. People say our drama program is one of the best in the city."

"It's great to see you so enthusiastic."

"I am."

"And you're reasonably happy?"

"I told you, Daddy, I'm fine."

"Nothing's bothering you or anything?"

"Just, you know, what I told you. Hassles with Mom." She suddenly narrowed her eyes suspiciously. "Why?"

"Like I said, I hate not being part of your life."

"Might as well get used to it." And then, perhaps realizing this sounded harsher than she intended, although it no doubt reflected her true feelings, she added, "It's not like you live in Tibet or something. We still see a lot of each other."

He nodded, deeply pained. She was a good kid, and she obviously felt nothing for him that wasn't benign. But it was clear the door had shut a long time ago. He might even have been the one to shut it.

～

AMY BALDWIN WAS SITTING alone in a dark-stained wooden booth with a drink in front of her. Toby briefly flashed on Piper Laurie in

44

The Hustler. This bar—her choice—wasn't crowded and was mercifully quiet. She hadn't noticed Toby yet, so he was able to stand in the narrow entranceway for a moment and watch her. She was wearing a dark turtleneck, navy or black, it was hard to tell which in this light and from this distance. An unremarkable-looking woman. It wasn't easy to explain why she'd had such an effect on him. It wasn't easy to explain his suddenly accelerated pulse. After a brief moment of internal preparation, like an actor's before going onstage, he entered the barroom proper. That's when she saw him and waved. That great smile. He smiled in response and approached the booth.

"Howdy, ma'am. You alone?"

"Just me and my thoughts, cowboy."

He leaned down to kiss her cheek, a socially sanctioned greeting even among bare acquaintances. "What are you drinking?" he asked.

"A cosmopolitan. Great drink. Gets you pie-eyed while curing your urinary infection."

"You have a urinary infection?"

"No, I generally avoid them. By drinking cosmopolitans."

"An ounce of prevention." He slid into the booth, across from her, and signaled to the waiter standing over by the bar. "How are you?"

"Why are you smiling?"

"I don't know. I can't help it. How are you?"

"Fine, thanks. How was your daughter?"

"Adolescent."

"How old is she?"

"Thirty-eight." And then, off her look, "She's seventeen."

"About as adolescent as it gets."

"Which is how she was." The waiter arrived. "Blanton's on the rocks, please," Toby told him. After the man moved off, Toby added, "She reserves the preponderance of her venom for her mom. Unfairly, but I can live with that."

"Divorce must be tough. All of it, but especially the kid part."

"Brutal. It's never not there. And if it isn't there, you feel bad about *that.*"

She nodded, and waited a moment to signal she understood this wasn't idle banter. Then she smiled and announced, "You'll be interested to hear Brad thinks you're gay."

Startled, all Toby could say in response was, "Really?"

"Mmm. Just lazy stereotyping…he hears the word opera, he figures any man involved must be queer. Except the baritones, maybe. Does that bother you?"

"Not in the slightest. Actually, it happens a lot. I even think my dad suspected it."

"Really?"

"Mmm. I wasn't what he expected in a boy. You know, sports and stuff. His ideas about such things were sort of primitive."

She waited a few seconds, and then said, "I didn't tell Brad you're not."

"You didn't? How come?"

She shrugged.

He processed the shrug, filing it away for future examination, and said, "But you're certain about that?"

"Give me a break," she said.

"That's very intuitive of you."

"Yeah, I'm amazing that way. You want to tell me about your divorce?"

Toby shook his head. "Uh-uh. Not now. Not yet."

"Are you waiting for anything in particular?"

She seemed to have a propensity for leaping in precisely where the ice was thinnest. "Well," he said, "for one thing, you have to make a donation to the opera first."

"You're getting down to business already?"

Toby looked directly into her eyes and held the stare for a moment. "I don't believe that *is* getting down to business," he finally said. "As far as I can tell, the opera stuff qualifies as preliminary small talk. Of course, I could be totally wrong."

This had the gratifying effect of causing her to break the stare and look down at her cosmopolitan. It was an ideal moment for Toby's drink to arrive, and it did, on cue. Toby thanked the waiter and took a sip. Nirvana. "Tell me about your business," he said.

"It's not very interesting. A web-based merchandising operation. Women's health products and services."

"So you sell cosmopolitans."

She smiled. "Can't, alas. The Feds won't let me. But pretty much everything else."

"Are you one of those computer whiz types?"

"Nah, I have an IT guy for the technical stuff."

"Is women's health a big topic with you?"

"Well, I'm a woman, and I don't like to get sick. But it isn't some big *cause* or anything. Not a Susan Komen kind of deal. I saw a business opportunity and took it."

"It's successful?"

"Pretty much. We did especially well during the pandemic, as you might expect."

"I don't really understand business. Despite being the opera's money man."

After a brief pause, she said, "Brad told me you gave him a hard time yesterday."

"Yep."

"He said, and I quote, you busted his balls."

"That was certainly my aim."

"You sound jolly pleased with yourself about it."

"Absurdly pleased. Childishly pleased." He took another sip of bourbon. "I mean, he was a total...Wait. Is this dangerous ground? If it is, tell me now."

She didn't answer directly. Instead, she said, "He doesn't scare you, does he?"

"No."

"A lot of people find him intimidating."

"I'm pleased not to be one of them."

"The reason I left that redwoods thing the other night—one of the reasons, anyway—is, I could see he was about to start in on you."

"Good."

"Good what?"

"Good you could see it. Good you didn't want to be there for it. Good you left before it happened."

She nodded, then stared down at the table with a thoughtful look in her eye. After a second or two she glanced back up at him. "Are you finished with your drink by any chance?"

"Finished?" He held up the glass. "I've barely begun."

"Well, bottoms up. Down the hatch."

"You mean we're done here?"

"I think so."

"Did I say something wrong?"

"The opposite."

He felt totally at sea. "I don't understand, Amy."

"Sure you do. Of course you do. It's been there all along. From the moment we said hello. So get the waiter, get the check, let's get out of here and go someplace we can be alone. Your place? My place? It doesn't matter. My place. Hurry. We've vamped enough."

She reached for his hand. He didn't say anything. He couldn't. His heart was in his throat.

3

NEXT MORNING, TOBY GOT to work an hour late. When he arrived at—virtually staggered into—the anteroom to his office, Daniel pushed his wire-frame glasses against the bridge of his narrow nose and regarded him quizzically. "Well, good morning," he said, his thin lips pursed. "You've had a few calls." He pushed a batch of pink slips in Toby's direction.

Toby reached across Daniel's desk and took them. "I hope you said I was in a meeting."

"Words to that effect. Which people usually take to mean you're in the bathroom. A really urgent meeting. Is everything okay?"

Toby had gone over to the Braun coffee machine and was pouring himself a cup. "Why do you ask?"

"Well...I don't want to say you look like something the cat dragged in—"

"No, that wouldn't be kind."

"Back in Minnesota, my mom would say you seem a trifle *peaked.*"

"Just a trifle? Things must be looking up since I shaved."

"Rough night?"

"Oh yeah." Then Toby realized this might sound like he'd had to dial 911, so he added, "You might say. In a manner of speaking." And wished he'd kept his mouth shut altogether.

Daniel blinked once, an uncomprehending look on his face. It's not that a possible sexual interpretation of Toby's words was beyond his ken, just that he couldn't believe a straight male might have an experience that left him, the next morning, looking the way Toby did now.

"Your schedule's relatively clear today," Daniel said, with a new gentleness, or was it new respect? "So that's good."

"It sure is," Toby agreed. "My brain is mush." He actually wasn't sure if his brain was mush. He hadn't tried to use it yet. Instead, he'd let it go where it chose—he'd given his brain its head—and it insisted on obsessively revisiting the previous night. A night of overwhelming, even transcendent lust, of unabashed, rowdy, carnal voraciousness unconstrained by any quaint notions of first-night seemliness. A veritable Whitman's Sampler of fucking. In addition, his entire world felt as if it had been turned upside down, and it was hard to say if that was a positive development or not. He'd had no complaints when his world was right side up.

Toby gave Daniel a little wave and escaped into his office. He removed his jacket and hung it on the peg on his door and plopped down at his desk. He took a sip of watery coffee. Daniel still hadn't mastered the Braun. It was probably unreasonable to expect mastery after only eight months.

He put his head in his hands.

Should he call her? Maybe not quite yet. He'd left her bed less than two hours ago, and he didn't want to seem weak-kneed and sappy. But she was going out of town today, so he'd better not play this *too* cool or he'd miss her completely.

To call or not to call? Jesus. Like a nervous teenager. Which is exactly how he'd felt last night, the first time they kissed, outside the bar, within several seconds of hitting the street. He'd taken the lapels of her cashmere coat in his hands and gently pulled her to him. It felt like they were melting together. He didn't give a damn about passersby, and she didn't seem to mind either. It was a delirious, dizzying first kiss. As was their second, in the Lyft on the way to her house.

Her house. It was nicer than he'd imagined, and he wasn't expecting a dump. Bigger, more elegant. A two-bedroom in Pacific Heights calling for a substantial reappraisal of her financial status. This was San Francisco, for God's sake.

"Very nice," he'd said. "Own or rent?"

"I sort of share it with the bank." She was putting her keys in a porcelain bowl resting on a rickety lacquered table in the entrance foyer.

A small, wiry cat of a lovely rich gray—a gray so deep it seemed, in the dim light, almost mauve—mewed and began circling Amy's ankles anxiously, pressing against her. The cat was all sinew and nerve, the life force within vivid, naked, fragile. Amy bent down and rubbed its neck and jaw, and it purred loudly. "Hi, Feeney," she said, her voice a lilting falsetto. "Hi, girl. Miss me?" The cat alternately mewed and purred. Amy gave its jaw another stroke and straightened up. Removing her coat and hanging it on a coat tree, her back to Toby, she said, "I'm a little nervous all of a sudden."

"Me too." More than a little. How to tell her, without sounding like some jaded roué, that he didn't usually feel nervous in this sort of situation anymore? "I was just thinking how, when we kissed before, you know, outside the bar, I was thinking I felt like a teenager. I guess I still do. And I don't think I've felt like a teenager since...since I *was* a teenager."

He couldn't think of an acceptable way to explain. Through his years of post-marital dating, he'd acquired what seemed to be an effective sexual repertoire, what Jonas occasionally dismissed, far too cavalierly, as "bachelor competence." But tonight everything felt different. In ways he couldn't describe, tonight felt like a new, totally novel phenomenon. The notion of going through the same routine he'd gone through so often before felt wrong, inadequate, unworthy. But such a scruple was almost immobilizing. He didn't know how to conduct himself other than the ways he customarily conducted himself.

"What?" she said.

Which startled him out of his reverie. "What do you mean? What what?"

"You were thinking something troubling."

"How do you know that?"

"I don't know." The cat was mewing for attention again, rubbing its head against Amy's shin. She knelt down and began to stroke it. "Some emanation. Not that I believe in that stuff." She rose again, looking him in the eye.

He met the stare. "Okay, swami, what am I thinking *now*?"

She laughed out loud, her throaty, unselfconscious laugh. "Too easy!" And waded into his embrace. "You're absolutely transparent at the moment."

"In my own corporeal way."

Now, sitting at his desk, a faraway look in his eye, he reached for the phone. She'd given him her card with her work number on it. But where had he put it? Oh yes, the breast pocket of his jacket, before leaving for work, in anticipation of this moment. He got up, found the card, went back to his desk, and punched in the number. The operation felt to him, in his present condition, akin to running the Boston marathon.

"Amy Baldwin's office," said a woman's voice at the other end of the line.

"Is Ms. Baldwin in, please? This is, uh, Toby Lindeman calling."

"May I ask what it's concerning?"

"It's, uh, personal. She'll know."

"She's out of town, Mr. Lindeman. She'll be back next week."

"Yeah, okay, thank you."

He hung up and slumped down in his chair. So she'd already gone. They'd exchanged several fervent goodbyes this morning, enough, ostensibly, to cover the entirety of her absence. But he felt bereft anyway. Especially since he'd asked her, at some point early in the morning, after a night in which, amid all the lovemaking and talking, they'd had no sleep at all, "Would it be possible to reschedule this trip of yours?"

"Uh-uh. I just can't."

"You're sure?"

"If I could I would. Leaving now seems…it seems almost perverse. But it's too late to change my plans."

"This trip…it isn't really a business trip, is it?"

"No."

He hadn't pursued it further. No need.

He could call her cell, of course. That number was also on the card. But he didn't want to risk putting her in an awkward position, and *really* didn't want to be treated as a wrong number. The symbolic stigma of that would be too painful. He sighed, swiveled his chair ninety degrees, and booted up his computer. Maybe he could get some work done at least.

There was mail. Much of it spam, asking for political contributions or offering him a better mortgage and a bigger penis. But there was also something from Doris. He opened it.

To: Toby Lindeman
From: Doris Raskov
Subject: (No subject)

Toby—

Two things:

I'm now prepared to concede that yesterday, when I threatened to forcefully separate you from your testicles, I may have been overreacting. Brad phoned this morning & tho it's hard for me to credit, he seems to have taken a shine to you. "A very bright guy, I don't know why he's wasting his time in that cockamamie job," is a verbatim quote. He said he'll transfer stock worth c. 5 mill subject to his approval of the opera the money is spose to fund. I interpret this last condition as a warning he expects some hand-holding, some palpable (and possibly ongoing) demonstration of respect and appreciation, rather than a serious intention to involve himself in the creative process. Since you're his new BFF, you are now official Hand-Holder-in-Chief. But that to the side, good job, well done, thanks from a grateful nation, & if you ever try anything like that again I'll wring your neck with my bare hands. Don't even try to guess what would happen, by way of preliminaries, to your testicles.

On a related matter: I've read & reread your email from yesterday & there are elements I find bothersome. I'm not familiar with Jeremy Metcalf for one thing tho the name sounds vaguely familiar. What do you know about him? Does he have a national reputation? What sort of music does he write? Has he written for voice? For the stage? (When I Googled him, all I got was a guitarist in a rock group called "Splosion." A different Jeremy Metcalf, surely.) Brian's opinion of course carries weight but it isn't decisive by itself. Brian mustn't think the company's his personal fiefdom. A show about the Castro might be specially right for this house but I'll need to know a lot more about the projected libretto before green-lighting it or even mentioning it to Brad. And while I'd prefer to proceed with alacrity I don't see a need for *haste*.

Please let me know your reactions to all this.

Doris

Uh-oh.

Once again, he had to acknowledge Doris's shrewdness. She had an instinct for when something wasn't kosher. It was foolish of Brian to underestimate her. He might be one of those guys, the brightest fellow ever to come from some little town in the middle of nowhere, who didn't realize that out in the great world there were other people as clever as he. A foolish mindset. A good chess player always assumes his opponent will find the best moves.

But Toby wasn't panicking. Doris's questions were reasonable and presumably could be answered reasonably. She wasn't saying no, and she wasn't a snob. Jeremy's membership in Splosion wouldn't automatically be disqualifying, especially not after she heard of his successes at Juilliard. She was open to Brian's basic proposal, which Toby had feared might be a deal-breaker. She said an opera about the Castro sounded provocative. That was good, right? Contemporary operas that weren't provocative tended to disappear. This one carried some obvious risks, so she wanted reassurance. Despite their different roles and sometimes conflicting areas of responsibility, she and Brian ultimately were after the same thing: An opera that made a splash, filled the house, and might eventually find a place in the repertory. And ideally, earn back its costs through other productions and maybe even a recording.

He made a mental note to talk to Jonas about this at racquetball later today. He might know the best way to explain the situation to Brian. Maybe, with a little cajoling, he would even agree to handle it himself.

Toby thumbed through the pink slips. There was one from Jessica, which was a surprise. And most likely didn't augur well. It had come early, at 8:59 a.m., according to Daniel's meticulous notation. That augured even less well. It suggested she'd been lying in wait, ready to ambush him the moment he strode through the door. She rarely phoned him at work. She rarely phoned him *anywhere*. And she certainly never phoned just to say hello. The closest she came was, "Hello, you're late with child support."

The other items weren't interesting. He couldn't handle standard-issue drudgery in his current compromised state, and there was positively no way he could deal with Jessie.

He hadn't had a sleepless night since college and wasn't used to this level of enervation; it wasn't entirely unpleasant, a languorous amorous fog, but it left him ill-equipped to cope with much else. All he could focus on was Amy. Would this feeling survive four days' separation, or was it chimerical, an erotic echo, an ephemeral fantasy? How could she possibly leave after what had happened last night, no matter how reluctantly she did it, what plans she'd made, or how long ago she'd made them? And why did he care? It was the sort of thing he *never* cared about. After the anguish accompanying Jessie's affair, it seemed wise never to let jealousy bother him again.

Even now, it wasn't jealousy exactly... The notion of feeling jealous of Bradley Solomon was too alien. Solomon *himself* was too alien. It would be like feeling jealous of a literal alien, an extraterrestrial. He and Solomon occupied different planes of existence. No, the truth was simpler: He missed her. Already. He ached for her, a dull constant throbbing. He ached for her only two hours after leaving her bed, having done so following a night of sustained lovemaking that left him sore, spent, and bone-weary.

He hadn't fucked like that in years. And even when he *had* fucked like that, it hadn't really been like that, just an expression of youthful pep. And he hadn't laughed like that in years either. Sometimes both happened simultaneously; at one point, they were laughing so hard he was actually expelled from her body. "Whoops," she said, which redoubled the hilarity.

God.

And what a great laugh she had. It wasn't what you would have predicted based on her public presentation. Not that a sense of humor was in question, even remotely—the ping pong ball always came flying back over the net, and with a devilish new spin on it each time—but it had seemed to Toby droll rather than uproarious, and she seemed to be the sort of person more likely to smile than laugh. The few times she *had* laughed in his presence, her laughter had been restrained, polite. Whereas in bed last night she'd surrendered to great whoops of glee.

Other surprises: She had an adorably fleshy little butt. Her parents were Republicans; she'd voted for Hillary and Biden but regarded herself as an independent. Her heart had been broken twice, once as an undergraduate in Ann Arbor, once in graduate school at Stanford. She liked to go horseback riding. She was valedictorian at her high school graduation. She lost her virginity in college, in her freshman year, more because the step seemed overdue than from any particular passion. She'd never married, although she'd been engaged once, for the better part of a year. She regretted not having had children but tried not to think about it too much. Her favorite movie was *Truly, Madly, Deeply*. She almost never read fiction except junk paperbacks on airplanes. She kept her eyes open during sex, and they seemed to glow, like hot coals, in the dark. She emitted a melodious, girlish little cry when she came.

At one point, deep in the middle of the night, they were lying close together, her hand was in his, her breathing led him to think she'd fallen asleep, and it suddenly and belatedly struck him as problematic that he had dealings with Solomon. Here were two related matters, Solomon himself and this *thing* with the man's girlfriend. Toby had somehow contrived to pretend they were separate. Pure self-delusion. They were never separate.

Later, with the etiolated light of a leaden March dawn just beginning to seep through her window, they finished making love for the final time. It was different from before, less impassioned, and yet oddly, tenderly greedy. Toby, sweaty and exhausted, collapsed onto her breast. She held his head, comforting him like a baby.

After a couple of moments, he raised himself up on his elbows so he could look her in the eye, and was surprised to see that, despite their frenetic lovemaking, her hair still looked very much as it had looked the previous evening, straight and simple, with just a few stray wisps sticking to her forehead. He smiled at her, and she smiled back, but the look in her eye was serious, almost solemn. He said, "You know, I started doing this almost thirty years ago, and it's always been one of my favorite things in the world, but...but this was so different it was like a first time. That's the literal truth."

"I know," she said. "For me too."

"I could barely breathe. Something in my chest kept...swelling."

After a moment, she said, "We keep tiptoeing around it, don't we?"

"There's time."

They smiled at each other and left it at that. It was then that he asked her about changing her travel plans, and within seconds the magic began evanescing. The intrusion of real life.

The intercom buzzed. "Your ex-wife is calling again," said Daniel, his voice freighted with significance. Did he suspect Toby had spent the previous night with Jessica?

Toby picked up the phone. "Hello, Jessie."

She came out punching. "What the hell happened between you and Cathy last night?"

"Huh?"

"I am sick to death being cast as the wicked witch, and I'm sick *past* death being out of the fucking loop. I insist you tell me what's going on."

"Wait," he said. He tried to collect his thoughts. "Let's back up a minute." He felt, as he often did where his daughter and ex-wife were concerned, unaccountably guilty, even though he had no idea what Jessie was upset about.

"Yeah, right, go ahead and stall."

"Tell me what the matter is. Please, Jessie. I'm totally in the dark."

"Stop evading and tell me what happened with Cathy last night."

"What happened? Nothing. We had dinner. She had a cheeseburger and fries. And a Diet Coke. Why she bothered to make it a Diet Coke, considering all the other crap she ate, is a mystery to me. Then I took her home."

"What did you talk about?"

"Jeez, I don't know. The usual. School. The drama club. Just...stuff."

"Did she talk about me?"

In the present context, it would be a blunder to dissemble. "She did the usual bitching. Nothing out of the ordinary. I tried to be understanding but still take your side. Which is what she accused me of doing, taking your side that is, in case you doubt my word about it."

"That's all?" Her tone was marginally less confrontational.

"She sounded sort of upbeat. Excited about the school play. I hadn't realized she was so involved."

"There's a lot you don't realize."

"I'm sure that's true, Jess. I try my best, but…listen, you want to talk about being out of the loop? It kills me, what I don't know."

Jessica's tone softened further. "It's hard for both of us, I do realize that."

"How about telling me what the problem is."

She sighed. "She was crying all night. Up in her room. I heard her all the way down the hall, but when I went in, but she wouldn't tell me anything."

At that precise moment, Toby's head started to ache, a solid throbbing behind his eyes. "She was crying?"

"All night."

"Shit." He rubbed his eyes. "She wouldn't say what was bothering her?"

"No. I assumed it must be something that happened with you. That wasn't unreasonable, right? It doesn't make me a bitch. She left smiling, and she came home in tears, so I figured whatever it was happened while she was gone. But I couldn't get an explanation from her, she ordered me out of her room. I didn't go, of course, but she just rolled over and turned her back on me. Didn't say another word."

"Jesus."

"I can't cope with this now."

Something in her intonation caught his attention. "Why now, particularly?"

She ignored the question. "I called you last night. You weren't home."

"You didn't leave a message."

"I was too upset."

"Is she having her period?"

It was the wrong thing to say. "Oh, for Christ's sake."

"Well, I mean—"

"You want to know the worst thing about the curse? The very worst thing? Worse than PMS, worse than cramps, worse than water-retention and bloating? It gives people like you an excuse to dismiss our concerns as meaningless hormonal craziness."

"I wasn't dismissing anything." His headache was growing appreciably worse. "I was casting about for answers is all I was doing."

"Well, you latched onto the wrong one."

"I accept that."

"So what do we do? I tried talking to her again this morning, but she wouldn't give me the time of day. She was all breezy and casual about the whole thing."

"What did she say?"

Jessica hesitated before speaking. "She said she was having her period."

Toby tried not to laugh. He controlled the impulse for just long enough so that Jessie laughed first. Thank, God. They both laughed for a few seconds, and the tension between them dissipated perceptibly. "Okay, okay," she said. "Fine. But that's not what this was about."

"I believe you."

"So what do we do? She blows me off. And..." Her helpless shrug was almost audible.

"I can try talking to her again. But not tonight. She'll think we're ganging up on her." He heard a snorting noise. "Jessie, you may find it incredible, but she thinks we're in cahoots. And you think she and I are. I seem to be the only non-paranoid in the family."

"We aren't a family."

A characteristic piece of Jessiana. He'd known her for over twenty years by now, and he still couldn't figure out whether it resulted from a tin ear or a constant undercurrent of anger. Either way, it extinguished whatever good feeling they'd managed to generate.

∽

ONE OF THE THINGS you wouldn't have figured about Jonas was how fiercely competitive he was at racquetball. Not at all what you'd expect from a gay Jewish violist. He played every point with naked aggression, as if his life were at stake. And he hated to lose. Sometimes, when he did lose—and he and Toby were fairly evenly matched, so it happened from time to time—his mood would sour unattractively, and he'd need up to half an hour to pull himself out of it.

There wasn't much danger of that today. Toby's reflexes were slow, his energy level below the flatline. While Jonas chased down every ball, shouted ferociously as he caromed it off a side wall, laughed triumphantly when his little lobs caught Toby flat-footed, Toby barely bothered to make an effort. The result was a rout, more so than even Jonas could savor.

"What's wrong with you?" he demanded as they left the court. "You played like a girl."

"I'm knackered, Jonas. This isn't an excuse, you won fair and square, but I'm beat and I've had a headache all day."

"Why didn't you cancel?"

"I thought the exercise might help."

"Exercise never helps."

Later, as they showered in adjacent stalls, Jonas said, "Feel like a movie?"

"I just can't. Let's grab a bite, but afterward I'm heading straight to bed."

Jonas peered at him over the shoulder-high tile partition separating their showers. "Coming down with something?"

"Nothing in the physician's desk manual."

"My, aren't *you* mysterious."

And later, while dressing, Jonas said, "Rough night last night? Is that it?"

"You might say."

Jonas's eyebrows went up. "Anyone I know?"

"Uh-uh."

"Jesus, this is like plucking fucking eyebrows."

Toby relented to the extent of saying, "I guess I'm not quite ready to talk about it yet."

"Wow. Sounds interesting."

"I'll go that far. Way interesting. Majorly interesting."

"Tease."

At the storefront Thai place they favored, after they ordered, Toby looked across the Formica table and said, "Delicate subject?" Asking permission to proceed.

"Okay."

"Don't look so eager. It isn't about last night."

"And now it's too late for me to retract permission. That was sneaky."

"It's about Brian's opera."

Jonas made a face. "Above my pay grade. I just play my instrument and keep my nose clean."

Was it fatigue? Toby's tone was sharp when he said, "It isn't my job either. I'm the money man. But this thing seems to have landed in our laps all the same, *both* our laps, so cut the Butterfly McQueen crap, okay?"

"But our situations are different." Jonas didn't take umbrage, his tone was mild. "You deal with the suits all the time. I'm just a drone in the pit."

"But you have unique and unfettered access to Brian."

"Get your mind out of the gutter."

Toby took a swig of beer. "Jonas, please. Brian is handling this business way too cute. He could make enemies when there isn't any reason for it."

"He likes to play his cards close to his vest."

Toby shook his head impatiently. "I'm trying to be straight with you."

"There's the problem right there."

Toby didn't give this evasive little joke a chance to count as a joke. "Only if you let it. This isn't an us-versus-them situation, no matter how you define 'us' and how you define 'them.'" Jonas started to say something, but Toby persisted: "Doris has already caught wind of something irregular. If Brian ends up alienating her, what has he gained? Even if he's doing it for shits and giggles, his position isn't so secure he can do it with impunity. He's the one who's on a sort of probation right now, the one who wants a longer-term contract and a grander role. I'm not carrying Doris's water when I talk to you about this. It's for Brian. I regard him as a friend in his own right, and more importantly I care about him because of you."

Jonas didn't say anything for a few moments. Then he said, "I hear you." Then, after another few moments, he added with a sigh, "Okay, the thing you should know is, there may be a little problem with the libretto."

"The libretto? It's a bit early for that, surely. Doris hasn't even approved the topic. She probably will, but it isn't definite. No librettists have even been proposed."

"Yeah, I know."

"Plus, we'll need Solomon's blessing. As a courtesy. So how can—?"

"Please, Toby, I'm in an awkward position here." He looked around the room, trying to get the attention of a waiter, something nobody had ever succeeded in doing at this restaurant until the waiter himself was good and ready to cooperate. After a few seconds, Jonas bowed to the inevitable and faced Toby again. "See, you're kind of dividing my loyalties."

Toby nodded wearily. "How bad is it? Whatever *it* is. Can you tell me that?"

"Not horrible. Necessarily. Just…it's a problem that'll have to be dealt with."

Toby's headache, which had been in abeyance for a while, came back suddenly, and with a splitting vengeance. "Jesus. I just wanted you to give Brian a heads-up. I had no idea there was anything else."

"It's nothing. Basically."

"I need you to get him to…to…Are you seeing him tonight?"

"Probably."

"Will you give him a message? Tell him to cut the funny stuff. Please. Tell him I'm on his side; I want him to have his opera. But it'll be harder if he keeps surprising me."

Jonas nodded. But the way he looked away, avoiding eye contact, wasn't reassuring.

~

DRINKING TWO BEERS IN rapid succession was ill-advised after forty hours of sleeplessness. Toby chose to walk the ten or so blocks home from the restaurant, hoping the cold night air might clear his head. It didn't. By the time he reached his building, he could feel every system in his body shutting down. Which maybe wasn't so terrible. There was so much not to think about, instantaneous catatonia held some appeal.

Back in his apartment, after he peed, he checked his landline voice mail. Two messages. One a hang-up, the other for a Chinese take-out whose number was similar to his; he got a few of those calls every week. Amazing how often his outgoing message, although clearly not from Beijing Palace, failed to dissuade callers. Sweet and sour duck, red-chili tofu, steamed rice.

Someone must be getting mighty hungry by now.

He was feeling a little depressed. More than a little. Four fucking days in Mexico. Jesus, she was sexy, though. The charge between them had been…*incandescent*. The way they'd clawed at each other. The way their bodies fit.

Stripping down to his undershorts, he climbed into bed. He pressed the "play" button on his bedside iPod dock and turned out the light just as the selection he had cued, "Soave sia il vento" from *Così fan tutte*, began to play. It was his favorite piece from any opera he knew. Music doesn't get more beautiful. Perhaps it would restore his spirits or lull him to sleep.

His phone rang again. Jesus fucking Christ.

He flicked on his bedside light, turned off the iPod, and reached for the phone. "Yes?" he demanded gruffly. It was only ten something; he had no grounds for indignation other than his own pissy mood. Grounds enough.

"Toby? Is that you?" The voice was so low it was virtually a whisper.

"Amy?" He was suddenly wide awake.

"Hi there."

"Where are you?"

"The bathroom."

"No, I mean—"

"Cabo. Can you hear me?"

"Barely."

"Oh, Toby…I miss you."

"Do you?"

"Mmm."

"Likewise."

"Really?"

"It's all I could think about today."

"Me too. Which was, you know, a little awkward at times."
She laughed. "Listen, I'm coming home tomorrow."

"You are? You are? How come?"

"The official story? Or the real one?"

"Let me hear the real one."

"For the reasons stated before."

"Wait. You're coming back because you miss me?"

"Mmm."

"That's so great."

"Can we see each other?"

"I don't see how we can avoid it."

"No. I agree. Only…there's something you need to know."

"Go on."

"You're not going to believe this." She hesitated, then said, "I have
a urinary infection." A single syllable of surprised laughter burst out of
him. "It's not funny, Toby. It *hurts*." But she was laughing too.

"You haven't been drinking your cosmopolitans, there's the
problem."

"Noooo," she said, "that isn't the problem."

"Are you suggesting—?"

"More than suggesting. According to the hotel doctor, it's pretty
much a medical certainty. They call it 'honeymoon cystitis.' Good thing
Brad wasn't in the room when the doctor delivered his diagnosis. I'd have
some 'splainin' to do." She sighed. "Is this forbidden territory?"

"I can handle it."

"So anyway, I'm not supposed to…you know…"

"Doctor's orders?"

"So…I mean, I'm coming back anyway, so if you want to wait a
couple of days—"

"I don't even want to wait till tomorrow. If you can teleport yourself,
feel free to materialize in my bed this second. I swear I won't lay a finger
on you."

"You don't mind I'm out of commission?"

"Well, less than you might think."

"Toby—" Her voice was suddenly a little tremulous.

"I know, sweetie. Me too."

"Isn't this amazing?"

"Completely."

Then, suddenly, in a very urgent whisper, "Oh shit! Gotta go!"

PART TWO

1

MAGDA WAS EATING HER oysters with unapologetic relish, spearing the unfortunate creatures, whose life up to now had surely been no bed of roses, with her delicate little fork, swallowing them whole, afterward slurping the liquor straight from the half-shell. Toby watched with admiration.

She noticed him staring at her across the table. Still holding an empty oyster shell in her left hand, she said, "What? Mascara? Lipstick? Something between my teeth?"

"Nothing like that. I was just…I approve of your gusto, that's all."

"Ah yes. My notorious gusto." She made a dismissive sound. "A dubious attribute. You'd be surprised how many men are scared off by it." She placed the shell back on the plate, carefully resting it against a small metal cup of mignonette sauce. Was it possible he'd made her self-conscious? Nah. Women like Magda floated blithely above self-consciousness.

"I *wouldn't* be surprised," Toby answered. "It *is* frightening. Has a 'put up or shut up' quality. Not many women dare eat oysters like that. It's too…too overt. Almost indecent. You learn something vital about a woman by watching her eat oysters."

Magda narrowed her eyes. "What the devil are you going on about?" she said abruptly and unaccountably irritable. "You're behaving very oddly, Tobias." She leaned across the table toward him. "Completely manic, nattering on about utter rubbish."

"Aw, I've always been a bubbly guy."

She waved that away. "Bollocks. A tad jaunty, maybe, but nothing like this. You're positively vibrating." An idea occurred to her. "Is it Christine? Has something happened there, finally?"

She was both entirely wrong and yet close enough, at least in terms of general area, to make Toby uncomfortable. "No, I haven't seen her in weeks."

Christine was a friend of Magda's, who for some unaccountable reason Magda seemed eager to see involved with Toby. She'd told each separately they'd be great together. One of the peculiar things about Magda, gleefully playing matchmaker while occasionally sleeping with one of the people she was matching. Was Christine aware of that last part?

"Why, for heaven's sake?"

"Oh, one thing and another." Her eagerness for him to get together with Christine had always struck him as a little creepy, and perhaps his sense that Magda was peering over his shoulder, figuratively speaking, had even slowed their progress. And now his attention was focused elsewhere. Was it ever! His attention had never been so focused. Future progress with Christine was no longer an option.

"Don't you find Christine attractive?"

"She's fine."

"But you're not pursuing this."

"Whereas you are." She looked hurt by this counterthrust, but it was definitely time to slip off the ropes. "What's your stake in it?"

"No stake. I know she likes you. She said you're hot, is how she put it." She suddenly peered at him sharply. "Damn it, you're barely listening."

"What do you mean? I'm all ears."

"Like hell. You're a hundred miles away. And while receiving a *compliment*. It's so unlike you I'm actually starting to worry. You're withholding something. I thought we were pals."

"Maybe it's a gas pain. Am I expected to report on every shooting gas pain I experience in your company?"

She smiled for the first time in several minutes. "Yes! That's what friends do."

"On a bad day, we'd talk about little else."

"It doesn't look to me like you're having a bad day, Toby. Quite the reverse."

Would he and Amy sleep together tonight? he wondered. Actual intercourse was clearly impermissible for medical reasons, but he longed for some intimacy. They could make out like teenagers, or hold hands, or lie on their sides staring into each other's eyes, or commit a few gross improprieties. Whatever happened would be fine. He just wanted to be with her. Unless, of course, his sudden erection suggested he was kidding himself.

"Is it Solomon?" she asked.

The question was startling enough to shake him out of his reverie. She kept scoring these near-misses that were also near-hits. "Solomon?"

"Did you get his check? Is that what you're smiling about?"

"Not exactly," he said.

"Not exactly you got a check or not exactly that's what you're smiling about?"

"Both."

"'Not exactly' would suggest somewhat, or almost, or approximately."

"I suppose it would."

"Well, congratulations. The way he cut you the other night, I figured you for dead meat."

"You underestimate me. We met again. Just me and the Bradster, no girls' claque to encourage grandstanding." Toby permitted himself a smile, and hoped it looked just smug enough to suggest his triumph without being obnoxiously smug.

"No wonder you're cock of the walk today." This could have come across as captious, but she actually sounded affectionate, even grudgingly admiring.

Later, as they were leaving the restaurant, she asked, "What should I tell Christine?"

He permitted himself his first outright show of annoyance. "You should tell her nothing. Let's drop the whole matter, okay?"

She nodded, deeply unsatisfied. "Don't think you can keep this nonsense up forever. At some point, you owe me an explanation."

He didn't understand the accounting principles underlying such an assertion but didn't argue. Given her normal tenacity, especially where gossip was concerned, she was letting him off easily. So he said, "Yes, okay," with a humorous shrug. Then he kissed her cheek—when they weren't in bed, they could be oddly formal with one another—and waited for her to walk away, hoping he wasn't being too obvious about it. He followed her departing figure with his eyes until she rounded the corner. Once she was safely out of sight, he turned on his heel and strode back into the restaurant.

"Yes, Mr. Lindeman?" said Serge, the maître d', when Toby approached his station. "Forget something?"

"I *remembered* something. I need a table tonight. Eight o'clock. For two." His heart produced a single mighty thump, followed by an alarming tattoo, as he said the words "for two."

Serge didn't bother to consult the reservation book. Toby, with his Opera House office a couple of blocks from the restaurant, was a regular customer who often brought potential donors to lunch or dinner here. Hayes Street Grill always took special care of him. One way or another, he would be accommodated. "Eight o'clock. We look forward to seeing you."

"A special favor, Serge?"

"Of course."

"Tonight is important to me." He felt his heart thump again. "I'd like it to be perfect."

"I understand. We'll do everything possible to assist, Mr. Lindeman."

"I'm sure you will. Thank you. But I have a specific request." He took his credit card out of his breast pocket and proffered it to Serge. "Could you swipe it and let me sign? Now, I mean? I'd rather not see a check tonight. Just add a twenty-five percent tip to the total. Is that all right?"

"Certainly."

"Will you be here?"

"Robert is on duty tonight. I'll make sure he understands the situation."

"I can rely on that?"

"Don't worry about a thing. It will be a perfect evening. We'll see to it."

Serge smiled chummily, man-to-man. That European attitude to pussy. Toby smiled back; the smile was an integral part of the transaction.

And then, pretending not to mind, he dug into his pocket, fished out a twenty, and slipped it into Serge's hand. A little insurance policy.

～

NOT THAT HE COULD afford to squander the time—it was another extravagance, like the twenty dollar tip—but Toby decided to take a walk down to the water before returning to work. The day was too nice not to. A young man's fancy and so on. All right, all right, a forty-four-year-old man's fancy. Get off my back.

It felt like spring, looked like spring, smelled like spring. The weather wasn't, perhaps, quite warm enough for spring, but if you were in the right mood, it provided a reasonable facsimile. Toby was in the right mood. He strolled downhill, admiring the trees that were just starting to bloom, listening to the cacophonous squawking of the seagulls, occasionally raising his face to the bright sunlight with its not-quite-kept promise of warmth.

God's in his heaven, all's right with the world.

Except for the fact that it wasn't eight o'clock yet. But it would be, eventually. Judging by past experience. You just have to give it time.

Easier said than done. Had he ever felt such impatience? It was a physical sensation, a fidgety imprisonment within his skin. Imprisonment on the last day of his sentence; awareness of impending deliverance occasioned his impatience but also rendered it almost pleasurable. There was something delectable about a restlessness that would decisively end within a few hours and at a point certain.

He smiled benignly at a group of young Catholic schoolgirls in their plaid uniforms coming toward him, and watched with chaste pleasure as they scrambled uphill past him, shouting and jostling each other. He stepped to the side to give them room, a chaos of bare limbs and plaid clothing and flying hair and unrestrained laughter. They were oblivious to him, and he liked that too, liked the way they surrendered to the exigent pleasures of the day, liked the way they were so caught up in their own exhilaration they treated him like an inanimate object. It was all so lovely, all the elements of the day fit together: The cloudless sky, the birds, the sun glinting off the bay, the girls in bud.

Les jeunes filles en fleur.

Wasn't it interesting that Proust wrote so fondly, so evocatively, of the winsomeness of young girls? You didn't have to be a pedophile to appreciate their charms—you could savor their pubescent allure without coveting their bodies—but Toby would have thought heterosexuality a minimal requirement. Apparently not.

A thought that brought him to Jonas and Brian and the multitude of other gay men within his purview. There was something about gay men, about the possibly erroneous presumption of unchecked unruliness in their sexual relations, that still had the power to discomfit him. As if he somehow knew more about their private lives than he had any right to know simply by virtue of their orientation. No doubt it was projection, or even envy, some notion of rampant male lust unrestrained by the white gloves and genteel bowing of the heterosexual cotillion.

But it was obvious to Toby that the Jonas he, Toby, was friends with was a different creature from the Jonas who used to go out cruising on Saturday nights. Jonas had no hesitation about being physically affectionate with Brian in Toby's company; that was safe, domesticated. But Jonas on the prowl was no doubt a different breed of cat. That was part of the alien universe to which a straight friend, even a very close straight friend like Toby, was denied access.

And yet, Toby's ruminations went on, who really knew what one's *straight* friends were up to? Maybe Lamont Cranston, but that would be about it, and you had to take his word for it. Private lives were full of surprises and secrets by definition. Everyone you met, everyone you passed on the street, straight or gay, buttoned-up or openly roguish, must have whole closets full of hidden urges and furtive longings.

Who, for example, would have guessed that a prosperous Midwestern Republican-reared entrepreneur like Amy Baldwin was, behind closed doors, an omnivorous little sexpot?

This thought made Toby laugh out loud with simple joy at his wonderful good fortune.

~

"Miss Baldwin isn't available. She said she'll see you at Hayes Street at eight."

He hung up, dissatisfied. Could she really be in meetings every single minute today? Well, it didn't matter, he'd see her in the flesh in less than five hours.

He suddenly jumped up, too restless to sit still. He didn't want coffee, and he certainly didn't need any, but he decided to go into the office's anteroom and get himself a cup. That should kill a couple of seconds.

He pushed the door open and stepped through. And was surprised to find Doris in conversation with Daniel. "Brian won't mind," she was saying. "Everyone who works here should do it. It's a precious opportunity." Then she saw Toby, and her face immediately turned stern. "We need to talk," she said flatly.

"Ah," he responded with bland irony, as if she were offering an interesting but impersonal news item. This was partly in self-defense; Doris would lose respect if he cowered too readily. It was also a way of saving face when it was obvious he was about to be called on the carpet in front of his assistant.

Doris gestured toward his office.

"Let me just get some coffee," he said. He glanced over at Daniel, who returned the glance with a small, sympathetic smile. *Teacher's on your case.* "Would you like some?"

"No."

Without a "thank you." This must be serious. Manners were not a minor matter to Doris. Still, he took his time pouring the coffee, and then ushered her through the door to his office.

She took a seat facing his desk, and he settled into his chair behind it. An anomalous bit of choreography. Here she was on his turf—she could have summoned him to her office, but hadn't—and occupying what would ordinarily be considered the inferior position, but with the clear intention of putting him in his place. She had enough personal force to make it work.

But he wasn't going to let himself be rolled. Maintaining a casual demeanor, he took a sip of coffee. She was staring at him levelly. He set his mug down. Her face gave nothing away; its very blankness was disconcerting, as it was no doubt meant to be.

He resisted the urge to say, "And to what do I owe the pleasure?" Flippancy would be a mistake. Instead, he waited, willing himself into a simulacrum of Zen-like calm. A charade, of course. Indeed, it suddenly occurred to him, with an irrational jolt, she might have learned about Amy, a prospect so chilling and at the same time so implausible he banished it from his mind. Play them as they're dealt.

Finally she uttered a single word, through very tight lips: "*Splosion*."

It was almost a relief after his lurid imaginings. "Jeremy Metcalfe's band," he said, nodding agreeably.

"How could you not have told me?"

"It wasn't a secret."

Her voice rose as she said, with a hint of incredulity and more than a hint of ire, "You expect me to green-light a commission for a guitarist in a rock band?"

"Not I, Doris. I don't *have* expectations. It's the music director's project."

"But I'm discussing it with you. Don't tell me it isn't your business. This is an unusual situation." She was keeping her wrath under a tight rein, but there was no mistaking it. "You're a friend of Brian's. You've established an amicable relationship with Brad, God knows how. And you clearly know more than you've shared with me. I need to be able to trust you, Toby. I need to know whose side you're on."

"You don't trust Brian?"

She flashed him a look of annoyance before replying, a look to let him know his question was out-of-bounds. Then, surprisingly, she answered. "Not completely, no. To be candid. He's a talented man and a charming fellow, and the board has confidence in him. I couldn't explain my misgivings if I tried. But that's a side issue. The point is, I *did* think I could trust *you*."

Toby still declined to rise to the bait, still refused to give any indication he took the conversation personally. He understood that in some obscure way it would constitute being outmaneuvered. "How have I let you down?" he asked calmly. "The only thing I can imagine your being upset about is I didn't answer your email yesterday. That was the first time something about Splosion came up. I was planning to get to it this afternoon."

"It was a fairly urgent email. In any case, it shouldn't have required an email from me for you to understand your obligations."

Time to give a little ground. Playing dumb with Doris was a bad strategy. Either she wouldn't believe it, and then she'd trust you even less, or, on the off chance she did believe it, she'd thereafter regard you as dumb. Lose-lose. He therefore conceded, "You're right. I should have let you know about it right away. I didn't want to do it in an email. I felt it was something we should discuss in person."

"You said you were planning to answer my email this afternoon."

"No, I said I was planning to get to it. I didn't say what form getting to it would take."

Which at last wrung a smile out of her. Quite a warm smile, really, if also reluctant. She preferred Toby to be forthrightly clever, even if it entailed losing the occasional point to him. "Okay, here I am. In person. Talk to me."

His answering smile was a little wan. "I had hoped for time to prepare."

"Tough sale, huh?"

"Not exactly. Complicated. Okay, tough. But I won't be bullshitting you, Doris. I believe my pitch, even if I am acting as Brian's mouthpiece."

"Let's hear it."

"Jeremy Metcalf *is* the bass guitarist and main songwriter in Splosion. A respected band on the art-rock scene, by the way." She started to object, but he kept going: "He was also a star student at Juilliard. Majored in double bass, but he plays keyboards too, and percussion and a variety of string instruments and God knows what. He took a lot of composition and theory courses. His musicianship is irreproachable. If you listen to the Splosion CD—"

"That won't be necessary."

"They're almost all classically trained. Not the drummer, I don't think, but the others. They aren't troglodytes. It isn't a garage band. Jeremy's been composing concert music all along. He won some sort of prize at Juilliard. A sextet of his was done at SoundBox last year. It got good reviews."

"As if that means anything. Reviews of new music are just hopeless guesswork." She sighed, unhappy at having been sucked into this line of discussion. "What sort of style?"

"Yes, see, that's the important thing."

"This should be rich."

"No, hear me out. He's quite conservative. I mean, tonal, and even kind of pretty. Not cornball, not Puccini-with-a-few-wrong-notes, but lyrical. He's learned something from writing pop songs, although he regards the two activities as distinct and uses a different idiom for each. But he knows how to shape a melody. That's what Brian says. He says Jeremy's been influenced by the minimalists without *being* a minimalist…"

She sighed theatrically.

"I'm not fancy-dancing, honest. Brian…it's not that he has trouble with thorny stuff, but where opera's concerned he's more traditional. His taste is more like the average operagoer's. He thinks opera needs to be tonal. Even tuneful. Otherwise, it's awkward for the voice and doesn't work as drama. He's not looking for some ugly, discordant horror our subscribers will walk out on. He doesn't want a scandal, he wants a hit. That's one of the reasons he's so eager for Jeremy to get the commission. He thinks Jeremy's approach is more likely to give us an opera that will be popular. And, of course, he has the highest regard for Jeremy's skills."

"His skills, right," she said drily, and snorted. "I'm sure that's what Brian likes best about Jeremy Metcalf, his *skills*." If Toby was interpreting her correctly, solely on the basis of her intonation, this was as close as he had ever heard her come to homophobia, which seemed profoundly out of character. But she was feeling excluded and beleaguered right now.

He elected not to address the implication. Instead, he went on in the same earnest tone, "And even if it's non-PC to say so, Jeremy's being Black was likely a factor in Brian's calculations. There's a notion opera's the exclusive preserve of rich white people. We're not getting young audiences, we're not getting…I mean, there are whole communities who would never *consider* attending an opera. And not just minorities. Despite the cliché, young gays are staying away in droves too. Brian hopes we can appeal to a new audience."

There. It was about as good as he could do. Not *too* shabby, he reckoned, considering the pressure she had put him under, and considering that he'd had no time to prepare his brief.

She was regarding him quizzically. "So," she said, "he thinks it would be smart for us to commission something along the lines of *Tommy*, is that it?" Toby noticed that, although her words were caustic, she no longer sounded quite so determinedly on the warpath.

"I suppose you can invoke *Tommy* if you like. But a popular opera doesn't have to be vulgar. Doesn't require Ann-Margaret rolling around in baked beans. It doesn't have to be a dressed-up musical, either. There are other precedents. *Porgy and Bess*, for example. Which, as I recall, the Met refused to mount. They apparently thought it was beneath them. Of course, George Gershwin didn't attend Juilliard."

Boom! He permitted himself another sip of coffee while he waited for her to respond. He realized the rigors of this little tête-à-tête had at least briefly taken his mind off tonight's rendezvous with Amy. Not much else could have accomplished that.

He noticed a slow smile stealing across Doris's face again. After a moment she all but growled, "You're lucky I have a weakness for smart men."

He coughed out a laugh of pure surprise. It was the last thing in the world he expected to hear. "Why, thank you. My goodness, that's the nicest thing you've ever said to me."

"I'm sure I'll regret it." She put her palms on her lap and stood up. He followed suit. "All my instincts tell me something stinks. But I have to admit you make a pretty good case. And God knows I'm relieved to hear there's *some* sort of rationale behind Brian's schemes."

"Absolutely."

She sighed. "I should've confronted *him*. I doubt he'd have been so persuasive."

"He'd have been more so. He knows Jeremy's music. I've only heard a bit of it."

"Splosion, or the concert stuff?"

"Splosion," Toby conceded. He instantly regretted having mentioned the matter.

"So that doesn't really count, does it?"

"I suppose not. That's why Brian would have been more persuasive."

"I have my doubts." She turned toward the door, and then turned back to face him. "Mind you, I'm not saying yes. Don't interpret this conversation as a go-ahead. Nor should you assume I'm happy. I wish the whole business had taken a different course. But I'll have to give it more thought. It may not be *quite* as nutty as I was inclined to believe."

"We'll make page one of the *Chronicle*. Hell, we'll get national coverage. You'll see."

She was willing to let him have the last word. She turned toward the door, and he quick-stepped to open it for her. When they emerged into the waiting area, Daniel was pretending to be busy, clicking away at his computer. But it was obvious to Toby where his attention and his curiosity were directed. He was careful not to look up. He didn't look up with a vengeance.

Doris, oblivious to all this, said, "From now on, volunteer information when you have it, don't wait for me to ask. And never leave me guessing. It will lead to bad blood between us."

"All right, Doris. Point taken."

She headed toward the stairs. Toby, relieved by the conversation's pacific outcome, but now more worried than ever about any stratagems Brian might be hatching, pivoted back toward his door and found himself confronted by Daniel's interrogative glance. You couldn't blame the guy for being curious, but neither were you obligated to *satisfy* that curiosity. "Tempest in a teapot," he said. The opera commission, Brian Hughes, Brad Solomon, Jeremy Metcalfe, all were none of Daniel's business. Hell, they shouldn't even have been Toby's.

"Maybe she's on the rag," Daniel suggested.

Toby was offended by this, maybe because it assumed a familiarity between them that didn't exist, or a shared male disdain for women in general, or more specifically a personal disrespect toward Doris. He answered quietly, "If I had to hazard a guess, I'd say those days are probably over for Doris. But I'd also say the subject's out-of-bounds."

Daniel frowned. He wasn't used to being reprimanded by Toby. He waited a moment before sullenly handing over a pink slip. "Your ex-wife called while you were in there."

Toby took the note, but didn't look at it until he was back in his office. It was written in pencil, in Daniel's small, neat hand. "Jessica. Important. Not re Cathy. Please return."

Toby slipped into his chair. And came to an unexpected decision: No. He'd never before failed to return one of Jessica's calls, return it promptly, and the reward for his conscientiousness was usually a litany of his failings as husband and man. Fuck it. Even if it took his mind off Amy for another minute or two, it wasn't worth it. He and Jessica weren't married anymore. And she'd cheated, he hadn't abandoned her. There was no guilt debt on his side. If there was a non-Cathy issue, it wasn't his problem. Let her find someone else to listen to her woes. And to blame.

This decision didn't make him feel especially good. He thought it might, but things didn't work out that way. Still, he intended to stick to it. Hard to know what to do instead, though. Cornelius Ryan's candidate for the longest day struck him as a poor second at best. Eight o'clock was eons away.

~

"Is GAY PORN LIKE straight porn, would you say?"

Jonas considered the question. "I guess. Sure. Not that I've seen a lot of straight porn, but is it short on plot? Short on passion? Lots of genital close-ups when you'd rather see faces? That's what the gay stuff is like. Why do you ask?"

"I killed a little time watching porn today."

"On your computer?"

"Uh-huh."

"In your office?" Toby nodded, looking a little sheepish. "Did you enjoy it?"

"Not especially. It was diverting for a few minutes, then I got bored."

"Not horny?"

"That strange unsatisfactory confluence of the two."

"Know it well. Another?" He was already signalling the waiter.

"No thanks. I want my head clearish."

"Another for me, nothing for my buddy," Jonas told the waiter. Then, back to Toby, "So what possessed you? To look at porn, I mean?"

Toby stole a quick glance around to see if Jonas might have been overheard. Probably not. "Couldn't focus on anything else."

"Your mind was already in the mud, was it?"

"Or environs."

"You weren't looking for a little inspiration?"

"Not necessary in this case. *Super* not necessary."

"Does all this relate to your wanting to keep your head clearish?"

"In a way."

"And it's also why we're here now? To provide temporary distraction?"

"Any port in a storm."

"Look, you might as well tell me, pal. You're dying to."

"I am, aren't I?"

"I'd say. Is it the same business as the other night?"

"Kind of. I mean, yes."

"Which must be epic. I've never seen you like this. Come on, cough it up."

Toby grinned. It was partly in response to his friend's avidity, but it was also an unfamiliar self-consciousness. "The thing to bear in mind is, this isn't a purely good thing."

"Tell your face."

"I know. See, it *feels* like a purely good thing. But it isn't."

"Okay, let's consider that fact established and proceed to the next step."

Toby sighed. "I'm fishing in troubled waters, Jonas."

"Someone's wife?"

"Not exactly."

"Someone's husband?"

"Hate to disappoint you."

Jonas laughed at that. At which point the waiter materialized at their table with the drink Jonas had ordered. As soon as they were alone again, he pressed on, "You want to keep playing twenty questions? I'm willing if you find it entertaining. But maybe you should just tell me."

Toby sighed again. "I'm relying on your total discretion."

"Of course."

"Why am I doing this?"

"Because you have to tell *somebody*."

Toby nodded, then blurted, "Solomon's girlfriend."

There was a short pause. Evidently it was a lot of information to take in, those two words. Jonas started easy. "Solomon's got a girlfriend?"

"Uh-huh. It's pretty widely known. Magda called it an open secret."

"And now you've got a secret of your own."

"Mine's not open."

"Does Magda know? About you and..."

"You're the first. The only. And in a half hour I'll be sorry I told you."

"Pish tush, I'm the soul of discretion." He tasted his drink. "Solomon's married, no?"

"Married, mega-rich, and has a girlfriend. It's unprecedented!"

Jonas put his glass down, looking serious. "Do you have any idea what you've gotten yourself into?"

"Not really."

"Do you think it's wise?"

"I'm not really operating on that level."

"Right. Obviously. Is the fact she's Solomon's girlfriend what makes this so special, would you say?"

"No, no. No. What makes it special is...her." He felt an accelerated heartbeat and a rush of blood to his head. Every fucking time he thought about her. "She's magic, Jonas. Smart and funny and sexy and...just incredible. *That's* why it's special."

Jonas, his head slightly cocked, regarded Toby appraisingly. He finally said, "Well holy smokes. Never thought I'd see the day."

Toby shifted uncomfortably. "No, listen, let's not go there. I'm in no shape to cope with the implications. I refuse to acknowledge them. I'm just...you know, letting the surf carry me where it will."

"Right. Sure. Whatever you say. What time are you meeting her?"

"Eight."

Jonas looked at his watch. "You'd better get going, chum. You'll be late."

Toby shrugged. "I've been counting the seconds all day, but now... maybe it'd be a mistake to be *too* prompt. I don't want to look desperate."

"Word of advice?"

"Sure."

"From someone who's been there?"

"I said yes."

"This sounds like it matters. Don't be an asshole."

≈

83

TOBY REACHED THE RESTAURANT at eight on the dot. It was Amy who was late. Seated at the best small table in the house—Serge kept his promise—close enough to the entrance to witness comings and goings but far enough away to be spared disruptive clamor, Toby, nursing a Tito's Gibson, sat and brooded for close to half an hour before she appeared at the entrance. She looked rushed and more than a little harried. When she saw him, she gave a small wave, and he waved back, aware of but unable to suppress a dopey smile.

He stood, rattling the crockery on the small table. His whole system felt flushed with adrenaline and desire. Under her coat she was wearing a trim gray pinstripe suit and a lavender blouse. No jewelry except simple silver earrings. The table was between them, so their kiss was more chaste than he would have liked. Still, her face felt wonderful against his, chilled and vibrant. He had to make a conscious effort to stop from touching her in some intimate way. Instead, he held both her hands in his while she offered breathless, agitated apologies. A late meeting, a crisis phone call, difficulties getting an Uber, terrible traffic, the standard downtown catalogue of woes. He assured her it was fine, no problem, he was just glad she was here. The waiter came by at the exact right moment, just as these exchanges were finishing—more evidence of Serge's beneficent influence, Toby guessed; someone was keeping an eagle eye on the table—and she ordered a cosmopolitan, she removed her coat and slung it over the back of her chair, and they both took their seats.

For a moment he just looked at her. Her face was a surprise to him, perhaps because he had difficulty picturing it in her absence. It was so... well, nondescript might not be the right word, but it was unmemorable, entirely pleasant without being especially pretty or striking. He could recognize in the abstract that she wasn't especially pretty, but she struck him as beautiful.

"What?" she said.

"Nothing. I just enjoy looking at you."

She nodded and looked away, surveying the room. "I've never been here before."

"It's near the opera, so I'm here all the time. They could charge me rent." He took her hand again. "How are you?"

"Unrelaxed." She freed her hand to take a drink of water.

"Rough day?"

"Oh boy. In addition to everything else, one of my programmers just gave notice. At six o'clock. Leaves me in a pickle. There's a lot going on these days. I've come to depend on her."

"The bitch."

"She's pregnant."

Was it his imagination or did he hear the suggestion of a rebuke in those two words? "Oh," was all he could think to say.

"Been trying for months."

"Temperature-taking and everything?"

"Worse. The whole painful panoply of reproductive technology."

"Jeez. So I guess that's good for her, then."

"Right." She craned her neck to look at the bar. "Where's my drink, I wonder?"

"You need it that badly?"

He intended this jocularly, but she didn't take it that way. "I don't *need* it at all. It's just, I ordered it, I'd like to have it."

"Would you like a sip of mine?" He proffered his martini glass.

She frowned and shook her head.

This wasn't going the way he'd planned.

"Listen," he said, but at the same time, she said, "So—" Which led to a little Alphonse-and-Gaston business, and after she prevailed on him to go first, her drink was delivered, either breaking his rhythm or letting him off the hook, it was hard to say which.

After she took a cautious sip of her drink, he asked, "Up to expectations?"

"It's fine."

Another not-quite-adequate response. Maybe it was nerves. He was pretty damned nervous himself. There had been so much intimacy so quickly, it was hard to situate oneself. Especially face-to-face.

Perhaps it would help simply to acknowledge the fact. Get it out there on the table where they could deal with it. He said, "Listen" again, and then, in a torrent, "this is strange, isn't it? In some ways I feel I already know you inside out." He wanted to kick himself for the unintentional double entendre, but raced on, "Do you feel that way too? It's like I've known you for years. All my life. It's an astonishing thing. But we don't know much

85

about each other at all, do we? I feel like we know the essentials, but maybe that's sentimental bullshit. And even if we do know the essentials, I don't know lots of other stuff, like what music you like, or how many siblings you have, or whether your parents are still married. Or are even alive. But I'm here, you're here, something's happened between us, and now I want to know everything. Even the boring stuff won't be boring. And I want to tell you everything about me. The good, the bad, and the Lee Van Cleef. For the first time ever, in my whole life, I want to be transparent. I don't know where an impulse like that comes from, but since I've never felt anything remotely like it before, I probably ought to trust it."

She looked down at the tabletop. The ensuing silence was palpable. He fancied he could hear the dying reverberations of his own voice along with the chatter at other tables.

"Maybe we should order," she said. "I wouldn't mind seeing a menu."

"Amy—"

The look she gave him was less than a hundred percent friendly. "Look," she said, "I've had a perfectly shitty day. Everything happened right at the end, totally fell apart, and I had to rush to get here, I'm frazzled, and now you're pressuring me to say something or do something or give you something, and frankly, it's not helping."

It was like a slap in the face.

"Are we having our first fight?" he asked, hoping to leaven the situation.

There was a long interval in which she continued not to meet his eye. Then she said, "No, we're having our *last* fight." She gave that a few seconds to sink in, and then looked up and continued, "It was wrong of me to lead you on, if that's what I did. This isn't a good idea. I've been struggling with it all day. It's been feeling like a huge mistake. Everything's so *serious* all of a sudden. It was supposed to be a lark. A respite from real life. And we had a great night, don't get me wrong. But we need to stop before it gets out of hand. If it hasn't already."

"But—"

"There isn't any point in discussing it. There's nothing more to say. It's over." She stood up. "I'm sorry if you're hurt, but I just can't do this." In one smooth move, she grabbed her coat, pushed her chair away, turned her back on him, and strode out of the restaurant.

2

T OBY HAD BEEN DREAMING, something indistinct but unsettling, a succession of elusive, apparently disconnected images fraught with indefinable menace. Then he suddenly wasn't dreaming anymore. First, a thought intruded on his dream: You can wake up whenever you like. Then another thought presented itself, alarming in its childlike simplicity: When you wake up, you'll be unhappy. And that completed the job. He was awake. His eyes were closed, but he was wide awake. And he most assuredly wasn't happy.

At which moment, the memory of the previous night, lurking fretfully at the periphery of his consciousness, suddenly burst into full view: Hi! Remember me? "Oh shit," Toby groaned aloud, and covered his head with a pillow.

He lay still for a moment, trying to assess the situation. The unhappiness seemed to have a specific locus, smack in the middle of his thorax. And yet it felt all-encompassing, reaching out innumerable tentacles wrapping around every aspect of his life.

He opened his eyes. There was no light at the edges of his window shades. That was bad. With an effort—an effort that seemed pointless, automatic, fatuous—he felt for his bedside clock. Once he had his hand on it, he picked it up, pulled it close to his face, and peered at the illuminated digits.

Four thirty-three. Jesus, Mary, and Joseph. Not much better than the middle of the night. He didn't have to get up for over two hours. And damn it, he needed sleep. Three nights ago, he hadn't slept at all; he'd been too busy fucking. And now he'd lain awake brooding till almost two. But sleep was out of reach. For all his fatigue, all the lethargy he was currently feeling and all the exhaustion he knew was sure to come, he was awake, awake with a vengeance, experiencing something like panic. His heart was beating violently. His mind was racing in frantic circles. He was awake with his unhappiness, and his unhappiness wanted company and wasn't going to let him absent himself from the party.

So what now? Just waiting out the dawn was unthinkable, an endless, unendurable vigil. He'd be counting the seconds. Like yesterday, when he was impatiently awaiting his date with Amy. The thought delivered a stab of renewed anguish. It was hard to believe yesterday was so recent; yesterday felt like something on the other side of a historical chasm.

Yesterday, he thought again, and heard music in his head. He recognized it right away: An acoustic guitar joined by George Martin's string quartet arrangement. Yesterday all my troubles seemed so far away. It was a song he promised himself never to listen to again. Except when he couldn't avoid it, like every time he stepped into an elevator and Sir Paul's personal cash register went *ka-ching*.

Hey, honey, they're playing our song.

Okay, let's get a grip. This *wasn't* a historical chasm. A woman I've seen three times in my entire life, and with whom I spent precisely one night, admittedly an extraordinary night but nonetheless a single night, just dumped me. Happens all the time. Barely counts as a dumping, the whole business was so brief. A one-night stand. An escapade. Just one of those things, just one of those crazy flings. What say we keep a sense of proportion?

Things seem worse in the gloom; small shapes cast giant shadows. That dark night of the soul when it's always three o'clock in the morning and so forth. Keep yourself occupied for a couple of hours and everything'll be fine. He kicked off his blanket and flung his lower body out of bed, planting his feet on the floor. Rise and shine. Up and at 'em.

But now what? Now that he was more upright than not, what should happen next?

Might as well go for a run, he thought, and congratulated himself on the inspired suggestion. Inspired, that is, under the unpromising circumstances. Weekday runs were a rarity; he usually didn't have the time for such a luxury. Consider it an opportunity. Lucky me.

Even though his entire being resisted, he abruptly stood up, which occasioned a nauseating wave of light-headedness. He ignored it, strode into the bathroom, brushed his teeth, and urinated in the dark, and then walked briskly back to his bedroom. We just need the proper attitude. The early bird catches the worm. When the going gets tough, the tough get going. He got down on the rug beside his bed and went through his stretching routine, then rose, pulled on some running clothes, put his key in a fanny pack, and headed out of his apartment.

Within a couple of minutes he was on the street, trotting down to the Marina. It was still dark, but cool rather than cold, and almost deserted. The Golden Gate Bridge looked majestic. It was kind of nice, if you were in the right frame of mind. Few pedestrians, only an occasional sad car. Zipping home in disgrace or fleeing home in desperation? Idle to speculate.

He had more energy than he'd expected; the initial lassitude when he began stretching hadn't lasted. Maybe he was already feeling better. Sure. Back to normal now that it was almost five. It was just the shock of last night's unexpected little amorous course-correction, and insufficient sleep, and those obscurely troubling dreams. In a few minutes he'd be right as rain.

The relevant question wasn't why she'd ended things with no warning but why he'd been so shocked. So distressed. Why had he invested so much in what was, after all, merely an unexpected adventure? She wasn't even especially pretty. Magda was prettier. Christine was prettier. Lots of women were prettier.

Although he did like her face. No point denying that. He liked looking at her. And oddly, he was now able to picture that face in his mind's eye, something he'd been unable to do before last night. Her intelligent, frank gaze. Friendly, candid, unaffected, but with a little ironic smile that put you slightly off-balance, let you know you underestimated her at your peril. There was shrewdness in that smile. An unsettling sort of knowingness. And then there were her eyes of course, those eyes that had stayed open in the dark during lovemaking and stared directly into his, audacious, unreadable, deep.

The memory almost made him stumble. It seized him around his chest and clamped down, it sucked the air out of his lungs, it tipped his internal gyroscope into a crazy wobble and made his knees go rubbery.

Get over it, for Christ's sake! He was far too old, and, if we're being honest, far too jaded, to believe in love at first sight. Now your life is in the same, eminently satisfactory place it was before. No fault, no foul. So stop moaning and count your blessings.

But that look of hers, those open eyes probing his, had to have meant something. It wasn't just bedroom etiquette. Couldn't have been. It went so far beyond the demands of bedroom etiquette it almost constituted a violation.

Think about something else. You've got plenty of other problems, why not brood about *those*? As Freud might say, shift your attention from neurotic misery to ordinary unhappiness. Take the opera; that's turning into a major headache. A veritable migraine. The opera. Brian. The mysterious Jeremy Metcalf, whom you've never met but defended so eloquently yesterday. Yesterday. All my troubles seemed so far away. Stop it! The opera. Brian. Jeremy Metcalf. Doris. Brad Solomon.

Brad Solomon. That son of a bitch. That unworthy, unforgivable son of a bitch. Does Amy look into *his* eyes the way she'd looked into mine? An intolerable thought. Was she sleeping soundly now? Did she have any doubts or regrets about last night? Or was it the emotional equivalent of sacking an under-performing employee, an unappetizing bit of business certainly, but one forgotten as soon as it was accomplished?

No, it simply wasn't possible. He wasn't that nuts.

Suppose she was suffering the way he was. Just suppose it for a second. For the sake of argument. As a working hypothesis. It was possible. Maybe she'd call him today to say it was a mistake, a crazy misguided overreaction to the awful day she'd just been through, she regretted it, she took it back, she took all of it back, she wanted to see him. Tonight. Immediately.

For a moment, he let himself believe it. But quickly realized it was impossible. A person doesn't make the speech she made last night on a whim. Not after what had gone before. She must have spent the whole day considering and reconsidering, she finally must have done all the reconsidering she was ever going to do and reached a definitive conclusion: Toby meets dumpster forthwith.

It was mysterious, though. She'd given him plenty of reason to think what he was feeling was reciprocal. She'd given intimations. Assorted hints. Not to mention fucking his brains out.

Approaching the Presidio, he encountered a couple coming in the opposite direction, a man and a woman a few years older than he but still fit, jogging rather slowly, side-by-side, absorbed in conversation. He caught only a snippet as he stepped to the edge of the road to let them by: She was saying, "...maybe we should skip Sea Ranch this weekend..." Brief as it was, this fragment was sufficient to refute his conceit that only rejected lovers were to be found in this venue at this hour. It was enough to make him feel empty and forlorn in a whole new way.

The domesticity implicit in what he'd just witnessed, a couple running together before their workday commenced, discussing plans for the upcoming weekend...Since his break-up with Jessie, such a scenario had had no appeal whatsoever. The very idea evoked not only the miseries of his unlamented marriage, but even way back to the despised constraints of boarding school. He'd found the latter so miserable that ever since he imagined he had an inkling what prison must be like. Today, though, right now, looking over his shoulder and watching the man and woman trotting slowly away from him, absorbed in and apparently pleased with each other's company, he felt sick with envy. That whole safe, boring, stifling intimacy, maybe it had something going for it after all. Maybe it was preferable to disconnection and isolation.

Jesus, what was happening to him?

～

THREE HOURS LATER, TOBY must have looked pretty much the way he was feeling, despite a bracingly cold shower and three cups of coffee. When he showed up for work and bade Daniel good morning, the latter, recovered from his sulks, looked Toby up and down, favored him with something close to a leer, and said, "Another rough night?"

Well, yes, as it happens, although not in the same sense as that other one. Its diametrical opposite, you might say. None of which concerned Daniel in the slightest.

"A bit of insomnia," he answered curtly. "That's all. Any messages?"

Daniel picked up a pink slip and handed it to Toby. "Jonas Glasman called a minute or two ago."

"Nothing from Doris?"

"Not yet. But the day is young. Which is more than you can say for Doris."

Toby resisted the impulse to respond with disapproval, and then relented even further, permitting himself a smile. The joke was innocuous; it wouldn't be fair to punish the guy because of his own foul mood. "I suppose we're all heading in that direction," he said. "And at the same exit velocity."

He already knew, had already known before he'd left his apartment, what he would do first today. Sometime during his post-run shower, he'd begun to feel remorseful about not returning Jessica's call yesterday. It wasn't that he suspected the Amy debacle had been karmic punishment for his dereliction, but he was feeling an unfamiliar humility, a fragility that made him more conscious of, and solicitous toward, the fragility of others.

So he went straight to his desk and punched in her number. Which used to be his number. "Jess? It's Toby. Sorry I couldn't call yesterday."

"Couldn't call? Or couldn't be bothered?"

He sighed. At least she was providing a useful reminder of why he'd procrastinated. "What can I do for you, Jessie? What's up?"

"Not on the phone."

"But it's not Cathy-related?"

"Right. Cathy's fine. Or rather, she's no worse than usual. But I need to talk to you."

"Yeah, okay." He pressed thumb and index finger into his forehead. This humility business could become a bottomless pit; each decent gesture led inescapably to another, and soon you realized you were confronting an endless series of ethical choices. No one could opt for decency every time; the horizon kept receding in front of you. "Lunch?" he asked.

"Let's make it dinner."

Jessica had never been constrained by shame; there was no distinction in her mind between personal preference and moral imperative. What a gal. "Dinner?"

"This is important, Toby. I don't expect you to understand—"

"How can I possibly understand?"

"—but this isn't a lunch-type conversation."

Oh goodie. "I didn't realize those categories existed." And then, "All right."

"Tonight?" she asked, although it didn't quite sound like a question.

He considered protesting, if only to let her know how pushy this was. But then he thought, might as well get it over with. My evening is free except for a few interminable hours of moping, and I can distribute those any way I choose. Maybe she'll even distract me. Mind you, a colonoscopy would distract me too, but that doesn't make it an attractive option.

"Sure," he heard himself saying, quite agreeably all things considered.

"I'll cook," she said.

Well! That was unexpected. Almost unprecedented. He stopped himself from saying something to that effect in the nick of time. She probably would have considered it snide. She wouldn't have been wrong.

"Can you be here at seven?" she asked.

"Sure. Does that mean Cathy will be joining us?"

"No, she has a rehearsal."

"Those famous rehearsals."

"There are a lot of them, all right. So it's just gonna be you and me, Lindeman. Think you can handle the caroming vibrations?"

"I'll be there at seven, we'll see how I do."

∼

It was a sudden inspiration—or rather a sudden anxiety about what Jessica would say if he arrived empty-handed—that led Toby, as he was walking up her street, to reverse course and take a two-block detour to the liquor store that used to be *his* local liquor store to pick up some wine. And he decided to cough up twenty-five dollars for a respectable bottle; Jessie might not notice, but you never knew. If he'd gone cheap, she wasn't above mentioning it.

The nice thing about his neighborhood was that it remained a true neighborhood. The man behind the cash register said, "Nice to see you again, Mr. Lindeman," as he swiped Toby's credit card. Toby hadn't been in for over five years. Maybe he still sympathized with Toby for having been married to Jessie.

If he could believe the reports that filtered back to him, Toby had won a large majority of the sympathy during his separation and divorce. Only a few of Jessie's more aggressively political girlfriends took her side, at least so far as Toby knew. She'd even lost a few friendships at the time; a number of the women in her circle had been too outspoken, both in their sympathy for Toby and their oddly conventional condemnation of Jessica's affair, for her to remain on good terms with them. People in groups impose a different, and more restrictive, set of moral rules than when they're on their own. Some sort of coercive primate instinct, evolved, no doubt, to preserve community cohesion and to discourage anyone in the herd from having conspicuously more fun than anyone else.

Doubling back to Jessie's street, he experienced the same little jolt he always experienced when he visited. There had been so many evenings just like this one when, carrying a plastic bag with some take-out dinner from a nearby restaurant, or something reheatable from the Italian delicatessen around the block, he'd followed this exact path home from work, seen these exact houses in this exact light. All of them more welcoming than his own.

He rang the doorbell. While waiting for Jessie to answer, he wondered idly if the day could get worse. Of course it *could*—there was no practical limit to those fresh hells invoked by Dorothy Parker—but how likely was it after a day of almost boundless misery? And the irony was, in terms of actual events the day had been pretty innocuous. No fresh hells to speak of. But the almost paralyzing weight of unhappiness he'd woken to hadn't lifted; almost every second of the previous fourteen hours was infused with it, sullied by it. So strange. Nothing in his life had changed and yet everything felt different.

Jessica, in faded jeans and a Brandeis sweatshirt, opened the door. He had to suppress the uncharitable thought that she could have made more of an effort, seeing as how he'd come at her behest. But suppressing the thought didn't prove difficult. Besides, she didn't look bad. Defiantly casual, yes, but jeans had always flattered her.

"You're on time," she said. "Come on in."

Again, he resisted the temptation to interpret her greeting as hostile. Getting around town at rush hour could be tricky. He'd made it on time. That might be all she intended.

He proffered the brown paper bag with the wine bottle inside. She took it out of the bag and gave it a quick glance. "Italian. White. Perfect. You read my mind."

"Never one of my specialties," he said.

She smiled. "No, I suppose we were always closed books to each other. That's how the marriage lasted as long as it did." She indicated the legend on her sweatshirt. "Brandeis offered a class in Gentile as a Second Language. Maybe I should have taken it."

"Did they offer it pass/fail?"

"No need. It was a gut course. Gentile for Jocks."

"Isn't that coals to Newcastle?"

"Not at Brandeis. But I thought Spanish would be more practical, coming from New York and all. Silly me."

"Might have spared you no end of misery."

"It was never misery, Toby. Just...puzzlement. Come in, sit down." She waved him into the living room.

He hesitated before taking his old seat on the larger of the two chocolate brown sofas, the one facing the stereo. He was aware, as always, that complicated territorial questions arose when he visited. But the space seemed to beckon, and he followed his instinct. As he sat down, she said, "Do you mind if we eat right away? I'd prefer to do this before Cathy gets home."

"Whatever you like."

"Make yourself comfortable. Won't be long."

"Nah, I'll join you in the kitchen."

"Like the old days, when we dazzled each other with our artistry at the microwave."

He laughed as he rose and followed her through the archway.

While she prepared pasta with pesto sauce, he tossed the salad. It really was like the old days, except that they seemed to be on good terms. Her rough edges weren't in evidence, and he was feeling too emotionally enervated to go looking for a *casus belli*. Also, he was curious to see what this evening was about.

But during the preparation, and during dinner itself, his curiosity remained unsatisfied. Conversation flowed easily enough, but they were clearly marking time. She told him stories from the public school where she taught, he told her a little of what was happening at the opera, leaving out his dealings with Solomon.

At one point she asked, "How's your love life?" It was a question she'd asked in the past, though it was never an effective gambit. What she hoped to gain by it was unclear to Toby. No answer could possibly please her, except, perhaps, "I've joined the Franciscans."

But, eagle-eyed as always, she noticed this time the question made him wince. "What? Trouble in your bachelor's paradise?"

"A mere perturbation on the mellifluent surface," he answered, hoping irony would keep her at bay.

"That's not nothing," she pressed. "Your surface doesn't perturb so easy."

"Mmm," he said, about as discouraging a noise as he could make.

"As you're demonstrating right now," she said, with a little laugh that combined frustration and affection. "You've got mellifluence coming out of your ass, same as usual."

After they'd eaten, they cleared the table together and rinsed the dishes and loaded the dishwasher. When they were seated in the living room, a brief moment of stillness inserted itself, and extended itself long enough to provide a full stop to what had gone before. They were complicit in this; for her to begin whatever she meant to begin, a smooth transition was out of the question, only a caesura would do.

"Okay, Lindeman," she finally said, "here's the thing. I found a lump."

At first—it was a matter of context—he was uncomprehending. "A lump?"

"In my breast. You remember my breasts, right? Those things you liked about me? Well, a while ago, during that self-examination thing we're supposed to do, I felt something small and hard in one of them."

A number of thoughts crowded in on Toby simultaneously. He wondered why he'd been chosen the recipient of this information. He wondered how he was supposed to respond. He wondered, through his almost total ignorance, how alarming this datum was. And he recalled something Jonas once said to him, that the most unsympathetic thing you can tell a friend who confides a medical problem is that they should see a doctor. "They know that already," Jonas said in his funny querulous whine. "They aren't coming to you for advice, especially obvious advice that translates as 'That ain't my problem.' Friends want solace, not a referral."

"Have you seen a doctor?" He wanted to kick himself as soon as he said it.

She shook her head.

"You need to."

"I know, I know...I've been putting it off. Trying not to think about it. I'm scared, Toby. I've never been so scared." And then she buried her face in her hands and began to cry. At first it was merely little whimpers, but after a few seconds those gave way to great wracking sobs, her shoulders heaving, her whole body writhing.

He'd never seen her cry before, not once, not during their marriage, not during the ravages of their breakup, and certainly not since. Strong feisty Jessica didn't cry. He was clueless what to do. He patted her shoulder, feeling awkward. She barely seemed to notice, and the sobbing went on, undiminished. He closed his hand over her shoulder, which seemed to make her sob harder. But it felt right to him nevertheless, and he didn't pull his hand away or ease his grasp.

"Jessie, listen...in most cases these things aren't as bad as you think. They're mostly false alarms. But you have to find out. If the news is good, what a relief. And if it isn't, you can see what your choices are and make some decisions."

She moved her head in a way that Toby interpreted as assent, but she went on crying. He put his arm around her shoulders. "It'll be okay. It will."

She shook her head. "This isn't..." she choked, and then tried again, "It's just, what happened to the life I planned on? Everything's so fucked up. And now this."

A facile response was impossible. He pressed his fingers over her shoulders and his thumbs between her shoulder blades, an attempt to provide a comforting but non-threatening, not-too-intimate human touch. She reached back to put a hand over one of his. "Hell of a thing, isn't it?" she said. Her sobs had begun to subside.

"Or not. You need to have it looked at."

"It just seems so...typical. Typical and unfair and predictable. Screw up your life and before you get around to correcting it, your time runs out."

"You're jumping to conclusions, Jessie."

"You know the really pathetic part? The part that proves what a mess I've made? The person I choose to talk to about this. Turn to for comfort. That's what spouses are for, isn't it? Not sex, not really. Not romance, maybe not even financial support. But when you have a spouse there's someone to drive you to get your wisdom teeth out, or pick up the Nyquil when you've got the flu, or listen to your obsessive panicky moaning when you find a lump in your breast. It's part of the job. And I don't have a spouse, so I called you. And, of course, I feel the need to apologize. Honestly, Toby, I know this isn't your problem. I'm sure it's the last thing in the world you need to deal with. We washed our hands of each other years ago."

"We're still friends."

"Except you don't like me. And I don't blame you, I behaved pretty abysmally. But in your passive, civilized way, you can be abysmal too. It didn't all go in one direction."

"I never claimed it did. And I *do* like you."

"I just sometimes feel we're still...you know, we're still joined at the hip in some funny way. Do you know what I mean?"

Toby did know what she meant, although he didn't really feel that way himself. Except for the enforced connection through Cathy, he felt their ties had been decisively severed. But this was hardly an ideal time to say so. "We married young," he said. "We'll always be imprinted on each other." He kissed the top of her head.

What surprised him as he did it was that, for all his feeling of separation from her, of disconnection, he also felt a wash of tenderness for her, or if not *for her* quite, then nevertheless encompassing her. All somewhat abstract, perhaps, the sort of thing one might feel for a bawling baby not one's own. But it was undeniably there. Was it her tears that did it? Or the fact that she'd exposed such vulnerability, such neediness, in his presence?

"Sometimes I think you might actually be a good person," she said.

"Let's not lose our heads."

She twisted around to face him. Her eyes were red and bleary, and the tears were still on her cheeks. But she was smiling a little, and without, thank goodness, self-conscious bravery. "When it comes to evasive action, you've got smoother moves than Fred Astaire."

He laughed out loud. He always liked it when she busted him. He might have married her for such moments.

She stood up. "Listen, is a hug out of the question? Not to be too New Agey about this, but I *really* need a hug. I hope that's not asking too much."

A millisecond of uneasy calculation, and then he took her in his arms. She pressed into him and rested her cheek against his chest. Even after five years, the feel of her body along his was familiar. As was her smell, and the texture of her wiry hair against his chin.

"You know," she murmured, "I still miss you sometimes."

While he was trying to come up with an appropriate reply, the front door burst open. Startled, Toby and Jessica stepped apart and turned toward the commotion. It was Cathy who had banged into the house, and now flung her books on the living room floor. "That fucker!" she shouted. "I hate that fucking Hank Ortega! I hate drama! I hate theater! I quit!" And then she noticed her parents and suddenly shut up, gaping at them.

They edged away from each other. Toby was thinking that they weren't only acting guilty, they obviously *felt* guilty.

"Well, well, well," Cathy said with a snarl. "Look at you two."

"Hello, Cathy," Toby said quietly.

"Next time, get a room, okay?"

"Now listen—" Jessica said, but Cathy had already turned her back on them and was clomping furiously up the stairs.

"I don't suppose," she shouted as she ascended, her voice wildly out of control, "this means Daddy's moving back? Or were you guys just gonna tear off a quickie for old times' sake?" And then, just before her bedroom door slammed shut, she shouted at the top of her lungs, "I hate my life!"

~

TOBY LAY IN BED in the dark. His head hurt. His stomach felt rebellious. Of course, during a long and difficult day, he'd been managing on almost no sleep; his present malaise was no great mystery. Small comfort. He felt a fatigue now that was beyond anything recognizable as fatigue. Just lying immobile felt like an effort.

The first act of *Così fan tutte* was playing quietly on the stereo. It was impossible not to recall the last time, only two nights before, he had lain in bed listening to the same opera. That thrilling clandestine phone call from Cabo San Lucas. Tonight, the music, for all its euphoniousness, was barely holding his attention. He recognized that some part of his mind, some small inner chamber walled off from the rest, was still covertly on the alert for the phone to ring again, even though the part of his mind that understood and negotiated with reality knew it would not happen.

Nothing could impinge on or displace or distract him from his misery. Not even Jessica's lump, which merited a far less selfish quality of concern than he'd been able to muster.

It was inexplicable. Here was something that, before he had it, he hadn't been aware of its absence. Then it had been granted him, very briefly, and snatched away again. And now that it was gone, he felt utterly bereft. He was no worse off than he'd been three days before, when he'd been perfectly content. Is this heartbreak? he wondered. Is it possible? In past amours, he'd had his feelings hurt, his pride buffeted, his vanity affronted. But the pervasive misery he was experiencing now was new. And damn if it wasn't as bad as country music claimed.

The telephone rang.

It shocked him like a jolt of electricity. He was groping for the phone even before his higher cerebral functions were involved in the process. He knocked his alarm clock off the side table and scattered a couple of books before his fingers closed around the receiver. The phone began its second ring before he pulled it off its cradle and up to his head. "Hello," he said. He tried to sound casual, despite the adrenaline surging through his system.

"Uh...yeah," drawled a male voice, "let's see. Some chicken with cashews, some sweet and sour prawns, uh..."

"You've got the wrong number," Toby said tightly. "And if you're too stoned to tell time, it's almost midnight. Which is too fucking late for a dumbass mistake." And then, in case his annoyance wasn't sufficiently clear, he added, "Stupid asshole," before slamming down the receiver.

His pulse was racing. In fucking neutral.

He drew a long, deep breath. And then he noticed that "Soave sia il vento" had begun to play. Something within him seemed to shift with the gentle opening pulsations, a slow grinding collision of his heart's tectonic plates. And then, no doubt for a variety of reasons—physical fatigue, emotional overload, pique, frustration, compassion, despair, along with the supernal, aching beauty of the music—he wept.

3

DURING THE NEXT TWO weeks, Toby went to bed every night confident he would wake up the next morning recovered from his strange mania. It had to be an illusion, what Jonas dismissed as self-hypnosis. He felt like a fool for feeling this way. A fool or a self-deluded adolescent. Only Jonas was able to offer balm on that score, balm in his characteristic, sardonic style. "You thought you were superior to the human circus?"

"Well," Toby answered, "I've managed pretty well so far."

They were in the back of a cab, heading through mid-town traffic toward Cathy's high school. It was a beautiful crisp Saturday, a little past noon.

"You never know when you'll be granted full membership in humanity," Jonas said. "Let me be the first to welcome you aboard."

"Why do people put up with this? It's awful."

"There's no choice, for one thing. You can't inoculate yourself. But also...the highs are worth a little misery."

"That wouldn't necessarily be *my* cost-benefit analysis."

"But you're not going through a high right now, are you?"

"My high lasted a day and a half, and I've felt lousy ever since."

"Give it time. Almost everyone recovers eventually."

"I've already been hurting a lot longer than the whole time she and I spent together."

"Ironic, isn't it?"

"Oh yeah, I'm really savoring the irony. It's exquisite."

"The point is..." Jonas was suddenly earnest. "Maybe it's not *her* exactly, or not *just* her. I'm sure she's all you say, but maybe what's bothering you is realizing something's missing in your life. A realization that wasn't there until you thought it wasn't missing anymore."

Toby processed this. "For a guy who plays the viola, you're not hopelessly stupid."

Jonas snorted. "Listen, smartass, I have actual wisdom to impart. The trap is thinking you've found and lost the person of your dreams. The person of your dreams doesn't exist. I can't tell you how many times I found the one person in the world created for me and me alone, if only he wasn't too bullheaded to see it. I was absolutely certain every time. Until I fell for someone else."

"So what's the traditional cure? Get myself back out there?"

"There are two conflicting schools of thought." Jonas sounded as serious, and almost as pompous, as a law professor distinguishing between a conflicting set of precedents.

"Go on."

"One says, Go for it, start dating immediately. And the other... There's a story about Joe Louis. Got knocked down once, I think it was in one of those bum-of-the-month fights he used to have. And he immediately jumped back up and won the round. After the bell, his trainer told him he should have taken the eight-count. And he got pissed, said that was ridiculous, he'd just slipped, there was nothing to recover from, he could take the guy no sweat. And his trainer said, 'Everybody saw you go down, Joe. You shoulda took the eight-count.'"

"So what's your point? I *shouldn't* start dating?"

"Well, that's the other school of thought. Grieving takes time, one way or another you have to go through it, there aren't any shortcuts, who do you think you're fooling?"

"This is a big help."

"No one said it was easy. It *isn't* easy, just normal."

Once again, Jonas was proving an exemplary friend, listening patiently when Toby needed to whine, offering sensible advice when asked. He'd even agreed to join Cathy's birthday celebration. Graciously disavowing any suggestion he was acceding reluctantly, assuring Toby he'd enjoy himself.

The invitation hadn't been entirely guileless. Cathy was likely to be more agreeable if Jonas was around. She'd always liked him, and this fondness seemed, if anything, to have increased of late. His being gay—and as her adolescence advanced, her growing understanding of what that meant—no doubt played a role. It conferred prestige. Terminally uncool in almost every way, Jonas still enjoyed a special cachet in Cathy's eyes based largely on his sexual orientation. An indication of just how far the zeitgeist had evolved in the last decade.

But it wasn't *only* his sexuality. Cathy appreciated that Jonas talked to her like an adult, refused to censor himself, never betrayed a hint of condescension. The two of them often whispered and giggled together in a way Toby even found disquieting, if only because it seemed purposely designed to exclude him. But since it was rare these days for Cathy to enjoy herself so openly, he tended to overplay his disapproval for comic effect, good-naturedly permitting himself to become the butt of their mockery. Let them have their fun.

Fun. Toby recalled a line from a Dr. Seuss book he'd read to Cathy when she was little and life was simpler. It went, "These things are fun, and fun is good..." An unostentatiously subversive sentiment to which Toby subscribed unreservedly. He wondered when, if ever, he'd have unalloyed fun again.

When Toby asked Cathy how she wanted to celebrate her birthday, she'd suggested a play. He teased her by responding, "So you don't hate theatre anymore?"

"You're referring to conniption night?"

"You said you hated drama—although God knows you were providing plenty of your own—and you hated the director, and you were quitting. Remember?"

"That was just temperament, Daddy. You obviously know nothing about women."

"That's for sure."

"Or about artists."

"Right. 'Cause I work at that hotbed of philistine insensitivity, the San Francisco Opera."

She was relaxed enough to laugh before saying, "I was just venting. It'd be great to go to a show. A matinee, maybe? With dinner afterward? That would be a perfect birthday."

"Any play you've got your eye on?"

"Well, not a musical. And not...you know, one of those dumb comedies that could be a TV show. With jokes and everything."

"Okay, I'll look for a comedy without jokes."

When Toby swung by in a taxi to pick up Jonas that Saturday morning, Jonas had an interesting addition to offer. "This business with Cathy, will it be going late?"

"Shouldn't think so. Matinee, early dinner in the vicinity, home. Why?"

"Well...Splosion's performing at Spats tonight. That venue in Berkeley, you know it? Restaurant/bar thing? Brian thought we might meet up later. Hear Jeremy's band, give you a chance to meet the guy."

"I'm game. Sounds like fun."

"We could bring Cathy if you like." When Toby made a face, Jonas said, "Aw, she's a great kid, Toby. Cut her some slack."

"I cut her plenty of slack. But I'm not taking her clubbing on Saturday night."

When the cab pulled up to her school, Toby told the driver to wait, and urged Jonas to stay in the cab. "It'll be less of a production," he said.

"I'm not sure you've got the ideal attitude."

"Look, if we both go in, imagine the introductions and folderol and showing off about her dad's gay friend, all that stuff. Extricating ourselves could be a challenge."

"I'm not arguing. But *chill*, okay? Today's supposed to be fun."

Toby nodded acceptance as he got out of the cab, then skipped up the short flight of steps into the building. She'd told him the auditorium was on the ground floor to his right. Now he wished she'd been a little more specific. He followed the green and white linoleum corridor around a couple of corners, and coming to a large set of double doors, pushed through.

He found himself at the rear of an auditorium seating perhaps two hundred. There were five kids onstage, including Cathy. The man Toby took to be the drama teacher was in front of the stage, talking to one of the students. When Cathy spotted Toby, she waved. Given the pressures on her to be cool in this setting, Toby was pleased, even touched, by the spontaneous gesture, and waved back. Everyone turned to look at him, and the drama teacher craned his head around to see what was going on. Toby, feeling self-conscious, strode down the center aisle toward the stage.

"Yes?" said the teacher. It wasn't unfriendly exactly, but neither was it welcoming.

Before Toby could answer, Cathy said, "This is my dad, Hank. He's picking me up."

"Hi," Toby said, extending his hand. "Toby Lindeman."

"Hank Ortega," the man said, and shook Toby's hand. "Nice to meet you. Cathy's doing terrific work here. You should be proud." Ortega looked to be in his mid-thirties. He was on the shortish side, perhaps five-eight, solid, swarthy, with thick black hair tied back into a little ponytail, and an earring in his right ear. "We're almost done. Take a seat, feel free to watch."

"The thing is…I wouldn't ordinarily do this, and I apologize for the disruption, but I understood the rehearsal ended at noon. There's a cab waiting outside."

Ortega stared at him. As the moment drew itself out, Toby found himself torn between feeling apologetic and irked. He knew he was on turf decidedly not his own, but still, there was no call for the fellow to engage in some bullshit battle of wills. High school high noon.

"Is it okay?" Cathy asked, giving Ortega the opportunity to break the stare without losing face. "It's my birthday today; my dad's taking me to a show."

Toby had the impression Ortega was as relieved as he to be provided a way out of the impasse. "Well, sure, I suppose so," the drama teacher said after a moment, forcing a taut smile. "Happy birthday."

She smiled back at him with a smile broader and far more genuine. "Thanks."

"What are you seeing?"

"*The Real Thing.*"

"Stoppard? It's supposed to be a good production. Have a great time." Only after this little exchange did he glance over at Toby. "Enjoy," he said, one notch above curtness, which was enough, but not by much.

"Thanks. Nice to have met you."

"Right."

A couple of minutes later, after Toby and Cathy had left the building and climbed into the cab, Jonas gave Cathy a big welcoming kiss, wished her a happy birthday, and then said, "Am I hallucinating, or are you thinner?"

She positively beamed. "I've lost seven pounds."

It was only after Jonas offered the observation that Toby realized he'd noticed it too, on some level below consciousness. The effect wasn't dramatic, but it was there if you looked.

"You look great, honey."

"Thanks, Uncle Jonas."

"What's your secret?"

"Don't tell anyone," she said, sneaking a mischievous glance at Toby, "but I've learned this special secret weight-loss technique known only to European royalty and Hollywood stars. It involves making yourself throw up a lot." She waited for Toby to look stricken, which took precisely no time at all, and then she laughed triumphantly. "Gotcha!" she exclaimed.

"'Gotcha' isn't enough," Toby said grumpily.

"It was a joke, Daddy. Throwing up is *gross*. I don't know how anyone can do it. I almost admire their courage. No," she went on, turning back to Jonas, "truthfully, I just mostly eat vegetables now. And some whole grains. It's the least glamorous diet there is, but it works."

"You haven't become some sort of vegetarian kook, have you?" Toby asked.

"Wow, there's no pleasing you, is there?" Cathy said.

She didn't sound querulous, but she wasn't teasing. While Toby was considering how to respond, he felt a nudge from Jonas. He interpreted it to mean, "Back off." Fighting his irritation, he decided Jonas's warning gesture was on-target. "You're pleasing me right now," he said. "You look great, and I'm sure you're healthier too. And even if none of that were true, I'm delighted we're celebrating your birthday together."

She colored. With pleasure, Toby hoped and assumed. Jonas caught Toby's eye, a quick, surreptitious glance that said, "There, that wasn't so hard, was it?"

"What possessed you?" Jonas asked Cathy.

"Oh, I don't know. The play, partly. There's no reason Kate Keller should be fat. The part isn't written that way. And the girls in the drama club are all hotties, so when I saw who I was hanging with, I started not liking the way I looked. Well, not started, 'cause I never liked the way I looked, but I decided I should do something about it."

"I feel that way whenever I pass a Calvin Klein billboard."

"You don't need to lose weight, Uncle Jonas."

"No, but I should have my cock enlarged."

More uproarious laughter ensued, in which Toby took no part. But this sort of grumpy disapproval was play-acting, really. Not that he was at ease with Jonas's amusing his daughter in this manner, but since it was done in part to provoke him, his letting himself be provoked was part of the game, and he was willing to play his role with a modicum of good grace. These things are fun—for somebody—and fun is good.

"Do you *mind*?" he muttered. He knew it would add to their merriment.

"Daddy prefers to think I don't know about cocks," Cathy said.

"Okay," said Toby, "that's enough. Let's *really* not go there."

And then Jonas piped up, "Trust me, honey, no matter what you think, you've barely scratched the surface."

Cathy said, "I realize I'm a mere apprentice in the presence of a master."

"It's like the viola. There's only one sure route to mastery. Practice, practice, practice."

"Stop!" Toby said firmly. He stole a glance at the cab driver's face in the rear view mirror. It was expressionless. Apparently, the only sensibility being assaulted was his own. "I'm laying down the law. A father's prerogative. Ixnay on the eenispay."

"Straight men are *so* uptight," Cathy said. "Don't you find?"

"Yeah, but you gotta love 'em," Jonas said.

They both looked at Toby fondly. He found himself smiling in spite of himself. "In your dreams," he mumbled.

～

SEVERAL HOURS LATER, TOBY walked Cathy up to Jessica's front door while Jonas once again remained in a waiting taxi. Toby felt a certain trepidation. He hadn't spoken to Jessie since their dinner and didn't know if she'd seen a doctor or had an answer to her worries. An indefensible cowardice had conspired with a slightly less reprehensible wish not to crowd her, and together they had kept him from phoning. He'd emailed once, but she hadn't answered. The house looked dark, and he felt an unworthy flush of relief at the thought she might be out.

Still, it had been a very good day. A perfect day, really. The play had been good, and Cathy enjoyed it as much as Toby and Jonas. Dinner had been fun too; Toby had chosen a popular steakhouse on Van Ness, and while both Cathy and Jonas expressed enthusiasm about the choice, Cathy ordered the steamed vegetable plate. When Toby tried to argue with her ("It's your birthday, you're allowed to have a treat"), Jonas had told him, pleasantly but firmly, to shut up, and he immediately did as instructed. Jonas's instincts in this regard were clearly superior to his own and merited deference. They'd laughed a lot. She seemed to like the earrings Toby had given her, and was intrigued by the set of Tom Lehrer CDs from Jonas. Toby allowed her to sip some of his wine. She'd declined the cake he suggested, and he'd desisted from repeating his earlier mistake of arguing. Throughout the meal, Jonas had been voluble and naughtily funny, Cathy had been titillated and amused, and Toby had been appropriately scandalized.

"Daddy," Cathy said now, as they walked to the front door, "this was the best birthday ever." She stopped him on the stone path and kissed him.

"I had a great time too," he said. "And so did Jonas, I could tell."

"I could too." And then, suddenly, impulsively, she cried, "You know what? I wish you were gay too. I wish you and Uncle Jonas were married and we all lived together."

It was one of those gut-wrenching moments. An unintentional confession of such pain, such loneliness and need. Cathy has two daddies. He pulled her to him and hugged her tightly, feeling hopeless, and almost criminally culpable. "Baby," he said, "I know I've let you down, I really do. There isn't a day I don't feel bad about it."

"Oh no," she said, "I wasn't blaming you. The opposite."

"I know. I know. But I blame myself."

"You're the best father there is." She slithered out of his embrace and began searching through her purse for her key. "Except, you know, you're a breeder."

"Is Mom out, do you know?" he asked, hoping it sounded casual.

"I'm not sure. She said she was going to a movie with Debbie. You know Debbie?"

"I don't think so."

"Lucky you." She made a face.

"Not a fan of Debbie?"

"She's a—" Cathy weighed her options, then said, "A bitch."

"Listen," Toby said, "are you okay being home alone? On your birthday and all?"

"Oh sure," she said easily. "I'm used to it."

Another little dart targeting his heart. She wasn't making a point, just stating a fact. Which suddenly struck him as intolerable. It was still early, and it was her birthday. Depositing her in this house now, regardless of how nice the day had been, was too uncaring. So despite what he'd said to Jonas, he blurted, "Want to come out with Jonas and me?" She looked startled. "We're going to a club in Berkeley," Toby explained, "seeing a band called Splosion. Jonas', uh, the guy Jonas—"

"The favored term is *partner*."

"Right. Jonas's *partner*—his conductor friend, Brian—is a friend of a guy in the band."

"I know who Brian Hughes is, Daddy."

"Come join us. It'll be fun."

"To be honest, I'm not nuts about Splosion. They're pretty old-fashioned."

"You know them?"

"It would be hard to have an opinion about them otherwise. Listen, it's like an extra birthday present that you asked, but this sounds like a grown-ups' thing, and I don't want to be a tagalong. So I'll just say thanks again for a perfect birthday and good night." She gave him another kiss, opened the door, and slipped into the house.

Toby felt an unexpected disappointment. But was it disappointment, in fact? It was *something*, and something nigglingly disagreeable. Her reasons for declining seemed admirably mature; she probably wouldn't have found it especially enjoyable to be in their party. But the thought of her alone in the house tugged at him unpleasantly as he headed back toward the taxi.

Bridge traffic was unexpectedly light; it was early when they got to Spats. Splosion's first set was still over an hour off, and there was no sign of Brian. But a table had been reserved for their party right near the stage, the latter already littered with electronic equipment and miles of wiring, and they sat down and ordered drinks. Jonas ordered a scotch-over, Toby a stinger.

"That's a pretty camp drink," Jonas said, once the waiter had moved away.

"A sign of how secure I am," Toby said.

"This isn't a gay club, you know."

"I like stingers. I'm not making a statement."

"If Cathy has her druthers, we'll get you yet." Toby had already told him about the conversation by the front door.

"Nah, I'm afraid this is just one more way I'm going to disappoint the girl."

"You're disappointing *everybody*."

"Not everybody, perhaps. Or so I'd prefer to think."

"How are you feeling?" Jonas suddenly asked.

"About—?"

"About everything. About anything. About how the day's gone so far."

"You mean with Cathy? Fine. Better than fine. Why? Did I miss something?" He no longer felt touchy about Jonas's insights. The guy's antennae were delicate; it would be foolish to ignore the vibrations they picked up. "Did I do something wrong?" He was careful to exclude irony from his tone. Jonas needed to know Toby cared about his opinion.

"Not at all. But Cathy's not the only one allowed to have emotions."

"I'm going to call her." Toby abruptly stood up.

"Solomon's girlfriend?"

"No, stupid. *Cathy*. I'm going to call Cathy. I can't call Amy."

"She's on your mind, though."

"Of course she is. But I'm trying not to think about her. Thanks for the reminder. Anyway, I meant Cathy. I feel bad about leaving her tonight."

"It was her choice. You invited her. Which I applaud. She said no. Accept it."

"Yeah, but…she's alone in that house on her birthday, Jonas. It doesn't seem right. I should have insisted."

"She's too old for that."

"Maybe. But I'm going to call. Just to tell her I love her."

"Jeez, Tobe, I barely recognize you."

"Me either. I'll be right back."

Toby rose and maneuvered among the tables toward the club foyer, where it was almost deserted. He fished his phone out of his inside breast pocket and dialled Jessica's landline. No answer. Odd. He tried Cathy's cell. Again nothing. Was she in the bathroom? He stepped away, planning to head back to the table, but then on an impulse called the cell one more time. Three rings and Toby was about to give up when Cathy answered.

"Hello?"

Toby could hear music in the background. "Honey? It's Dad. I just tried you at home."

"Oh. Yeah. Uh…I'm not there."

"Uh-huh."

"I went out."

"Where?"

"Uh…some of the kids from drama decided to get together. I'm with them."

"Was this planned in advance? Why didn't you just say so?"

"No, no, after I got home there was a text. I wouldn't have kept it secret."

"Where are you?"

"Starbuck's."

"Coffee'll keep you awake, you know."

"I'm having a chai."

"Do your friends know it's your birthday?"

"Yeah. I didn't have to pay for my chai. Good deal, huh? Is anything the matter?"

"I just wanted to say I love you, and tell you what a nice time I had today."

"Oh. Thanks. I feel the same way."

"And to renew my offer. To join us. But I guess you're okay where you are."

"I am. And I really ought to…"

112

"Sure, I understand. 'Night, Cath."

"'Night, Daddy. Thanks again...for everything."

He disconnected, oddly dissatisfied. Something about the conversation felt off. Oh well, whatever. At least she was with friends rather than stuck in an empty house.

When he returned to the club proper, he saw that Brian had arrived during his absence, wearing tight-fitting jeans and a tan cashmere sweater. He looked good, as he always did, handsome, vital, with the golden aura that always seemed to envelop him. The latter a product, most likely, of nothing more mystical than blond hair, a tan, and good posture, although magazine profiles often attributed significance to it. But no one who didn't recognize him would peg him as music director of the San Francisco Opera. He looked like a guy who belonged in a hip club in Berkeley. He rose when Toby approached the table. "The Money Man!" he said. "Always good to see the Money Man!"

Toby shook Brian's outstretched hand. He kept a smile pasted on his face, but he wasn't thrilled at the greeting. It pigeonholed him, deliberately and rather unflatteringly, and defined him by the role he played in Brian's professional life. It also—a natural corollary—underlined the difference in their respective status. Or maybe he was reading more into the two words than they deserved. He couldn't deny he was sensitive where such issues were concerned, excessively conscious of the opera's pecking order and his place in it. That someone like Doris could recognize and value his qualities despite his nominal rank was a rare thing of which he was no doubt insufficiently appreciative. "It's other people's money," he said, attempting to sound good-humored. "I just pick their pockets. How are you, Brian?"

"Doing well."

Toby sat down. His stinger had been delivered while he was away. He took a sip. Nice. The bartender hadn't been too generous with the crème de menthe, a common mistake that made the drink taste like mouthwash.

"How was Cathy?" Jonas asked.

"Not home. I got hold of her on her cell. She's with some friends."

"Sounds good." He turned back to Brian. "We were out with Toby's daughter. It's her birthday."

"I see," Brian said, with a patent lack of interest. "What I *don't* see, however, is someone who can take a drink order."

"I can go find somebody," Jonas offered.

"It's okay. Somebody'll show up." He turned to Toby. "What did you do to celebrate this birthday?" Making no effort to camouflage the effortful good manners behind the query.

Which led to a small quandary: Answering fully would likely invite a further, insulting display of boredom, while not answering, or answering curtly, would make Toby himself seem gratuitously rude. Who was to blame? Toby wondered. Somebody was certainly doing damage to the mood, and Toby couldn't absolutely dismiss the possibility the culprit was himself.

"Theater and dinner," Jonas said, filling the small gap. "We had a good time."

"Sounds nice," said Brian. His eyes were wandering all over the club, looking to connect with a service person. Then he said to Toby, "Have you heard Splosion?" To Toby, it didn't sound as if he were putting much energy into this question either.

"The CD," Toby said.

"The CD's pretty good, but it doesn't give you much idea of what they sound like live. You're in for a treat."

"Good, huh?"

"Well, yes. That's what 'you're in for a treat' was meant to signify."

Toby turned away without responding. He was tempted, but there were too many constraints on him, professional and social. At least his earlier question was answered: It was Brian being shitty, not himself being tetchy. Still, the strongest response he permitted himself was to ignore this latest thrust. If Brian perceived the implied rebuke, fine. If not, at least Toby had preserved his self-respect by not saying anything ameliorative.

He wondered if Jonas was aware of what was happening. Probably. Jonas didn't miss much. And besides, he probably was aware—as Toby himself suddenly recognized, with a thud of belated insight—that he, Jonas, was the innocent, indirect cause. This whole business was junkyard-dog territoriality on Brian's part. An assertion of proprietary rights. Wholly pointless. Unlikely to impress Jonas, and definitely the wrong way to deal with Toby, even if—especially if—Brian's aim was to establish primacy. Toby didn't mind being considered a beta male, but he refused to kiss alpha ass.

Turned away from the table now, Toby saw the club had filled considerably during the last few minutes. Splosion evidently had a Berkeley fan base. But, he wondered, would they troop across the bay to see an opera?

A waiter arrived. Brian ordered a stinger—a choice Toby found interesting, given the unacknowledged tension, and even, just possibly, an eccentric little olive branch—and Toby ordered a refill. He'd gone through his first too fast. Now that he'd reached the requisite two-drink minimum, it would be a good idea to nurse the second.

For the next few minutes, he kept quiet, responding only if Jonas or Brian addressed a comment to him. These little games were obnoxious— initiating them was beneath contempt—but sometimes you had to play by refusing to play, especially with someone like Brian who believes he holds all the cards and enjoys abusing the advantage. Or, the thought occurred to him, like Solomon at that redwoods event, and Toby instantly understood his present prickliness. His tussles with Solomon had given him pleasure back when things with Amy were on track. He'd refused to take the man's shit and it worked out great. Now, though, the memory rankled. Not just rankled: festered.

Eventually, the lights dimmed and the PA system announced the opening act, a singer Toby didn't know named Lilly Hammond. To polite applause, she took the stage, holding an acoustic guitar, stepping carefully around the drum kit and electronic equipment en route to the microphone. Once she planted herself there, she was so close to Toby's table he could almost reach out and touch her. Which seemed to create a sense of distance rather than the reverse; she was so near, and yet, alone on the stage, bathed in a spotlight, so obviously differentiated from everyone else in the room, as if she'd been translated to another sphere. Also, she seemed to exist in a sort of time warp; with her long straight blond hair, her angelic freckled face, her frail body, her tight jeans and peasant blouse, she could have played a club like this fifty years before. Except fifty years before she would have had to wait twenty years or so to be born.

Toby whispered to Jonas, "You know her?"

Jonas whispered back, "I don't know anybody."

115

She began to tune her guitar. "Hi, everybody," she said with a rather studied artlessness. "Y'all having a good weekend?" She tentatively strummed a couple of chords, and then adjusted the tuning on one of her strings. "It's nice to see you all here tonight." And then, without another word, she began a fast, intricate vamp. After a few bars, she began to sing. Her voice was clear, reed thin, and dead-on pitch. Reminiscent of all those sixties folk angels. Born too late, poor girl.

Her set consisted exclusively of her own songs, several of them explicitly about sex. A few were startlingly frank, close to pornographic, with none of the indirection, or sniggering adolescent allusiveness, that characterized an earlier generation's songs on the same subject. These weren't risqué, weren't intended to provoke naughty laughter or knowing smirks; they just described what they described, take it or leave it.

The audience grew very quiet as she proceeded through her thirty-minute set. Even after several decades of the supposed equalizing impact of second-wave feminism, it was striking when a woman dealt with her sexuality so forthrightly and so publicly. The songs, though, were too blunt to be especially titillating. Toby admired the woman's courage. Or was it chutzpah? It was tough to gauge the extent to which she'd premeditated the impact. Calculation or simple unfettered honesty? Either way, innocently or shrewdly, one or two of the songs did suggest a special fondness for oral sex. Go argue.

After she finished, took her bows, and left the stage, Jonas cupped a hand over his mouth, leaned in toward Toby, and murmured, "I'm surprised she didn't sing 'Blowin' in the Wind.'"

Toby laughed—any other reaction would have been churlish—but he felt obliged to register a small protest: "I liked her, though."

"She was all right."

"I thought she was better than that."

"You like she's a slut."

"I liked her voice, too. And she's got balls."

"If only," Jonas said.

Which was the moment the woman in question appeared at their table. Jonas started, and then raised his eyebrows and suppressed a giggle, like a junior high school student caught passing a naughty note. Meanwhile, Lilly Hammond was leaning over and giving Brian a kiss on the cheek. He stood up, returned the kiss, whispered something—presumably a compliment—then put an arm around her shoulders and said, "Guys, say hi to Lilly. She's a good friend of Jeremy's. Lilly, that's Jonas over there, the one with the terrible posture, and the dish next to him is the Money Man."

Toby frowned, but met her eye and managed a smile. "Toby Lindeman," he said, half-rising. "I enjoyed your songs."

She smiled back. "Thank you."

"Just FYI," Brian said, "Toby's our token straight."

"*And* a dish? *And* the Money Man? This must be my lucky night."

"Go sit by him, why don't you?"

"Excellent idea." With a mischievous smile, she went around the table and took the chair next to Toby's. He felt discomfited. The byplay, hers and Brian's, made it hard to act natural.

"It was Toby?" she asked. He nodded. "Nice to meet you."

"Likewise. Those were very gutsy songs." He kept his voice down. He didn't want their conversation to become a performance piece.

"So people tell me."

It was hard to figure where else to go with this topic. "How do you know Brian?" he therefore asked. She gave him a funny look. The look was so pronounced he couldn't ignore it or even pretend to. "What?" he asked.

"That's it?" she said. "That's all you're going to say about my songs?"

The question puzzled him. "What do you mean? You want more praise?"

Which made her laugh. "Well, sure, always, but that's not what I meant. Most guys, they hear those songs, I'm subjected to several hours of blowjob banter."

"I had no such plans."

"Sometimes it's cleverish, mostly it's hopeless. The name Monica Lewinsky comes up a lot, apparently that's still a guaranteed yock after all these years. You sure you're straight?"

It was Toby's turn to laugh. "Pretty sure. More sure than most, I'd guess."

"How you figure?"

"Well, I've had ample opportunity to consider the alternative. Because of my work."

"Oh? What do you do?"

"I'm a drag queen."

"Yeah, right." She smiled politely, to show she recognized a joke when faced with one. Which made him ache for Amy with renewed force; it reminded him just what, and how much, he'd lost. "Why did Brian call you 'the Money Man' before?" Lilly asked.

Toby tried to shake his head free of distracting mournful thoughts. "You misheard him. He said 'monkey man.' I have a prehensile tail."

"Come on."

Toby sighed. "I'm a fundraiser. I'm not really a money man, not in the sense of having much myself. I separate actual money men from their money. The rest is Brian's little joke."

"You don't sound crazy about our maestro."

In fact, even after all the time he'd known Brian, Toby wasn't sure *how* he regarded him. But he had no intention of saying anything negative now, not to someone he'd never met before, especially someone who'd greeted Brian with a kiss. "How did you say you know him?" he asked.

"I didn't. Through Jeremy. The club scene's a tight little world, everybody knows everybody. Brian and I aren't pals, I just see him around. When a classical guy comes slumming, it's kind of noteworthy in scuzzy circles like ours."

"He's a man of broad tastes."

"I'd say so."

This was the point where one or the other of them would have to stake out new territory if they were going to sustain the conversation, so it wasn't unwelcome that the waiter chose the moment to take orders. Toby held up his glass and shook his head, indicating he wasn't ready for another. Lilly asked for a Coke, and then said to Toby, "Just 'cause I'm working. There's a second show at eleven. Gotta stay sober."

"Far be it from me to judge."

"I don't want you to think I'm a teetotaller or a prude or anything."

"No chance of that. I heard your songs."

She smiled, the same dutiful smile as before, and it gave his heart another twinge. "I usually have some wine afterward, to unwind. Or a little weed."

Was this an invitation for him to issue an invitation? If so, how did he feel about it? Before he could begin to decide, the house lights dimmed and the voice over the PA announced it was the club's pleasure to present Splosion.

To an eruption of applause, five men ambled onstage. Only one of the five was Black, so it was obvious which was Jeremy Metcalf. Very tall, maybe six-five; extremely thin; very dark; with a narrow, sculpted face, fine, sensitive features, a wide mouth, and large Ethiopian eyes; wearing tight jeans, sneaks, a close-fitting yellow T-shirt, and a red do-rag around his head. He was the one who immediately compelled attention, the one impossible not to watch. When he crossed the stage and then bent down to pick up his bass guitar, his movements had a slow balletic grace. Once the instrument was in his extraordinarily long, thin hands, he seemed to caress it delicately for a moment before adjusting the tuning. Only then did he look out toward the audience. When he saw the group at Brian's table, he offered a quick bright smile and a nod.

"Are you a fan?" Lilly whispered in Toby's ear.

"I don't know their stuff that well. You?"

"Uh-huh."

Up on stage, Jeremy Metcalf turned to face his bandmates. They nodded to him, he nodded to them, and he counted out a bar *sotto voce*, one-two-three-four, and...bam! The attack was sudden, ear-splitting, and thrillingly unanimous.

It wasn't Toby's sort of music, but you'd have to be tone-deaf not to recognize they were very good. The melodies were catchy without being obvious, taking many a wayward harmonic turn, the lyrics weren't embarrassing—not a negligible achievement in this sort of repertoire—and the playing was extraordinary: Fabulously tight ensemble, intricate skeins of independent melodic lines (even Jeremy's bass seemed to be playing melody), solid gut-punching percussion, and good vocals traded off between Jeremy and one of the two lead guitarists.

Their set lasted almost an hour. They never said a word to the audience, and barely acknowledged the ovation greeting each song, just stood immobile waiting it out. When they were done, they offered a quick, unsynchronized, perfunctory bow, Jeremy said, "Thank you," and they loped off the stage. No curtain call, although the applause went on for several minutes.

Lilly turned to Toby, and said, "Well?" It wasn't quite as coercive as saying "What did I tell you?" but the intonation was almost identical.

"Great."

On Toby's left, Jonas was nodding. "They're awfully good, aren't they?" He spoke slightly louder than usual and cast a quick glance in Brian's direction.

"Aren't they?" Brian agreed warmly. "They got screwed on their first album. The worst promotion job *ever*. No radio play, no ads, no video, no nothing. Fell into a sinkhole. Barely outsold my *Poppea*. They're looking for new management, of course. They ought to be huge. With proper marketing, their next drop will get them over the hump." He turned to look at Toby. "Would that help promote the opera, you think?"

"Opera?" said Lilly. "What opera?"

Brian, too late, registered Toby's warning glance. He said, "It's just… just a fundraising thing. Right, Money Man?"

"Whatever." Dismissively. Toby was tiring of these little shots from Brian, which he wasn't supposed to notice were barbed, nor to answer in kind.

He rose abruptly, and without excusing himself went over to the bar to get another drink. While he waited, Lilly Hammond materialized at his elbow. "You hate that 'Money Man' stuff, don't you?" she said. And then, to the bartender, "Another Coke when you have a sec, Steve."

Toby shrugged. "Brian has some little drama going on in his mind, and I resent being cast as a supernumerary. I don't object he's the star—we're all the stars of our own dramas—but I resent the way he expects the rest of us to see him that way too."

"I know what you mean," she said.

Maybe. Or maybe this was what linguists call "phatic communication," designed less for content than to signal one's sympathetic presence. No matter. "The other thing is, he must see it bugs me. But he keeps doing it. So that's a wee bit hostile. But honestly, we're giving this more attention than it merits. Brian's fine. I'm mostly just in a snit so I'm letting it get to me."

"Why's that?"

Uh-uh. No moseying down that road. "Stuff. Nothing to do with Brian." He had his stinger in hand by now, and Lilly was taking her Coke from the bartender. "I'll get this," he said, reaching into his pocket.

"An empty offer, partner," she said. "I get comped, and you're on Brian's tab."

"Well, I hope I still get credit for my handsome gesture." Why was he flirting? Habit?

"Of course. Very handsome. Lots of credit."

She led the way back to their table near the bandstand. Where, seated in what had been Toby's chair, was Jeremy Metcalf himself, leaning across the table toward Brian, and occupying an enormous amount of space. A moment of hesitation while Lilly seated herself, and then Toby swiveled toward a neighboring table, put his hand on an unoccupied chair, made eye contact with the two women sitting at the table, and raised his eyebrows interrogatively. Both of the women offered friendly nods. Toby hoisted the chair and brought it over, placing it to the immediate right of his old position, where Jeremy was now sitting. That's when Jeremy noticed him, or gave a sign of noticing him.

"Did I take your seat, man?" he asked. His voice was velvety and grave.

"No prob. I've got another right here."

"Didn't mean to usurp your seat," said Jeremy, rising. He rose and kept rising, towering over Toby when he finally was upright. "I can scooch over," he added, with a quick neutral glance in Lilly's direction. It wouldn't be accurate to call his manner effeminate, but there was something close to it in the graceful way he held his impossibly long body, in the elegance with which he moved his enormous hands, and in the deep lilt of his voice. Something regal, yes, but the unworthy adjective that occurred to Toby was "queenly." Metcalf, impossibly tall, resplendently Black, startlingly handsome, in any case had star presence. "Jeremy," he said, extending his immense, delicate right hand, and offering a friendly smile.

"Toby." Toby grasped the hand and shook it. Despite its delicacy, the hand was strong, the grip firm, the skin hard and calloused. "You guys were terrific," Toby said.

"Thanks." And then there was a flash of recognition in Jeremy's eye. "Wait. Toby *Lindeman*? You're the guy getting funding for the opera?"

"Trying to."

"The famous money man! This is a pleasure. How do things look?"

Toby glanced toward Lilly. She didn't seem to be paying attention; she was saying something to Brian. So he answered quietly, "Promising. But it isn't a done deal yet."

Jeremy gestured toward the chair he had just vacated, and while Toby sat down, Jeremy squeezed himself into the empty chair next to him. "I have to tell you," he said after this was accomplished, his deep voice youthful and enthusiastic, "I'm licking my chops. Writing opera, that's all I ever wanted to do. Since I was a kid, when I first heard those Saturday morning Texaco broadcasts with my mom, way before I even knew what opera was."

"I'm doing my best."

"Brian says there's no one better."

"Does he?" That was a surprise. Brian likely regarded anything he considered *his* as automatically being the best simply by virtue of its being his.

"If there's anything you need from me that might help, let me know. Tapes of my other music, recommendations, reviews, anything."

"I don't think that's necessary. Or advisable. Letting potential donors hear your music would invite trouble. They like this piece, they don't like that one, make sure it sounds like this instead of that, etc. Opens up a whole can of worms."

"I see what you're saying."

"You and Brian should just keep your heads down and let me do my job." With luck, this warning would get back to Brian. "And keep things under your hat."

"I'm just, you know, hungry for it. And we've got this great libretto. The whole thing's gonna kick ass."

A waiter suddenly appeared. "Ms. Hammond, table six wants to buy you a drink."

Lilly turned. And offered Toby a sheepish grimace before saying, "Tell him thank you."

"Another Coke?"

"What a waste, huh? Unless—" She looked to Toby. "You want another?"

"Thanks, but this is my third, so it better be my last. Besides, it seems wrong, a guy sending you a drink and me taking it."

"Right. Bad karma. It's probably unevolved of me even to accept, since I'm not gonna fuck him. Make it a Coke, Mike."

"Does this happen very often?" Toby asked.

She shrugged. "It happens."

"That must be flattering."

She seemed to give the matter serious thought. "If I weren't performing, they wouldn't give me the time of day," she finally said. "Being up there...it confers...I don't want to say glamour. A seal of approval, maybe. Strangers don't hit on me that much in civilian life."

"Maybe it's the blowjob songs," Toby suggested.

"Maybe that's it." And then, with an abrupt alteration in tone to signify she was changing the subject, "Listen, you plan on sticking around for the eleven o'clock show?"

A long train of thought took only a few seconds to play out. It wasn't hard to guess what would happen if he stayed. He and Lilly would have a drink or two in the club after her second set. The others would probably leave, but he and Lilly would linger. Then she'd suggest they share an Uber back to the city. In the back of the car their knees would occasionally touch, sort of but not entirely accidentally. Then he'd finally kiss her. She'd say something nice. He'd kiss her again, and then one or the other would suggest they just go back to his place or her place. She'd probably, out of some residual sense of territorial caution, suggest her place. Where they'd pour some wine or fire up a joint, put on some music, and start making out.

Soon afterward they'd go to her bedroom and fuck, and though neither would feel overwhelmed by passion, the novelty would be exciting enough to make the experience seem worthwhile. At worst, his vaunted bachelor competence would provide a simulacrum of passion that could pass for the real thing, and anyway, it's always interesting to discover how somebody new behaves in bed. A privileged peek. And not until he came—but at that point it would be instantaneous, virtually simultaneous with orgasm—would he think of Amy and feel the sinking sensation of loss and loneliness that was bound to follow. Once it arrived, though, it would settle in and make itself comfortable while he tried to ignore it in order to observe one-night-stand decorum.

Odd he used to enjoy the experience. Not just enjoy it. Organize his existence around it.

"I'd like to," he told her, "but I just can't tonight."

~

ABOUT FIFTEEN MINUTES LATER, alone on the street outside the club, shivering in the cold, waiting for the Lyft he'd ordered, Toby realized something had been gnawing at him from somewhere just beyond consciousness for some time. Something specific that happened at the club. Not Brian's bullshit either. There was nothing unconscious about Toby's reaction to that. This was something else.

Not Amy, not Brian, not Lilly...

And then he knew. It was something Jeremy had said when they were talking earlier. Toby should have noticed it right away. There were so many distractions at the time, it hadn't quite registered.

We've got this great libretto.

Fuck.

124

4

WHEN TOBY WAS USHERED into Brian's office, he was displeased to find a photographer and reporter there. Toby had made this appointment specifically to ensure a private chat with no audience Brian might be tempted to play to or hide behind; the presence of virtually anyone else was going to make things more difficult, and of all the unwelcome eavesdroppers, press people were hands down the least welcome. Another of Brian's games, or simply a result of his crowded schedule? The man himself was sprawled in a corner of one of the room's two plush sofas, posed carefully with a score on his lap, studiously trying to appear to study it. The photographer was alternately looking at a light meter hanging around his neck and making adjustments to his lamp and reflecting screen. The reporter, an attractive young woman, was in an easy chair facing Brian, a pad of paper in her lap, a pen in her hand.

Brian turned to Toby and waved. "Morning. Sorry about this. *People* magazine. Not the Sexiest Man Alive issue, oddly. Quite a disappointment. Bit of an insult, even."

"Scandalous." Toby gamely played along, but he was nonplussed. A photographer alone might have been okay. Photographers seemed invisible and one assumed, perhaps erroneously, didn't listen closely. But reporters were intrusive and snoopy by professional obligation.

Brian gestured toward the reporter and said, "This is Linda. She's asking me a bunch of personal questions. She's already figured out I'm gay, for example."

"She must have mystic powers of divination," Toby said. "Hi, Linda, nice to meet you."

Linda had dutifully turned her attention to Toby. "You are—?" she asked.

"Oh, sorry," Brian said. "This is Toby Lindeman. Our director of development."

She wrote this down. "You seem to have an easygoing relationship with Brian," she observed.

"Everyone has an easygoing relationship with Brian. He's an informal guy. None of that 'maestro' stuff with him." Laying it on with a trowel.

"That must be nice."

"Am I still fired, Brian?"

Brian smiled. As did the photographer. That was a lesson worth remembering.

"So," Linda said, "let's get a picture of the two of you conferring, okay? Sit over there, Toby. And give me some idea what you're conferring about."

Toby took a seat where she indicated, on the sofa next to Brian, who cooperated by laying his score aside. "We're conferring about…about funding new projects," Toby said carefully. Brian nodded his agreement, or maybe it was his approval of Toby's discretion.

"What does that mean?" she asked.

The photographer took their picture.

"It means…sometimes projects progress at an unexpected pace, and the left hand of the organization doesn't know what the right hand is doing. When that happens, it can lead to misunderstandings." He stared at Brian until the latter felt compelled to meet his eye. "Which can have an adverse impact on our ability to fundraise, so it's my duty to keep the music director apprised."

"I appreciate the heads-up," Brian said, his tone neutral.

But did he really understand what Toby was driving at? Best to be sure. "I thought you needed to know about it," he said. "See, someone I met the other night let something slip without realizing he was doing it…about an Italian book, you might say." There, he thought. Brian can fill the room up with strangers to discourage me from speaking freely, but he can't stop me from trying to circumvent his little dodges. "I found it distressing. Very."

"Right," Brian sighed. "Got it."

"Are you guys talking in code or something?" the reporter asked.

"Or something," Brian said curtly. He was miffed, and unable or unwilling to hide it.

"Okay, that's all," Toby declared. "Message delivered." He stood up. If Brian was upset, well, too damned bad, it was his own damned fault. "Sorry about interrupting the interview," Toby added, and then couldn't resist a parting shot: "I expected to find you alone."

"Wait up a sec," Brian said. He rose too. "I'll be right back," he told the reporter, and, draping an arm across Toby's shoulders, walked with him out of the office and into the waiting area just beyond the door. He was careful to shut the door behind them. Toby turned to face him. Brian's assistant, at his desk a few feet away, looked up curiously for a moment, and then back to his computer screen.

"Jeremy said something about the libretto? Is that the deal?" Brian's vanity winning out again; he wanted to show he was smart enough to decipher what he'd been told, even at the price of having to deal with it.

"Yeah. To be precise, he said there *is* one."

Brian, very briefly, looked abashed. Then he said, "Well, that's not strictly speaking true." He coughed. "Jeremy's let his enthusiasm run away with him a little. There's an outline of sorts, there are some provisional drafts…"

"Who by?" Toby demanded. "No one's been authorized to hire a librettist. No funds have been approved. That's leaving aside the fact that the subject hasn't even been accepted."

"Yeah…See, the thing is, Jeremy and I have been messing around with it a little ourselves. No risk to the house. If it's crap, we'll toss it and no one's the wiser."

"*I'm* the wiser. And I'm going to have to say something to Doris, of course."

Brian looked stricken. "Aw, come on, Tobe." His voice was uncharacteristically wheedling. "No one's out a cent, so who cares if Jeremy and I fiddle with a few ideas on our own time? If Doris finds out, she'll blow a gasket for nothing, I'll be pissed at you…" He paused, and then added, "Permanently." He let the word resonate for a second, and then added, "Plus, it could set the opera itself back by several months. What's the percentage in that?"

"The thing is, I work for the company. I report to the general manager."

"Don't be an asshole," Brian said.

"I try not to be. It's an ongoing struggle."

"I thought we were friends," Brian had the nerve to say.

Not a good time to air petty grievances or exact revenge for petty slights, Toby quickly decided. "We are. And you're my best friend's partner, and I don't take that lightly. This isn't about spite, Brian. I'm not *snitching*. But I have to give Doris a heads-up. I'll make it as bland as possible, I'll put it in the most favorable light I can, but I'd be remiss if I said nothing."

"I hope you know what you're doing."

"I hope *you* know what *you're* doing. There's no reason for all this subterfuge. Doris could be an ally if you'd take her into your confidence."

Brian's answering nod didn't signify agreement, merely acknowledgment a point had been made.

Doris's office was only a short distance down the same corridor. Toby could feel Brian's eyes on his back as he made his way toward it and went in.

"Is she inside?" Toby asked Sherry, Doris's assistant. Sherry was about Doris's age, efficient and brusque. Toby had never succeeded in establishing a personal connection with her, but he didn't take it personally. He doubted there was a personal connection to establish.

The door suddenly opened, and Doris emerged, dressed for the street, with a lightweight wool shawl draped over her business suit, and looking preoccupied. She almost bumped into Toby, but recovered quickly. "Oh, Toby. I'm off to a lunch meeting. I'm late."

"Listen, Doris—"

"Not now. I'm in a rush."

"Can I walk you out of the building?"

"Yes, okay." As they left the office, "Actually, it's good you're here. There's something I need to tell you, now's as good a time as any. Come on."

She strode briskly toward the stairs, and Toby scrambled to keep abreast of her.

"I just—" he began, but she interrupted to say, "Are you busy tonight? If you are, cancel. This is more important. Brad's office called. He wants you as his guest at a function tonight. You have to accept."

"If it was about me, why did they call *you*?"

"Oh, please," she said, "don't start. Do not start. They didn't call you because they called me. Brad believes in going directly to the top of the organizational chart, okay?" They started down the stairs. "The fact you're invited should be enough. I'm sure he wants to discuss the opera, but he could do that anywhere. He invited you to this thing because he's taken a shine to you. It's a good sign. Phone his office for details."

"What's the function? What member of the plant kingdom are we saving this time?"

She hesitated, only very briefly, no more than a fraction of a second, but long enough for it to register on Toby. "No plant," she said. "It's political."

"Political? What sort of political?"

"Republican fundraiser." She kept her voice studiously uninflected.

"Forget it," he said flatly. "No way."

"Don't be a child." She sounded cross. "I expect you to act professionally."

He had a sense she'd rehearsed this conversation. His reaction wouldn't have come as a surprise. They'd first met during the Hillary campaign; Toby was fundraising and the Rastovs had made a hefty contribution. Hefty enough that Toby, as a courtesy, kept in touch over the following weeks. And he'd evidently made a good impression; at the funereal election night gala, she sought him out and invited him to work at the opera.

"Would *you* go?" he demanded.

"Of course I'd go," she said. "I do that kind of thing all the time."

They reached the lobby. She stopped and turned to face him. "This is about keeping a major donor happy. Our loyalty is to the opera, not our own politics. If I only dealt with people who vote like me...I mean, Jesus, people with money are often Republicans. Even out here."

"But—"

"And anyway, nobody at this thing will give a damn about you or your opinions, to be perfectly blunt." Perhaps realizing how harsh this sounded, she continued quickly, "Brad's probably paid for several tables, he needs to fill them. You're basically a warm body."

"I'm not sure how warm I'm going to be."

"You'll be warm. See to it. There's five million dollars at stake."

"Aw shit, Doris…You know what it'll be like. They'll tell stupid, smug jokes about Biden, Kamala, AOC. And laud Trump as if he isn't a malevolent buffoon. It'll be awful."

"Just like a Democratic fundraiser, only with different villains."

"Uh-uh. Republicans are meaner. Less tolerant. As a group. I firmly believe that."

As they walked toward the front doors, Doris said, "I don't agree, and more important, I don't care. I can't allow myself to care. It's got nothing to do with our business. And by the way, right now you sound a lot less tolerant than any of my Republicans friends. But that's not the point either. The point is, you're going, you'll be there on opera business as the guest of a very generous friend of our organization, and you'll conduct yourself in a respectful and professional manner. Is that clear?"

"Yes." He felt as if he were about ten years old.

"Now excuse me, I'm late for lunch." She pushed the door open and left the building.

Toby stood at the entrance, staring out of the glass doors, watching her descend the steps to the street. And realized he hadn't had a chance to tell her about the libretto.

"MR. SOLOMON WILL BE delighted to hear you're coming, Mr. Lindeman. The event is at the Fairmont. The Crown Room. Cocktails at seven. He suggests you be prompt. Security will be tight, there may be delays getting in."

"I'll do my best. My name's on a list?"

"Yes. Be sure to mention you're with Mr. Solomon."

"You can count on it."

"By the way, I don't know if you were told, but it's a black-tie affair."

"Not a problem."

"And also…" The woman cleared her throat. "Mr. Solomon will be joined by Mrs. Solomon, and he said…that is, he said to let you know that if you have…if you have a special friend, he's also welcome."

Toby resisted the temptation to laugh. He wasn't amused, really, just startled. He'd forgotten Brad thought he was gay. Remembering also reminded him ineluctably of Amy's telling him about it. A memory accompanied by that sensation with which he'd become much too familiar, a sudden, sharp stab of anguish. Brad's misapprehension and Amy's refusal to correct him had colored everything that happened thereafter. Her telling Toby about it that night was an inflection point. An implicit invitation. And little more than an hour after that...

In fact, though, even while experiencing the pain of the memory as a sort of background hum, Toby had to acknowledge this was a rather handsome gesture on Solomon's part. To be fair to the man. In San Francisco being gay was hardly scandalous, even in Republican circles, but still, it was thoughtful of him, and it would have been easier *not* to make such an offer.

On the other hand, fuck him. He probably was desperate for a few more *warm bodies*.

"Tell him thanks," Toby said, "but I'll be solo."

~

WHILE DRESSING THAT EVENING, standing in his small bathroom carefully tying his bow tie, Toby decided, with relief, that Amy would most assuredly not be at tonight's event. Zero possibility. A respectable businessman, a pillar of the community, wouldn't parade his mistress at a Republican fundraiser, especially one to which he was bringing his wife, and at which he'd be surrounded by political honchos and friends and associates, many presumably with their own wives in tow. It just wouldn't do. NOCD.

Guys like Solomon played by the rules. So continued Toby's sour reflections. They wrote the rules to favor themselves, same as they did with financial regulations, and then they played by them. They took their wives to formal functions and their girlfriends to Cabo. They had the cash and the sense of entitlement to lead two distinct lives, one of stolid social respectability, the other of covert gimme-gimme selfishness. Separate bedrooms and the dutiful fortnightly fuck for the wife, something hot and gamy with the mistress. If the wife found out and refused to accept the situation, well, that was too damned bad. She had a mansion in Pacific Heights and a weekend place in Tahoe and clothes and jewels and a limo and driver. Wasn't that worth a slightly unromantic marital arrangement, especially since nobody acknowledged it? And if the mistress wasn't content with *her* end of the deal, well, gee whiz, no problem, there were plenty of girls clamoring to replace her, to enjoy the posh treatment, the gifts, the exotic vacations. Everyone understood the bargain. Only the churlish dared complain.

Guess I'm in a bad mood, thought Toby, catching himself in mid-musing. Quite the grump. Now why would that be?

He slipped on his trusty Hardy Amies and checked himself out in the full-length mirror on his closet door. Pretty darned dashing. Every gentleman looks handsome in a tuxedo, so they say. I look handsome in a tuxedo. Ergo, Socrates is a man.

God he was dreading this evening. Solomon resplendent in personal triumph. Hail the conquering hero (only that wasn't *Solomon*, it was *Judas Maccabeus*). And rich people, rich *Republican* people, wherever one turned. Well, no use whining about it, it was too late to back out. Backing out was never a realistic option. Not if he wanted to keep his job. Time to grab keys, cash, and credit card, and take it like a man.

He left his apartment a little before six thirty and got to the Fairmont by ten to seven. Wandering through the hotel lobby, he felt conspicuous in his dinner jacket, but he had no intention of being an early arrival. Not at this event. So he went to the news kiosk and flipped through a few magazines to kill time. Nobody was going to demand he buy something. A white guy in a tuxedo doesn't get harassed.

He waited until a little after seven before putting *The New Yorker* back on the rack and following the signs to the Crown Room, the largest and grandest of the hotel's banquet facilities. By now, lots of affluent-looking people in their fancy duds were bunched together at the welcoming tables near the doors, jostling each other to get their name tags and their table assignments. In front of the doors were metal detectors and X-ray machines for ladies' purses, and there were menacing-looking plainclothes security personnel eyeing the crowd. Some important Republican luminary was obviously going to be speechifying tonight. This crowd would accept no less. They'd forked up big bucks.

Finally inside the room, Toby put his name tag and his table assignment in his right inside breast pocket and immediately had another struggle on his hands, getting to the bar. He was pretty sure he'd need a fair share of fortification tonight. But getting to the bar, and getting the bartender's attention, required highly developed urban skills; it was a contact sport, damned near. But he finally managed it. The only bourbon available was Wild Turkey, so instead he requested a scotch-rocks, and quickly amended his order to a double. He'd try to be a good boy and nurse it, but he sure didn't want to have to make this struggle more often than necessary.

He took a quick sip of his drink and then reached into his inside breast pocket to check his table assignment. He withdrew the small cream-colored envelope, opened it, and removed the card nestling inside. Not the easiest thing to do while holding a glass filled to the brim with scotch and ice cubes. The single digit 1 was hand-written on the card, in green ink. Impressive. Table 1 presumably wasn't Siberia.

Toby glanced around the room, vaguely curious but eager not to meet anyone's eye lest he be forced into conversation. He didn't recognize anyone noteworthy, no celebrities or local pols. In San Francisco, anyone answering to either description was likely to be a Democrat. Everyone looked affluent, but otherwise normal. Doris had been right on one score, at least: at these socioeconomic elevations all fundraisers looked the same.

He took another sip of his drink. And cautioned himself, Slow down, boy, there's a long night ahead. A night when, among other things, you'd be well advised to mind your manners. The last thing you need is your inhibitions so suppressed that you blurt out what you're really thinking.

And then he saw Amy.

She was standing about twenty feet away. Next to Brad Solomon, in animated conversation with another couple. Wearing a black velvet dress, cut simply, off the shoulder. A glass of white wine in her right hand, with a small cocktail napkin bunched around its base.

He felt his heart sink. Not just an expression. He actually felt his heart—or at least *something* in his chest, something large and serious— sliding downward toward his solar plexus. But it couldn't be his heart because it was making its presence known in the same place it could always be found, beating so violently the entire world seemed to shudder with each throe. He briefly feared he might be undergoing some sort of coronary event. He reached over and grasped the back of a chair. It was hard to breathe.

Amy laughed at something Brad said.

Goddamn.

She looked away for a moment, still laughing, and noticed Toby. Their eyes met. Her face fell. In a way, it was gratifying his presence had any effect on her at all, but a falling face wouldn't have been his first choice. She recovered quickly and turned back to Brad with the same amused smile she'd been smiling before.

Toby tried to arrange something similar with his own face, tried to banish the pained, stricken frown it had assumed, tried to replace it with something genial and bland. He had the impression he was managing his transformation less convincingly than she. Still supporting himself with a hand on the back of a chair, he looked across the room toward the dais—anywhere but at Brad and Amy—and thought, You can never predict how you'll react in this type of situation. You might think you can, but you're kidding yourself. He'd known, of course, that something like this was bound to happen sometime, and he'd known, of course, that it wouldn't be pleasant. But he hadn't anticipated its being as bad as this. The feeling was almost childlike in its utter naked bleakness: He felt like a little boy who'd been assaulted for no reason by a neighborhood bully.

Maybe he *really* couldn't stand it. A whole evening of this promised to be unendurable. Maybe he had to leave. He'd explain to Doris tomorrow that he'd shown up at the event but had suddenly taken sick. Hell, singers at the opera did it all the time, abruptly cancelling performances, claiming indisposition when everyone knew it was for other reasons. Why shouldn't the staff enjoy the same privilege? He could invent something very specific and very unpleasant to lend the story verisimilitude. An attack of diarrhea, something along those lines. Doris wouldn't exactly believe him, maybe, but neither could she be positive he was lying. She certainly couldn't penalize him. Hell, she might even feel obliged to offer sympathy. Given their unfortunate conversation on the stairs—why, oh why hadn't he kept his mouth shut?—her suspicions would no doubt be aroused, and their relations might be strained for a while, but it would probably be temporary and certainly wouldn't approach the breaking point.

He'd do it. Sometimes self-preservation has to outweigh professionalism. He was going to get the hell out, and pronto. He set his drink down on the nearest table.

"Toby!" It was Solomon's voice, braying his name. Caught! Was it possible to pretend not to hear? "*Toby!*" Even louder, with the unselfconscious bumptiousness of the privileged. Toby was well and truly trapped. He forced his face into a smile—it felt so false to him from the inside he could only wonder what it presented to the world—picked up his drink, and slowly turned. Solomon was grinning at him, waving him over. Amy was looking down at the floor.

Toby's feet moved of their own accord. Crossing the few yards separating him from Brad and Amy was like a march to the scaffold.

"Good to see you, my boy," Brad said when Toby arrived. "Delighted you could come."

"Hello, Brad," Toby said, and shook Solomon's outstretched hand.

Solomon grasped Toby's arm with his free hand and said, "You've met Amy Baldwin, I believe." And then, hastily, "She and I just bumped into each other."

Toby turned to face her. Her bare shoulders. He had kissed those shoulders. He had held them roughly in his hands, he had forced them down into the mattress while taking her from behind, grinding his thighs against hers, feeling her buttocks along his belly, hearing her melodious little cries. Now he had to ignore all that, had to smile politely and meet her glance.

"Yes, that's right," he said. His voice was steady. That was a surprise. The first and no doubt only welcome surprise this particular evening was going to offer. "Nice to see you again."

She met his eyes levelly. No hint, no private glint, not a fucking thing. "Yes, very nice."

Solomon kept a firm grip on Toby's bicep. "I'm guessing you're not a Republican," he said, smiling. "Your demographics fairly scream Democrat. I appreciate your coming tonight."

"I am a Democrat, yes."

"I shouldn't have used the word 'scream.' Didn't mean anything by it."

"No offense taken," Toby said, trying to ignore the pounding in his head. It wasn't easy to think. Was Amy amused by this exchange? He wasn't going to meet her glance to find out. He didn't want to risk encountering that cold, level gaze again; it was like a second rejection, or a decisive confirmation of the first.

"I used to be a Democrat myself," Solomon said pleasantly. "Still vote that way sometimes. Couldn't stand Trump, for example. Went for Biden. None too happily, but it was the only choice." He lowered his voice. "Please be so kind as to keep that under your hat tonight."

"Sure," said Toby.

"Are you all right, son?" Solomon suddenly asked, peering at him closely.

He apparently wasn't doing a perfect job of concealing his discomfort. Fuck. The last thing in the world he wanted was for Amy to see him struggle.

"I'm fine," he said. "Just a little light-headed, for some reason."

"You want a glass of water?"

He held his glass of whisky up to Solomon's view. "This should do the trick."

"Why don't you sit down?" Solomon suggested. "Our table's over there." He pointed.

Toby took the few steps over to the table, found his place card, and collapsed into the chair. He now had a throbbing headache in addition to his other symptoms. At this rate, he'd be leaving the event in an ambulance. He glanced at the other place cards around his table. Amy's card was to his immediate right. Worse and worse.

He leaned his head into his cupped right hand and closed his eyes. After two or three minutes, he felt and heard a body placing itself in the seat next to his. Amy's seat. He lowered his hand and found Solomon peering at him.

"I'm okay," Toby said. "It's passed, whatever it was." He'd force this to be true by dint of will. There was no alternative. At some point, the evening would be over and he could go home. Until then, all that remained was to endure.

"This happen often?"

"Uh-uh. Must be political. A kind of allergic reaction."

136

Solomon smiled thinly, then said, "Are you up to talking a little business?"

"Okay."

Solomon nodded, evidently approving of Toby's game attitude. "I've been rethinking this opera thing, and you know, I'm not sure I'm comfortable dealing with artists. They aren't like businesspeople. They don't behave in rational, predictable ways. I'm starting to worry I'm buying a pig in a poke."

"You're afraid the opera will suck?"

"Not that I'd be able to tell. Nor would anyone else, is my guess. The whole business is so subjective. But yeah, that's part of it."

"What else?"

"This idea you mentioned the other day, a piece to celebrate San Francisco, is fine in the abstract. But what aspect? We've got a colorful history. Is it going to be about the Gold Rush? The Barbary Coast? The earthquake? Beatniks? The folk scene? The rock scene? I need more information. I don't believe in writing blank checks."

It was inevitable Solomon would decide to get shrewd on this night of all nights.

"I'm not saying I'm pulling out," Solomon continued, making Toby's blood run cold. He'd had no idea they were on such thin ice. "Not yet. But to be frank, I'm beginning to feel I need a reason not to." His tone seemed bullying again, the way he'd sounded the night of the redwoods dinner. He'd certainly chosen a propitious moment to strike, when Toby was feeling so diminished and vulnerable. He must have sensed as much.

Toby, fighting to keep the weariness out of his voice, said, "I hear you."

"Don't just hear me," Solomon said. "I know you can hear me. I want an *answer.*"

Toby looked up and met Solomon's gaze, and no longer had the energy to hide his resentment. Where had Amy gone? he wondered. Maybe she still preferred not to witness a round of bullying, simply on general principle. After all, he couldn't fight back, definitely couldn't answer the way he had that day in Solomon's office. He'd got away with it once, but he'd have to be irredeemably stupid to expect the same leeway a second time. That had been sheer luck, giving vent to his annoyance on the one occasion Solomon was feeling either vaguely tolerant or vaguely remorseful.

And now, in addition to all his other ailments, Toby realized he was sweating heavily. A classic get-me-out-of-here reaction. What a nightmare. Was there any reward he could give himself when the evening ended? Too bad he didn't smoke crack. "You understand there's no project yet," he said, trying to sound matter-of-fact. "None's been presented to Doris. All we have is a concept, an opera about San Francisco."

"Then what am I paying for? Some airy-fairy promise of something wonderful in the unspecified future?" Then he added in an ill-tempered grumble, "I shouldn't have said 'airy-fairy.' I'm not being personal. But you see my point."

It was all backing up on Toby. He could feel the dangerous decision being made without his conscious participation. Fuck it all. Solomon with his browbeating, Doris with her maternally tyrannical style, Brian with his pointless mendacious games. Amy. Hell, Toby didn't even like opera all that much. Let them fire him if that's where this was headed. Solomon seemed determined to wring something out of him, so just fucking give it to him and get it over with. This was how interrogators secure confessions. Capitulation is a relief.

"Something *is* under discussion," Toby said. "I'm not saying it's certain. It's at a preliminary stage. But the idea seems to be gathering steam."

"Will you please just fucking say it already?"

Toby didn't exactly gulp, but he steeled himself before proceeding. "They're considering something about the Castro." What the hell. Solomon was going to find out at some point.

Solomon's face darkened. "As in…as in what? The *gay* history of the Castro?"

"Maybe not only. But…yeah, mostly."

"You want to do an *opera* about that?"

"Not me, but—"

"Of course not you. The company. People up there on stage belting out arias about police harassment and butt-fucking. Have I got that right?"

"I wouldn't put it exactly that way." Doris was going to regret forcing Toby into attending tonight's banquet. She was going to wish with every

138

fibre of her being that she'd let him stick to his political principles and stay home.

"Wasn't there already something about Harvey Milk? Didn't I read that some time ago?"

"There was. But this would take a…a more panoramic view."

Solomon didn't say anything for what seemed like forever, but probably was only about ten seconds. He bit his lower lip, he shook his head, he started to say something and then restrained himself. Only after all that did he say, "Okay. I approve."

"What?"

"I mean, as a subject. Who knows what it'll be like? But it's maybe worth the risk. The world's changed a lot, homophobia's going the way of racism or maybe it's already gone that way, and maybe it's time to celebrate that. I like it. I like it much better than some bullshit I-heart-SF pageant. In fact, I *heart* it, if you want my bumper sticker reaction. And I appreciate your being straight with me." And then—but this time he meant to be funny—he interrupted himself to say, "Or shouldn't I put it like that?" He waited, anxiously Toby thought, for Toby to show some amusement. Toby dutifully laughed. "Seriously, partner, tell Doris I'm on board."

"Will do." Toby's head, already throbbing, was now also spinning.

"I'm glad we spoke. You know, I'm fine with the gay thing. Some of my best people are gay. I was offering partner benefits and so on before they were standard. It's none of my business where a guy puts his dick. Within reason. Besides, gays are like Jews, they use humor as a way of dealing with life's dreck. I like that. Now, where's Amy at? I told her to leave us alone for a bit."

So much for Magda's theory that Solomon needed a female audience when he broke a guy's balls. He seemed perfectly content to do it in private.

"I'm going to hunt her up," Solomon said. "Want to come along?"

Oh, that sounds jolly. "I need a men's room. I'll see you back here."

"All right, my boy." Solomon stood, clapped Toby on the shoulder again—it was easier for him to do when he was standing and Toby was seated—and then waded into the crowded banquet room. A moment later, Toby rose, drink in hand, and set out in search of a bathroom.

He didn't have to relieve himself, but he definitely needed to splash cold water on his face. A sauna and shower would be even better, but those amenities were unlikely to be available.

When he returned to the table a few minutes later, all but two seats were occupied, the other tables in the room were full, and the bigwigs at the head table up on the dais were seating themselves. Solomon now did the honors, introducing Toby to his dinner table companions, and Toby obediently circled the table, shaking hands and saying hello. A real estate developer, a tech guy, and some sort of finance guy, all in their thirties, and a judge who must have been in his seventies. Plus their wives. If the wives had professions they were left unmentioned.

Toby sat down in his assigned place. He noticed that the seat directly across from him, the one next to Solomon, was empty.

"And you know Amy Baldwin," Solomon was saying.

"Yes." Toby turned to face her. "Hello again."

"Hello." The same blank look. A slight social smile, in which her eyes played no role.

On Toby's left was the wife of the finance guy. She was young, blond, pretty, and stacked. Whether she knew it or not, whether she welcomed it or not, she was about to become the recipient of all of Toby's conversational energies. He could only hope she'd be receptive. Her looks, which ordinarily might have been enough to hold his interest, meant nothing to him tonight. All he sought was shelter from the storm.

"Hi," he said.

"Hello." She smiled pleasantly. "You're a friend of Brad's?"

He hesitated. "Yes. I mean, sort of. We're doing some business together."

"You're in real estate?"

"No, I...I'm at the opera."

She looked at him suspiciously, wondering if he was joshing. "You're a singer?"

"No, I'm in the administration."

"The *Biden* administration?"

This was certainly going smoothly. "The SF Opera."

A waiter arrived with a bottle of white wine and began filling their glasses. While this operation proceeded, Toby stole a covert, sidelong glance in Amy's direction. She was staring down at the empty plate in front of her, frowning slightly. He turned back to the woman on his left, who had just said something he hadn't caught. "I beg your pardon?"

"I asked if you're a donor."

"To the opera?"

"To the party."

"Oh, I see. No, I'm not." And then he added, unnecessarily, "I'm a Democrat, as a matter of fact."

This was evidently more information than she needed. She pursed her lips. "Well," she said, "it's a free country." It wasn't clear in the present context if she regarded that as altogether a good thing.

The evening was looking longer and less endurable with every passing second.

On his right, he heard the judge saying to Amy, "I've never used social media. Don't understand it. An old dog like me, it's too late to learn these new tricks."

And then a cell phone at the table suddenly rang, with a piercing, insistent electronic chirp. Solomon held up his hand like the winner at a bingo game, withdrew his phone, and then swivelled his chair away from the table and began speaking sotto voce.

Toby took a sip of wine, and, for want of anything better to do, glanced down at the ornate menu lying beside his place card. The first course was a salad with crabmeat, avocado, field greens, and a drizzle of balsamic vinegar. The entree was a choice of filet of beef in a glaze of red wine and cèpes or grilled salmon in a creamy dill sauce. Dessert was an ice cream concoction with a French name. The thought of food was sickening.

Another waiter came around, offering rolls. Toby declined.

Solomon had pulled his chair around so he was facing the table again. His face was uncharacteristically flushed, a deep, mottled red. "Toby," he said, his voice tight, "I need a word with you, if you don't mind."

Toby felt a shiver of apprehension. Something in Solomon's voice seemed grounds for alarm. "Okay," he said, pushing his chair back and rising.

Solomon was out of his chair too. He croaked, "Excuse us, please," and gestured to Toby, who followed him a short distance from the table, till they were almost against a wall, as far from any potential eavesdropper as was possible in such a crowded room.

"Man-to-man?" Solomon said.

"Works for me," Toby answered. It probably wasn't the right time for flippancy, but he didn't imagine he had much to lose.

"This is damned awkward. I'm in a jam here. The thing is..." He sighed. "You've probably already guessed—I'm relying on your discretion—"

"Sure."

"—you've probably guessed there's something between the Baldwin gal and me. Of a personal nature, I mean."

Toby felt the blood rush to his head. He could only hope that Solomon was too self-involved to notice. He made a non-committal noise.

"We try to be discreet. She wasn't going to come tonight, for example. We aren't necessarily fooling anybody, but it seems like the decent thing to do, not rubbing people's faces in something they'd prefer to ignore. You know what I'm talking about?"

"I imagine so."

"Right. So, that phone call just now..." Another sigh. "It was Judy. My wife. She'd told me earlier she was feeling kind of under the weather, thought she'd give this evening a pass. So that's when I suggested... Well, anyway, she's apparently feeling better all of a sudden, so there's been a change of plans. Called me from the car. She's on her way. Almost here."

"Ouch."

Solomon regarded Toby with annoyance. But for once he wasn't in the driver's seat, he couldn't afford to give vent to the feeling. "I can't have them at the same table, can I? I mean, I can't have them in the same *room*. If you've ever felt cornered, you'll understand how I feel. Have you ever felt cornered, Toby?"

"Oh yes."

"So you understand. More or less. I'm about to ask a big favor. I hope it's not out of line, but even if it is..." He evidently didn't know how to finish this sentence, because, after a brief hesitation, he started a new one. "Could you escort Amy home for me? Act like you and she

142

are leaving together and take her home. My car's downstairs. My driver will take you."

It was too much to absorb. Toby stared at Solomon blankly. Was there no limit to the punishment he'd be subjected to tonight?

Solomon added helpfully, "I know you're not too eager to be here anyway." What exquisite sensitivity, Toby thought. The fellow's almost psychic. Solomon continued, "So you can go home before the speeches, which is where you want to be, right? And it'll put me deep in your debt, which if you're half as smart as I think you are is where you want *me* to be." He forced a chummy smile. It was painful to behold. "What do you say?"

There was no gracious way to refuse. "All right."

Solomon sighed with relief, then said, "One other thing…Can you explain to Amy what's going on? If I pull her aside now, just before you guys leave and Judy arrives…I mean, Jesus, the whole thing will be so obvious I might as well put a big scarlet 'A' on my tux."

When Toby didn't answer immediately, Solomon added, "She won't make a fuss, if that's what's worrying you. She's good about stuff like this. Comes with the territory, you might say. But if you're the one to tell her, it might avoid a certain…public crassness."

"Frankly, Brad, I doubt many people will be fooled. Like you said earlier."

"No, but it'll preserve appearances. You'll do it?"

Oh man. What a horror show. But at least it would hasten the evening's end, so maybe that could be put on the plus side of the ledger, count as some small compensation for the mounting pile of grotesquery on the other side.

Brad was looking into Toby's eyes as beseechingly as he was capable. Toby met the look and held it. "Before I say yes, I want us to be clear about something. I'm not your beard. Or your lackey. I'm doing this as a personal favor because I *choose* to. Not because I have to or you have any right to expect it. Is that your understanding as well?"

"Yes, yes, of course. But time's getting short, so please say yes and do it already."

Toby's heart was going rapid-fire again as he made his way back to the table. He hadn't looked directly into Amy's eyes once tonight, and he hadn't addressed a word to her beyond the minimal greetings appearances required. Now, as he slipped back into his seat, he turned to her. Keeping his voice very low, he murmured, "What I'm about to say isn't my doing, okay?" She almost jumped when he first addressed her. He kept on talking. "When Brad called me out just now, it's 'cause his wife's on her way, he asked me to take you home." He waited for a couple of seconds, giving the message a chance to sink in, and went on, "There was no reasonable way to refuse. It's probably worse for me than it is for you, although I'm sure it's rotten for you too. But let's just do it and be done."

"Now?" She was, as he already had reason to know, quick on the uptake, she got the picture, she didn't need to have anything repeated.

"The sooner the better is my understanding."

Frowning, she stood up, placing her napkin on the table, and retrieved her purse from the floor. "'Night," Toby muttered to the table at large, "something's come up, we have to go." He gestured for Amy to follow him and marched between the rows of tables toward the main doorway. He resisted the impulse to take her arm; he didn't think he could stand touching her.

Not saying a word, they left the banquet room and briskly crossed the carpeted area toward a bank of elevators. As Toby reached over to press the call button, an elevator arrived with a ping. The doors opened. Emerging from it was a young man pushing an old woman in a wheelchair. She was well-dressed, her makeup was carefully applied, her hair was dyed a plausible shade of yellow, but the left side of her face bore the frozen aspect of a stroke victim, and her left hand lay gnarled in her lap, a useless claw.

He might have guessed anyway, but Amy's sudden intake of breath confirmed it: It was Judy Solomon. As he and Amy stepped back to allow the woman to be wheeled past them, and as they stepped into the elevator, he heard Brad behind him saying, "Judy! I'm so glad you changed your mind. We've got some nice people at our table, I think you'll like them."

So much, Toby reflected, for his dyspeptic ruminations about the sloppy appetites of wealthy men with their wives and mistresses. Solomon's situation was clearly more complicated than he'd been willing to imagine. Pity. He preferred to think of Solomon as a son of a bitch pure and simple.

When he and Amy turned around inside the elevator to face the doors, Toby caught a glimpse of Solomon pushing his wife into the banquet room, whispering something into her ear. Toby pressed the button for the lobby level. The doors closed.

He still didn't say anything. There was nothing to say. Amy too seemed disinclined to speak. But Christ it was stressful being alone with her in this small box where he could easily reach over and touch her... He had an intimation that later tonight, when he was alone, this was the moment that would occasion the most searing retrospective pain.

The elevator reached ground level in seconds. As they stepped out into the hotel lobby, he had no choice but to speak. "Brad said his driver would take us. Do you have any idea how we're supposed to find his car?"

"Let's just get a cab." She said it flatly, without looking at him.

He shrugged his agreement. He didn't care. He wasn't sure he cared about anything anymore except getting away from this place and this situation as soon as possible. They crossed the lobby, exited the hotel through revolving glass doors, and emerged onto the entrance plaza. The uniformed doorman said, "Taxi, sir?"

"Please."

There was a queue of cabs waiting. The doorman gestured to the cab at the front of the queue, it glided up to the entrance, and the doorman opened the door. Toby slipped the fellow an unearned five-spot and slid into the back seat after Amy. The door slammed shut.

"Two stops," he told the driver. "The first on Washington, then over to Pierce Street."

"Okay, mister," the driver said. He had an African accent. Somalian? Eritrean?

The taxi pulled out into traffic. They sat in the darkness, saying nothing, barely moving. Toby stared straight ahead at the posted cab license unreadable in the gloom. His headache had grown worse. He could hear Amy's breathing, inches away. This was a special sort of agony. It didn't have the tumultuous quality he'd been experiencing earlier, but had, rather, a strange gentleness. He almost felt like crying, but his heart was beating normally, and though his head was pounding, his brain didn't feel as if it were bristling with static. He found himself wishing he could have some idea, even the tiniest hint, what she was thinking or feeling. Resentment? Embarrassment? Nothing at all? He'd never know. The ride would be over soon enough, and then, no doubt, a different variety of misery was in store.

Traffic crawled. Damn. He desperately wanted this to end. And he wanted it never to end. It was unimaginable he'd ever be alone with her again.

Several minutes went by. He continued staring straight ahead, not moving. The silence was becoming intolerable. The last time he'd seen her was at the Hayes Street Grill. The time before that they'd been naked in bed. How had they gone from that to this so quickly, from uninhibited intimacy to frosty unbridgeable distance?

Her breathing remained audible, making her unmoving presence beside him achingly evident. He risked the briefest of glances. Her silhouette was softened by the darkness, her profile gently smudged. He turned away. "It'll just be a few more minutes," he heard himself say, his voice thick with weary bitterness. "And that'll be that."

She stirred beside him. Then he felt her hand on his thigh; it was like an electric shock. And then, a breathless second later, she was on him, she was all over him, her legs were straddling his lap, she was kissing his face. His arms went around her waist of their own accord. She kissed him. Her face was wet against his. Was this really happening? "Wait," he said. It was a feeble enough protest, God knows, but all he could manage. "What's going on?"

She kissed him again. He kissed back. It was impossible not to. After they separated, she whispered, "Oh God, Toby, these last weeks have been awful."

"They have?"

"God, yes."

"For me too."

"I got scared," she said. "I got spooked. I'm so so so so sorry." She rested her face against his neck. Beneath his hands, her body felt as fragile and tremulous as a bird's.

"But—"

"Shhh." She put a finger to his lips and then kissed him once more. Then she pulled her head back and stared at him unblinkingly, and her eyes were indeed glowing, exactly the way he remembered. His chest

146

began to expand, as if joy were some sort of volatile gas. After a few seconds, she said, "What?"

"No, nothing. Believe me. I'm just flabbergasted. Speechless."

"And I was here to witness it." Then she shifted away from him, and said, in a totally different tone of voice, "Driver, forget that second stop."

"Yes missus," the driver said with a little laugh, "I figured."

She laughed too, a thick honeyed chuckle, and then took Toby's right hand in both of hers and brought it up to her mouth and kissed it. "Toby," she said. "Toby Toby Toby."

PART THREE

1

I T WAS A GOOD thing Toby was feeling imperturbably jolly these days, because Monday threatened to be awful. He'd told Daniel to keep his morning clear so he had time for first Jessica and then, right after that no doubt delightful tête-à-tête, a potentially explosive confab in Doris's office. Hell of a way to start a week. But maybe this concentrated dose of nastiness was a sort of happiness tax imposed by a jealous cosmos. If so, he was willing to pay. He was a Democrat, he had no principled objection to taxing the rich.

Jessica had picked a café on Van Ness, so at least it wasn't too big a schlep. He'd have to nurse a cup of coffee for the duration of their conversation; he'd already had breakfast. There was at least one chance in thirty Jess wouldn't take this as a personal slight, and where she was concerned those weren't bad odds.

It was a bright spring morning; he was delighted to be out of doors. He arrived five minutes past the agreed-upon hour. With anyone else, that would qualify as on time. With Jessie, who knew? He braced himself for a scolding as he pushed into the restaurant.

But he'd prepared himself for the wrong assault. When he entered and scanned the room for Jessie, a woman seated at a Formica table toward the back of the place rose and waved both arms at him. He was embarrassed, and tried to ignore her, since she looked like a typical downtown crazy; among other things, she was completely bald. It took him a few seconds to realize the lunatic was his ex-wife.

His reaction came in two discrete stages. First was the simple shock that accompanied recognition, shock merely at the sight of Jessica with an exposed white pate, so white it was almost fluorescent in the gloom of the deli interior. It was slightly asymmetrical too, with a minor declivity on the right side. Toby's second reaction—lagging a second or two behind the first, just long enough to register as a separate event—was a belated, appalled understanding of what the baldness signified.

"Jessie!" he said, trying to keep dismay out of his voice. He strode through the almost empty room toward her table at the rear.

"Hell of a thing, isn't it?" she said. But her voice sounded strong, and there was a smile on her face. Not a brave smile, just a smile. She gave him a hug when he reached her. "Thanks for coming, Lindeman. Hope you don't mind being seen with Yul Brynner."

"Not at all. Makes me feel like Deborah Kerr."

"Sit down, sit down. You eating?"

"Just a cup of coffee."

"'Cause I'm ravenous. I haven't been eating—couldn't keep anything down for the past few weeks. Now I'm starving. Feeling good, too. My energy's back."

"I'm glad. You look—"

She was smiling at him fondly, waiting to see how he was going to end the sentence.

"—bald," he finally said. She laughed. "And thin. But good, Jess. I don't know quite how to say this, but you have a healthy look."

"I'm feeling okay." She looked at him, a frank, level, assessing gaze. "You're shocked."

"Well, yeah."

"I'm done with the first cycle already. The doctors didn't think dawdling would be wise. And now...well, the last test was encouraging. But I'd prefer not to talk about it." She frowned. "That came out like a rebuff, didn't it? I didn't mean it that way. It's just, cancer's all I talk about these days. It's boring. *Literally* boring, I'm not being noble. A deeply dull topic. I'll make the good fight and hope for the best. There's nothing more to say."

"But—"

"The details are a yawn. I feel fine. And I'd rather—" She reached across the table and took his hand. "I feel alive, Toby. Connected to life. My own life and the people in my life. So I wanted to tell you I don't want you *out* of my life. That's why I called. Don't worry, you don't have to be a nurse or caretaker, I've got people for that. But we have a daughter in common, and she needs us both. So I'd like you to be around occasionally. Not just for her, for me too. And not because I'm dying. Because I'm living. Okay?"

"Sure."

"And I have a mad craving for lox, eggs, and onions. That doesn't sound like a dying woman, does it? The only lethal thing about me will be my breath."

~

It DIDN'T LOOK LIKE a judicial proceeding, but Toby, watching quietly from the periphery, couldn't construe it any other way. Both Brian and Doris, each without the other's knowledge, had asked him to be present, although he had no official role to play. Thankfully. It was a relief not to feel responsible for the events unfolding before him. He could sit quietly in a straight-back chair against the wall and observe dispassionately, a non-participant with no stake in the outcome, nothing to contribute and nothing to lose.

Unless he was kidding himself.

"We could have picked something harmless and bland," Brian was saying. He was feeling the heat and keeping his usual jaunty arrogance in check. "And we still can, if that's your preference. But it's a choice I think we'd regret. This city is full of complicated history, that's part of what makes it vital. Our Gold Rush origins. Italians and Jews, Bohemians and beatniks, rock music and comedy, and yes, of course, gays. We were the gay capital of the United States once upon a time. A Joan Rivers punchline, a right-wing target. The new opera should reflect some of that energy. Otherwise, why bother?"

No one said anything for several seconds. Then the president of the board, a banker who usually kept a low profile when artistic rather than budgetary matters were under discussion, said, "What's your thinking, Doris? Brian's eloquent, but some of us are still a little at sea here. Can you help clarify some of these issues?"

Doris took a couple of seconds before answering. "I won't say I *like* it. My tastes are a bit old-fashioned. I didn't like *Nixon in China* either. Struck me as an absurd subject for an opera. That doesn't mean it wasn't valid. It may just mean my imagination is limited." She looked down at the hands folded in her lap. "The truth is, I'm a little torn." She glanced up at Brian. "I feel we've been presented with a virtual *fait accompli* by the music director, and frankly, I resent it." Brian started to speak, but she cut him off. "I'm sure you see it differently, Brian. I'm sure you can make a plausible defense of your conduct. I'm just mentioning the matter in passing. Doubtless it's had an impact on my thinking, and doubtless it shouldn't. I'm trying to guard against it."

"So is it yes or no?" the president pressed.

"I'm in a quandary, Paul. I'm still processing. If it weren't for Toby here, I wouldn't even know about it and we wouldn't be discussing it."

Oh great, thought Toby. She's thanking me for being a snitch. That should help a lot in my dealings with Brian.

"Well," said the board president, "at the end of the day, it's your call."

"I don't want to be rushed into anything. The good news is Brad Solomon, who pledged five million dollars to the project, has agreed in principle. Enthusiastically, in fact. I'm not sure how Toby managed it. Anyhow, that's got to be weighed in the balance now. It may limit our options. If we say no at this juncture, Brad might take it ill."

"He kind of talked himself into it while I sat there," Toby said.

Doris blinked, an all but invisible warning to Toby not to be ironic about Brad in front of others. And, of course, she was right. It was tough for Toby, for reasons no one in this room would ever understand, to be respectful toward Solomon, but that didn't make it less necessary.

"So we have a donor who's enthusiastic. I referred to that as good news a moment ago, but it ultimately depends on whether the *opera* turns out to be good news. It would be an exaggeration to suggest our hands are tied—I don't believe they are, quite—but Brad's feelings are a factor we'd be foolish to ignore." She permitted herself a rueful smile. "I wouldn't have predicted this. Someday, Toby, you must tell me what led you to take the plunge with him. From where I sit, it looks like a big gamble."

"He was going to find out eventually," Toby said. A non-answer.

Doris turned to Brian. "How far has this thing gone? Has any music been composed?"

"Uh-uh," Brian said. "Or if it has, I haven't seen any."

Was he lying? Toby wondered. His hedge was a troubling indicator. It wasn't hard to understand why, if Jeremy had indeed begun composing, Brian wouldn't want to admit knowing it. Doris was annoyed enough with him already.

"At this stage," she said, "I'd almost be relieved to hear the damned thing is *finished*. At least it would get us off the dime."

"Nothing like that. But we do have a head start, if you decide to go forward. On the libretto, I mean. There's a draft Jeremy and I have been working on, and I don't think it's too bad. I can't honestly tell you about anything else."

He *is* lying, Toby decided. He's volunteered more information than she asked for, which is probably meant to compensate for what he's withholding. And if that's true, it suggests Jeremy has already written a chunk of the score. Jesus. These guys sure like to live on the edge.

Doris was nodding at Brian. Toby couldn't tell if she'd just gone through the same thought process and come to the same conclusion. He did know she'd deliberately sent Brian a signal that he could come clean without fear of recriminations if he had more information; Toby wasn't sure, though, if Brian was perceptive enough to have noticed, or trusting enough to have relied on it if he *had* noticed. Brian might be the sort of person who suspected a trap even when none had been set, even when—especially when—he was explicitly assured none existed.

"Listen, Brian," she said to him now, "if you're holding any hole cards, I beseech you to turn them face up. We're not betting against each other."

"I believe that," he said. "I agree. Absolutely. And I'll keep you abreast of developments, you have my word."

"That would be refreshing," she said. About as critical a statement as she had ever permitted herself to make directly to Brian. She stared at the wall for a few seconds. No one budged. Then she said, "Maybe there's no profit in delaying any further. At a certain point you know what you're going to do even if you kid yourself the question's still open. We'll give Metcalf the commission." She waited for Paul's nod of confirmation, then turned to her deputy. "Connie, call legal, tell them to talk to Metcalf's representative. Let's negotiate a contract and get this thing going."

Brian looked elated, although he was smart enough not to crow. "I think it's the right decision. It'll be great."

"Well, it's always a crapshoot, isn't it? Let's hope for the best."

A few minutes later, when she was ushering everyone out of her office, she asked Toby to stay behind. After shutting her door, she turned to face him, leaning her weight against the door behind her, and exhaled. "He was lying. Don't you think?"

"That was my impression." He quickly added, "But maybe at this point it doesn't matter so much."

"Still, I'd prefer to be able to trust him. Anyway, the die is cast. And now your ass is on the line, buster."

"*My* ass? Why *my* ass? I'm just a go-between."

"I know. It's terribly unfair, isn't it?" Only then did she grant him an affectionate smile.

~

TOBY WAS GATHERING UP his papers and preparing to leave for the day when his phone rang. He almost didn't answer. After all, the day was over, and most news was bad news. But his conditioning was too thorough to ignore the stimulus. He grabbed for it. "Yes?" he said. He kept his voice brusque to discourage any casual harbinger of ill-fortune.

"Daddy?"

"Oh, Cathy, hi."

"You didn't sound like you."

"No, I…I'm just leaving. Meeting Jonas at the gym. What's up?"

"Good news, Daddy. Great news!"

"Tell me." And then, before she could begin, he said, "No, wait. First, I've got to ask why you didn't tell me about Mom. I saw her today. You should have warned me."

There was a brief silence before she responded. "I wanted to. I would have. She said not to. She wanted to tell you herself."

"Okay."

"I was in a difficult position."

"It's all right, Cathy. I understand. Tell me your good news."

She grimaced. "I think the moment's sort of ruined now."

"Aw, don't be punitive. I'm not giving you a hard time. You did the right thing. It was just a shock, that's all, seeing her like that."

"Which is probably the effect she was aiming for."

He was about to reprimand her, but he didn't want to douse her enthusiasm any further, and besides, the observation struck him as likely on-target. "Tell me your news."

"I got into Berkeley." Her tone was a little flatter than it might have been.

"Berkeley? That's great!"

"Yeah, I'm excited."

"Was it your first choice?"

"Or UCLA. But Berkeley's better. Especially now, with Mom and all. I'll be nearby."

"That's just great. We have to celebrate."

"Sure."

"Did it come as a surprise?"

"A little. I wasn't a shoo-in or anything."

"What made the difference, do you think?"

"Who knows? The interview went well. The guy turned out to be a theater fan, so that probably helped. And Uncle Jonas and Hank wrote really good recommendations."

"Jonas wrote a recommendation?" The information, coming so long after the fact, almost felt like an indictment.

"A glowing one. Lied through his teeth." She laughed.

"You asked him?"

"I figured a musician would bolster my arts cred."

"Why didn't you tell me?"

"Tell you?" She sounded genuinely puzzled. "I didn't think you'd be interested."

Another wound, all the more hurtful for having been inflicted unintentionally. "It's great news, honey. And I'm thrilled you'll still be in the area."

"Right, I think Mom's going to need me."

He didn't explain that that wasn't what he meant. Cathy's interpretation, although it left him out of the equation, was more caring and more compelling than what he'd intended.

But her assumption that her whereabouts were a matter of indifference to him continued to rankle while he and Jonas played racquetball. Their third game, the tiebreaker, turned into a protracted, cutthroat affair with a seemingly endless series of deuces, which Jonas finally managed to win, following what Toby suspected was a shady line call.

Afterward, when they were sweating in the sauna, Toby said, with studied casualness, "I got a call from Cathy today. She got into Berkeley."

Jonas, on the pine bench below him, said, "Terrific. I'm delighted."

"She thought your rec might have made the difference."

"Isn't it pretty to think so?"

Which is when Toby finally surrendered to the irritation he'd been feeling for the past few hours. "Why didn't you tell me?"

"Tell you what?"

"That you wrote a recommendation. That she asked you to."

Jonas sounded surprised. "I assumed you knew. Didn't you?"

"Nope. I didn't even know what schools she applied to."

"And you're blaming me for that?"

Hmm. His point. No shady line call required. Toby wiped his forehead with a towel. "I'd like to," he said. "There are so many loops, and I'm out of all of them." Which, by a process of association, prompted him to say, "Oh my God, I forgot to mention this, but Brian's opera got approved this afternoon."

"Did it? Really? He must have been over the moon."

"He was. But he was smart enough to play it cool. The right approach. Doris has plenty of misgivings. It was a close-run thing."

"He's been worried sick about it. It's all he talks about." Then, in a different tone, Jonas said, "Listen," and then hesitated, which caused Toby to think, Uh-oh, more bad news, some terrible new secret about the opera. "I've been waiting for the right moment, but it never comes, which may mean there isn't one, so..." A second to collect himself. "See, Brian and I have decided to get married. And I'm not asking you to give the blushing groom away or anything, but would you consider being the one who stands beside me during the ceremony? Kind of a best man deal, except there are no responsibilities. Is this out of line?"

"Of course not, Jonas. I'd be honored."

"Yeah? That means a lot to me. This whole thing's gonna be so fraught. Crazy-making. I'm moving in with him this week, that's scary enough. And my parents are coming, and they're pretending to be pleased but deep down they're totally freaking out. This tells them there's no hope, no road-to-Damascus moment where I'm blinded by revelation and fall to my knees and cry out, 'O Lord, the scales have fallen from my eyes, I like tits!'"

Toby laughed.

Jonas reached up and took Toby's hand. "You're a good friend, Tobe."

Toby had the unworthy concern that somebody might come into the sauna and see the two of them like that, but forced himself to shrug it off. "Have you set a date?"

"Not yet. We're aiming for the end of the year sometime." He released Toby's hand.

Toby was relieved. The politics of hand-holding can be a complex business. "What about *his* parents? Will they come? Has he told them?"

"They won't like that I'm a guy," Jonas said. "And they won't like that I'm Jewish. So there are two strikes against me. I have a cock, and it's circumcised."

"Is he out to them?"

"To his mom. She's not thrilled, to put it mildly, but she hasn't disowned him or anything. She says she prays for him. She also tells him to say hi to me when they talk on the phone, so maybe that's progress. She won't let him tell his dad, says it would kill him. Literally. The Hughes family doesn't use figures of speech. She's never traveled alone, and we have to keep Dad away at all costs, so I don't know if she'll come or not." Jonas snorted. "Families!"

"Everywhere you look," Toby said.

"And not a functional one on the planet. Anyway, with the engagement and the opera, Brian and I will be celebrating tonight. You free for dinner? Or seeing Amy?"

"Seeing Amy." The words, and indeed the thought, were accompanied, as always, by a palpable thrill, a small adrenaline rush. Jonas was the only other person in the world to whom Toby could utter them.

"Boy," said Jonas, "for a straight guy, you sure get laid a lot."

WHEN TOBY ARRIVED AT her house, Amy was waiting, framed in the open doorway, a smile on her face and a wriggling, nervously resistant Feeney in her arms. She was barefoot, in jeans and a thin navy pullover. She had on a pair of glasses Toby had never seen before, with heavy black frames, less ugly than Cathy's but definitely unflattering. It didn't matter. There was nothing she could do to make herself unattractive to him.

"Hi there," she said.

He held up the brown paper shopping bag he was holding. "Dinner," he said.

"My hero."

He took the short distance separating them quickly and wrapped both woman and cat in an embrace. "Hi, sweetie," he said.

She put her face to his. He could smell the sandalwood soap she used; he could feel her glasses against his temple and her breath against his cheek. Her lips brushed his face. "I've been looking forward to this moment all day," she said.

"Me too. Everything in my life that isn't you is just a pointless interruption."

Feeney was struggling vigorously, mewing with unmistakable annoyance. Amy backed across the threshold, and Toby followed, kicking the door shut behind him, at which Amy knelt and released the cat from her grasp. It went skittering off into the depths of the house.

"As pleased as ever to see me," Toby said.

"She's just shy. Also, she hates you." She reached up, folded her arms around his neck, and urged his head down toward hers for another kiss. A long kiss. He put his hands over her buttocks and pulled her against him. When their mouths separated, she had a little smile on her face. "And what do we have here?"

"Where?"

She reached down and moved her palm against his stiffening cock. "Here."

"Oh, that. A little tribute to your allure."

"Not so little."

"You know how to sweet-talk a boy."

160

"Sweet talk's the least of it. Come to bed."

He laughed. Her ardor always tickled him. "Why don't we eat dinner first?"

"Aw…"

"I just played three sets of racquetball, and all I had for lunch was a smoothie. I'm weak-kneed. Let me have some nourishment. We'll both benefit."

She was handling the front of his trousers again. "I'm getting mixed messages here," she said. "Which do I heed?" She dropped down to her knees and unzipped him. He couldn't bring himself to protest as she freed his cock and started to suck. After about a half minute of this, she stopped and looked up at him. "Am I making any headway?" she said. Her eyes were guileless, opened wide.

"That's exactly what you're making. But I'm still hungry."

"Killjoy. Okay. Consider this what's called 'a lick and a promise.'"

He took her hand and helped her to her feet. "I feel ridiculous," he said.

"And so you should."

"No, I mean…" He gestured to himself. "…Undignified."

"Put yourself together and come to the kitchen. What'd you bring? Besides *that*."

He hoisted the shopping bag and followed her to her spacious kitchen. As he placed the shopping bag on a granite counter, he said, "I stopped by an Italian deli. Melon, prosciutto, rosemary-and-sea-salt focaccia, Soave, and a couple of biscotti."

"And no cooking required. Full marks."

As he was reaching into the drawer under the counter for a corkscrew to open the bottle of wine, she suddenly put a hand over his. "Toby?"

Surprised by her tone, he looked over at her.

She hesitated. "It's nothing really. Only…when I saw you coming up the street, I felt happy."

Something hot and alarming was occurring behind his eyes. He took her in his arms. Her body against his, its warmth, its compactness, its soft contours, felt like a safe haven, a natural mooring. Her scent, a combination of sandalwood and something her own, was both aphrodisiac and balm.

She pushed him back a little to search his face. Her hands were on his shoulders. "This is…you know what I'm trying to say. This is a big deal."

"I'd say so."

"Creeps up on you, doesn't it?"

"That isn't how I experienced it."

"How did you experience it?"

"Krakatoa 1883."

"I think we need some wine."

"Coming right up," he said, and reached into the drawer for a corkscrew.

"Tell me about your day. I want to know everything. It's amazing. I gave up on expecting this sort of thing years ago. Preparing dinner in the kitchen, describing what sort of day we had while secretly wanting to hop into bed. I thought it'd only happen to other people. So how was it? Your day, I mean."

"I hardly know where to begin."

"A real humdinger, huh?"

"'*A real humdinger*?'" He had been removing the foil from the top of the wine bottle with the point of the corkscrew, but now he stopped. "Did I just hear you say 'a real humdinger'? No fibbing, now."

She reddened, and then laughed. "I refuse to answer."

"Jeez. Or perhaps I should say, 'Jumping Jehoshaphat.'"

"I'm from Michigan, damn it. That's how we talk."

Toby suddenly thought he saw something briefly flicker behind her eyes. So his tone changed when he asked, "What?"

"Nothing."

"No, something happened. You had a disturbing thought."

"It's nothing. Really." Then she gave in with a shrug. "It's just…what you were saying just now, it reminded me of something I thought you'd find funny, but then I thought maybe you wouldn't. Brad sometimes says I'm the most *shiksa*-like *shiksa* he's ever met." She looked down at the floor. "I guess it's funnier when he says it."

"Context is everything."

"Aw shit, I've ruined the mood."

He pulled her to him and held her close. "Nothing can ruin the mood. It's indestructible. We both know the situation. It's part of the package. We can't let him become unmentionable. I refuse to give him that power. Brad Brad Brad Brad Brad Brad...See? The sky's still up there. Brad Brad Brad. We can say his name. We can acknowledge his existence."

She smiled crookedly. "Okay. But..." And then she shook her head. "But nothing. Just okay." She kissed him, a quick peck. "I want to hear about your day. I want to know everything that's happened to you."

"Every goldern thing?"

"Cut it out!" Laughing, she brandished the large knife with which she had been ready to slice melon. "Make fun at your own risk, pal. I'm armed. And I'm from Michigan."

"You're a one-woman militia."

"Damned right."

"A real humdinger."

"And a real handful."

"Let me see about that."

Only minutes later, in bed, he whispered, "You are *so* beautiful."

"Don't say that now, Toby. Really. No one should think about what they look like when they're doing this."

A few minutes later, he said, "You want to know why I'm a lucky, lucky guy?"

"Tell me."

"I've fallen in love with a great lay."

She made a little rumble of amusement. Then she said, "You are too." And then, after a long pause, she added, "I have too."

"There. Was that so hard?"

"Nothing about this is easy."

Several minutes after that, lying side by side, Toby said, "I wish we weren't so excluded from each other's lives, though. I'd like you to meet the people I tell you about."

"Jessica?"

"Maybe not Jessica."

"Because I *would* like to meet her. The girl you married."

"It was another lifetime."

"All the more interesting. Like looking at your high school yearbook."

"I'd like you to meet Jonas, my best friend. And I'd be curious what you'd make of Doris."

"You mean Doris Raskov? I already know her."

Toby was startled. "You do?"

"Sure. She and Mike are friends of…"

"Just say it."

"Brad. I've met most of Brad's friends by now."

"Isn't that awkward?"

"It doesn't seem to bother him. I figure it's his decision."

"She's a tough cookie."

"Judy?"

He grimaced. "Doris."

"Really?"

"Isn't that your impression?"

"I don't see her in a professional situation."

"Tough and smart."

"When I see her, she's mostly just Mike's wife. She has an unusual job, of course, but no one really knows what it consists of."

"It consists of being tough and smart."

She rolled toward him. "You like tough, smart women, don't you?"

"I haven't been offered many alternatives. They're the ones I meet. I might prefer soft and stupid if given the chance." He rose on a forearm and peered down at her face. "What does Doris think of you, would you say?"

"I'm sure she disapproves. But it wouldn't be personal. She and Judy are old friends."

After a moment he said, "So…what do we do now?"

"Exactly what we're doing."

"No, I mean—"

"I know what you mean. But…" She bit her lip. "Please, Toby, let's not turn this into a struggle. A tug of war. Let's just…This is so amazing. Isn't that enough?"

He didn't answer. Instead, after weighing several alternatives, he said, "Do you think we can eat now? I'm famished."

2

Toby was restless. Once upon a time, working late was fine with him. During the last year or so of his marriage, he even welcomed it. A valid reason to postpone going home. Now, though, it was agony, at least on nights he was going to see Amy. And such nights—it was enough to make him touch wood—were lately more rule than exception.

He hadn't pressed for an explanation. Most likely, Solomon was busier than usual, or traveling. With copious apologies to Amy for his absence, no doubt. The son of a bitch was so full of himself he probably thought she felt deprived. Well, Mr. Big Shot, guess again.

He checked his watch. He was awaiting a business call scheduled for seven, and it was twenty past. Christ. He felt the way he had eighteen years ago, waiting for Cathy to make her painstaking, grudging entrance into the world. Just do it already!

Ironically, the call he was expecting was from none other than Brad Solomon. He hadn't decided whether to tell Amy. Something like this might amuse her or it could cloud her mood. As a subject Solomon was far from neutralized.

He impatiently rose from his desk, paced over to the sofa, picked up a copy of *Opera News*, a magazine to which he felt honor bound to subscribe even though he rarely read it. And then someone knocked on his door. "Yes?" he called. "Come in."

It was Brian. "Your guy's gone, what's his name, Daniel, but I saw your light was on."

"I'm expecting a call, but come on in." Toby walked over to Brian and shook his hand. Interesting which friends' hands you shake and which you don't have to bother.

Brian entered the office, crossed over to the sofa, and plopped himself down. "I'll make myself scarce when the phone rings. Just wanted to personally say thanks. I didn't get a chance the other day. You've shepherded this project very skillfully, and I appreciate it."

Toby shrugged. He felt the mistrust he always felt with Brian, but he chose not to say skill would have been unnecessary—no shepherding would have been required—had Brian been more straightforward. He'd already made the point several times. Now it was moot.

"I've been noticing how you work," Brian went on. "Get the job done with a minimum of fuss, no grinding of gears. I admire that."

It made Toby uncomfortable to be praised for stealth, as if Brian regarded him as some sort of kindred spirit. "I just deal with things as they arise."

"And leave no traces."

What the hell was this about? Some kind of indirect apology for making threatening noises the other day?

"I'm sure I leave traces," Toby said. "I've found transparency is the best policy." He permitted himself this little dig.

"Yes, yes, I wasn't implying anything." Brian smiled winningly. "I just wanted to say I value your help. I'm prepared to admit that when we differed, you were right and I was wrong."

"I'm glad it worked out."

Brian shook his head impatiently. This evidently wasn't what he was after. "I'm not just talking about Jeremy's opera," he said, his voice lower, his tone confiding, even insinuating. "There's life after Jeremy's opera. I think we both have a future in this house. Not just for a year or two or five. For a long time. A lifetime. Someday I expect—that is I hope—to be artistic director, not just music director. This isn't a secret. Doris knows, though I doubt she approves. I'd love to have the opportunity to try to create a unified style for our productions. To have responsibility for what a San Francisco production *is*. We've become sclerotic, we need a sense of adventure, and that requires a housecleaning. I'll need a team I can rely on, given the resistance I'm bound to encounter when I start shaking things up. Some people will have to go, some new people will have to be brought in. But when that happens, you're one of the ones I'll keep. Not just keep. Promote. Your talents are being wasted. It's criminal the way you're underutilized. I don't see any limits to how far you can rise in this organization."

Toby didn't know what to say. If he was interpreting Brian right, he was being invited to participate in a whole new level of disloyalty. But the invitation was couched in such general terms it was impossible to demur. "Glad I make the cut," he said, keeping his voice uninflected, as if oblivious to subtext.

Brian was going about it crudely, seemingly inviting Toby to join a cabal, but he was pressing the right buttons, raising issues that Toby had long been finding worrisome. In his mid-forties, he still wasn't sure whether his job at the opera was a career or a way station. And if the latter, to where? He had practical concerns as well, about salary and security and tenure. The job paid well enough, but was it going to take him anywhere beyond itself? It wasn't going to make him rich or ensure an affluent retirement. It definitely wasn't going to put him on a level with the people he dealt with on a daily basis. Solomon was too rich to count, he was in a class by himself, but to most donors, probably even to Amy, Toby was a drone, a salary-man. And Doris, for all her collegiality and appreciation of his competence, never so much as hinted at advancement. The metaphor struck him unpleasantly: Under the present regime, he was a serf, valued for his skills but unwelcome at the master's table.

It was a good thing Brian was so maladroit at manipulating Toby. Had he been more deft, Toby might have been susceptible.

"Listen," said Brian suddenly, "after this phone call of yours…you want to get a drink? There's lots to talk about. Or come to my place? Jonas is out, we could pick up some takeout."

Toby felt intimations of alarm. Was it possible Brian intended a sexual undercurrent? Were there no limits to the betrayals Brian could propose in a single conversation?

"Can't," Toby said evenly. "I have a date."

Brian smiled. "Lucky girl."

The phone rang, sparing Toby the onus of finding an innocuous answer. He knew how to dissimulate obliviousness—it was a tactic that often saved him from embarrassment—but he'd been doing it for a while now, and Brian was unlikely to buy the act much longer.

"Go ahead," Brian said easily. "There'll be other opportunities. Have a good evening. Play safe." He managed a leer before heading out the door.

Unsettled, Toby picked up the phone. "Hello?" He kept his voice cool and professional, which is precisely how he didn't feel. Did he have an obligation to tell Jonas about this conversation? Or would that just be fishing in troubled waters?

"Toby Lindeman," purred a female voice. Another member of Solomon's harem, no doubt. Her honeyed voice, all by itself, told you she was beautiful.

"Speaking." He rubbed his forehead hard, as if trying to force out any residue of the distressing exchange with Brian.

"I have Maynard Jacobson on the phone."

"Maynard Jacobson? I was expecting—".

"Toby?" a male voice interrupted. "Maynard Jacobson here. I handle Mr. Solomon's finances. He told me to phone."

"Did he? He told me *he* was going to phone." Toby kept his tone cordial but guarded. The call was forty minutes late and not the one he'd been promised. Nobody thought they owed a serf anything. Not even common courtesy.

Jacobson was unruffled. "Brad's out of town, but he would have referred you to me anyway. He's a genius businessman for sure, but that doesn't mean he manages the books." Jacobson chuckled at the very thought. "Anyway, it's late, you're probably impatient to go home, so let's get down to business. I understand Brad's offered to make a gift to the opera. You're the point man on this, have I got that right?"

"I suppose you could say that. I'm director of development." A quick calculation told Toby to use Solomon's first name when referring to him; it might leave this Jacobson fellow confused about the nature of their relationship, suggesting the possibility they were social friends and maybe social peers. If Jacobson thought that was the case, he'd be less likely to make difficulties. "Brad's promised to help fund a new piece. He offered us five million dollars." He was careful not to hesitate or stumble over the figure or pronounce the words "five million" like Carl Sagan, with an orotund note of wonderment at their daunting immensity. Part of his job consisted of naming vast sums as if they were chump change.

There was no immediate answer at the other end of the line, leaving the impression Toby either had his facts egregiously wrong or had committed some gaffe. Why, Toby wondered, do people play these games? He'd been forced to play them for long enough, and with a wide enough variety of donors, that he'd acquired a few relevant skills and had no difficulty letting the silence extend itself. No matter what Jacobson was trying to convey by not responding, Toby was unfazed. The man was blowing smoke, probably because it was automatic, habitual. It wasn't his money, and it wasn't his decision how to spend it.

Jacobson finally, inevitably blinked. Probably not more than five seconds had gone by. "Brad mentioned a figure in that range. You understand this won't be a cash gift, yes?" It was Toby's turn to remain silent. The ball was still in Jacobson's court. "I'm authorized to transfer stock valued at approximately the amount you named," Jacobson added.

"Fine," Toby said smoothly. "But I hope you intend to proceed with alacrity. These discussions have been ongoing for a while. It would be helpful to have the transaction completed." Sounding ever so slightly impatient, perhaps even a tiny bit skeptical about Solomon's intentions. Toby was an old hand at this; he could play his part in his sleep.

"Of course," said Jacobson. "I'll set the process in motion in the morning."

"Excellent. Is there anything else you need from us?"

"That should do it."

"Then I'll bid you good evening. When you speak to Brad, tell him I missed hearing from him." A little parting shot.

Rather than replacing the receiver in the cradle, Toby mashed the disconnect button, released it, and as soon as he heard a dial tone, punched in Amy's cell number.

She picked up after one ring. "On your way?"

"Not quite. Still in my office."

"Me too."

"You are?"

"Minor crisis. Software glitch. Won't take forever. An hour, maybe."

"Should we—?"

"Hell no. Every fuck is precious. Just let yourself in, I'll meet you there."

She'd given him a key a week ago. Casually taking it out of a kitchen drawer and sliding it along the granite counter toward him while they were preparing dinner, saying, "This might come in handy sometime. Just promise not to steal my jewelry." Despite her offhand manner, it had struck him as momentous.

"You'll find a menu from a Thai place on the fridge door," she said. "Beneath one of those magnet thingies. They deliver. That work for you?"

"Fine. Perfect. Anything."

"Order whatever you like. But could you feed Feeney?"

"Happy to." More precisely, overjoyed to. He relished the domesticity implicit in the request. He still wasn't used to this, still found the prospect of seeing her thrilling. The ardor of their lovemaking was undiminished. How long could they sustain such heat? Not forever, surely. But neither could he picture it abating.

~

HE FELT LIKE A felon unlocking the door to Amy's house. Apprehensive, as if a cop might suddenly appear and demand an explanation. But Feeney was the only one to greet him as he stepped into the foyer. And while there might have been something accusatory in her mew— some suggestion of "What kept you?"—he believed her preponderant emotions to be pleasure and relief.

Of course, Feeney was such a nervous specimen it wasn't easy to tell. She brushed up against his leg, mewing, circling, mewing again. But when he knelt down to pet her, she dashed off into the darkness of the interior. "Feeney!" he called. "Come back, kitty."

She returned a few seconds later, padding in warily from the dark recesses of the house. He knelt and scooped her up with one hand under her belly. Suddenly panicked, she wriggled to escape his grasp, a slender, sinewy gray packet of terror. He brought his other hand up to support her hindquarters, and said, "Relax, pal, I come in peace."

He deposited her on the floor and off she scampered again. He took a deep breath. It was odd to be here alone. His first time. Turning on lights as he went, he headed for the kitchen. When he opened the refrigerator door, Feeney sidled into the room, feigning indifference.

Toby smiled at her disingenuousness as he squatted down and peered into the refrigerator. A quart of milk, two bottles of white wine (one of them a third empty and recorked), a jar of mustard, strawberry jam, cherry-flavored Greek yogurt, ketchup, half a sandwich encased in Saran Wrap, a can of Diet Coke, a head of iceberg lettuce that had seen better days, a lemon, and a can of cat food, the top of which had been all but completely severed, its edge tilting slightly above the rim of the can. He grabbed it and removed it from the refrigerator. The smell, fishy and somewhat reminiscent of garbage, was unpleasant but not awful.

Feeney started to purr excitedly—her reaction to the smell was evidently more positive than Toby's—twirling in a circle a few times and then rubbing her jaw against his leg. "Calm down, puss, it won't be long now," he said. He located a bowl and a spoon, ladled the contents of the can into the bowl, and placed it on the floor. Feeney dashed over to it and began eating noisily. He stroked Feeney's neck, but the bitch, now that she'd got what she wanted, ignored him. He located a bin under the sink and tossed the empty can into it.

He took the few steps back to the refrigerator to find the menu Amy had mentioned. There were several magnetized plastic doodads on the door; one of them, in the form of a Harlequin head, held a photograph of Solomon and Amy (the latter in sunglasses and straw hat) smiling from a Venetian gondola, shielding their eyes from the sun with their hands. Further inspection yielded a menu from something called The Bangkok Kitchen. He took it down, glanced through it quickly, found the kitchen phone, and ordered, almost randomly, a chicken dish, a noodle dish, a vegetable dish, and steamed rice.

What now? Well, the first item on the agenda was using the bathroom. Was this a reaction to that Venice photograph, an atavistic impulse to mark the turf with his urine? Or was it merely a result of his bladder being full, one of those times when a cigar was just a cigar? He chose the bathroom off her bedroom rather than the one near the foyer, so perhaps territoriality did play a role. While peeing—or, as he preferred to think of it, leaving his spoor—he noticed a small pile of magazines on the hamper by the toilet. An unanticipated window into someone's intimate moments. After finishing his own operation, he poked through the magazines: *Vanity Fair*, *The Economist*, *Business*

Week, The Atlantic. He replaced them on the hamper, and the thought occurred to him that he might, during this brief solitary interval, permit himself a little private exploration around her apartment. He didn't want to be accused, even by himself, of out-and-out snooping, so he formulated a few ground rules for himself: He wouldn't examine her medicine cabinet or look at personal papers or correspondence, but anything in plain sight was fair game.

Once he got started, the exercise proved disappointing. Her bookshelves contained little of interest. Books about business and finance, a few about computing, several dozen broken-spined paperback thrillers, an oversized paperback guide to movies on television. She'd warned him she wasn't much of a reader, but it puzzled him anyway; how could someone with such an interesting mind not read?

He moved on to her CDs. No special enthusiasm was in evidence here either, no sign of idiosyncratic taste. It was all perfectly good, but could have been purchased by the yard. Some Ella, some Barbra, Sinatra, Tony Bennett, Johnny Hartman and John Coltrane, Beatles, Stones, Paul Simon, Aretha, a Motown compilation, Radiohead, Lady Gaga. A handful of classical: Three Beethoven sonatas with nicknames, the fifth and ninth symphonies, one of those appalling "best of" collections devoted to Mozart, another to Rachmaninoff, a Yo-Yo Ma sampler. How could someone who made love like Amy have such generic taste? Clearly, he would have to reexamine some prejudices. A certain mutual tolerance was going to be necessary over the years.

Over the years? He caught himself. Were they looking at years, in fact? It was tough to imagine otherwise if the strength of his feelings meant anything. But this was an issue she wouldn't address, cutting him off if he went near it. Their future was muzzy because the present was undefined, and the present was undefined because of that fuckhead Solomon.

He plopped down on one of her sofas. I'm head over heels in love with this woman, he thought. Obsessed and besotted. She intrudes on all my waking thoughts, including thoughts where she has no rightful place. I can hear her voice in my head, its intonation and rhythms, at will. I want to ravish her, and I want to talk with her till we're hoarse. Everything about her appeals to me, even the unappealing things.

Her happiness is as important to me as my own. Unless her happiness depends on that fuck-head Solomon, of course. I can't imagine life without her. And I know what that feels like, I've been there. But does she feel the same? She says the right words (sometimes without being prompted), but "love," that key word, is a tricky beast. We love our friends, our parents, our siblings, our pets, our favorite movies, our iPhones. "All you need is love," the Beatles sang, and a very young Toby didn't have a clue what they were on about, and still didn't. Or consider: "I *do* love you, just not that way." How many times had *those* words been uttered? Toby had uttered them himself on occasion.

The phone rang, interrupting these reflections. Toby froze. After three rings there was a click, cutting off the fourth, and he heard, "Hi there, this is Amy, leave a message and I'll get back to you." Then the familiar beep. Her old-fashioned answering machine. A male voice said, "Hi, honey, it's me, I'm still in LA." Solomon! Toby stiffened, but couldn't bring himself to scurry out of earshot. "It's been one holy hell of a day. I think we got a deal. I spent the whole fucking day battling with the mayor, called him a schmuck to his face, walked out on him twice, pulled the life-is-too-short routine, and each time he called me back. Some people shouldn't be allowed in a negotiation, not that I'm complaining, fish are always welcome at my table. Anyway, I have to go to dinner with some local poo-bahs in a few minutes, union guy, planning commission guy, gal from the mayor's office. I doubt it'll go late, but who knows, for some of these folks it beats going home. But I wish I wasn't coming back to an empty suite and an empty bed. I really miss you. Maybe I'll call when I get back if it isn't too late. 'Night, honey. Love you." Another click.

Toby had to remind himself to breathe. Wow, that was strange. Solomon sounded so different. Warm. Confiding. *Intimate.* Taking reciprocal intimacy for granted. And weary. Needy. Human.

Toby tried to pretend Solomon was just background noise, playing a role in Amy's life like the one Jessica played in his. Part of Amy's past, germane only as an impediment. But life kept reminding him that wasn't the case; Solomon was a factor, he was *there.*

The message light on the phone console was now glowing red. It too was a reminder that Solomon was part of the equation.

Feeney padded into the living room, wandering aimlessly for a few seconds, pretending indifference once again, as if Toby's presence had nothing to do with her entrance, as if she wasn't even aware he was there. She licked a paw, she stretched, she licked a paw again, and then, after a few seconds, warily approached him in his easy chair. He was willing to indulge this charade. "Hi, Feeney," he said. "Come join me, I'd appreciate the company."

She cocked her head, considering her options, then leapt onto his lap. She moved around a bit, positioning herself, trying to get comfortable, trying to assert some sort of occupant's authority over his lap's acreage. Then she gave in and started purring, licking a paw once more and rubbing it repeatedly across her face. "Suffer from OCD much?" he asked. He caressed the tight fur behind her ears and under her jaw. She closed her eyes, looking blissful, and moved her head around to ensure the right areas received proper attention. "Do you act like this with Brad by any chance? Does he have a clue how to please you?"

The front door opened. Feeney froze for a second, then mewed once and leapt off his lap, scampering toward the foyer. He heard Amy's voice, saying, "Hey, Feeney! Hi girl! How are you? Did Mr. Toby give you dinner?"

He sat quietly. He heard Amy's approaching footsteps. She appeared in the living room archway, carrying Feeney. "Finally made it," she said. "Hi there, Mr. Toby. Sorry I'm late."

"It's okay. The food isn't here yet."

"You ordered?"

"And fed your friend."

"I wish my employees were so dependable."

"I'm dependable all right."

She took a tentative step into the room. "Is something the matter?" she asked.

"Uh-uh."

"Good. Enough's going to hell at work. Here things should be perfect." She set the cat down—Feeney promptly dashed out of the room—then approached Toby's chair and kissed him. "Give me a minute, okay? Let me take a quick shower, get out of these clothes."

"I'm not going anywhere."

She gave him a funny look, but didn't push it. It was only after she left the room that he realized he was angry. It wasn't fair; Amy hadn't done anything, she couldn't know about the message he'd overheard, and besides, the message didn't change anything. But there it was. The situation was inherently unstable, and occasionally things were going to tip this way or that.

Feeney entered the living room again. "Crawling back, huh?" Toby said. "You think I'm that easy?" The cat approached, purring. No shame, no remorse.

Looking up, Toby noticed that the answering machine light was no longer glowing. Amy must be listening to the message. How did she react to such things? Was it a problem for her, hearing one set of intimacies while another was waiting in the next room?

The doorbell rang. Toby jumped up and walked to the front door, opening it to a young, very thin Asian man in jeans and a denim jacket. He was carrying two white plastic bags.

"Bangkok Kitchen?" Toby asked.

"Bangkok Kitchen," the young man declared. It didn't have the rhythm of a confirmation. It sounded like it was being offered as a fresh piece of information.

"Yes, good," said Toby. "How much?"

The man handed Toby the bags, and then reached into his pocket and withdrew a bill. He held it up for Toby's inspection. "Thirty-two dollars," he said.

"Okay," said Toby. "Only…" He raised the bags slightly, to indicate to the man that holding them prevented him from reaching for his wallet. The man nodded and took one of the bags from Toby, who reached into his pocket, fished out a wallet, and then realized he needed the use of both hands. He handed the other bag to the man as well, and then fished a twenty and two tens out of the wallet. "There," he said. "That's fine."

The man handed a bag back to Toby, which freed one hand to take the money from Toby. Then he handed the other bag to Toby.

"You want change?" he asked.

"No. It's fine."

Toby carried the bags back into the kitchen, set them on the counter, and emptied them, setting the cartons on the granite central island. Then he opened the refrigerator and removed the one-third-empty bottle of white wine. He was about to get some plates and bowls down from the cupboard when Amy appeared in the doorway. Her hair was damp and tousled. She was barefoot, wearing a pair of black jeans and a white T-shirt. No bra. Looking at her, noticing her unassuming but perfect little nipples against the thin white cotton fabric, Toby knew it would be tough to sustain his anger for long.

"Let's have some of that wine," she suggested.

"Yes, ma'am," he said.

As he turned to the cupboard to grab some wine glasses, she said, "Something *is* wrong."

"Hard day." He didn't have the stomach for a serious discussion. His anger was still there, still exigent, but so was the way she looked, and the food, and his weariness.

After a moment, she declared, "But something's bothering you. You want to tell me?"

She was too fucking sharp. He considered his own mood and wondered whether to accept her invitation. "Not if we're just going through the motions," he finally said. He could hear the edge in his voice.

As, of course, could she. "All right, I know we're going to have to talk eventually. About you and me and Brad. But...look, it's complicated, and this thing between you and me still feels very new. Can it wait a while? That's all I'm asking."

"Right," he said. He could feel his anger starting to rise again. Why was that? Maybe because postponing the discussion was in her interest but hell for him. He said gruffly, "Forget Brad for a minute. Let me ask you something else."

"All right."

As she filled the wine glasses, he said, "Have you done this a lot?" He knew he was taking a chance. But he felt entitled.

"'This?'"

"Seen other guys."

She looked at him coolly. "You mean while I've been with Brad?"

"That's what I mean."

Still holding the stare: "What's a lot? You're not the first, if that's what you're asking. Or the second."

"Or the third?"

"Let's leave it at not the second. So this doesn't turn into an auction."

"He's never found out?"

"No." Pause. "Well, once." Pause. "It wasn't good."

There was something in her tone; not exactly hostile, but closed-off, wary. "Is this out-of-bounds?" he asked.

"Whether it is or isn't…is there anything else you want to know?"

He was in too far to retreat. "Just…*why*? I mean, more than two, that sounds like…like policy, not impulse."

"It's a fair question. I guess." She offered him one of the wine glasses. "I didn't think it through or anything. It wasn't a philosophical proposition." She took a sip of wine. "Brad's married. He wasn't—isn't—always available. Sometimes it bothers me, sometimes not, but…So that's one thing. And the other guys were so different from Brad. Close to my age, unattached, with life experiences more like mine. They didn't… they didn't *impinge* on Brad. And they happened to be attractive to me. I thought I had a right. With Brad, there was—I mean there *is*—that's a sort of interesting slip, huh?—an asymmetry. Maybe that's just an excuse, but I felt it gave me some sort of license. Jesus, I loathe talking about this."

"And with me? What happened with me?"

"Does it matter? Here we are. Clearly, this isn't some frivolous escapade."

"But I want to know. What were you thinking? *Was* it an escapade at first?"

She hesitated. "In the beginning maybe. You were cute, you seemed like fun, I felt like playing." She frowned. "But no. Now that I say it, I know it isn't true. It may be what I told myself, but things felt different right away. The way we talked to each other…it was like great sex all by itself. Which was, you know, novel. Intriguing. More than that. Like we weren't just flirting, although we obviously were flirting. I don't even know how to describe it. Like we were looking into each other. *Seeing* into each other. It was almost scary. In a good way."

"You felt that from the first?" But he knew the interrogation was effectively over; the last of his anger was all but dissolved, both by her candor and because her answers were getting him aroused. An unfamiliar sort of arousal, centered in his heart rather than his groin, but the outward effect was indistinguishable.

"Yeah. At the redwoods thing, when you were such a babe in your tux and Brad was such a bastard. It was immediate, like that song, 'This Could Be the Start of Something Big.' Now, do you think maybe we can fuck? I've been pretty patient."

∽

AT SEVEN-THIRTY THE NEXT morning, Toby slapped his hand down over his clamorous alarm clock and then promptly fell back into a deep, dream-suffused sleep, and stayed that way until the ringing of his telephone woke him again almost two hours later. Another reason to hate the current arrangement: Not being able to spend whole nights at Amy's house—which meant he couldn't keep a toothbrush and change of clothes there—which meant he was constantly suffering from lack of sleep. For several nights running, he hadn't left her bed before two—a miserable business, leaving that cozy warmth when his body was limp with fatigue and her body within easy reach—and hadn't fallen asleep in his own bed until almost three.

He grabbed for the phone, barely remembering where he was, barely remembering *who* he was, and said, "Hello?" Trying to sound alert when he wasn't even *compos mentis*. He glanced at the clock and felt a stab of panic. Almost ten. Was it a weekday? Of course it was.

"Toby? Where the hell are you?"

"Nora?" Nora was in charge of Major Gifts. She was, at least nominally, his subordinate. She didn't seem to see it that way.

"There's a problem, Toby."

"For a change."

"Why aren't you here?"

"I—" He briefly considered lying, but what was the point? "I overslept." His head was clearing fast. "What's the problem?"

"We've just received a transfer of stock from Brad Solomon."

"Already? That's fast. I just talked to Solomon's accountant yesterday."

"Uh-huh. Terrific. Swell."

"What?"

"Well, I don't know what the stock was worth when you talked to him, but today it's worth approximately two million six. Didn't he promise five million? Wasn't that the deal?"

Toby groaned.

3

BRAD SOLOMON GLARED AT Toby across an immense kidney-shaped mahogany conference table. "Why are you wasting my time with this shit?"

"Maynard Jacobson says he isn't authorized to resolve it," Toby said calmly. A better question was why Solomon was wasting his *own* time. If he wasn't determined to be a dick, they could fix the problem in minutes with a call. And even if he did intend to be a dick, was Toby's physical presence really required? He could be just as dickish over the phone. And why were they using a conference room rather than Solomon's office? Was it meant to intimidate? It didn't. You expected Bradley Solomon to have a spectacular conference room with a great view and lavish furnishings.

"But I wonder why you still want me to jump through hoops," Toby went on mildly. "You summon me to your office, then ask why I'm wasting your time. Look, the situation may be a little awkward, but it isn't unusual, and it's no disaster. You pledged five million, and we've ended up with half that. It's your money, we don't have legal recourse, but if you mean to keep to your pledge you'll make good on the difference. End of story."

"It was the full amount when I transferred it."

"Ah."

Solomon hunched forward, elbows on the table, and smiled. It was a vulpine smile, but that didn't mean he wasn't amused. "Are you insinuating something?"

Amazing the courage Toby drew from having fucked Amy two nights ago. He met Solomon's stare. "Nothing vile. I'm sure it's natural, when you're deciding what stock to transfer, to prefer to unload the stiffs."

Solomon didn't dispute the notion head-on. "I had no idea they were going to fall like that. Or at all, in the allotted time frame. Took me completely by surprise."

"And yet it happened."

"People who don't have a lot of money can be awfully cavalier about large sums. Two and a half million dollars isn't chopped liver."

"I wasn't suggesting it was."

"If the stock had appreciated overnight, would you have returned the difference?"

It was Toby's turn to smile. Good shrewd question. Solomon smiled back. He enjoyed having scored a point. Toby nodded, a small acknowledgment, and said, "While that's an interesting and valid question, it really isn't relevant. And what the stock was worth the night you transferred it isn't relevant either. I see the appeal of taking a $5 million charitable deduction just before your stock plummets, but we're not involved in arbitrage, we're trying to put on an opera. Developing and producing a new piece takes money, and your pledge was a crucial part of the budget. Do you see? *We need the money.* You offered it, we counted on it, and now there's a gap."

Solomon slowly tilted back in his chair. Chin held between thumb and forefinger, he was regarding Toby with frank curiosity. After a few fretful seconds had ticked away, he said, "Tell me something, Lindeman: You a Jewish boy?"

Toby was startled but tried not to show it. "No."

"So what are you?"

"Not much of anything really. My mother was raised Catholic, my father was some sort of Protestant. They weren't churchgoers."

"Not that it matters. How much you make in this opera job?"

"I beg your pardon?"

"I'm asking how much you take home per annum."

"I have two reactions to that question, Brad. The first is, what's the relevance to our discussion? And the—"

"And the second," Brad interrupted, "is, how is that any of my business?"

"I might have phrased it a little more gently, but yeah."

"No relevance, none of my business. So what's your salary? Two hundred k, three hundred k, something in that range?"

Toby sighed. He'd registered his protest. "That's the ballpark."

"Peanuts, in other words."

"To someone like you. I find it adequate."

Solomon grinned, enjoying Toby's discomfort. "Take the broom out of your ass, my friend. You're going to get the other two and a half mill. You made the right arguments, I'm convinced. I'll talk to Maynard this afternoon. We're discussing something else now."

A relief! Solomon hadn't been easy to read. "What's the something else?"

"I'd like you to consider working for me."

Toby's mouth fell open.

"Whatever they're paying you," Solomon continued, "I'll start you out at more. With opportunities to increase it over time. Increase it *a lot*. Or don't you want to be rich?"

Toby, nonplussed, forced himself to look away, and his eye fell on Solomon's hands resting on the table, the interlaced fingers short and thick, a tangle of black hairs on the knuckles. "I don't know anything about real estate," he said.

Solomon waved that away impatiently. "You'd pick up the basics in no time. I want bright people working for me. Like JFK said, you can't beat brains."

"Well, I'm flattered, of course..." And horrified. The idea was unthinkable.

"Look, don't say yes right away, don't say no. Let it percolate. And by the way, I haven't mentioned anything to Doris about this—she'd eat my liver if she knew—so let's keep this between ourselves for the time being, what do you say?"

~

WHEN TOBY STEPPED INTO the elevator, he immediately, automatically, pressed the "L" button. But when he stepped out into the lobby, acting on a sudden, reckless impulse, he crossed to the bank of elevators facing him, entered one, and jabbed the "Four" button. When the car stopped at the fourth floor, he hesitated for a fraction of a second, and then exited. A sign posted on the wall indicated that suites 400–430 were located to the left. He headed in that direction.

The door to suite 425 had a plaque reading "Femacopia." He opened the door and entered. After Solomon's penthouse, this anteroom looked downright dinky, although it was quite nice in its way, with olive carpeting and cherry furniture. A chubby young woman with incandescent purplish hair and some sort of rhinestone in her nose was sitting behind the desk. She seemed startled that someone had entered the suite. She narrowed her eyes. "Can I help you?" she said. The familiar offer that translates as "Go away."

"Is Ms. Baldwin in?" Toby asked.

"Is she expecting you?"

"No, it's a surprise."

She grimaced. "Who should I say is here?"

"Toby Lindeman."

"Oh! Toby!" Her smile was quick and friendly. "I'm Priscilla, we've spoken on the phone. Hold on, I'll tell her you're here." She picked up the phone and pressed a button. "Amy, Toby Lindeman just strolled in." She hung up a second later. "She'll be right out."

Less than a minute later, Amy appeared. "This is a surprise," she said. Toby thought her tone was less than totally welcoming and her smile betrayed a measure of vexation. "You want to come back for a minute?"

That "for a minute" was a clear indication he wasn't welcome. He could take a hint. "It's just, my cell died, I need to make a call. I was just wondering if I could use your phone."

She nodded and ushered him toward the back part of the suite. He followed her down a short corridor to her office, a small room with several framed Hockney reproductions and a Mapplethorpe flower poster on the walls, a sofa, and a big amoeboid steel desk.

"I guess this was a mistake," he said, opting at the last moment not to kiss her. "I was in the building, thought I'd say hello."

"Just makes me uneasy," she said.

"I can see that."

"You were meeting with Brad?"

"Uh-huh."

184

"Did it go all right?"

"Mmm. In fact…" He hesitated, then said, "He sort of offered me a job." She didn't say anything. "You don't find that amazing? In a creepy sort of way?"

"He likes you."

"Well, okay. But still…"

"Was it a firm offer?"

"More like a probe."

"What'd you tell him?"

"He said not to give him an answer right away. But I mean…"

"Are you going to consider it?" Toby had no response to that. She filled the gap: "I mean, of course it's a terrible idea, but maybe it's worth some thought. A real job. With real pay and a real future."

"Amy—"

"I'm just saying."

He felt a twinge of annoyance. Were these issues for her? "Christ. I mean, leaving everything else to the side, would *you* be comfortable with me working for him?"

She relented with a little laugh. "It'd be awful."

"Thank you." He didn't feel particularly assuaged. She wasn't disclaiming all of it, just the unimaginable part.

"Now…Did you really want to use the phone?"

"Well…as long as I'm here."

She gestured toward the console on her desk. "You want privacy?"

"Nah. I wouldn't call my other girlfriends from here. That would be insensitive."

No visible reaction. "I need to talk to somebody down the hall anyway. Leave a dime on the desk." She gave him a quick peck on the cheek and left the room.

What an unsatisfying little interaction *that* had been. He went to her desk, seated himself in her generously padded leather chair, picked up the console phone, and punched in Doris's direct line. After two rings, Doris picked up. "Yes?"

"Doris? It's Toby."

"Lindeman?"

"You know some other Toby?"

"What the hell is Femacopia?"

Shit! Caller ID. He was momentarily nonplussed. "It's…uh…I'm…" Think of something! "It's…it's in Brad's building. My phone's out of juice, they were nice enough to let me use theirs." Jesus, what had he been thinking? This was the kind of carelessness that could get everyone concerned in the deepest conceivable shit.

"You must have used the famous Lindeman charm on their receptionist. Why didn't you use one of Brad's phones?"

"I…uh…"

"What is Femacopia anyway? Sounds like an escort service. Have you wandered into a whorehouse, Toby? Seems in character, somehow."

He laughed. "I don't believe so." Get off the topic, damn it. If she kept pressing, the implausibility of his hastily improvised story would become apparent. "Listen, I talked to Brad. We're fine." He felt a stab of conscience, not telling her about the job offer. But since accepting was unthinkable, the issue was moot. "He promises he'll make up the difference. Today."

"Did he give you a hard time first?"

"Started to."

A warm, affectionate chuckle. "The guy's a notorious hard-ass. How do you manage?"

"The chemistry of these transactions is always volatile. Sometimes only chaos theory can explain it."

"I give you more credit than that. Handled wrong, this could have been a major pisser." She cleared her throat. "Toby, there's something I've been meaning to say to you for some time, I keep forgetting or get distracted."

To Toby's ear, she sounded embarrassed. His radar started beeping. The way she'd effected the segue seemed both awkward and portentous. "Okay," he said warily.

"It's nothing really. It's just, Mike and I have a place in Carmel, and with the kids grown, we hardly use it anymore. We're there a few weekends a year at most. Fourth of July, Labor Day, that's about it. We sometimes rent it out, but we often don't bother." This all came out in a torrent. Amazing how ill at ease she sounded. "So I was thinking, if you ever want to use it, it's just sitting there empty most of the time.

Could make a lovely romantic weekend for you and a date, or a great place to unwind. So just say the word. Anytime."

"Why, Doris, that's so nice of you." He was thinking, Is this my payoff for handling Solomon? A thank-you, and perhaps also a sort of promotion, from flunky to peer, from person you don't have in your house to person you do? Whatever. He felt gratitude all the same.

And thought, Wouldn't it be splendid to get Amy away for a whole weekend? Maybe even *this* weekend. After Cathy's play on Friday, his weekend was clear. The Raskov place was likely sumptuous. The weather figured to be glorious. To be alone with Amy for two full days, to drive down to Monterey Bay with her, go walking in town, drink a leisurely cup of morning coffee on the deck while passing sections of the newspaper back and forth, sit on the beach side by side listening to the waves and soaking up carcinogens, go shopping together, prepare and eat dinner together, drink gin-and-tonics, and watch the sun set...bliss. Like the most pathetically romantic personal ad ever posted.

And then there was the fucking to consider.

"I'm likely to say yes if you really mean it," he told Doris.

"Of course I mean it. I wouldn't have mentioned it otherwise."

"You're the best boss a little boy could have."

"Keep that in mind next time I scream at you."

After they hung up, he left the office, going out to the reception area. Priscilla was behind the desk, as before, but now hunched over her desk reading *People*. A classic employee-with-time-on-her-hands. She glanced up when Toby appeared.

"Done?"

"Yes and no. Do you know where Amy is?"

"Tom's office. Want me to buzz her?"

"Nah, I'll call later." He'd already annoyed her once today by barging into her territory uninvited. Interrupting her during a meeting was a guaranteed uh-uh.

But as he was heading for the door, Amy appeared in the reception area. "Leaving without a goodbye?" she asked.

"I didn't want to bother you."

"Don't be silly. We were just going over some numbers." A frown. "Come back for a minute."

Again "for a minute." But he wasn't going to take umbrage. As they walked along the corridor to her office, he whispered, "Is a quick blowjob out of the question, d'you reckon?"

It got a laugh out of her. She actually nudged him in the ribs. "Let's have none of that," she said. "This is a place of business."

"That's why I called it a job."

"I'm afraid you're going to have to wait for a more auspicious moment."

They had reached her office. She let him in. This time they embraced, body against body. "Mr. Toby," she whispered.

"I won't do this again," he said into her neck. "I can see it makes you uncomfortable."

"It isn't personal, sweetie. It's situational."

"Absolutely."

He tried to back away from her, but she giggled and held the embrace. "I won't let go until you prove you're glad to see me."

"Tease."

"Of a certain legendary kind."

He managed to extricate himself from her grasp, despite having failed to produce the requested physiological reaction. He wanted to see her share his pleasure. "How'd you feel about Carmel this weekend? I've got the use of a house."

Her reply was prompt. *Too* prompt, and insufficiently regretful. "No can do. I'm going away with Brad."

"You're saying no?" He hadn't even considered the possibility.

"I have to." Now her tone did sound slightly regretful, or at least apologetic, but it was like a facile social regret, not remotely adequate.

Toby felt his mood plummet. "We'd have had a great time," he said. He heard a whiney quality in his own voice and resolved to control it.

"I'm sure that's true," she said.

"So where are you going?" he asked. As soon as the words were out of his mouth, he realized he didn't want to know. But it was too late to recall them.

"London."

"For the *weekend*?"

188

She shrugged. "A long weekend. We leave Thursday. There's a dinner on Saturday. In the country. Oxford. One of Brad's associates. We'll see a show Friday. And we're—"

"Okay," Toby interrupted sharply. "I don't need the whole itinerary."

She absorbed the blow. "No, I guess you don't."

"I won't expect a postcard." He took a step toward the door.

"It's part of the situation, sweetie. These things are going to happen from time to time."

"Right." Another step.

"Wait...Toby..."

He turned to face her. "What?"

She looked into his eyes. Whatever she was looking for, she didn't find it. "Nothing."

~

MAGDA WAS GIVEN TO dramatic entrances. It could be a nuisance, but this afternoon Toby welcomed the diversion. She flung open the door to his office without knocking—poor desperate Daniel a step behind, trying vainly to restrain her—and demanded, in her lightly-accented, seductive contralto, "Have you been avoiding me?"

Toby, seated at his desk, staring into space, had been startled by the rather violent opening of his door, but he was too down-in-the-dumps this afternoon to register much in the way of shock. "Magda." He forced a smile. "No, not avoiding you. I just haven't seen you."

"Nor called."

"Nor called. But neither have you."

"Yes I have, dear boy. I don't leave messages. It puts one in an intolerable position."

The presence of Daniel hovering just behind her made Toby feel self-conscious. "It's okay, Daniel. She isn't dangerous. Despite appearances."

Without so much as a smile, Daniel withdrew, closing the door after himself. Then, to Magda, Toby said, "Come in, sit down." And wondered if his arrival at Femacopia earlier today had felt to Amy the way this unannounced visit felt to him. Like an intrusion.

Magda took a few steps into the room. "Don't you intend to kiss me?" she asked.

He rose and gave her a kiss on each cheek, European-style. "It's very good to see you."

"Is it? One would hardly think so from your recent behavior. Where have you been? What's happened to you?"

"Oh, I…Jeez, I don't know, Magda. Life gets crowded, things clamor for attention. My daughter, the job, Jonas…one thing after another."

"You're not being candid. This is pure prevarication. Are you in love? That might explain it." She wagged a finger at him, as if to forestall a response. "In any event, I'm taking matters into my own hands. I've come to whisk you away for the afternoon. There's a show at the Martin Lawrence Gallery I want to see, and you're coming with me."

Toby weighed his options. He'd certainly been remiss with regard to Magda since getting involved with Amy. It wasn't intentional. There was much less time available, and—if he was being honest—he felt less drawn to spending it with her. Had the sexual component been an important part of their relationship after all? It hadn't felt that way for some time, but how else to explain his recent apathy? "My afternoon *is* sort of free, in fact," he said. "Except I'm expecting an important call." Maynard Jacobson. "One I can't miss."

"When do you expect it?"

"I don't know. All they said was, sometime today."

"That's rather discourteous." She bit her lip thoughtfully, then said, "Well, see here, you probably wouldn't enjoy the photos anyway, they're German, very stark, very homo, with sort of sado overtones—not your thing at all." She waited for him to confirm this assumption, which he did with a nod, although he had no idea if it was true. Who knew from sado overtones? "Just walk me to the gallery, all right? It's a beautiful day. The exercise will do you good, and if the call comes while you're gone, your chap can say you'll be back within the hour."

He stood up. "Let's go."

Out on the street, Toby inhaled deeply. "Beautiful day."

She smiled at him. "Gorgeous. I love it here. Maybe my favorite of all the cities I've lived in."

They walked wordlessly for several steps, and then she abruptly stopped, gripped his shoulder, and said, "Now listen, Toby, seriously, I don't like not seeing you. And I don't like being treated like a stranger."

She sounded untypically earnest. None of her habitual European irony. "When are we going to get together? When are you going to tell me what's been happening to you?"

"We're together right now."

"Now doesn't count. How about tomorrow night?"

"Cathy's school play is tomorrow night."

"You have to go?"

"Of course I have to go."

"Saturday?"

It occurred to him he could invite Magda to Carmel in Amy's stead. She was fun, and they were thoroughly comfortable with one another. It wouldn't be romantic in the same way, but it could be diverting. Even its likely placidity appealed. How much *sturm und drang* was a fellow supposed to tolerate? And it would serve Amy right, going off to London with Solomon.

Amy never asked him about other women. Because she was sure of him, or because she didn't feel she had the right?

He toyed with the idea briefly. But no, while he knew he could justify it to himself, he also knew he'd regret it. Dinner was an innocuous alternative. "Saturday works," he said.

"I feel like I'm forcing you," she muttered sourly.

"Not at all. Saturday night was going to be the loneliest night of the week."

"Yes, now that you mention it, I wouldn't have expected you to be free."

"Nor I you."

"Ah, but I'm not. I shall have to disappoint someone."

~

TOBY HAD TO TALK Jessica out of going to Cathy's school play bald. When he came to fetch her, she opened the door to him dressed for the evening in a black pants suit, now rather baggy on her, with her head smooth, pale white, and naked.

She wasn't looking too good anyway, far less good than the last time he'd seen her. She'd lost a noticeable amount of weight in the intervening weeks; thin before, she now looked gaunt, frail, almost spindly.

The vivacity he'd noticed in her eye the last time was gone. Now her gaze could almost be described as haunted.

"You wanna just go?" she suggested, after giving him a peck on the cheek. "Cathy'd kill us if we're late." She was already reaching for an overcoat on a coatrack by the front door. "Is it warm out?" she asked, noticing Toby wasn't wearing a coat. "Not that it matters," she grimaced. "I'm always cold these days."

"It *is* cold," he answered, as if this might supply some solace. "I made a mistake, not wearing a coat." And then he heard himself blurting, "Don't you have a wig or something?"

She frowned. He knew he was on thin ice, but he wasn't going to let this go, even if he usually went to extravagant lengths to avoid her wrath. If she showed up uncovered, it could ruin Cathy's evening, and if it did, sooner or later Jessica's evening would be ruined too. Cathy would see to it. And so, of course, would Toby's, although that would simply be collateral damage. Better to head off the disaster at the pass, whatever the risk.

"This is who I am now," she declared defiantly. "This is how I look."

"I accept that, Jess. But is that what tonight's about? Who you are and how you look?" He didn't believe he had ever confronted her so directly before. It wasn't the way their relations were conducted. "I thought it was about Cathy."

He braced himself. This was where things could get ugly. But they didn't. Maybe she didn't have the energy, or maybe she realized he was right. She sighed, she offered a small smile, and she said, "Oh, all right, I won't argue."

That was a first.

"Do you have something?" It occurred to him that, given her attitude, she might have chosen not to buy herself any covering. "A hat or scarf will do in a pinch."

"I've got a few wigs, in fact. Went on a shopping spree a couple of weeks ago. I haven't worn any of them yet. You can tell me which one you like. We'll have a cancer fashion show."

"That's okay," he said, forcing a smile. "Just pick one."

"The Marilyn?" She laughed when she saw his reaction. "Relax, I don't have a Marilyn. Give me a sec."

When she came back a minute later, she was wearing a chestnut-colored, neck-length wig. The effect was convincing. but also disconcerting; he was used to seeing her under her own wiry black mop with its Susan Sontag streaks. "What do you think?" she asked.

"Very nice."

"Does it do anything for you?"

It was a canny question in its flirtatious way. She looked the same to him but also subtly different, just different enough to dim unpleasant memories. It helped him recall finding her sexy. "Whether it does or doesn't," he answered lightly, "we don't want to be late."

She shook her head, amused and balked at once. "Houdini strikes again."

~

HE DROPPED HER OFF at the school before parking in a nearby garage. When he finally walked into the crowded auditorium, Jessica was on her feet, waving to him from the middle of the fourth row. He exchanged greetings with various parents as he made his way down the aisle and then along the row toward her. When he took the empty seat she had saved for him with her coat, she said, "We've got great seats."

"Yep. Won't miss a moment of theatrical magic."

She regarded him fondly. "People are whispering, seeing us together."

"You reckon?"

"I do."

"The very words that got us into this fix."

It took her a second, but then she rewarded him with a smile.

"Hey, Toby, glad you could make it," came a voice from a couple of rows in front of him. He turned and saw Hank Ortega smiling back at him in jeans, a pink shirt, and a colorful tie. The ponytail was still in place, as was the earring. Toby forced a smile; it didn't come easily.

"Hank. Good to see you. You know Jessica, Cathy's mom?"

They exchanged greetings.

"Excited?" Toby then asked.

"I am, yeah," Ortega answered. "I think it'll be a good show. I hope that doesn't jinx it."

"That's not the relevant superstition. You're just not supposed to whistle or mention…the Scottish play. I believe that's the crucial rule." It was tough to exchange friendly banter with someone you instinctively mistrusted.

"Anyhow, the kids have worked hard, so we're all pretty pumped about this. I just saw 'em backstage. They're rarin' to go. Cathy more than anyone."

"Do you say 'break a leg' to the director?"

"Can't see why not. Enjoy the show."

Toby turned back to face Jessica. "The director," he said.

"I figured." She lowered her voice. "You don't like him."

He laughed out loud. She did have his number. "He and I had a weird bit of aggro a couple of weeks ago. On Cathy's birthday. But he seems okay."

The house lights dimmed. Jessie reached over and gripped his hand. He was touched and discomfited. It reminded him of the time Jonas had taken his hand in the sauna; his first thought then, as now, was concern about how to engineer the moment of letting go. The audience applauded as the curtain went up, so an excuse for unclasping came early. The set was pretty good, the Keller backyard. There were two boys onstage, both made up to look like older men. The applause died down, one of them said, "Where's your tobacco?" and the action began.

Cathy didn't make her first appearance for ten or fifteen minutes. It was enough time for Toby to relax a little—also to realize how tense he'd been—and even, unexpectedly, to enjoy the play. He found himself admiring its skillful construction, the way key bits of information were revealed almost imperceptibly. And the kid who played Joe Keller, a short, burly boy who probably wasn't older than sixteen or seventeen, was very good, a convincing older man with an interesting combination of hearty bonhomie and barely disguised anxiety.

Cathy's entrance, when it came, was deliberately low-key. There was applause as she emerged from the Keller house onto the back porch, but of course the audience consisted entirely of parents, teachers, and friends, so every entrance was applauded. It seemed to throw her for a moment—she said her first word into the thick of the noise, when it was inaudible—but she then got a grip on herself, waited for the applause to abate a little, and repeated, "Joe?"

It was hard to be objective. The talcum powder in her hair and the lines drawn in her face did make her look older, even from the fourth row. To Toby, it was also obvious she'd lost weight; this didn't affect the quality of her performance, but she was looking better than she had in years, even with old-lady makeup. She read her lines competently, she moved on the stage comfortably, she didn't emote in a blatant or vulgar way. But as the first act went on, it became distressingly clear to Toby that neither was she especially good; despite all the work she'd put into rehearsals, despite her professed commitment to theater as a calling, she seemed like an intelligent amateur without noteworthy talent. He knew this judgment was harsh, and he knew he was given to harsh judgments where Cathy was concerned, but because the boy who played Joe was so very good—probably already professional caliber—the rest of the cast seemed like…well, like students in a high school play. Cathy included.

Or was Toby just being Toby-like with respect to Cathy—anxious, hovering, critical? He wondered what Jonas would say. Jonas was a useful reality check in this sort of situation.

And he wished he could talk to Amy. Not so much for a reality check; Amy didn't know his relationship with Cathy well enough for that. But she was a good listener, quick to comprehend and quick to offer discerning sympathy. Her assessments of people were consistently shrewd. Any observation she had to offer would be worthwhile. But no, she wasn't available, she'd chosen to sashay off to London with Brad Solomon instead.

Once Cathy was onstage, it was harder for Toby to enjoy the play. Harder even to follow it. He had to force himself to focus. At the intermission, when the lights came up, Toby regretted he wasn't at a Broadway production where he could freely express his opinion without risking giving offense to everyone within earshot. And Jessica made matters worse by asking the natural question, "So, what do you think?" even while the applause was still cresting.

"Very nice," he said, after the briefest of pauses to gauge the complexities of the situation. "Terrific."

She gave him an unfriendly look in return. "Jesus, Toby," she said.

Why was he always in the company of women who could see right through him? "What?" he whispered, feigning wounded innocence when he felt guilt.

"Nothing. Just…nothing. I need the ladies' room. Right away. I'll meet you back here." She stood and fairly bolted past him toward the aisle. It was clearly an emergency.

Brownies and an unidentifiable purple drink were on sale in the open area outside the auditorium. This was neither the snack nor the beverage he wanted, but he stood in line to buy some all the same. While he waited, a number of people came up and congratulated him on Cathy's performance. He thanked them, and when it was offered by another cast parent, returned the compliment. There was a little quadrille you went through at these things; deviation from the approved choreography was unthinkable. Check your irony at the door and your critical judgment along with it. That's not what these evenings are about.

Jessica appeared. She looked worse than before. Not just pale, but faintly green. She stopped to lean on a chair or table every few steps. Toby approached her.

"You okay, Jess?"

"Struggling a little. Can I have a sip?" She gestured toward his Dixie cup.

He handed her the punch. She drained it. He asked, "Do you want another?"

"I'm not sure. Let's see what happens to this one." She managed a wan smile.

"Are you going to make it? If not…Cathy won't blame you. She'll understand."

"I can manage. I don't want to miss this." Alarmingly, her eyes suddenly reddened. "I'm sorry you're not enjoying it, Toby."

"I *am* enjoying it." Then he amended the statement. "I'm very glad to be here. And I'm very glad we're seeing it together."

"Just don't give her a hard time afterward."

"Of course not. What do you take me for?"

She put a hand on his upper arm. It wasn't a sign of affection; she needed the support. Still, to an outside observer it probably looked affectionate. Parental tongues would be wagging tomorrow.

These private schools were like small towns. She was staring at him. Her eyes were still red, but no tears were appearing, thank God. "I'm so fucking sorry to have missed all this," she said. "This corny enforced family togetherness. It's a complete sham, maybe, but it's also the most important thing there is."

"At least we're here now. Unlike a lot of divorced couples who don't see each other again until the kid gets married. We've stayed on reasonable terms."

"Yes," she said. "We've managed that."

Toby understood what she was feeling. It was hard not to experience a pang at events like these. The life they hadn't led. The whole Grover's Corners deal, the community going through its predictable, reassuring rituals. That Cathy was counting down her final few weeks of high school, after which she would presumably fly the coop for good, made everything that much more poignant. Along with Jessie's awful illness. He gave his ex-wife's waist a squeeze. "We've done okay, Jess. With Cathy, and with each other."

"I didn't used to think so. Lately, maybe I do." She kissed his cheek. Oh boy, the gossip would be flying thick and fast.

"How are you doing?" he asked.

"Never better. Can't you tell? But you'd better get me another cup of punch, Lindeman. You're still the hunter-gatherer in this duo."

The rest of the play, when it resumed, presented no big surprises. The kid who played Joe continued to dominate the stage; Cathy continued to be adequate, but to Toby's eyes no more than that. She had some big scenes, but she didn't show, nor did she elicit, big emotions in them. The play itself provided its share of dramatic wallops, although Toby felt it was perhaps a little anticlimactic by the end; yes, selling defective airplane parts to the military in wartime is a bad thing, and so is letting your partner take the rap for it. Hard to argue.

Still, as these things go, the production could be considered a triumph. The kids all got huge ovations, and then Hank Ortega bounded to the stage and got a huge ovation too. And the cast didn't merely applaud him when he came onstage, they hugged him and kissed him and pumped his hand and even tousled his hair. He was evidently that sort of high school teacher.

Afterward, the audience members milled around in the area outside the auditorium. Toby found Jessica a chair and brought her a cup of punch. Compliments were freely shared with other parents. A number of them went out of their way to praise Ortega as some kind of miracle worker. Toby knew his part; he echoed every sentiment.

Within ten minutes or so, the cast and crew started to emerge into the area as well. They were still in costume, still in their makeup, and were all in a state of high excitement, laughing, chattering, and sweetly eager for praise. Cathy wasn't in the first wave. "Can you handle this?" Toby asked Jessie. "We've done our duty."

"For a while. Not much more than that, though."

"There's probably a cast party later, at which we're certainly not welcome. So after we congratulate Cathy we can safely vamoose."

Jessie nodded. Then she closed her eyes. She looked to be in serious distress.

More castmembers dribbled out, and other kids who were presumably stagehands and tech crew. Cathy was in this group. Hank Ortega followed, and he entered the area with the bouncy gait of someone on top of the world. When he passed Toby and Jessie, Toby made himself say, "Great job, Hank."

He whirled around toward them, smiling. "Thanks." Then he recognized Toby, and his smile broadened. "The kids were terrific, weren't they?" A little stab at self-effacement. "Did you enjoy the show, Mrs. Lindeman?"

"My last name is Galfand," said Jessica. "But call me Jessie. Yes, it was great." She tried to look animated while saying this, but the effort was visible.

"So glad you came," said Ortega, and off he moved to accept more congratulations from other sets of parents. Tonight, in this setting, he was a star and acted like it.

Jessica made a face. "There's something icky about that guy."

"I agree."

"I know. And you've always been a better judge of character than me."

"My feminine side."

"Irresistible. Always has been. Most guys don't have a clue about that."

198

It was at this moment that Cathy spotted them and approached. "Hey, Moms, Pops," she said. The Americanisms were intended satirically.

"That was lovely, Cath," Jessica said.

"Very nice," said Toby, and then added, "Just great," as Jessie surreptitiously nudged him. By this time, Cathy was directly upon them.

"Why aren't you mixing with everybody?"

"Mom's not feeling well," Toby explained.

"Oh. I'm sorry, Mom."

"It'll pass."

"You must be thrilled," said Toby. "The thing seemed flawless."

"Well, almost. A couple of minor screw-ups. It felt good, though. I mean, there's nothing in the world more fun!" She was obviously over the moon. "If I could act in plays full time, I wouldn't even bother sleeping."

"Was Hank pleased?"

"I think so. He said he was. He's sure acting like it." She turned to Jessie. "Can I get you something? Some water or punch or something?"

Jessie shook her head.

It was hard to know what to say next. Then the boy who played Joe Keller passed by. "Nice work," Toby said to him.

"Oh, thank you," he said. The compliment momentarily broke his insolent adolescent strut. "You enjoyed the show?"

"Very much," said Toby. "Congratulations."

"Thank you," the boy repeated, and then he moved on.

Cathy was staring at her father now, and her glance could almost be described as suspicious. "Did you really think he was good?"

Careful, Toby told himself. The ice could be thinner here than you realize. "I did."

Cathy shook her head. "He was indicating all over the place. That's a major no-no. Hank had a lot of problems with him in rehearsal."

Toby chose not to press it. Let her be the expert. "Everybody was good," he therefore said. "And you were one of the standouts."

She nodded, and declared, "I think so too."

He glanced at Jessie, hoping for a cue about how to react. But what he saw gave him no guidance; Jessica's eyes were shut, and she was gripping the seat of her chair tightly.

"Jess?"

"I'm okay," she said.

From a group of kids standing together across the open area, someone called Cathy's name. She looked at Toby interrogatively.

"Go ahead," he said. "We'll try and catch up with you before we go."

"I'm sorry you're feeling so lousy, Mom," she said.

Jessica nodded, but didn't open her eyes.

After Cathy moved off, Toby said, "You should get into bed."

"To be honest, I don't even feel steady enough to walk. Just give me a few minutes, okay? These things come in waves."

"Do you want anything?"

"Maybe a glass of water. I'm sorry to be such a bore, Toby."

"Don't be silly."

He walked over to the table with the brownies and the punch. A couple of students were behind the table handing out goodies, and there was a short line. Short but slow moving, as the kids, once they got to the front of the queue, seemed to debate with their conscience about whether or not to indulge in a brownie. Toby itchily waited his turn, and when it came, asked if he could have a cup of water.

"We don't have water," a boy with bad acne told him. "Just punch."

The girl standing next to the boy offered, "There's a water fountain down that corridor to the right." She pointed.

"Do you think I could take a Dixie cup?"

"Sure," she said, "help yourself."

He grabbed a cup and set off in the direction she had pointed. The water fountain was in a small alcove about twenty feet down the corridor. He took a sip of water himself, filled the cup, and started back toward the central area outside the auditorium. A number of parents greeted him as he went, and he answered politely, occasionally offering congratulations or insincere observations about the play. Then, as he approached Jessica, he noticed Hank Ortega standing at the center of a group of students, who were all looking at him and laughing at something he was saying. Standing right next to him was Cathy, and

Ortega's right hand was cupping the rather generous curve of her butt, and moving up and down over it. The fondling was covert—it wouldn't have been visible to anyone but Toby, and that only because of the angle from which he happened to view it—but it also looked casual, and casually proprietary. As far as Toby could tell in that shocking split second, Cathy was either ignoring the intimacy or pretending to. But she was looking directly at Ortega, just like the other students in their little circle, and she was manifestly neither startled nor offended.

Toby felt rage start to boil inside himself almost instantaneously. It was a novel sort of anger for him, fierce, consuming, compellingly physical. He could feel an urge to violence with the same precise, palpable clarity as hunger or thirst. He took a step in Ortega's direction. As he was about to raise his voice, no doubt as prologue to doing something irremediable, he heard some sort of commotion to his left, a loud thump, followed by a collective gasp and a startled shout. He turned and saw that Jessica was on the ground, on her hands and knees. The chair on which she'd been sitting had toppled over. Their eyes met. As she opened her mouth to say something, she suddenly and spectacularly vomited, an awful explosion of bilious sludge.

4

"THIS IS RIDICULOUS," JESSICA said. "It was just a reaction to the chemo. Happens a lot."

Toby was brusque. "Quiet." He'd had to tell the Uber driver to stop three times. The third time, when there was nothing left in her stomach, she knelt on the sidewalk for several minutes, retching helplessly. There was no comfort he could offer; all he could do was look on impotently. "At least they can give you something for the nausea."

"I've got something at home," she said.

"Something that works."

"Daddy's right," said Cathy.

Toby glanced at his daughter and then quickly looked away. Too many difficulties there to deal with, too many even to think about.

They were in the UCSF emergency room. Fortunately, it was still early. On a Friday night the place was likely to start filling up as midnight approached and the car crashes and ODs began in earnest, but now there was only one other patient awaiting attention: an elderly man with chest pains. Jessie's name was called in under a quarter of an hour. After she went in, unsteadily following a nurse through the swinging doors, Toby sat down on one of the pastel plastic chairs, and Cathy took a seat facing him. He wished she were sitting next to him; it would have been easier to avoid meeting her eye.

"I hate this," she said.

"Mom's probably right; it's probably not a crisis." That was about as reassuring as he could manage.

"I've never seen her this bad."

"We'll see what they say." He knew he sounded curt, but it was hard to know how to deal with Cathy now, and hard for him to make an effort to soothe her.

She started to cry quietly. He leaned forward and patted her knee. Not far from where Hank Ortega had been stroking her tush. He pulled his hand away.

About half an hour later, a young-looking doctor in light blue scrubs appeared. "Mr. Galfand?" he said to Toby.

"It's Toby Lindeman." He shook the doctor's hand. "I'm Jessica's former husband." And then, more as a warning than out of politesse—to prevent him from saying anything too alarming—Toby indicated Cathy and said, "Our daughter, Cathy."

The doctor's eyes widened at Cathy's old-lady theatrical makeup and talcum powdered hair. "How do you do. I'm Dr. Friedman. I didn't realize it was Halloween." He bestowed a friendly smile on Cathy, then turned back to Toby. "We'd like to keep Ms. Galfand overnight."

"Is something wrong?" Cathy asked.

"Well, she is quite dehydrated. But it's mostly just to observe her."

"I'm sure she accepted that with good cheer," Toby said.

The doctor reacted with a crooked smile. "She wasn't thrilled."

"Can we talk to her?" asked Cathy.

"Sure."

He led them through double doors, down a linoleum corridor, past a nurses' station, to an area that was more like an alcove than a room. There was a blue screen in front of it, on wheels. The doctor pulled the screen aside, revealing a very wan Jessica on her back on a narrow bed. She raised her head slightly and said to Toby, "You should have taken me home, damn it."

"I'm sure we'll be able to send you home in the morning," the doctor said.

"Who asked you?"

"Stop being childish," Toby said. "This is clearly a sensible precaution. If you're worried about Cathy, I'll stay at the house tonight, we'll be fine."

He felt rather than saw Cathy react to this statement, a slight start or twitch. Meanwhile, Jessica briefly looked as if she were preparing to argue, then gave up. "What a pain in the ass," she muttered, almost inaudibly.

"Just get a good night's sleep," Cathy said. "You'll feel a hundred percent better tomorrow." She leaned down and kissed Jessica on the forehead.

They didn't speak during the Uber ride to the house or the short walk up to the front door. When they reached it, Toby said, "I don't have a key." The sound of his own voice was startling to him.

Cathy didn't answer directly, but reached into her purse, extracted a key, and opened the door herself. Only after they were inside did she speak, saying, "This is weird."

Toby couldn't think of an answer.

"I'm just going up to change my clothes and get this makeup off," she added, heading for the stairs.

Toby stood in the foyer for a moment, feeling, he was certain, considerably weirder than Cathy. But he would have to spend the night here regardless. Might as well make himself at home. He walked into the kitchen, knelt, opened a cabinet, and was pleased to discover the liquor where it had always been. The cabinet was less well-stocked than it used to be, though. Jessica had no taste for spirits. Nevertheless, that bottle of Blanton's she'd bought for his visit weeks ago was still there, and untouched since. He put it on the counter, got a translucent blue plastic tray of ice cubes out of the freezer, urged several into a glass, and poured in a healthy splash of bourbon. The ice cracked with satisfying solidity, a molecular event writ large. He replaced the tray and the bottle and then carried his drink into the living room.

He took his once-familiar seat and only then permitted himself his first sip. Blissful. You could spend the rest of an evening trying to recapture the pleasure of that initial jolt.

He suddenly realized he was ravenous. No food all evening. But he was too weary to go foraging in the kitchen for food. He closed his eyes. What a night this had turned into.

About fifteen minutes later, he heard Cathy on the stairs. He opened his eyes as her legs appeared—now clad in khaki cargo pants—followed by the rest of her. A loose gray shirt over a skinny maroon sweater. She looked okay, even to Toby's critical eye.

"I'm going to the cast party," she said. "I'll be pretty late, so don't wait up for me."

He set his drink on the floor. A bubble of anger—not a bubble, a gusher—was rising, was *erupting*, inside his chest. "The hell you are," he said. His voice remained level.

But Cathy knew him well enough not to be fooled by his semblance of calm, to recognize the menace in his taut, even tone. Once upon a time it would have intimidated her into instant submission. No longer. She responded preemptively with a slightly hysterical anger of her own. "You can't stop me!" And then, her voice rising higher, "You can't fucking stop me!"

"I really don't think you should go," he said, still quiet.

"So what?" she cried contemptuously. "I don't give a shit what you think." She was breathing heavily, but at least she had ratcheted the volume down a few notches.

So he chose to ignore the provocation in her words. "Don't you think it would be inappropriate to go to a party on a night like this?"

"Why? I did my part...I went to the hospital with you and Mom."

"You expect credit for that?"

She shook her head at his obtuseness. Or maybe it wasn't obtuseness, maybe it was what she perceived as deliberate unfairness. Still, she spoke almost calmly. "Not credit. But let's face it, this wasn't how this night was supposed to go. The opening night of my play, I went with you to the hospital, it was the right thing to do, I didn't think twice about it, and I'm glad I did. But now...For God's sake, Daddy, I've worked with these people for months. We're like family. I don't want to miss the celebration. And I can't imagine why you think I should."

He started to answer, but she cut him off. "It's not like we can do anything for Mom tonight." She sounded reasonable, persuasive, adult. "I don't see how it helps for me to stay home." Then, almost snarling, she added, "And I don't get why you're staying here tonight either. I can manage just fine. I don't recall *asking* you to stay."

Of course she was right. If you disregarded a crucial datum, her arguments were valid. So there was no avoiding it, the dreaded business had to be confronted. On some level, he had known all along this was so, but he'd been hoping for time to prepare an approach.

"And Hank Ortega?" he said. "Will he be at this party too?"

Cathy wasn't stupid. She recognized a warning shot when it sailed across her bows. She took a beat to compose herself before saying, "I'm not sure. Probably." Employing all her deficient thespian skills in an effort to sound casual and unworried.

He earnestly wished someone else were here to have this conversation with her. Or at least to assist. WWJD? What would Jessie do?

"Cathy, please, let's not bullshit each other. I saw him. Him and you."

"What do you mean?" She was starting to color.

"I saw him handling you."

A fierce blush. Bull's-eye. But she wasn't quite ready to give up yet. "Handling me?"

"Fondling you."

"Just what are you talking about?" Displaying a little bit of steel. There was no conviction behind it, though.

"Tonight. That's what I'm talking about. Just before Mom, before Mom…" He gave up the search for a euphemism and started afresh, saying, "I insist you tell me what's going on."

"Oh, Daddy." She forced a laugh that was meant to sound sophisticated and amused and superior. It didn't sound like any of those things. "Hank is…I mean, jeez, he's a physical guy, a touchy-feely guy. It doesn't mean anything. He's always patting people, giving them back rubs, mussing their hair. Guys as well as girls. I suppose it could get him into trouble, those things are frowned upon these days, but he's a theater guy, you know what they're like."

"He isn't a theater guy, he's a high school teacher." Toby let that one resonate for a few seconds. "And the way he was touching you…" He wasn't sure how to continue. He'd always had a frank relationship with Cathy, but this was awkward. But then he pictured Ortega's proprietary, smug hand taking its stately landlord's ramble along Cathy's sizable rump, and the resultant rage provided him with the momentum he needed. "You're sleeping with him," he declared flatly. Saying it out loud was almost physically sickening. "I'm forty-four years old, Cathy, I've learned a little bit about how people behave with one another in that time. It isn't *all* a closed book. You're having sex with your drama teacher."

"What?" Starting loud, with a rising intonation and a crescendo. Intending to convey indignation, disbelief, outraged innocence. But it sounded hopelessly false. "That's ridiculous!"

"Is it?"

"Of course it is."

"Why am I not convinced?"

"Because you're deluded."

"You're saying you don't have a sexual relationship with Hank Ortega? Is that what you're telling me?"

"That's exactly what I'm telling you."

"You're lying."

"Now you're calling me a liar? How dare you!"

She shouldn't have pushed her luck like that. "How dare I?" echoed Toby, and his voice wasn't even slightly level, his tone not even slightly subdued. He was bellowing. *"You have the gall to say that to me?"* He hadn't yelled like this in years. At anyone, under any circumstances. There was something cathartic about it. He noticed he was on his feet, although he didn't recall standing up. "Is this the kind of crap Jessie puts up with? Go to your room! I don't want to talk to you! I don't even want to look at you! Go! Get out!"

She was staring at him, open-mouthed. A combination of fear and chagrin and shock could be read on her face. Her voice veered crazily out of control as she shouted, "I'm going to the party! You can't stop me! I'm eighteen years old, I can go where I want! So fuck you! *Fuck! You!*"

Fighting tears, she started toward the door.

"I forbid it!" He took a step toward her. It was almost a surprise he could still walk; he felt as if he'd taken a bullet, been shot in the heart point-blank. Never before, in all their contentious history, had she spoken to him like this. "Do not go near that door!"

"Or what?" she jeered. "You'll ground me? Or maybe you'll spank me? Oooh, I'm so scared!" She opened the door. "Fucking asshole!" She stepped through the door. "Go home, asshole. Or call one of your girlfriends, maybe it isn't too late. I won't be coming back tonight." She slammed the door shut.

The sound of the slamming door was remarkably reverberant. While the echoes caromed around the room, Toby briefly considered pursuit. But then what? She was right; she was eighteen, he had no coercive power at his disposal. She was legally allowed to drive, allowed to vote, allowed to enlist in the armed forces. She could legally consent to sexual intercourse.

It was all beyond his control.

He felt powerless, but right now he mostly felt...wounded. Deeply, deeply hurt. He had always been Cathy's favored parent. She was still an adoring daddy's girl in some ways, within the constraints of her notion of cool. Until tonight, he'd believed himself forever exempted from the full force of her teenage contempt. It never once occurred to him that she might say "fuck you" to him, or call him an asshole. Her doing so changed everything, altered the fundamental architecture of his universe. It had become a less hospitable place.

He needed to talk to Amy. He needed her advice. He needed the solace her presence offered. But she was in London—in fucking London!—with that bastard Brad Solomon.

He fell back into the chair. And then remembered, with something that approximated relief, the glass of bourbon on the floor, mere inches from his hand.

~

WHEN YOU WENT TO a restaurant with Magda, she usually ordered the way you'd expect a stylish woman to order. She usually chose salads or a plate of steamed vegetables or a piece of salmon. (What was it about women and salmon? Their appetite for it seemed limitless. Is it that the male dies after spawning?)

But when she dined at home, different rules obtained. She favored hearty central European fare, old family recipes she prepared with great skill and no apologies. Tonight she'd insisted on cooking for Toby. She was keen to make him her spicy goulash with noodles, the formula passed down through generations of Szerlys. She accepted with thanks the pricey bottle of wine he brought and promptly put it away in the small wooden wine rack she kept in her kitchen. She'd already selected a kick-ass Bull's Blood as the only possible accompaniment.

Toby stood in her kitchen, sipping the Jack Daniels she'd handed him—not exactly his drink of choice, but a reasonable approximation—while she put the finishing touches on the meal. Although strands of her hair were sticking damply to her forehead, and although she wore an old-fashioned white apron and a big oven mitt, and although she seemed a tad frantic as she went about her business, turning the fire down under one pot and up under another and stirring the contents of a third with a big wooden spoon, she still contrived to look glamorous.

Toby had offered to set the table, but she'd declined. "Just keep me amused, that's your assignment." She slurped a bit of sauce from the wooden spoon. "Mmm. Fabulous! You're a lucky boy, Lindeman."

"I realize that."

"I don't go to this much trouble for just anybody."

She'd certainly gone to some trouble. When he was seated at her dining room table, he noticed she'd put out her good china and silverware and glassware, along with stiff linen napkins. There were a couple of candles burning. The lights were set ominously low.

Looking around, waiting for her to join him, he thought again what odd contradictions she embodied, and how precisely her apartment reflected them. The rooms were papered in rust-colored wallpaper, the furniture was heavy, dark, echt-Biedermeier—inherited from her parents when they went home to Budapest, no doubt—and yet the art on the walls was contemporary, including a couple of Mapplethorpe photos of nude Black men with erections. She was a woman caught between two worlds. At home in both, or neither?

She entered carrying a big flame-colored casserole. As she placed it carefully on a wooden trivet, she said, "I've made a ton. You'd better have seconds. Possibly thirds."

"Let's take it one helping at a time." He poured her a glass of wine and one for himself. It seemed to emerge slowly, reluctantly, from the bottle, as if it were too viscous to flow easily.

"To friendship," she proposed, raising her glass and clinking it against his.

Several minutes later, after he'd praised the goulash a couple of times, and she'd told a rather pointless story about her mother's having made it for the embassy staff in London during some crisis or other, she suddenly announced, "You might be interested to hear Christine's getting married."

It took him a moment to place the name: the woman Magda had been so eager for him to hook up with. "That's nice," he said.

"I guess you missed your chance."

"I guess I did. Do we approve of the guy?"

Magda shrugged. "He's not terrible, I shouldn't say. Treats her quite liberally. He looks a bit soft to me, a bit…what's the word? Do you say doughy? Like that awful Pillsbury advert. But when a woman selects a life partner, the choice isn't usually made on the basis of his body."

"It's different from choosing a lover?"

"Of course."

"I thought she just wanted to have fun. Isn't that what you told me?"

"She must've changed her mind." Little smile. "At the first opportunity."

He put his fork down and looked at Magda, facing him across the table. Her eyes sparkled in the candlelight. There were deep, mysterious shadows at the top of her cream-colored silk blouse, which was opened to the second button. Her breasts, as he had good reason to know, were larger than one first expected, full, heavy, womanly. For whatever reason, she usually dressed to camouflage them rather than show them off. She probably regarded them as unfashionable. It was Toby's impression that women dressed with the unforgiving assessments of other women in mind rather than the admiration of men—men, after all, were easy, they were pushovers—and women could be especially competitive, scathing really, about breasts.

He said, "The thing is, Magda, I barely know this woman. But…I don't know, I get the impression you expect me to have some sort of reaction to the news."

"No, you've missed the point of my telling you."

"I guess I have. The point is…?"

"The point is, *I've met him*." She looked him in the eye and held the stare. "She thought her good friends should meet him. She thought he should meet her friends. Such things matter."

"I see."

She took a sip of wine before saying, "Okay, who are you seeing, Toby? It's perfectly obvious there's *someone*. It's equally obvious it isn't casual. Is it someone I know? Or perhaps some obscure little greasy-spoon waitress you're ashamed of? An ignoble display of *nostalgie pour la boue* on your part? Why the secrecy?"

The calculus confronting him was too complicated; he prided himself on his fast tactical reflexes, but there were too many factors to calculate before assessing the optimal response. "Magda, I just can't tell you. You're going to have to take my word for it. It isn't personal…by which I mean, if I *could* tell you, I would. Please don't ask me to explain."

"So you haven't told Jonas?"

"No. Not Jonas either." The lie was a no-brainer.

She raised her wine glass, but didn't bring it to her lips, simply stared at it, apparently lost in the contemplation of the candlelight's reflection glinting in the glass. "So she's somebody's wife," she announced after a few seconds.

He hoped he managed to keep his face expressionless. "I'm not going to answer any questions."

"Has to be." She nodded. "And the husband is probably more successful than you, since practically all the straight men with whom you come into contact *are*." She nodded again. "Oh Toby, you're going to get hurt. You do realize that?"

"I don't want to discuss this, Magda. Really."

"I mean, be realistic. To her, whoever she is, you're a *divertissement*. I'm not saying this to be insulting."

"And yet you're managing."

"A very special *divertissement*, of course. I'm sure she's enjoying herself immensely."

"That doesn't help."

The briefest of hesitations. "Then I'll be quiet."

"Yes."

"I'm just concerned for you." Before he could answer, she added, "But enough." She changed her tone when she said, "Are you ready for seconds? Pass me your plate."

"No thanks. I've had enough."

"Don't sulk, dear boy. I'm dropping that other matter. Perhaps you'd like me to entertain you with another gripping story about goulash?"

His answering smile was grudging. She had drawn blood, no question about it. "No to the story, no to the goulash."

"Well, *I'm* having more. I wish you would as well. I made far too much to freeze."

"Okay, just a little," he said, giving in with a sigh. It was pure good manners on his part. He had no appetite. Besides, it wouldn't do to reveal the extent to which she'd struck a nerve.

Some twenty minutes later, after he helped clear the table, she said, "Don't you dare offer to wash them. Grab your glass and the bottle and plant yourself on the sofa. I'll be right in."

He didn't argue. He was feeling awfully weary all of a sudden. The liquor, the *divertissement* business, Jessica, Cathy last night…they'd taken a toll. He carried his glass and the wine bottle into the living room—the lighting there was as subdued as in the dining room—and dropped onto her overstuffed, chocolate-brown sofa. Not a lot of lumbar support, but otherwise luxurious. Maybe those central Europeans knew something Danes didn't. He poured some wine into his glass and then placed the bottle on the floor.

Magda entered the living room, wine glass in hand. "Music?" she offered.

He shook his head.

She sat down on the couch next to him. Close, but not crowding him. "Hit me," she said, extending her glass. He reached down, hoisted the bottle from the floor, and poured. She brought the glass to her mouth and observed him over the rim for a moment through lowered eyelids—a coquette's glance—before taking a sip.

"You're staying tonight, yes?" she suggested after lowering her glass.

A question he'd been fearing since he'd noticed the apartment's dim lighting. He took a second before replying. "I don't think so. It doesn't strike me as a superb idea at this juncture."

"Because of what I said before?"

"Uh-uh. Because—"

"—you're in love," she finished for him, and laughed, briefly and falsely. "I assumed you were more sophisticated than that."

"You make so many assumptions, Magda."

She leaned in to him and put a hand on his thigh. "What difference will it make? We're pals. She never has to find out. And I was here first."

He looked at her and couldn't deny he felt a stirring. The debate got rolling in his mind; she'd brought him to that point awfully quickly, awfully easily. Did he owe Amy fidelity, especially when she was off with Solomon? Wouldn't it be lovely in his present fatigued and slightly inebriated state to slide into bed beside Magda rather than heave himself out into the cold? It was tempting. At the moment the contest was too close to call.

Magda slid her hand up his leg. One knuckle was touching his cock, whether or not she was aware of it. Whoops, all of a sudden she couldn't not be aware of it. The gaze she was directing his way was level, unblinking, and, with those slightly parted lips, undisguisedly lascivious.

His cell phone rang.

They both froze. She suddenly got a disgusted look in her eye. "Go ahead," she said.

Quick calculation: It could be Jessica with medical news. He hadn't managed to get hold of her today despite repeated attempts. Or Cathy, who hadn't been answering her phone; he'd called several times unsuccessfully (never certain what he'd say if she answered). It probably *wasn't* Amy, since it was after 7:00 a.m. in London. "I think I need to," he said. "It might be an emergency." He withdrew the phone from the breast pocket of his jacket. "Hello?"

"Sweetie?"

It could have been worse. He could have been in bed with Magda when the phone rang. If he was honest, the evening had been tending in that direction. "Yeah," he said, "hi."

"Say it."

"I can't."

"You're not alone?"

"That's correct."

"Are you on a date or something?"

"Or something."

"Ah." He could almost hear her thinking. She eventually said, "Is this payback?"

"It isn't, no."

"I'm not saying you don't have the right."

"Nor am I. But it isn't."

An awkward silence. Then, "I guess calling wasn't such a hot idea. I was missing you. I'll call when I get back."

She hung up before he could say good night. He clicked off his phone and reluctantly turned to face Magda.

"Everything tickety-boo?" she asked.

"It wasn't an emergency," he admitted. "I thought it might be Jessica. Or Cathy." The situation was awkward enough that he felt he owed her an explanation.

"You might as well go," she said. "If there was a moment, it seems to have passed."

"Yes."

"There *was* a moment."

"I'm not denying it, Magda. We'll always have chemistry." It was only after he said it that he realized how valedictory it sounded. Rick to Ilsa.

She rose. He rose. She let him kiss her on both cheeks, she accepted his thanks for dinner, she saw him to the door. A few seconds later, while standing alone on the landing waiting for the elevator, and feeling none too pleased with either the situation or himself, he suddenly recognized with an unpleasant jolt that Magda was bound to guess Amy's identity sooner or later. She was sharp enough, interested enough, and he'd provided enough clues. It was only a matter of time.

Toby didn't always attend pre-show cocktail events for donors, but he was expected to. If he failed to turn up several times running, it would be noted. He went as often as he could bear. At least doing so was a way of amortizing the exorbitant cost of his Hardy Amies.

As he crossed Van Ness, the Opera House in front of him, City Hall behind, he felt again the grandeur of the American Renaissance-style civic complex. It was easy to take for granted, he was here every day, but seen lit up at night, immense and imposing, it was stirring. He quick-stepped up the stairs and pushed his way into the building. The reception was being held in the capacious lobby. There were already forty or so people present, plus serving personnel with trays of champagne and wine. The women in gowns and jewels, the men in tuxes. Conversation loud and animated, occasionally punctuated by laughter. How many of these people genuinely enjoyed opera? How many of the men prided themselves on hating it?

Sometimes it struck Toby that a guy like himself, with some vestige of inherited class resentment, was in the wrong job. Still, it was psychologically healthier and morally preferable to nurture the resentment than surrender to the value system of the class you served and make the mistake of thinking you belonged. Many of Toby's colleagues had fallen into that trap, and it was an ugly thing to behold. They fancied themselves aristocrats when in reality they were barely tolerated by those whose manners they aped.

Toby grabbed a glass of champagne off a passing tray. He didn't like the stuff much, but it was helpful at events like this to have a glass in one's hand. Something with which to busy oneself during awkward silences and stray moments of solitude.

He scanned the room for a familiar face. To find or avoid? Hard to say. He was in an uneasy, disconsolate mood. That thing with Magda last night; he felt oddly guilty for not fucking her and oddly guilty for having been tempted. No word from Cathy. No answer at Jessica's.

"Toby!"

Startled, he looked toward the voice. It was Carol Macelli, a mezzo in the company. They'd had a one-night stand several years ago. Or had it been two one-night stands? Or one two-night stand? Hard to keep track. She wasn't the only woman in the company with whom he'd had a meaningless dalliance on one occasion or another. As one of the few straight men in the organization, he was convenient pickings as evenings were ending and parties winding down. Last call. Toby was a dependable port in that storm. The times with Carol had been entirely pleasant, including, Toby suddenly recalled, an unexpected and dandily dirty afternoon blowjob in his office; Daniel seemed oblivious when Toby showed Carol out into the reception area afterward. (The sexual arrogance of gay men! As if only they manage anything taboo.) Some of the specifics of what he'd got up to with Carol might be hazy now, but it remained untainted by any toxic admixture; it had all been good fun, no hard feelings, no recriminations. Both retained a jolly memory of the liaison, plus, when their paths crossed, some small lingering vibration of potential energy.

"You're not singing tonight?"

"No. Thank God. My throat's a disaster, I'm fighting a cold."

"You don't look it. You're looking good."

"You too. Handsome as ever." She grinned, offering him the kind of look you give someone when you share a secret.

"Helps me bilk the crones."

She put a hand on his upper arm and squeezed lightly and moved off. Seemed kind of abrupt. But they'd never had much to say to one another. Made the sex all the more compelling.

There was a station with canapés across the room. Toby wasn't hungry, but it was something to do. As he made his way toward the table, he was greeted a few times by donors and company members. He returned the greetings amiably, smiling, offering a little wave, but making sure to keep walking. He was only a few yards from the food when he encountered Doris, standing next to her husband, Michael, and an elderly man Toby dimly recognized. Tall, bony, leaning on a cane. Bushy eyebrows, hairy nostrils, oversized ears. Toby couldn't remember the man's name, which, given the nature of his professional obligations, came close to malfeasance. Some rich dude—of course—who'd given 100K last year, Toby now recalled, although they'd expected more. Fucking tightwad.

"Hello, dear," Doris said. She seemed relieved at the interruption.

"Hello, Doris." He kissed her cheek. Something he would never have done in a work environment. What strange, arbitrary rules social life imposes. Paging Margaret Mead!

Doris introduced Toby to her husband, although they'd met several times—which came as news to Mike Raskov, but he recovered gracefully—and then to the old guy, who extended the limpest hand Toby had ever grasped.

"Weren't you at Princeton?" he asked Toby peremptorily.

"No."

"Ah. I'm mistaken, then. I thought I recognized you."

Who knew what that meant? Toby smiled a bland, generic smile and stepped over to the food table. What an evening! Hard to believe some people came to these events for pleasure. Or did they?

He took one of the small white plates in a neat stack—the size of the plates definitely discouraged hoggishness—and surveyed the goodies. Not too appetizing. An expensive chef had no doubt prepared them, but they looked like they came from the freezer compartment at Costco. He reached over and manhandled a miniature crab cake.

"Should've known I'd find you with the free food," came a voice. It was, astonishingly, Brad Solomon, bestowing a fond paternal smile on him.

Toby did his best not to react. "Brad. I'm surprised to see you here."

"Why's that?"

Because Brad had spent the weekend in London with Amy and it was Sunday night. He couldn't have been back more than a few hours. But Toby had no acceptable reason for knowing this. "You've never been to one of these events before, have you?" The question provided an answer of sorts.

"Now I have to. I'm a fucking patron of the arts." He drained his champagne glass, put it down, picked up a full one, and took a healthy sip. "Right alongside those Medici momsers."

Toby gave Brad a quick, surreptitious once-over. His skin was ashy, and his eyes were bloodshot, and he seemed unsteady on his feet. His thick, stolid body looked like a dead oak tree ready to topple. He was clearly very tired, and he might be drunk. He certainly *sounded* drunk, slurring his words, speaking too loudly.

"Noblesse oblige," Toby said.

"It isn't noblesse in my case. Plain cold cash does the obliging."

"Looking forward to tonight's show?"

"Oh God. No way. Been travelling. And this champagne's hit me like a ton of bricks."

"You've been travelling? Where to?" Play dumb.

"Back from London this afternoon. Quick trip. Two fucking days. Damned draining."

"Business?" There was no way to opt out of the conversation once it was in motion.

"Little bit. Mostly pleasure. Not that I had much. Spent more time getting there than being there, damn near. Could barely sleep. Stomach trouble. It was like a forced march. Up the bloody Bataan Peninsula."

Toby felt a slight shiver of satisfaction. Unworthy, maybe, but he wasn't saintly enough to repent. Meanwhile, Solomon was staring out at the crowd, and after a couple of seconds blurted, "Tell me something, Lindeman. Do you understand evening gowns?"

"I'm not sure I follow."

"I mean, what's the point? Are they supposed to be elegant and classy, is that the deal? Ladies wear 'em to embassy balls and opera receptions and court levees, right? So there's that. Or are they supposed to be sexy? By exposing all that cleavage and crap. A lot of the women here, they're almost bursting out of their gowns, have you noticed? So is that some sort of glamor thing, boobs tumbling out of dresses, or is it supposed to be hot and provocative? 'Cause to my mind it ain't either. Much too slutty to be elegant if you ask me, slutty and sloppy, even if the gowns are studded with fucking diamonds and shit. And in most cases..." He finally turned his head to face Toby, and shrugged humorously. "In most cases, all that burstage, too goddamn much of it, acres of it, endless, like the steppes of central fucking Asia, at least with the gals you usually find wearing the fucking things. It was different at our high school proms, those pert little buds, little glimpse of nip if you were lucky, I get that one hundred percent. But these fucking dowagers, they shouldn't be allowed within a mile of the things. It's like Vesuvius, only bozooms are erupting instead of lava. Gonna bury fucking Pompeii in tits, every last inhabitant, a slow, agonizing death by mammary inundation."

Toby had been gaping blankly at Solomon during the first part of this recitation, but eventually gave in and laughed. He had never seen Solomon in such extravagant, manic, comic flight, had no inkling he was capable of it.

"'Course, *your* prom was probably different," Solomon allowed. "Did they already let same-sex couples go?"

Toby laughed again, and shook his head.

"What?" Solomon had a goofy grin on his face. "Is something wrong? Like, 'This is your brain, this is your brain on jet lag?'"

Toby laughed again. "Maybe something along those lines."

"Jetlag and champagne," Solomon said. "And an Ambien for the plane. Killer combo. Can't recommend it highly enough." And then, "Aw shit, I better get home."

"Might be advisable."

"Five hours of krauts killing swans and bleeding and cutting off their dicks and bellowing about the fucking Holy Grail...can't face it."

"No jury would convict."

Solomon drank down the last of his champagne and put the empty glass on the buffet table. Then he turned to face Toby. "Listen, kid. Before I go. You give any thought to that thing we talked about? You know what I'm referring to?"

"I do. And I haven't, really. Or rather, that is—"

Solomon interrupted him. "It'll wait." And then, "You're good people, Lindeman. Aces. But right now I'm getting the fuck out of here. Don't tell Doris. Don't tell her *anything*."

"Need a cab?"

"I've got my car."

"I'm not sure you're in any shape to drive, Brad."

The look Solomon gave him seemed almost pitying. "My car *and* driver."

"Right. Of course." And then, "Going straight home?" Toby hoped the question seemed natural in context, although there was nothing remotely natural about it. He needed to know Solomon's destination.

"I'm not heading off to the Cat Club to disco the night away, if that's what you're getting at. Gonna give Judy her present, then collapse. Got her a bracelet from Asprey's. Hope she likes it. Her life's no bed of roses." He sighed, and it wasn't for show; a world of pain was comprehended by that mighty sigh. "You and me, we'll talk. Meantime, take care of yourself."

Another pat, and Solomon wobbled away through the throng. Toby, observing, was filled with misgivings. The last thing in the world he wanted was to start liking the man.

~

TOBY AND AMY WERE in bed. He was on his back, she was on her side, curled in toward him, her head resting in the curve of his left arm, her

219

mouth against his chest. "I'm not saying I wasn't tempted," he murmured. "Don't want to pretend to be more virtuous than I am. But I didn't. And I was glad. Relieved, even."

"Me too," she said. She was so tired, her defenses were so enfeebled, her voice had a soft, high-pitched, little-girl quality. "Although it'd be hard to blame you. Magda Szerly's a beautiful woman."

"Yeah, but…" But what? There were so many buts. He opted for the simplest. "But I'm not in love with her."

She made a sighing noise and nuzzled her face against him. "For what it's worth, Brad and I…the whole thing was so rushed, way overscheduled, no fun at all. By the end, we were barely speaking." She suddenly yawned mightily.

"You must be exhausted." Don't enjoy her problems with Brad too much, he cautioned himself. Or at least, don't let her see you enjoying them.

"Never been exhausteder."

"You're not alone. At the opera, Brad was staggering around like a wounded wombat."

"He got more sleep than me. Took an Ambien and napped on the plane."

"Private jet?"

"Guys like him don't fly commercial." Then, her voice dreamy, "Listen, Mr. Toby, don't let me fall asleep, okay? Wake me if I doze off."

He kissed her. Hard to believe this was the same person as the brusque businesswoman he'd seen in her office two days before. "It's an amazing thing," he murmured. "Right here, right now, for maybe the first time in my life, I'm totally content. No desires, no appetites. A Buddhist would say I've achieved satori."

"Satorial splendor." She snickered into his armpit and then said, "At lunch yesterday…I kind of zoned out, and I was having this fantasy about you. Majorly dirty. And the look on my face must have been rich, because Brad suddenly said, 'What the hell are you thinking about?'" She snickered again. "Not only didn't I tell *him*, I'm not even going to tell *you*."

"Maybe you'll show me some time."

"Much better idea." She yawned again. "Now remember, don't let me fall asleep."

A second later her breath had become deep and regular. Toby lay quietly beside her, his arm under her head, his heart full to bursting. He let her sleep.

5

"JESUS, I HATE THESE THINGS," Jessie said. "It's like they need to remind you you're sick."

Toby pushed the wheelchair out through the hospital doors, which had obligingly opened when they approached. "Sit tight for a sec, okay? I won't be long. Just have to find a taxi."

Her bald head nodded. "I've got all the time in the world."

A few minutes later, in the cab to her place, she asked, "Have you been sleeping at the house all this time?"

"Uh-uh. Cathy didn't feel it was necessary." And said no more. He didn't want to burden her with Hank Ortega. She had worries enough.

"She's a big girl, she can manage. And besides—" She considered for a second "—I think she's got a boyfriend. She hasn't said so, but I've picked up emanations, you know? Probably one of the boys in the play is my guess. Don't you think that makes sense?"

She seemed to expect an answer, so he said, rather lamely, "I don't know."

"Of course not. But it seems likely, is all I'm saying. So she probably *prefers* an empty house. Bit of a luxury for her. Doesn't have to sneak around. Not that she'd have to, but she must enjoy the drama. Adolescent girls love thinking they're Juliet." Jessica smiled fondly; Toby guessed it was at the idea of their big strapping daughter bearing a resemblance to that sylph-like Capulet kid. She'd probably never seen a production of the Gounod opera; Juliets come in all sizes, even jumbo. "I'm surprised she didn't physically shove you out the door."

222

"She practically did," Toby answered. He tried to match her jocularity, but there was nothing amusing about the girl's situation. Jessica was comfortable with Cathy being sexually active. Fair enough. She was being true to her ideas about adolescent sexuality and to her own stormy sexual history. Toby agreed in theory. But how would she feel if she discovered who Cathy's partner was? He knew Jessica Galfand well enough to be sure of the answer: Hank Ortega's testicles would be in dire and imminent jeopardy.

In the ensuing silence, Toby decided to risk asking, "Why did they keep you so long? I thought it was supposed to be overnight."

"They wanted to do some additional tests. I protested—"

"I'll bet."

"—but they were pretty insistent. They called my doctor, and she agreed."

He waited. He waited a long time. The full duration of a red light. Only when the car resumed moving did she speak again: "It's spread."

He glanced over at her. He didn't know what to say next. "Is it—?" He stopped, confused about how to finish the sentence, not even sure what he'd meant to ask when he began.

"It's bad," she said. "If that's what you wanted to know. Stage four."

"Oh Jessie."

"Life's a bitch, huh? I thought I was beating this thing."

"I'm sure there are still plenty of weapons left in their arsenal."

"I'm sure there are." No drama. "I have an appointment on Wednesday with Sharon. My doctor. We're going to decide what to do next."

"You like her?"

"Yeah, she's good. She understands the human side of this. A lot of them can't get beyond the cellular."

They said nothing further until they reached her house. As he helped her out of the car, he said, "You need a hand?"

"Honey, you have to believe me, I feel normal. That's what's so surreal about this."

They walked to the front door. She got out her key and opened it. As they stepped through, Cathy rushed toward them. "Mommy!" she said, "I've missed you!" and gave Jessica a hug. While doing so, she directed a glance at Toby, over Jessica's shoulder, that could only be described as poisonous. Too bad. Cathy didn't usually nurse a grudge.

"I've missed you too, sweetheart." Jessica hadn't noticed the look.

"I'll be upstairs. When Daddy goes, you can tell me how you are." The acidity with which she said this was unmistakable.

After she had left, Jessica asked quietly, "What was that about?"

"Adolescent rage."

"Had your first dose, did you?"

Toby was relieved Jessica didn't want details. "Full blast," he said.

"Put it down to hormones. It's the only way to keep from throttling her."

Hormones indeed. Toby, to change the subject, said, "Can I get you some tea or coffee?"

"Thanks, but…but no, I just want you to sit with me for a minute. Is that okay?" She seated herself on the sofa, reclining against one of the armrests, and he took his old seat, facing her. They looked at each other for a moment. Then she burst out, "Oh Toby, I'm so scared."

Without thinking, he stood, crossed to her, and sat beside her. "Me too."

She took his hand. "You know what I miss most about you? Just sitting. Not talking. Not doing anything. You were always so contained, which is a nice way of saying *withholding*. I could never tell what you were thinking or feeling. But there were times I didn't mind. It was a comfort just having you around."

He remembered evenings like that. When they were first married, sitting in this very room, on this very couch. Listening to music or reading or merely staring at the fireplace. What *had* he been thinking and feeling?

"I really loved you," she went on quietly. "Couldn't believe my good luck. I was crazy about you, Toby."

"And I you," he said. And wondered if it were true. It didn't matter, it was the only thing to say, but still, interesting he didn't know. He remembered Amy had once asked him if he'd loved Jessica. He'd been unable to answer then too.

But now, sitting beside her, holding her hand, he suddenly and unexpectedly *did* remember. Memories were flooding in. Memories he'd buried long ago, buried deliberately after all the acrimony and wild accusations and personal indictments and the wrenching pain of her affair. How wounding that affair had been, even though he always claimed, to himself as well as others, that, after the initial shock, it had been a relief, had freed him, had given him the wherewithal to make an escape that was years overdue.

And maybe it was true. Partly true. But he could now also recall the pleasure of sitting beside her on quiet evenings. The subtle pleasure of being with someone because he wanted to be and knew she felt the same. He remembered the tenderness he'd felt, the novel joy he'd found in her messy, unfettered, rambunctious companionship. Her noisiness compensating for his reserve. Her in-your-face insistence overwhelming his lifetime of diffidence. It was a revelation to him, an education in acceptable misbehavior. And his first experience of feeling truly at home. Perhaps the thing had been fleeting, but it had been real. He'd loved her for her toughness, and for the neediness he descried beneath the toughness. He'd loved her. And the tenderness he was feeling toward her now seemed to efface the intervening years.

All these connections. Like loose netting. You ignore them for years, you deny their existence, but sooner or later you find yourself entangled.

He squeezed her hand.

∽

TOBY SQUARED HIS SHOULDERS before pushing into the high school auditorium. No way this wouldn't be ugly.

As Toby entered, Hank Ortega was sitting on the lip of the stage, his legs dangling down. He was wearing tight jeans and a tight black V-neck tee. Getting closer, Toby could see his ponytail, the small gold cross hanging from a gold chain around his neck, and a single earring. Toby also noticed the girth of the man's forearms and biceps, bulging with muscle. Like post-spinach Popeye. Had he deliberately worn the T-shirt to intimidate?

Ortega offered a friendly wave from the stage when he saw Toby enter the auditorium. "Yo!" he called out. Bravado? He must have suspected this visit didn't augur well, even though Toby, when he phoned to make the appointment, hadn't offered a preview.

"Sorry about the venue," he said when Toby was close enough to have entered his social space. "They don't give me a classroom. This is my base of operations, by default." He leaned down and offered his hand. "It's more private than the teachers' lounge, that's the good news. We won't be disturbed."

Toby briefly considered not shaking. But not shaking hands is a major statement. Refusing to shake would have made further conversation more difficult, and things were difficult enough. Toby grasped the hand, doing his gentlemanly duty.

Ortega gestured toward the front row. Toby took a seat, wondering if Ortega planned to remain sitting on the stage. It would give him the advantage of height, and would put a certain distance, psychological as well as physical, between them. But Toby didn't think such a positioning would matter; he enjoyed the sufficient intrinsic advantage that little finesses couldn't have much effect. And then Ortega surprised him by also taking a seat in the front row, just one away from Toby's own.

The two men shifted their bodies toward each other and their eyes locked. Kasparov vs. Karpov. Toby registered Ortega's Aztec cheekbones, his copper coloring. Then Ortega raised his eyebrows interrogatively, as if to say, You've got the white pieces, make your move.

"Would you care to characterize your relationship with my daughter?" Toby demanded abruptly. He kept his voice low.

The slightest flicker in Ortega's eyes. The salient question about this conference was answered; it wasn't an innocuous visit, nor a thank you for the Cal recommendation. He smiled thinly, perhaps in tribute to the clever way Toby had initiated hostilities. Not with a direct accusation, but with an open-ended question. Refusing to tip his hand. Toby knew Ortega must be wondering if he was working on suspicion alone, or a telltale piece of evidence, or even a teary confession from Cathy. It was up to the drama teacher to guess, and to contrive a response.

"I'm very fond of her," he said. "She's one of my most promising students."

Toby let the answer resonate in all its inadequacy for a few seconds. Then he said, "I believe you know that isn't what I'm asking."

"Maybe you could be more specific?"

226

Toby didn't flinch. "Has there been sexual contact between you and Cathy?"

"Sexual contact?"

"Look, you can stall if you want, but there's no way you're going to run out the clock. We've got plenty of time. And—to avoid wasting more of it—we don't need to discuss what the meaning of 'is' is. My question was clear enough."

"Does Cathy know you're here?"

"We can talk about that later. There's a question on the table. Mind you, I haven't heard any outraged denials, so I guess I can take that as implicit confirmation."

Ortega nodded. He'd made up his mind. "Not much point, is there?" He suddenly smiled. Smiled rather easily. "But let me ask…was this guesswork on your part, or—?"

"Or what?"

"Well, doesn't matter. Either way, we seem to be in a situation, don't we?"

"That's one way of putting it. *You're* in one, that's for sure."

Toby was surprised to discover he was feeling no rage. Which was peculiar, since he'd experienced so much when anticipating this meeting. But now, in the thick of it, he felt calm and dispassionate. Maybe because Ortega was being sensible about not making things worse. Credit where credit's due, Toby thought; he must sense how little it would take to set me off. Lying outright, say, or accusing Cathy of leading him on, or emitting even the faintest whiff of machismo. But the conversation was young, there were still plenty of opportunities for him to go wrong.

Ortega was saying, "Fair point, I'm the one in the situation. But it involves us both."

"It involves more than just us, Hank. It involves you, me, Cathy, her mother, the school, the headmaster, the teachers' licensing board, the police…"

"*Not* the police, in fact," Ortega said. "I don't believe any laws have been broken. But I don't mean to get technical. The ramifications are serious enough."

Interesting what a tightrope the guy was managing to walk. No show of bravado, but no groveling or sniveling. A serious man having a serious conversation with another serious man.

"You've done this often?" Toby asked. "Diddled a student?"

"No."

Had he wanted to provoke Ortega? It wasn't conscious, but he couldn't imagine why else he'd posed the question so crudely. "In that case, assuming you're telling the truth, why was Cathy the lucky one? What made you single her out?"

"Look." Ortega gestured to Toby, hands up. Not a surrender, more a request for a parlay. "Before we continue, can I ask your intentions here? Are you looking for a real answer, or are you doing this to harass me and vent some spleen? I mean, either way, I don't have any basis for arguing. But it might affect how I respond."

"Just answer the fucking question, Hank."

Ortega sighed. "I didn't mean for it to happen, okay? I wasn't a *predator*. She…you're not going to like this…"

"Keep talking."

"Look, your daughter was a sad case in a lot of ways. Unhappy with the way she looked, unhappy with her life. Lonely. She…forgive the psychobabble, but for kids that age, self-esteem's a major deal, they're all convinced they're unattractive and unlovable, and Cathy felt it more than most. For whatever reason."

Toby sniffed significantly. "Is that supposed to mean something? 'For whatever reason.'"

"Divorce hits kids hard. Some divorces hit harder than others."

"Jessie and I separated over five years ago."

"And the melody lingers on. What can I tell you? I see a lot of these kids. You want to make a snide comment go ahead, but the fact remains, I deal with kids on a daily basis, I know what I know. A lot of the kids in my classes, their parents are split, I see the effects. It's easy to tell who they are without being told. And I'm sorry if you don't like hearing it, but Cathy was one of the worst. I mean hurting the worst. I'm not saying it's your fault."

"Gee, thanks."

"Okay, fine, maybe it *is* your fault. How much time do you spend with her on average? Couple evenings a week?" It was less than that, but Toby let Ortega continue rather than confess this dereliction. "Do you have any idea what she cares about? Her favorite books? Her favorite music? Movies? Her worries and concerns? Do you know any of that?" Before Toby could answer, Ortega went on, "Because I do."

"No, I guess I don't," Toby conceded. "Not most of it. She doesn't confide in me that way."

"I admit kids that age don't always talk to their parents, but...well, in this case, I don't think it's only that. I *listen*. I pay attention."

"I listen."

"Did you know she went through a bulimic phase last year?"

Toby didn't. This news, in fact, hit him like a blow to the solar plexus. Was he really so clueless? He wanted to lie, but instead just stared at Ortega.

"No, huh? That's a pretty big thing not to know, wouldn't you say?" Ortega leaned toward him. "So when you ask why her, there's no single answer, but her eating issue is how it started. Not how it started, but...I mean, I could see right away she was damaged. Also funny and talented and smart, all the things I hope you're aware of and proud of. But so sad, and kind of cut off from everyone. What caught my attention was, she kept going to the bathroom all the time. More than anyone should. That's a tricky situation for a male teacher with a girl student. There's menstruation and so on, and kids are self-conscious about all their physical functions anyway, you have to step carefully. But *something* was clearly up, and I finally talked to her. She flatly denied it at first, but I finally got her to admit she'd been bingeing and purging."

This little chat wasn't going the way Toby had expected.

"So I let her have it. Real tough-love stuff. How she could be ruining her life; how she could injure herself permanently. How, if she was so concerned about her weight, she should do something sensible instead of destroying her body. And I put her on a healthy diet. I mean, I didn't *put her on it*, I'm not a doctor, but I recommended a sensible approach to food, I told her some healthy ways of eating while controlling calorie intake, that sort of thing. Common sense stuff everyone knows, but it helps when they hear it from someone they think is cool. And bless her, she listened. She agreed to try it, and she stuck with it. Stopped the bingeing, stopped the purging, started eating right. Maybe you haven't noticed, but she's been losing weight."

"I've noticed."

"And not on some crazy fad diet. Check out her complexion some time, it's *improved*. And look, I'm no dietician, I'm not a therapist, this is something she'll have to stay on top of. I'm not claiming I worked miracles. But I do believe I helped. She eats lots of fruits and vegetables now, plenty of whole grains, lean protein…And no junk. So anyway, that's how we started talking, her and me. And she trusted me, and I—"

"Abused that trust," Toby interrupted.

"—enjoyed her company too, is what I was going to say." His eyes flashed with sardonic amusement. "She's a terrific kid. Mature beyond her years, even if she's also a crazy teenager. Very intelligent, very perceptive, an original. Sometimes I get the feeling you don't see that. So does Cathy."

"She does?" Toby was aware of having lost the initiative, but this didn't seem like information he should disregard.

"Mmm. She adores you, she looks up to you, she thinks you're the coolest dad in the universe. But she feels you don't respect her, you don't find her interesting. Which leads her to believe she *isn't* interesting."

"Well, that isn't true."

"You don't have to convince me. I'm telling you how *she* feels."

"So I guess she was a sitting duck, huh?"

Ortega shook his head. It took chutzpah, but he managed to convey he was disappointed in Toby's reaction. "If you want to look at it that way," he said. "She was starved for attention and approval from a male authority figure. But as I said, my intentions weren't amorous. I was concerned. But the thing is…Aw hell, let's face it, she's not a child anymore. I know she's in high school, but she's obviously not a kid. Once she and I started talking intimately…" He shrugged again. "Things changed. No one intended for it to happen."

"Don't you have a professional obligation not to give in to that sort of thing?"

"Yes. I messed up. Big time. Or at least that's one way of looking at it."

"There's another way?"

"I think so."

"Go on."

"I'm happy to keep it to myself. Something tells me you're not especially eager to hear my side. You'd deem it self-serving. And it's not like I'd blame you. God knows I'd probably feel the same if it was my daughter."

"I said go on."

He sighed, as if to say, What's the use? "A few months ago, she was miserably unhappy; I'd say clinically depressed, that's my layman's diagnosis. She was suffering from an eating disorder, she had no close friends, she was a lost soul. She wasn't very attractive by conventional standards, she didn't like herself much. Whereas now she strikes me as pretty cheerful; she appears to be recovering from the disorder or at least dealing with it responsibly. She's discovered this great enthusiasm for theater; she's been accepted at a terrific college. And what's the downside? She's involved with one of her teachers. I realize that's a major no-no, but honestly, Toby, she'll be done with high school in a few weeks. It's not child abuse, she isn't a child. You surely didn't expect her to be a nun after graduation. She was going to be sexually active soon enough one way or another." His voice was starting to rise; he was warming to his theme. "It was only a matter of time, months probably, so what's the big deal if it happened a little sooner rather than a little later? Where's the harm? I've treated her well, much better than some high school kid would have. I've tried to be a good influence, I've been considerate of her feelings, I've looked after her, I think I've been good for her in almost every way. And meanwhile, where have you been? You're her father, but you didn't even know which colleges she applied to. Where the fuck do you get off acting aggrieved?"

The anger still wasn't there, but Toby, disappointed in himself, tried to gin it up a little. "You expect me to thank you for seducing my daughter? For exploiting your position?"

Ortega had too full a head of steam to answer Toby directly; instead, he continued, "You know the one unethical thing I'll cop to? The one thing I maybe shouldn't have done? I wrote her a more laudatory recommendation that I might have otherwise. I still would have praised her to the skies, but I might have been more restrained about her acting talent. You care to complain about that? The way I see it, she clearly belongs at Cal, it's great she got in, and if I told a little white lie to help, I don't imagine I'll burn in hell for it. I don't think I'll burn in hell for *anything* I've done with Cathy, and yes, you bet, that includes sex with her. Okay?" Ortega's eyes were flashing. He had gone a lot farther than he'd intended.

"Tell me this," Toby said quietly. "Is she in love with you? Or maybe I should say, does she think she's in love with you?"

Ortega rolled his eyes humorously. As if he and Toby were suddenly buddies. "No way, no how. And I mean…look, of course it's a relief she isn't, it's a huge relief, but I also have to tell you, a guy goes into this profession, it isn't because he's immune to adolescent adulation. Other teachers may lie about it, but we enjoy being admired. So it's a relief, but it's also almost insulting the way she tells me she isn't going to fall in love with me under any circumstances, it isn't in the cards, she hasn't and she won't, she's off to college in September and that'll be that, goodbye, it's been swell, good luck, adios." He laughed outright. "I'm probably crazy to level with you like this, but the fact is, I'd like to go on seeing her. Why not? We'll both be living in the same area, we have some common interests, we're fond of each other. I'm *very* fond of her. And to be crass, she's looking better with every passing week. It's like Pygmalion getting the brush-off from Galatea. But she doesn't think it's wise, so that's that. A whole new life's about to begin for her. You can put your mind at ease. I'm never gonna call you 'Dad.'"

Toby laughed. He didn't intend to. It just happened. Ortega laughed too. "Maybe we *are* both in a situation," Toby said.

"Maybe so. You *want* to want to kill me, but somehow, you find that you don't. Right?"

"I haven't decided."

"Yeah. Well…" Ortega cleared his throat. "If you want to end my career and ruin my life, it's in your power. No point pretending otherwise. I mean, it doesn't matter how *I* see it, the zeitgeist will think I did something unforgivable. And look, I was never going to be a theater professional, but I'm a good teacher, we do good work here, the kids enjoy it, the theater department has a good rep. You can end all that. Get me fired, and I'll be unemployable in the profession. I hope you won't. I don't think it would be good for your relationship with Cathy, but of course, my reasons aren't selfless. It would be worse for me."

"Uh-huh."

"But I won't beg. I'm a big boy. I messed up. I knew the rules, and if there are consequences, I'll just have to accept them."

Toby stared at the man. He was beginning to understand what Cathy saw in him. "I haven't decided," he finally said. "I honestly don't know what I'm going to do."

"I understand. You'll do what you think you must."

Toby nodded. "My intentions were—"

"I know. You were planning to take my head off. So I guess I should count myself lucky. My head's still where it's always been." He smiled. "Up my ass."

Toby found himself smiling back. He said, "Word to the wise?"

"Please."

"You ever call me 'Dad,' you won't know what hit you. I mean it."

They both laughed. That's when Toby realized he wasn't going to bust Ortega.

∾

"WAS THERE ANY MOMENT—I don't really understand testosterone, so I'm just asking, no attitude implied—when you thought you'd hit him?"

At Toby's suggestion, he and Amy were in the bar where they'd met the night they first slept together. He reckoned she must regard it as safe, since she'd chosen it all those weeks ago. And it had sentimental pull, of course. He'd called her within minutes of leaving Ortega. He needed to see her; he'd been through an emotional wringer. No, she said, she wasn't free for dinner and she wasn't free after. But she must have heard the urgency in his voice, because she volunteered she could probably manage a quick drink at six.

"Before I got there," he answered. "But I haven't been in a fight since sixth grade, and that one was more like ineffectual flailing. Compared to the Baltimore toughs I went to school with, I was a pantywaist. My dad thought I was a sissy. Testosterone is a mystery to me too."

"You get its primary effects."

"You're too kind."

233

They smiled at each other. Then she said, "I just got a scrunch."

"A scrunch?"

"This thing that happens. When I'm with you, or sometimes just when I think about you. A kind of…sensation, sort of a little spasm kind of thing, localized in my…you know."

"Your cuntal regions?"

She laughed. "Precisely. My cuntal regions. You're certainly conversant with female anatomy. Have you made a study?"

"Mostly field work." He took a sip of bourbon. "Listen, bantering aside…I need your counsel. This Ortega guy. What he did, abuse, harassment, whatever you call it…it's the unforgivable abomination *du jour*. Our witchcraft. Am I wrong if I don't rat him out?"

She peered down into her cosmopolitan and considered for a second. "You want my opinion?" He nodded. "Okay. If you're really torn, my question would be, do you believe him that Cathy was his first? Or is he a serial student-seducer? 'Cause if he is, it's a no-brainer."

"I believe him. He was convincing."

She put her hand over his. "Cathy isn't a child anymore, Toby. He got that right."

"I know."

"Speaking as a former eighteen-year-old girl. Whatever this was, it *wasn't* child abuse. Lots of girls are sexually active in high school these days. *Lots*. Most of them, quite likely."

"I know, I know. When I was in high school, the challenge was figuring out which."

"If you do turn him in, Cathy sure won't thank you. She might never forgive you." She looked thoughtful. "Another question is whether you think he exploited his position somehow."

"Of course he did. Whether he meant to or not. You can't separate his position from what happened. A handsome guy takes advantage of his looks simply by having them. A rich guy takes advantage of his money, not by flashing it, but because certain options are available to him. A celebrity takes advantage of his fame by being famous. And someone in authority takes advantage of his power even if he's conscientious about not using it. It's part of the equation." After she nodded, he added, "For me, the salient question is, did he do her harm? Has she been injured by the relationship?"

"And—?"

"To hear him tell it, quite the opposite. He seems to think he effected some sort of miracle cure. Rescued her from a shitload of adolescent angst."

"You must have wanted to strangle him."

"Uh-uh. I *wanted* to want to strangle him, but…it rang true."

She stared at him, a frank, open gaze. "You're a remarkable guy, Toby."

"Nah. I'm a deficient father who's trying to come to terms with his deficiencies." He went on, "The thing is…that sort of relationship is so demonized, but if you call it mentoring instead of exploiting, what's different? Just sex. The Greeks thought these sorts of transactions were noble. Does sex automatically make it evil? If both people like each other and enjoy the relationship and get something from it?"

She squeezed his hand. "Cathy's lucky to have you, Toby. Whatever you say. You understand. Most guys wouldn't, not if it's their daughter. But when a charismatic older guy is willing to give a bright young woman his time and attention, she can bloom."

"Speaking from experience, are you?"

He had never seen her blush before. She hadn't seen it coming. She mumbled, "I suppose I must be."

"And all of a sudden it's out in the open, isn't it?" He waited, but she didn't say anything, or even change expression. "How old were you?"

She sighed. It was out in the open all right, and she wasn't happy about it. "Older than Cathy." She stopped, as if hoping that was all the response required. But he kept looking at her, conspicuously waiting for more, and she gave in with another sigh. "It was after I left business school. I was looking for a job, trying to figure out what to do with my MBA. One of the places I interviewed was Solomon Enterprises. They offered me a position, but I turned it down. Real estate seemed so yesterday. Compared to the high-tech stuff, it seemed…too real. I was going to say 'too concrete,' but that seemed like a stupid pun. I guess 'too real' is too. Anyway, there's nothing virtual about a building, and I thought the future was virtual. But I guess I'd made an impression on

Brad, we'd talked in the latter stages of recruitment, and when I turned down the gig, he invited me to lunch."

"Had some vigorous mentoring in mind, did he?"

She frowned and shook her head, unamused. "His intentions were honorable. I wasn't his type. I don't have the flash. Had even less back then. It was almost a point of pride with me. Flash was for unserious women."

"But one thing led to another?"

"We got along. He thought I had potential. He liked the way I caught on, the way I wasn't cowed by him or anyone else. We made each other laugh. And if you're not too jaundiced to be objective, you've noticed how smart he is. I'd never met anyone like him."

Toby waited. After a second, Amy went on, "He gave me good advice. Said I was probably right not to join his company. Asked about my family. Told me about his background. He's a good listener—at least he used to be—and a wonderful storyteller. We laughed a lot, like I said. We had fun. He told me to call whenever I felt like it."

"Did you?"

"Uh-uh. I didn't want to impose, and I wasn't sure what the lunch had been about. It didn't feel like he was hitting on me, but sometimes it's hard be sure. And then, after a week or so, he called and suggested dinner."

"Ah hah."

"No, it wasn't like that. We just had dinner and talked some more. It was months before anything happened."

"Months of lunches and dinners?"

"And telephone conversations, and email, and…and lots of things. He made some calls on my behalf, steered me in certain directions, prepped me for meetings. When I started my site, he gave me some seed money. Said he was investing in *me*, not my idea. He was very helpful. We got in under each other's radar. Neither of us felt anything romantic was happening so we let our guards down. And even then… you know Brad, he isn't shy about saying what he wants. *Getting* what he wants. But he never even hinted at anything. It was my doing. I told him…" And then she abruptly stopped. "I'm giving you way too much information, aren't I? And besides, it's late, I need to go."

"You told him—?"

She hesitated, then said, "All right. I told him I'd fallen in love with him. Which I had." Toby felt a sudden shortness of breath. "And that whether he knew it or not, he'd fallen in love with me." She drained the remainder of her drink, then firmly placed her glass back on the wooden table with a little thunk. "I have to go. Brad hates to wait." She stood up.

"Hold on," he said. It was too much to deal with, or even absorb, in the seconds remaining. He inhaled deeply before asking, "What about now? What about me?"

"It's a mess. I told you this isn't easy." She picked up her coat, draped over the back of an empty chair.

"Yeah, but—"

"To be continued. I have to run." She shrugged the coat onto her shoulders, leaned over, and kissed his cheek. "I think your instincts about Ortega are right. As for the rest...we'll come back to it. I promise." She pivoted away from him and scurried toward the exit.

~

CATHY HAD SUGGESTED LUNCH. A first. And she offered to meet Toby near the Opera House. Hayes Street Grill seemed a little too fancy, so he picked Max's Opera Cafe; it was nearby, and fundamentally a deli with pretensions.

Cathy ordered a salad, Toby a bowl of matzo ball soup. The latter caused Cathy to say, with a smile, "I guess Mom left some small imprint on you after all."

They made small talk for a few more minutes after ordering, but they obviously had a serious conversation ahead of them and someone had to make it happen. The transition wasn't going to take care of itself. So after no one had said anything for long enough to be noticeable, Toby said, "You haven't been answering your phone. I've called a lot."

"Yeah. Well, I've got Caller ID."

Toby grimaced. "I was worried sick about you. And about us."

"I kind of enjoyed thinking so."

"You wanted to hurt me?"

"I didn't think that was possible. But I thought I might be able to frustrate you, at least."

"You hurt me very much."

237

Cathy shook her head. She wasn't making a point, she simply didn't believe him. "You're just not used to being balked," she said. "At least by me."

Not an argument worth winning. "Well, I'm glad you finally relented."

"I wouldn't have. Hank told me to. He said I wasn't being fair."

A spoonful of soup was halfway to Toby's lips. He set it back down and looked at her. She looked back. There was nothing innocent in her telling him this, and she was making no attempt to hide her amusement. After a few seconds, she went on, "He said you must be worried about me. He said I *owed* you a call. And an explanation." A mischievous grin. "He's apparently taken a shine to you."

"Because I didn't bring the law down on his sorry ass."

"I'm sure that's part of it." It was fun for her, having power to wield. Toby didn't begrudge her. "But maybe it speaks well for you that you didn't. Hank thinks so."

"I wish I knew how."

"Give yourself some credit."

He took a slurp of soup. "Not many people would agree."

"That's one of the reasons Hank admires you. He knows it would have been easier to go the other way. He says you listened, you kept an open mind."

Carol Macelli was passing their table with another singer in the company, a new hire. When she noticed Toby, she pulled away and approached him.

"Hey, stranger," she said. And after he returned the greeting, "Is this your daughter?"

"Yeah, yeah, it is," he confirmed, and made the introductions.

After Carol rejoined her companion, Cathy said, "Who's that?"

"Singer with the company."

"You've slept with her, haven't you?"

Toby sighed. And lied. "No, I have not. Listen, kiddo, the fact that you're, you know, a woman...that doesn't automatically give you x-ray vision about grown-up relationships."

"Whatever." She was smiling. "She likes you, anyway. And why not? You're a hunk."

"Whatever." He was smiling back, in spite of himself.

"So look," she said after a moment, "I want to be sure we're okay." The rest followed in a torrent: "And when I say 'we,' I mean *you*. I want to be sure *you're* okay with who *I* am. 'Cause who I am now is pretty much who I'll be from now on. I'm grown up, more or less. More more than less. So I'm going to be having sex, you need to get used to that. I've discovered I like it. A lot. And I mean, heck, I had to get used to *you* doing it, and I was a kid at the time. It was hard for me when you started dating. So now it's your turn. Plus, I'm going to get drunk occasionally. Not excessively, but it's bound to happen now and then. And I'll smoke weed. No, before you ask, Hank doesn't, he doesn't like it, the times I've done it he wasn't around. But I *do* like it. And I'll be out all night sometimes. I'll have friends you disapprove of. I know you give me money, and maybe you think that gives you some say over how I lead my life, but it doesn't. That isn't why you do it, and doing it doesn't give you that kind of power anymore. If that's what you think your money is buying, then keep it. It'll be difficult for me, but I'll figure something out."

He stared at her. Her tone wasn't hostile, merely categorical. She'd obviously rehearsed these topics in her mind. "Gee," he said, "I'm glad we're having this robust exchange of views."

"I want us to be friends, Daddy. It's important to me. But I don't see how we can be friends if we're gonna have the same fights over and over, especially about really basic stuff. The way you and Mom do. Always the same fights. So why not declare a truce?"

"Is that what Hank recommended?"

She raised her eyebrows. "Sounds like you're jealous."

"I probably am."

"This has nothing to do with Hank. I just think we're better off with a holistic approach instead of confronting disagreements one by one. There's never any closure that way."

"And by 'holistic approach,' you mean I acquiesce in everything you do?"

"Close." She grinned. "Only…it can't be good for you to know this, but the truth is, you still have a lot of influence over me. I care about your opinion. You just don't have veto power anymore."

"Jesus, this is going to take some getting used to," Toby said. He was thinking: Who *is* this person? If this is the real Cathy, then when—how—had she become so poised, so mature, so self-assured? For all his chagrin at how she'd outmaneuvered him, and how she blithely informed him she felt free to disregard him whenever she chose, he also found himself admiring her cool, droll adroitness. Had it been developing steadily while he'd been too preoccupied to notice? Or was it a recent, abrupt development, punctuated evolution? It was enough to make him break into a chorus of "Gigi." Toby leaned back in his chair, smiling faintly. "I see I'm going to have to make some adjustments," he said.

"That's life, I guess," she answered, not unkindly.

Something unexpected came over him then, something unexpected and sweet. He got up from his chair, went over, hooked an arm around her neck, and leaned forward to kiss the top of her head. After he released her and sat back down, she laughed, a little puzzled and no doubt a little embarrassed, and said, "What was *that* about?" And then, "Oh look! Isn't that Brian Hughes?"

Toby turned to follow Cathy's gaze. It was indeed Brian, alone, on his way out of the restaurant. When he noticed Toby, he waved and changed course to approach their table. Toby girded himself for the inevitable charmless charm offensive.

"Hi," Toby said. "Have you met my daughter, Cathy?"

"I was wondering who this was," Brian responded with his familiar leer. His instinct for the inappropriate. "Nice to meet you. I'm Brian."

"Yes," Cathy said, "pleased to meet you."

Brian turned to Toby. "I'm glad I bumped into you. I've been meaning to tell you...It seems Jeremy's been composing. For months. Didn't tell anybody, just started doing it."

"Uh-huh," was all Toby said.

"He just told me."

"Right."

Brian chose not to acknowledge Toby's all-but-overt incredulity. "He must've been too enthusiastic to wait for official word. I haven't seen any of it yet, but he's jazzed."

"Okay." Keeping his voice uninflected. "Does he have a projected finish date?"

"Jeez, I doubt it. An opera's a big undertaking."

"So they say."

Brian frowned. Finally. "I thought you'd be pleased."

"I am."

"I just heard about it. Honestly."

"I'm glad it's moving ahead."

"Please tell Doris. She seemed impatient last time we talked."

"I will."

Brian looked less cocky than before, a fact Toby noted with satisfaction. "Nice meeting you," he told Cathy. "At first, I wasn't sure *who* you might be. For a second there, I even wondered if you were Amy, but, of course, you're much too young." He patted Toby on the shoulder. "See ya, Money Man." And then moved off toward the door.

Cathy waited till Brian was out of earshot, and then asked quietly, "Were you rude to him on purpose?" And then, with sudden concern, "Is something wrong?"

∽

"Look, I'm sorry," Jonas said. He sounded more defensive than apologetic. "But I mean, Brian and me, we're *engaged*. We talk. We don't have secrets. We discuss people we know and what's happening to them. That's how relationships work."

Toby made an effort to suppress his irritation. He didn't much like being lectured about relationships, not by anyone. No one knows how relationships work. Except that they usually don't. He leaned back in his chair and switched the phone to his other ear. When he swiveled to look out the window, dark, ominous clouds were gathering. Appropriately enough. Like in a Russian novel.

"It's not like I was *totally* indiscreet," Jonas added, sounding more than a trifle defensive. "I didn't mention her last name, I don't think."

"You don't *think*?"

"No, I didn't. For certain."

"Or—?"

"No, not that either. If you were about to say something about Solomon."

"Of course I was."

"I didn't. I did say she was involved with someone. To explain why it's complicated. But I didn't say who."

"Are you sure? If not, please, tell me." Toby turned his body away from the window and back toward his desk, the better to slump despairingly across it.

"I'm sure. With the opera connection and all, I figured I should be discreet."

"I think *less indiscreet* is the best you can hope for."

"Okay, okay. The thing is, in all likelihood Brian and Solomon are going to meet someday, so I chose not to mention his name." He sounded like he wanted Toby to give him credit.

"Which means Brian is also likely to meet Amy," Toby pointed out. "She and Brad go places together." Jonas had nothing to say to that. "Sooner or later Brian's going to meet a woman named Amy who's involved with someone I have dealings with, and he already knows I'm involved with someone named Amy who's involved with someone else. You see where I'm going with this? The dots will all be there, waiting to be connected. Brian isn't stupid."

Another silence. Finally, Jonas said, "You can trust him."

Getting to the nub of the problem, Toby *didn't* trust Brian. Far from it. "I hope so."

"He's my fiancé, Toby. Plus, he's a good guy, and he knows you and I are friends. And he considers *you* a friend. And an ally. There's no reason for him to jeopardize all that."

Toby nodded, although Jonas, at home in his apartment, couldn't see it. This was, in fact, the sole reason not to panic: Even if Brian cared to make trouble for its own sake, because of that incomprehensible nihilist streak of his, the resultant brouhaha would inevitably backfire on him. Not only would he lose a valuable ally, he'd alienate someone bankrolling a cherished project. Even a loose cannon like Brian would hesitate before doing anything *that* nuts.

"Can you tell him we've broken up?" Toby suggested. "Tell him we're no longer seeing each other. Confuse the issue. Say she's moved out of state or something."

"I won't do that."

"Why?"

"Because I don't lie to Brian. But relax. You have nothing to worry about."

~

"PRISCILLA THINKS YOU'RE SEXY. Did I already tell you that?"

Toby stopped chopping the onion. "Your receptionist?"

"You're a stud muffin, is how she put it. I think she's guessed there's something between us." She put a can of tuna into the electric can opener. As it spun slowly with a low whirring noise, Feeney padded into the kitchen, mewing excitedly. Amy's face lit up with amusement. "Kitty! Hate to disappoint you, but this is for Mr. Toby and me."

Feeney circled Amy's legs, undeterred.

"What makes you think so?"

She considered. "Maybe the fact she's never asked who you are? She's usually pretty nosey, and you and I talk on the phone every day, so you'd think it might make her curious. And how she sounded when she said you're a stud-muffin. Like she was congratulating me. And the way she acts like she's being discreet. *Conspicuously* discreet, if you see what I mean."

"Does it bother you?"

"Not so much," Amy said, removing the can from the contraption. "She'd never say anything to Brad. And I think she enjoys the intrigue. This is like a romance novel to her."

"To me too."

Feeney's mewing became more importuning. Amy ignored the cat as she crossed to the center island and dished the tuna into a bowl.

"Although," Toby added, "I *don't* enjoy the intrigue." He carried the chopping block with the diced onions on it over to the bowl and dumped them in, using the knife to guide them.

There was a sudden flash of lightning outside, followed a few seconds later by a long clap of rolling thunder. Toby looked toward the window. A downpour. No preparation, just instant deluge. As if the sky had been torn open and water was gushing through the rift.

Amy was at the refrigerator, removing a bowl of new potatoes she'd boiled the previous night. Feeney was still under her feet, still mewing. "No, sorry, you've already been fed."

"But *we* get sashimi grade. She can tell the difference. She resents being treated like a second-class citizen."

"Tough shit. She's a cat. Here, slice these, would you?" She handed the bowl of potatoes up to him.

As he took the bowl and the wooden chopping block back to the granite island, he asked, "And you? How do *you* feel about the intrigue?" He tried to keep his tone casual.

"I could live without it."

"But is it a net plus?"

"Not anymore." Still squatting in front of the refrigerator, she was withdrawing a couple of hard-boiled eggs and a tin of anchovies. "It might have been part of the excitement at first."

Was this ominous? "Things are less exciting now?"

She straightened up. "No, no. But it's about *us* now, not the situation." She put the eggs and anchovies down on the counter and went to him, putting her arms around him from behind, her hands around his waist, her face nestled into his nape, her body pressed against his back. "I'm in love with *you*. Drama doesn't add value."

A perfect answer. "Full marks," he said, and turned to face her. His arms went around her body.

"You must know how I feel."

"Well, there are…you know, ambiguities."

"I'm unambiguously nuts about you, Mr. Toby."

Feeney was complaining again. Amy broke from the embrace and knelt to comfort her. "Aw, puss, this ain't your night. Toby gets the love *and* the yellow tail. Not to mention the tail."

She cradled the suddenly purring cat in her arms. Toby approached and ran his fingers along the line of Feeney's taut jaw, exposing her incisors, which gave her a fierce aspect. His other hand loosely gripped the back of Amy's neck. He wanted to convey his boundless delight in the entirety of their dealings: Her, of course, primarily her, her body, her mind, her laugh, the way she kissed, the way her eyes glowed when they made love; but also her life, her work, her house, her cat, everything. Everything except that bastard Solomon.

"Poor Feeney's feeling forsaken," Amy said. "What with you, and London, and trouble at work…there's been less time for Feeney here."

As she set the cat down on the floor, Toby asked, "Things are bad at work?"

She crossed to open the tin of anchovies, and said, "I've been operating at a loss for a while. Since the pandemic things have slowed down a lot." She attached the tin to the opener's magnetized grip mechanism. As it whirred into action, she said, "If it's short-term, Brad's a safety net. I won't go under right away. But I'd rather not take anything from him if I can avoid it. He helped me get started, and he's been very helpful in all sorts of ways. But…"

The whirring ceased. She took the tin over to the island. "Do you prefer your anchovies in teeny-tiny bits, or are you okay with chunks?" The sound of the opener, or perhaps it was the smell of the anchovies, had drawn Feeney back again. The cat pressed against Amy's ankles and mewed a few demands. But her tone was plaintive. She no longer entertained high hopes.

"Did he ever offer to leave Judy?" Toby asked. It just popped out.

She reached into a drawer and withdrew a cocktail fork and a sharp knife. In the silence between them, the pounding rain outside was suddenly audible to Toby, clamorous and insistent. Apparently deciding she owed him an answer, she said, "We talked about it a little," she said, her tone flat. "In the beginning. Idle chat, nothing more. And after the stroke, it was unthinkable. Unmentionable." She prodded Feeney away with her foot. The cat quickly returned, rubbing against her calf, mewing aggressively.

"May I offer a suggestion?" he said. Amy stiffened. "Not about Brad. Relax." She exhaled. "About your business. If it isn't too presumptuous."

She exhaled. "Go ahead."

"Have you ever considered offering vibrators?"

"Are you nuts? It's a health site! Respectable. Dignified."

"Hear me out. I'm not suggesting you *feature* them. Or turn the whole site into a toy dispensary, with herbal menopause specifics on the side to preserve your integrity. But with all those medicaments and supplements and things…it's a safe venue for women to buy something like that. And it gives the transaction an aura of respectability, keeps it private and anonymous."

Amy was smiling. The smile was opaque, impossible to interpret. "You're out of your mind," she finally announced.

"Okay."

"You know, I've never used one."

"Really?"

"My hand to God. As it were."

"This is your big chance. You have a professional obligation to exercise due diligence."

"I could ask Priscilla. She probably owns several." She looked pensive. "You know, it's not a completely insane idea. I'm resisting, but…I could offer it as a massager, maybe."

"You wouldn't be fooling anybody. Call it a 'personal tension reliever.'"

She snorted, then said, "Okay, Lindeman, it's worth considering. I'm hesitant because it's so different from the way I conceive of the site."

"You have to start thinking…I believe the expression is *outside the box*."

"Stop it!" They were both laughing. "I'll think about it. You may be on to something. Now…are you okay with big chunks of anchovy?"

A couple of hours later, in bed, she murmured, "I don't need a…a 'personal tension reliever.' Not if I have access to this. And these. And in an emergency, *this*."

"They're yours as long as you want them. But I forbid you to offer them online."

"No chance. They're mine, all mine." She pushed him back down on the bed and straddled him, positioned herself over him, and slowly lowered herself down with a drawn-out, aspirated sigh. "Oh God, Toby," she whispered, "this is just…"

A phone rang.

"Shit," she said, freezing. After the second ring, she said, "It isn't mine."

"It's mine," he said.

"Ignore it?"

"I can't."

She rolled off him. "Okay." No rancor in her voice. She understood.

He stumbled out of bed and toward the easy chair where she'd unceremoniously dumped his clothes after ceremoniously removing them. Feeling around in the dark, he located his trousers and fished his cell phone out of the rear pocket. "Hello?" he said, trying to keep any hint of irritation out of his voice.

"Daddy?"

"Cathy?"

"Where are you, Daddy? Where are you?" Her voice sounded quavery, with an almost hysterical edge.

"What is it, honey? What's the matter?"

"Oh, Daddy..." A deep, raspy intake of breath. "It's Mommy..." And then the sobbing began.

~

Dearest Toby,

I realize getting this letter is bound to seem macabre. It may even arrive after I'm six feet under if you were considerate enough to follow Talmudic law. But no matter what you think, I'm doing it for practical reasons, not dramatic effect. I don't want to compromise a certain person who's helped me, at considerable risk to her career and possibly even her liberty. Please don't show this note to the police or let on that you received anything from me. Burn after reading. It's nobody's business anyway. I'll leave another note to throw them off the scent.

Something tells me you won't need an explanation about why I'm doing this. If you were in my position, you'd probably do the same. The cancer has spread; it's only a matter of time—probably not much time—and it wouldn't be pleasant or useful for me to hold out to the bitter end. I don't even know if this is the brave way or the cowardly way, but it's the way I've chosen. End of story.

There isn't a whole lot more to say. Just three things. One is that I still love you and never stopped loving you. No guilt trip, I swear. After all, it's not like there's anything you can do for me now. I just thought you should know. Two is, please please please take good care of Cathy. Give her everything you've got and then a little more. She needs you. She needs us both, is my honest opinion, but she can't have us both, so the ball's in your court. Fucked again, eh, Lindeman? Well, you seem to have softened lately, maybe you won't mind as much as you once might have. Three is, I'm leaving Cathy everything of course. I'm sure you expect that and approve. Not that there's much, but it isn't quite nothing either. Randi Weingarten gets some of the credit, and I've been frugal. But there is one exception. I'm leaving you the house. We bought it together, we lived in it together, it was something we shared during the short time we were happy with one another, and you can probably use it. Besides, I don't think Cathy needs the headache of property ownership just yet. But I forbid you to sell it, at least until Cathy decides it's time to move out. You ever make her feel unwelcome, I'll come back and haunt you. That's a promise. It'll be *bad*. It'll make our marriage seem like a Sunday frolic in Golden Gate Park. Cathy stays in the house till she's good and ready to leave. At that point you can do what you want with it.

I think it's traditional to end this kind of note by saying how you're reconciled to your fate, you accept it, nobody should feel bad for you, etc. Well, 'fraid I'm not there yet. This has all happened much too fucking fast for me to be able to lie like that. I hate what's happened, I cry on a regular basis, I curse the God I don't believe in. But what can I do? Some diseases don't ask for your consent, they just go ahead and kill you.

You're a decent man, Toby. A tight-ass of course, but a pretty good guy. You should try to let people touch you occasionally, though. It wouldn't kill you.

All my love,

Jessie

PART FOUR

PART FOUR

1

IT STILL GAVE TOBY a small jolt to wake up in this house that had been his years before and now was his again. Cathy had been good about letting him have the master bedroom; perhaps she was more comfortable remaining in the room that had been hers all her life.

He took a quick shower, shaved, and dressed. He left his bedroom and walked along the short, uncarpeted hallway, down the short flight of uncarpeted stairs, and through the living room to the kitchen. And encountered an unwelcome surprise.

Cathy was seated at the small table in the breakfast nook, a cup of green tea and a bowl of fresh fruit in front of her. Seated across from her, a mug of coffee in his paw, was Hank Ortega. They had the *Chron* between them, a sugar bowl, and a carton of cream. Hank was reading the front section of the paper, Cathy was paging through *Datebook*. Toby hesitated at the threshold. Cathy looked up and greeted him with a smile and a jaunty, "Top of the morning."

"'Morning," Toby grunted. What choice did he have? He stepped through the doorway into the kitchen. "Hank."

"Hi, Toby." Ortega had a morning stubble darkening his chin, and his thick black hair was a riotous mess, with a couple of rebellious cowlicks thrusting up in different directions. No neat hip ponytail this morning. The bottom of his blue cotton work shirt was out of his jeans. He looked like a man who'd just vacated a bed. It was impossible for Toby not to picture him all over Cathy. Those mitt-like hands, that ropy, compressed body.

Hank at least had the decency to look sheepish. Cathy, on the other hand, seemed unfazed. "I made coffee," she said.

"I see."

"You can probably use some caffeine." A mischievous smile. "Sleep well?"

"During the brief period I was asleep, very well, thank you."

Her smile broadened. "What time'd you get in?"

"Is this a rhetorical question?"

"No, I'm curious. I didn't hear you. We turned in early."

Rubbing his nose in it? Or did she feel so casual about it that she was oblivious to Toby's discomfort? Toby's *and* Hank's, to the latter's credit. Hank grimaced and said, "I'd better get going. Long day ahead."

He rose, took his mug to the sink, gave it a quick rinse, wished Toby a good day—this time with a humorous what-can-you-do look in his eye—and left the room joined by Cathy. Toby heard them murmuring in the foyer, and then he heard the front door open and close.

Moments later, she was back in the kitchen. By then he was pouring himself a cup of coffee, so he had his back to her when she entered, sparing both of them his immediate reaction.

"Seriously," she said, "what time did you get in?"

As if this were all normal, as if Hank's presence at the breakfast table required no explanation, as if the only question worth asking involved Toby's nocturnal habits. Since she wouldn't be able to put him off forever, he chose to answer. "Two-ish."

"I don't know how you manage. This was, what? The third night this week?"

He laughed out loud. "Hey, I'm supposed to be the one who asks the questions. Believe me, I've got a few."

"My life's an open book."

He took a sip of coffee. "Hardly. I don't even know what you do with yourself all day."

As he started to rummage in the refrigerator for something to eat, Cathy said, "Just tell me this and I won't ask anything else. Is it the same girl every night? Or are you out there tomcatting around and taking potluck?"

He found half a grapefruit and some English muffins. He removed them from the fridge. "Why should I even consider answering?" he asked.

"Why shouldn't you? Afraid you'll be a bad role model?"

"As a matter of fact, I'm *not* a bad role model. Not only is it the same girl—or as we enlightened types say, *woman*—it's serious. So there."

"Serious? Really?"

He couldn't tell whether she was pleased or upset. Lately, she seemed to have acquired the emotional opacity Jessica had always attributed to *him*. "Yep. First in a long time."

"Since Mommy?"

"I guess that's right. Since...Jessica." Mentioning her name was hard. Harder for him than for Cathy. Cathy seemed to need to bring Jessica's name up occasionally, as if to reassure herself that her mother had really existed.

"What took you so long, do you think?" she asked.

"I don't know."

"Didn't you feel something was lacking?"

"Not while it was lacking. And now it isn't."

"So who is she? How long has it been going on? How come I haven't met her? Why do you drag yourself home in the middle of the night?"

He'd separated a muffin with a fork, and was putting both halves in the toaster. "Maybe her dad doesn't like bumping into me first thing in the morning," he said.

Cathy laughed outright. "That bothered you?"

"Of course it bothered me."

"A lot?"

"I haven't decided."

She graced him with a silly, affectionate smile. "So okay, what's the story? Come on, throw a girl a crumb."

"You're asking an awful lot of questions."

"There's really only one question."

"We're not going to talk about this anymore."

A mistake. He should have just made up a name. "Sadie Glotz, you don't know her, she's a machinist, her shift starts at five a.m." A mystery was bound to pique her interest. It's what mysteries do.

She looked annoyed for a moment, and then laughed and said, "You're a real pain in the butt, you know that?"

"You've got your secrets, I've got mine."

"But I don't have any left." She hesitated a moment, then said, "Look, this morning will probably be repeated. So we ought to talk about it. I'm not asking permission…"

Toby made a face, but said, "Understood." This was how the Grand Canyon was carved out of the Rockies. Grain by grain. He put the toasted muffin and the grapefruit half on a plate, picked up his cup of coffee, and headed over to the table.

She waited for him to sit down before continuing. "I mean, Hank and I could handle things like you do. Sneaking around. But why bother?"

"To spare my sensibilities?" He dipped a spoon in the grapefruit. "I was under the impression you weren't going to see Hank after graduation. I thought you planned to end it."

"Where'd you get that idea?"

"Him."

"Oh, yeah. I did tell him that. Way back. When he was sort of freaking about everything. Like, what had he gotten himself into? It was to ease his troubled mind."

"You didn't mean it?"

"I meant it at the time."

"Uh-huh." He took a sip of coffee. "This has been going on all summer?"

"There was a gap of a week or two. Then I started to miss him. It wasn't a big secret. I mean, maybe I didn't volunteer the information, but if you'd been less busy you'd have noticed."

"That's a bit disingenuous. If I didn't notice, you must have arranged it that way. Waited till I was out, et cetera."

A half-smile tantamount to confirmation. "The point is, me and Hank, we're basically friends with benefits. No hearts and flowers. Buddies who have sex. Like you and Magda."

Whoo! You never know which pigeons will come home to roost. "Magda was never my high school teacher," he pointed out.

"Yes, there is that difference." She grinned, and there was something triumphant in the grin: These thrusts of his no longer drew blood, and she was pleased to let him know it. "But maybe that's not the key thing. Maybe it's ancient history, especially seeing as how he isn't my teacher anymore. Maybe it's the present relationship that's under discussion."

"Maybe."

"And I start college in a couple of weeks. I'll be living in a dorm. Everything's up for grabs after that. But for now, well, you'll be bumping into Hank from time to time."

Toby sighed. "So I should expect to be greeted by the same happy vision tomorrow?"

"We haven't made any plans."

"Want to come to a party? The Raskovs. You know who she is, right?"

"Your boss."

"General manager of the company. It'll be glitzy. They know everybody."

"Nah. Those grown-up parties aren't for me."

"The mayor might be there."

"Ooh!" She permitted herself an eye roll, and it got a smile from Toby. "Look, thanks for asking, but I'll either hook up with Hank or make it an early night." Then, suddenly earnest, "Listen, can I ask you something? Something serious. Before she died…did you tell Mommy about Hank?"

"Uh-uh. Seemed to me she had enough on her plate. She guessed you had a boyfriend, and she was happy about that. I kept the details to myself."

"That was considerate." She reached across the table and took his hand. "She would have hated it, wouldn't she? She would have died furious. And I'd always worry I'd had something to do with her decision."

"I didn't know what she was planning, obviously, but…I thought it was better she not worry about it. For everybody's sake."

She gave his hand a squeeze. "You're turning into an okay guy, Toby."

She had never called him Toby before. He wasn't sure how he felt about it. He stood up.

She was startled by the abruptness of the gesture. "Where are you going?"

"To change my shirt." The freshly laundered one he had on was soaked through.

∽

WHEN HE ARRIVED IN his office forty-odd minutes later, Daniel greeted him with news his lunch appointment had been cancelled. It was one of the few items on his calendar this late-August day, and Toby was relieved. He'd been scheduled to meet with a wealthy widow who enjoyed making potential recipients of her largesse jump through hoops; she was too rich to ignore, but God, what an annoying person. She had a reputation in the fundraising world, taking delight in summoning young development directors of arts and human rights organizations to dance attendance upon her. She disbursed relatively modest amounts periodically to keep the game in play, but what everyone was jostling for was a substantial bequest in her will. The whole fandango was a travesty worthy of Ben Jonson.

But Toby wasn't proud. You couldn't be proud in a job that, however you dressed it up, involved scrounging for cash. He'd dance attendance upon her with the same energy and solicitude and feigned enthusiasm as his rivals. It was his impression the woman liked him; she might be conveying that impression to everyone else as well, but Toby had the notion he'd wormed his way into her good graces. But the effort required! And the dissimulation, as they discussed everything in the world except her money: the barbaric ugliness of modern music, the vulgarity of modern literature, the greed of San Francisco's unions, the philistinism of her grandchildren. He was more than happy to forgo the experience.

But once behind his desk, he found himself unaccountably restless. Why? And then he suddenly realized: Today was Jessica's birthday. It was a long time since he had celebrated it with her, God knows, but it was a date that ordinarily stayed in his memory.

Acting on a sudden impulse, he reached for the phone and punched in Amy's number. After the customary banter with Priscilla—which had grown more elaborate since their face-to-face meeting the previous spring—he was put through. "What's up?" Amy asked.

He couldn't tell whether she was being breezy or brusque. "Almost nothing at my end," he said. "Bad time at yours?"

"On the contrary. We're having a good month. The last one wasn't too shabby either."

"It must be the vibrators."

"They didn't hurt. We sold a bunch. And other stuff along with them. It was an inspired suggestion, Mr. Toby. Vibrators have been a lifesaver. The rising tide that lifted all my boats."

"I'm not going near that one." After she laughed, he said, "Listen, I'm going to issue a weird invitation. This bizarre impulse just came over me. Feel free to say no."

"I'm not ready for midgets and chains."

"You weren't listening. I said it was weird." And then, "Can we be serious for a sec?"

"Sure."

"See, I haven't...ugh, this is too crazy. Forget it."

"Go on, Toby. At worst, I'll say no."

He hesitated, then plunged in. "See, except for the unveiling of Jesse's headstone, I haven't been to her gravesite. And this whole idea may be irrational and atavistic, but today would have been her birthday, and...I suddenly felt I should go. And this is even crazier, but..."

"You want me to come? Is that what you're asking?"

"That was the general idea," Toby admitted. "But I don't know what I was thinking. Let's pretend this conversation never happened, okay?"

"You were going to...introduce us?"

"Nothing *quite* so nuts. Maybe I just wanted company. Or maybe I thought you two gals might hit it off." He waited for a laugh; he had to settle for a sort of audible smile.

"Tell you what. Throw in lunch and the answer is yes."

"Really?"

"It could be interesting. In a bizarre sort of way."

A couple of hours later, they were standing together at a plot in a Jewish cemetery down the peninsula with a view of the Pacific and far enough from the freeway so you could almost pretend it wasn't there. The headstone gave only Jessica's name and dates. Cathy and Toby had discussed the possibility of a quotation or some sort of characterization—"Beloved Mother and Noodge" was Cathy's suggestion—and decided against it.

After a few minutes during which neither uttered a sound, Amy took his hand and said, "What are you thinking?"

He looked over at her. Her tone was solicitous, not lugubrious. "Remarkably little."

"Okay, what are you *feeling*?"

"Not nearly enough." He hesitated, then went on, "I don't get this whole business. It's not like I think Jessica is *anywhere* anymore, her soul or consciousness or whatever. I believe it all ends with death, insofar as I believe there's a soul, it's a physical phenomenon, an interaction of chemicals. And if she actually *is* somewhere, it definitely ain't here. So it's peculiar to visit the site. I mean, we're not going to sing 'Happy Birthday' or anything."

"You're reading too much into it. It's a natural place to think about the person who died. A peaceful spot to think benign thoughts."

Toby nodded. "I'm starting to feel bad we didn't put more on the headstone. Just the name and dates…as if her life was just…"

"It probably isn't an appropriate place for a character sketch."

"It's all so uncanny. We were together for more than ten years. And because of Cathy, we were never out of each other's lives. It's hard to accept she doesn't exist."

"Do you miss her?"

"I wouldn't put it that way. She was a tremendous presence. Had a lot of vitality, a lot of force. I can still hear her voice. It's easy to guess how she'd react to things. I've dreamt about her." He was under the sway of an emotion so bittersweet, so unfamiliar, he couldn't describe it. "If she hadn't had such a big chip on her shoulder, she'd have been more lovable. But then she wouldn't have been *her*. Truth is, I sometimes even found the chip on her shoulder endearing. My mom and dad were…they were big ones for emotional evasion, you know? Not Jessie. She never felt a need to dissemble."

They relapsed into silence. Toby inhaled deeply; the air was freshened by the proximity of the sea. He felt strangely calm, and melancholy in a way that was almost pleasant.

After a minute, Amy asked, "Would we have gotten along?"

"You and Jess?"

"Mm. If you weren't in the picture, I mean."

"Well, *she* would have liked *you*. You're irresistible."

Amy smiled. "You might be prejudiced."

"No, you're the type of person she went for. She valued directness. She liked women who didn't preen, who said what they meant, who didn't act girlish or incompetent." It struck him this was an odd conversation to be having by Jessica's grave. But it didn't feel like a desecration. "Not sure what you would have made of her. She had a lot of edges. And she was political. Very. Self-righteously. If you didn't agree with her, you were either mean-spirited or stupid. She was great in lots of ways, brave and tough and honest, but she wasn't easy. And she didn't *make* things easy, not on herself or anyone else."

Amy suddenly embraced him. Touched by the gesture, he put his arms around her and held her close. Time seemed, for one magical moment, to freeze into stasis.

"Here's what I think," she said quietly, into his chest. The earth started to turn again. "You grew up with her, really. She had a big hand in making you who you are. I have to like her for that."

He stepped back, his hands still on her shoulders. "If she was being honest, she'd look at you and say she was surprised I had such good taste."

Amy pulled him down toward her to be kissed. And then he heard a voice from some distance away calling, "Toby!" Startled, feeling caught, he pulled away. The "Toby" business threw him; it took him a moment to realize it was Cathy. He stepped away from Amy, at the same time swiveling toward the sound of the voice. His daughter, unaccompanied, was approaching down the gentle incline from the main path some yards away.

"Cathy!" He smiled, and it wasn't entirely feigned. But this could be awkward. If his daughter were feeling possessive about Jessica, and about their intertwined lives, she might regard Amy as an interloper. On hallowed turf.

"I didn't expect to find *you* here," Cathy said, still approaching.

"Nor I you."

"Well, it's Mom's birthday. It felt like the right thing to do."

Toby nodded. "I had a similar feeling."

Cathy was abreast of them, looking at Amy inquisitively. It had to be faced. Toby, with a certain formality, made the introductions.

Amy offered her hand. "I'm so sorry about your mother," she said.

There ensued a moment that extended itself just a fraction of a second beyond what was socially acceptable, the outward sign of an internal tussle. Cathy looked Amy up and down, as if trying to make the picture coalesce. Then, to her everlasting credit, she smiled and took the proffered hand. "Thank you," she said. "It's very nice to meet you. And it's nice you came." She turned back to Toby. "Is this your first time since the unveiling?"

"Uh-huh."

"I've been a few times. Not sure why. Just to remember her, I guess. Try to imagine what she'd say about this and that." She turned to Amy. "My mom and I fought all the time, but we were really close. For a long time, we only had each other."

"You must miss her."

The two women continued looking at each other without saying anything further. It wasn't uncomfortable exactly, but it was, to Toby, an odd interlude. It probably didn't last longer than ten seconds altogether, but it felt like an eternity. Were they sizing each other up? Were they considering what role each might play in the other's life from now on? The moment seemed significant. For Toby too. These were the two most important women—the two most important people—in his life. Whatever their preference in the matter, and whatever they thought of one another, they were now, willy-nilly, in each other's lives as well.

He recalled the day Cathy was born. He'd been in the delivery room, in scrubs and mask, for the final forty minutes of the seemingly endless night, when Jessie finally relented and grudgingly assented to the caesarean the obstetrician had been urging for several hours. After the procedure was over, the pediatrician on duty conducted a brief examination of Cathy, flashed Toby a thumbs-up, probably to indicate he'd found the standard complement of digits, and then brought the infant over and placed her in the arms of a shell-shocked Toby. He held her, and, looking into her face, saw two huge, wide-open blue eyes peering back at him in what appeared to be a frankly inquisitive stare. Of course, he realized it was nothing of the kind—those eyes might not even be capable of sight yet, for all he knew—but still, it seemed to him this tiny neonate was aware she was meeting her father for the first time and was coolly sizing him up.

Something similar seemed to be happening between Cathy and Amy now.

It was Amy who broke the silence. "Toby and I are going to get some lunch. Someplace casual. Will you join us?"

Cathy glanced anxiously over at Toby. It was touching, really: She seemed to be checking for some appalled reaction from him, some indication the invitation was out-of-bounds or she wasn't welcome.

"Yes, do," he therefore put in quickly.

She hesitated. "I'm going to say no," she finally said. "I need to get back to the city."

"We could give you a lift," Toby said.

She looked sheepish. "I've got a car, in fact. Hank lent me his." She noted Toby's grimace with a half-smile and went on, "And he needs it back. I'm just down the road a ways. Walk with me?"

"Right now? You just got here."

"Oh, for Christ's sake, Toby," Amy exploded with an exasperated little laugh, "she wants to talk to you!"

Cathy laughed too, exchanging a brief, amused look with Amy, and then took hold of Toby's arm and led him up to the winding road away from Jessica's plot. After they'd gone about twenty yards, Cathy said, "All I wanted to say is, she's great. I mean really, really great."

"You think?" Toby felt a rush of relief and pleasure, although he kept his voice calm.

"Fabulous. Not your type, of course. No Magda swagger." Cathy made a face before continuing, "She's just...I mean, we exchanged about two words altogether, so what do I know, but she has a quality...there's something completely lovely about her."

"I'm so glad you see it." He pulled her into a hug. "But how did you know...?"

"Oh, puh-leeze."

"It's that obvious?"

"You're nuts about her."

"Head-over-heels."

"That's exactly how it looks. And she likes you too, it's easy to see." Cathy's eyes narrowed shrewdly. "So what's the big secret? Why the two o'clock homecomings?"

"I can't tell you."

"Ugh!"

It was Toby's turn to laugh. Then he said, "You really liked her?"

"I'm prepared to say it as often as you want."

261

"It means a lot to me, kiddo."

"And now your turn: How do you feel about Hank?" As Toby inhaled sharply, Cathy laughed with glee and cried, "Gotcha!"

Toby managed a wan smile. "Yeah. Although, for the record... Listen, not so long ago, I couldn't stand the guy. But maybe he's okay. I'm not sure."

"Whatever. I'm not head-over-heels nuts about him, so it doesn't matter. He *is* a great lay, though." When Toby's mouth fell open and he made a sputtering noise, she yelled a second, triumphant, "Gotcha!"

~

THE RASKOVS' HOUSE WAS on Broadway near the Presidio: a grand old house resembling a Venetian palazzo. When you entered the black and white marble-floored foyer on this particular evening, a butler welcomed you, and another, holding a salver, asked if you wanted a glass of champagne or white wine—evidently no spirits were on offer, to Toby's disappointment—and then indicated the elevator, which whisked you up to the second floor, where the party was in progress.

The art on the walls was museum quality. Mostly post-war American, Rothko, de Kooning, a big Lichtenstein; but Toby, as he strolled down a corridor past the large living room, also noticed a Utrillo and a Chagall. In the library off the dining room, a string quartet was playing, or appeared to be; from the hall, the music was inaudible above the hubbub of conversation. All over the house, serving staff in black-and-white uniforms were circulating with drinks and canapés.

The party was announced for eight o'clock. Toby had made a point of not arriving before nine, but, although the decibel level suggested otherwise, guests were just beginning to dribble in. Which meant Doris was able to spot him as he was about to step into the library, glass of wine in his hand, wondering what he was doing here and how awkward he would find the evening. It also meant she could afford the time to swoop down on him.

"Toby! So good of you to come." She was wearing some sort of pants-and-toreador-jacket get-up, gold and black. It flattered her. The tight trousers revealed disconcertingly good legs. The gestalt was startlingly different from the frumpish way she presented herself at work. Her hair was different too, unbunned and free.

She offered a cheek to be kissed. He did what the situation required. "So good of you to invite me," he said. The invitation was a first; he'd never been to her house before, and never to any of her parties other than the office Christmas party, which didn't count. "This place is magnificent, Doris."

"Thank you." She gave him a curious look, as if she were seeing him for the first time. It *was* odd to encounter each other outside of the Opera House and to be engaged in something other than opera business.

"It's like a palace."

"Well...we're rich." She laughed, as if surprised at herself for blurting out a tightly held secret. Toby laughed too. "Not like your pal Brad, but rather disgustingly all the same. But we have a motley crowd coming tonight, not just Mike's boring money friends. Arty types and media types, etc. Plus the inescapable opera types. So I hope you'll manage to enjoy yourself."

"I'm sure I shall."

She frowned. "Christ, I feel like such a fucking *hostess* at these things!" Sounding more like the Doris he thought he knew. "Ignore me till I get a little wine in me, I won't be nearly so stiff after that." She plucked a glass of champagne from a waitress who was passing by with a tray and took a quick sip. "One other thing before I send you off to work your wiles on every lady in the place. It's business, I'm afraid."

"Okay."

"I'm anxious to get a look at the libretto Brian and Jeremy have cooked up."

"Have you asked them?"

"I've asked Brian. Of course. Repeatedly. He says yes, but then does nothing or makes up an excuse. He's coming tonight—so's Metcalf—but I despair about getting him to comply. You seem to have a facility for dealing with impossible people. Brad, and Brian, and, and *me*." A quick smile. "Let's face it, the world is *awash* in difficult people. Will you please put a flea in Brian's ear about this? Impress upon him I regard the matter as vitally important."

"Sure thing."

"I have a legal right to demand a copy, but it shouldn't have to come to that."

"Clearly. I'll talk to him."

"It doesn't have to be tonight. But soon, yes?" He nodded. "Good. Now scoot. Deploy your charm. Stay away from the married ones, though. I don't want an ugly fracas in my living room."

"Yes'm."

She patted his arm and moved off. He stood rooted in place for a moment, at a loss, then continued into the library. A passing waiter had a tray of sushi. Toby took a slice of California roll, dipped it in a bowl of soy sauce, and gobbled it down. Delicious. He grabbed another and then stepped further into the room.

A splendid room, lined from waist to ceiling with antique leather-bound books. Green leather furniture. Persian carpeting. A large fireplace with a roaring fire. There were a few small conversational groupings in the room already, but none seemed welcoming. The quartet was playing "Night and Day." Some songs can withstand anything. Toby took a few further steps into the room and plopped down on a sofa to collect himself before embarking on any social adventures or misadventures.

As he was draining his glass of wine, he heard his name called. He looked over toward the doorway to the dining room. Magda had just come through it, bearing down on him.

"What in the name of God are *you* doing here?" she demanded. Her manner was as extravagant as always, but also, perhaps, less friendly. She spoke loudly enough so that several people glanced her way.

"Hi." He hadn't seen her since the ill-fated goulash night. Would there be any awkward residue? "I work with Doris, remember. But how about you? These aren't your people."

"*Everyone's* my people. I know them all." Still standing, she leaned down toward him.

"You have a face-pass?"

"When all else fails. I never get turned away. But tonight a date brought me."

"Where is he?"

"We've fanned out. A wise policy at parties, I find. Being observed cramps one's style."

"Anyone I know?"

"I shouldn't think so. Not your sort of person at all."

"I wonder what that means."

Her lips were smiling, but there was no amusement in her eye. Indeed, to Toby, her look was almost malevolent.

"Should I be jealous?"

"Not much point, is there? Besides…" She frowned crossly. "To be frank, I don't find empty flirtation gallant. It's just boring."

Toby was stumped for a response. He held up his glass. Under the circumstances, its emptiness could be regarded as serendipitous. "I need a refill," he announced, and stood. She granted him a dismissive nod.

He crossed into the dining room. A group of servants were there, setting up chafing dishes. Their busy presence discouraged socializing; the room was otherwise empty. He kept walking, emerging into a corridor, and then turned left toward the large living room.

The house was fuller than when he'd arrived, and, as he could see now, more people—a veritable clown's car worth—were debouching from the elevator. The noise level was commensurately higher, and the temperature inside the house had climbed perceptibly.

As he was entering the living room, he noticed out of the corner of his eye that among those exiting the elevator were Brad and Amy. He felt a jolt but didn't stop walking, just turned sharply away. Interesting that neither he nor she had mentioned the party during the day's visit to the cemetery, their lunch at an Italian joint in Hillsborough, or the hours of indolent lovemaking at her apartment. Probably because they arrived here from regions of their lives independent of the one they shared. The only point of contact was Solomon.

The sight of Amy and Brad together, while unwelcome, wasn't intolerable. They hadn't all been together under the same roof since the epochal Republican fundraiser almost six months before, when everything changed so radically. But he'd known something like this was bound to happen at some point, and while he'd anticipated discomfort, he'd been living with the prospect long enough, and their affair itself was going well enough, he guessed he could manage.

As he stepped into the living room, a waiter, wandering by with a large tray of drinks, almost collided with a woman who had pivoted around suddenly and heedlessly. The resultant collision wouldn't have been a minor mishap; only the waiter's quick reaction, a fancy sidestep deftly executed, averted catastrophe. Not a drop was spilled. He looked at Toby and beamed. With relief, yes, and also pleasure in his own balletic reflexes. And possibly with a flirtatious little suggestion to Toby. Toby found gay attention flattering. There was something pure about it; it was usually free of any agenda beyond itself.

Except where Brian was concerned.

"Smooth," he murmured, reaching over for a fresh glass of wine.

"Glad I had a witness," the waiter murmured back.

Toby pushed farther into the room and saw Mike Raskov at the far end, champagne in hand, talking to a group of four people. Mike waved him over. He finally seemed aware he knew Toby, although it was an open question whether he knew how or why. And waving at a guest in your own home was pretty safe. No points for Mike yet.

Toby noticed a very tall Black man standing by the matte black concert grand in a far corner of the room. It took him a moment to recognize Jeremy Metcalf. The only other time they'd met, Metcalf had been in jeans and a T-shirt with a red bandana tied around his head. Now he was wearing a loose-fitting cream-colored linen suit and an open-neck white silk shirt. He looked like a male model, implausibly tall, implausibly lean, exotically handsome, elegantly posed. But he also seemed lost, standing alone, sipping from a flute of champagne, surveying the room and apparently not knowing where to turn. It awakened Toby's fellow-feeling. Two lost souls. Toby headed in his direction.

When he noticed, Jeremy broke into a wide smile. "Toby!" he exclaimed in his deep, slow voice. "Great to see you, man." He grasped Toby's extended hand and shook it. "What a relief! I'm a fish out of water among these rich folk."

"Me too, Jeremy."

"I would've thought this was the Money Man's natural habitat."

"They let me pick their pockets, but they rarely allow me into their homes."

Jeremy put his champagne glass on the piano. "I haven't had a chance to thank you. Brian says the commission wouldn't have happened without your help."

"I'm glad it worked out. How's it coming?"

Jeremy hesitated. Then he said, "Brian says not to talk about it. But it must be okay to tell you it's coming along. I'm working hard. Having a blast." A slow smile took hold of him.

"I can't wait to hear some of it." And then, remembering himself, "By the way, Doris Raskov wants to see the libretto."

"That's fine."

"She says she's asked more than once."

"I'll mention it to Brian. I don't have a problem with that."

"She's legally entitled, you know."

Jeremy had looked away and was now reaching for his champagne glass resting on the piano. Was Toby wrong in thinking he perceived something furtive in the way Jeremy had broken eye-contact? Probably just his own mindset; nothing about this project had been straightforward from the get-go.

It was at that moment that Doris herself glided up. "You must be Jeremy!" she declared.

"What makes you say that?" asked Jeremy.

"Well...I mean..." And then she realized she was being teased and smiled. "Somebody mentioned you were tall." Which had the ice-breaking effect of causing Jeremy to smile back. Toby made the introductions, and Doris said, "I'm glad to meet you finally. It's overdue."

Jeremy bowed slightly. "I want to thank you for inviting me tonight. You have an exquisite home, Mrs. Raskov."

"That's because she's rich," Toby put in mischievously.

She gave Toby a playful—largely playful—swat on his upper arm. "That wasn't to be repeated, Toby."

"It's okay," said Jeremy, "I'd pretty much worked it out for myself."

Doris made a face. "Yes, well, nobody's perfect."

Jeremy laughed, a low, honeyed chuckle. This encounter, Toby reflected, was going okay. It wasn't without hazards. Then Jeremy said, "I was just admiring your Bösendorfer. It's a beauty."

"Would you like to play it?"

"You mean…now?"

"If you feel like it. It isn't a requirement or anything."

"Wow! Sure!" Sounding very boyish. As he walked around to the keyboard side of the piano, he added, "Not that I'm a real pianist. Not like Brian. I just…tinkle." He pulled back the piano bench and sat down.

An interesting moment, Toby thought: What would the guy play? Splosion? Something classical? The opera? Brian would be apoplectic if *that* happened.

Jeremy pushed up the lid of the piano, played a tentative chord or two.

"I just had it tuned," Doris said.

Jeremy nodded, and played a couple of additional chords to test the piano's touch. The sequence sounded hymn-like. In the room, conversations were stopping. People were turning toward the sound.

"Beautiful action," Jeremy said. "Plush. A fur coat." He played a few more chords, and then, without any noticeable preparation, launched into an intricate little figure with his left hand, bouncy, staccato, off the beat. No pedal. After a couple of bars of this vamping figure, he slammed down two stabbing dissonances with his right hand, seemingly unconnected to the bass-line, did the same thing again a bar later, and then slyly segued into a melody. It was so embroidered with filigree that Toby needed a few seconds to recognize it: "I Feel Pretty."

The choice made Toby laugh out loud. Jeremy probably did feel pretty; hell, he *was* pretty. And it was a perfect choice in this setting, sophisticated and familiar. Who would have figured that, along with everything else, Jeremy knew show tunes? And Jesus, the guy could play. That earlier show of modesty was absurd. His chops were incredible. Close your eyes, you could almost think you were listening to Art Tatum.

He stopped after about five minutes, abruptly, mid-phrase, with an embarrassed laugh. "Well…anyway…" he mumbled.

The room erupted in applause. He shook his head uncomfortably. Considering that he was a professional performer—and his magnificent leonine stage presence the night Toby had seen Splosion—it was odd how awkward he appeared.

"That was wonderful!" Doris said. "Fabulous!"

"Thanks…I was just…"

"More? Will you play some more?"

"No, no, I…maybe later…" He closed the piano lid and slowly stood, unfurling his long body. When he stepped away from the piano bench, people began to crowd around him. Well, thought Toby, now he's in for it. But maybe not, maybe the modesty was an act, maybe this was the way he went about establishing himself.

Doris sidled up to Toby and murmured, "Okay, I'm not too stubborn to say it: *Wow.*"

"He's very talented."

"And gorgeous! We have to feature him in the promotion campaign. A face like that could bring in a lot of new people."

"And launch a ship or two."

She unexpectedly kissed his cheek. "You did good, Toby."

"I had nothing to do with it," he protested, but somebody was pulling Doris away from him. Probably to ask about Jeremy.

Feeling claustrophobic in the growing press of people, he squeezed his way out of the room and back toward the library. It was becoming harder to move around now that the place had filled up. The library itself was a good deal more crowded than it had been before, but the sofa remained unoccupied. The people who were in the room were standing in little clumps, talking. Toby took a seat, facing the string quartet. He recognized the players from the opera pit. The cellist nodded to him as he seated himself, and he nodded back.

A few minutes later, he felt someone sit down on the sofa next to him. He looked over. Amy! She had a napkin and a plate of food on her lap and cutlery in her hands. The food seemed to be some sort of curried chicken and basmati rice, pleasantly aromatic, and a salad.

"Hi there," she said with a smile when their eyes met.

He returned the smile. Couldn't help it. And immediately recalled their lovemaking earlier that day. The slow, sweaty languor. The delicious, transgressive dirtiness that made them both laugh out loud at their bold mischief as well as startled pleasure. Her melodious little cries when she came. And now here she was beside him, composed and respectable in a simple navy dress, dignified, self-possessed, almost distant (except for those sly sparkling eyes).

"Well, hi," he said. "They've started serving?"

"Yep," she confirmed. "Long line. Like flies on carrion in there."

"Attractive image," he said, and then, more quietly, "I saw you and Brad before. That's why I wasn't surprised just now."

"You've been avoiding me?"

"Something like that."

She took a bite of food. "I won't take it personally."

"You shouldn't. What you should take personally is what happened earlier."

"I remember." The salacious look in her eye suggested she remembered it vividly. She lowered her voice. "I can still feel you. The notorious phantom dick phenomenon."

"Ah." He felt a distinct stirring, which, paradoxically, reminded him they were in a public setting. He stole a quick, apprehensive glance around the library.

She caught it. "Brad's in the other room. Ran into some guy from City Hall, they're having a lively chat about zoning."

"Pity to miss that."

After a brief moment, in a different tone of voice, she said, "It was great to meet Cathy today. I liked her very much. It was a tricky situation, and she handled it with total grace."

"Yeah, she's turning out okay." He realized with a little start of pleasure that he meant it. She *was* turning out okay. A force to be reckoned with for sure, but more power to her. "She liked you too. She said so, but I could tell before she said a word."

"I'm glad. I'd hate for her to think of me as an interloper."

"She said you were lovely. That's a quote. I'm starting to worry you two might like each other so much you'll run off and leave me."

"Unlikely. There are benefits only you can provide. I think you know the ones I mean."

"Mmm."

Lowering her voice further, she said, "You're getting hard, aren't you?"

"Why do you say that?"

"You make that noise when you start to get hard. A kind of growl." An affectionate, almost complacent smile was spreading across her face.

"Do I?" He was grinning back at her. "I'd better learn to control it."

"Not on my account. Helps me get my bearings."

They smiled at each other. It was like an electric current between them, so palpable Toby could almost hear it humming. "Come home with me," he said quietly.

"You know I can't."

"I know you won't. I don't know you can't."

He suddenly felt the weight of a hand on his shoulder. It nearly made him jump. He looked up, craning his neck to the right. Standing behind the sofa was Brad Solomon, leaning over them both, one hand on Toby's shoulder, the other on Amy's. "Hello, you two."

How much had he overheard? Christ. His tone sounded mocking. Toby forced a smile. "Brad." He could feel adrenaline jolting up his spine.

"You two look mighty cozy. Enjoying yourselves?"

"Very much so," said Amy. A cool customer.

"When'd you get so chummy?"

"You remember," Amy said. "Some function. You asked Toby to take me home. Hasty departure. A few months ago."

"Oh yes." Solomon colored at the memory.

"We bonded making our escape from all those Republicans," said Toby. This was a slightly bold stroke, but boldness, suggesting insouciance, might be the right tack.

It got a thin smile from Solomon. "Standing there in the doorway, watching you two—" Brad chuckled. "If I didn't know better, I'd start worrying."

"Guys like Toby are the ones you *should* worry about," Amy said brightly, opting for boldness as well. "They know how to talk to us girls."

"I'm not worried about talk," said Brad. "Go ahead, compare fashion tips and beauty secrets to your hearts' content."

"Brad!" exclaimed Amy. "Honestly!" She contrived to sound indignant on Toby's behalf. "That's just completely not okay."

Brad shrugged, then turned to Toby. "No offense. I was just *ootzing* you."

"Of course." Toby forced a friendly smile. But the face looking back at him wasn't smiling, and didn't seem especially friendly. Not *un*friendly, quite, but thoughtful, wary, alert. Hazard lights were definitely flashing.

"All right," said Toby, standing up abruptly, "I'm hungry. Can I get you anything, Brad?" He made the offer so he wouldn't seem to be running away, although, of course he was.

"No thanks." And then, a second later, "Listen, was I out of line? It's hard to know these days what's okay to joke about and what's off-limits."

"No problem," Toby said. "Water off a duck's back."

A sitting duck if he wasn't careful.

He left the library and pushed into the dining room. There were a number of large chafing dishes on the buffet table, with plates, napkins, and cutlery at one end. The long queue of people was moving slowly. He positioned himself at its tail.

When he finally reached the food, he helped himself to some salad and accepted a portion of rice and curry being ladled out by a waitress. Then, while sprinkling coconut flakes over his curry and taking a glass of wine, he noticed that Brian and Jonas had joined the rear of the queue. Plate, napkin, and cutlery in one hand, glass of wine in the other, he went to greet them.

After a quick hello, he said to Jonas, "I need to borrow you. It'll only take a minute."

"Borrow me?"

"Just for a minute. Please. It's for a noble cause."

"Me too?" Brian asked.

"Nope. This is for Jonas solo."

"Violists don't get many solos."

When he had Jonas some distance from the table, Toby said in an undertone, "I'm going to introduce you to Brad and Amy."

"I finally get to meet her."

"Yeah, but that's not the point. Just listen, okay? I'm not going to say anything that isn't true—that would be too reckless—but I am going to leave a false impression. And when I do, don't look startled, and don't contradict me."

Jonas was staring at him curiously. "Is this an emergency?"

"I don't think it is, quite. But a train of thought is about to leave the station, and I need to switch it onto another track before it gathers steam."

"All right, here's the deal." Jonas said. "I'll do whatever you ask provided you promise never to use a metaphor again."

Toby harrumphed and, still holding his plate and cutlery and wine, led Jonas into the library. Brad and Amy were on the sofa. Amy was eating, and Brad was talking to her. Toby guided Jonas toward them. They looked up. "Brad, Amy, I'd like you to meet Jonas Glasman. Jonas, say hello to Bradley Solomon and Amy Baldwin."

Brad didn't sound especially enthusiastic when he said, rather curtly, "Hello." He offered his hand, but he didn't rise.

While Jonas shook Brad's hand, Toby said, "Jonas is…well, I guess you'd call him my best friend. My special friend. I thought you all should meet."

It worked. A little something, some sort of process, was visible behind Brad's eyes, and then, sounding friendlier, he said, "Oh! I see! Pleasure to meet you."

Jonas looked amused, but he stayed in role. After exchanging a quick nod with Amy, acknowledging the oddity of the situation, he said to Brad, "I've heard a lot about you. But you don't seem that bad." Which won him a grin from Solomon. Then Jonas said something about getting something to eat, and the deed was done.

After he and Toby returned to the buffet, Jonas muttered, "Shrewdy-pants."

"Just buying a little insurance. That was excellent. Thank you."

In their absence, Brian had been joined by Jeremy. Both had plates in their hands. Toby and Jonas approached them. "What was that about?" Brian asked.

"Toby wanted me to meet someone," Jonas said. Bless him, he was opting for discretion.

"Straight?" Brian's suspiciousness seemed intended humorously.

"Hundred percent."

"There's no such thing. But I'll settle."

Jonas said, "Give me a minute, I need food," and went to rejoin the buffet line. Toby nodded to Brian and Jeremy and moved off. Every seat in the room was occupied. He leaned against a wall, placing his glass of wine on a side table, and ate what was on his plate, although the food had gotten cold. He was feeling uneasy. Secrets are vulnerable things. It's easy to forget that until life reminds you.

He drained his glass of wine, and realized he didn't want to stay. The party was just kicking into gear, but he was confident he could slink off without attracting notice. He was anxious, though: Jonas certainly hadn't been invited, he was here as Brian's date. If Doris took it into her head to introduce Brian to Solomon, and Jonas was somehow included... Calamity! Well, it was a worst-case scenario, no point brooding about it. It was beyond Toby's control in any event. Too fucking much was beyond his control.

He set his wine glass on the side table and left the room, heading down the corridor toward the elevator. He was near it—freedom within his grasp—when he came face to face with Doris. Bad timing. She'd observed his trajectory.

"You're not going?" she asked.

"Have to, Doris. It's a terrific party, but I have to be somewhere."

"The mayor's in the other room. Don't you want to meet her?"

"I just can't."

"Have a date, do you?" She smiled affectionately. "Oh, Toby, you're going to come to a bad end." They both laughed, although Toby had to force it. Still, her attitude seemed so benign he briefly considered asking her not to introduce Brian to Solomon. Invent some reason why it would be a bad idea. But no reason he could offer would make any sense. "The life you lead must be awfully draining," she added.

"You have no idea." He gave her cheek a light kiss. "Thanks for having me."

She touched his face: A benediction.

He stepped into the elevator. Just as he pressed the down button, Magda slipped into the cage, followed by a man whose hand she was holding. About Toby's age, taller than Toby, blandly handsome, Brooks Brothers head to toe. The elevator door closed. Toby said hello. Magda nodded, but didn't introduce her companion.

The elevator made its short descent. As the door was opening, Magda caught Toby's eye, shook her head, and said, "Oh Toby...I knew it had to be bad, but this is even worse than I imagined."

274

2

TOBY WAS STARTLED AWAKE by a ringing telephone. At first, barely conscious, operating automatically, he was confused by his whereabouts. He reached for the phone with his left hand and found nothing, just empty air. His head was clearing. He flopped to his right and his hand encountered the bedside table. A little more groping and he found the phone. Oh yes. He was in Jessie's house. His house. He lived in Jessie's house. Jessie's house was his house.

"Hello?" he said. And opened his eyes, and saw the time on his bedside clock. 2:57 a.m. Christ. Who could be calling at this ungodly hour? His first thought—he was still half-asleep—was that it must be some crisis with Jessie.

Then he remembered Jessie was dead—this happened in under a second—and thought, with a nasty internal jolt that fully woke him, it must concern Cathy. Something bad. No one calls at three a.m. for anything good. Even as he was going through this groggy process, he heard a male voice saying, "Toby? I'm really sorry, this is…" Whoever was calling had started crying, or perhaps hyperventilating, it was impossible to tell which.

Could it be Jonas? It sounded like him, almost. The voice was stretched so taut it was hard to be sure. "Jonas?"

"Can you get over here? It's an emergency."

"Where is here?"

"Brian's house. Our house. His and mine."

"Is everything all right?"

"No."

"Is everyone alive?"

"Yeah, it isn't life-and-death anymore."

Anymore? "Give me a minute."

Toby went through the motions like an automaton. An *efficient* automaton: He pulled on jeans and a sweatshirt and gym shoes, grabbed his wallet, left the house, fortuitously managed to get a Lyft almost immediately, and made it over to the Haight, all in under half an hour. His speed was motivated by curiosity almost as much as concern. What the hell was going on?

When he reached the house, the front door was ajar. He knocked, received no answer, entered, and, hearing voices down the hall, followed the sound, soon reaching the kitchen.

The first thing he saw was two uniformed cops: a burly, sandy-haired guy and a short Hispanic woman, so short Toby figured they'd relaxed the requirements to let her join. Then he noticed Jonas, leaning back against the sink, a dreamy half-smile on his face. And then Brian, seated at the kitchen table, his face a shocking bloody mass of bruises and abrasions. His right eye was swollen closed, his nose caked with dried blood, his lower lip cracked and puffy.

Toby, stifling a gasp, tapped the doorframe as a kind of symbolic knocking. Everyone turned in his direction. The two cops eyed him warily. Brian's expression—as far as you could tell through the gore—was blank. No one said anything.

"Anyone care to shed a little light here?" Toby finally said.

"Who the fuck are you?" the male cop snapped.

"It's all right," said Jonas. "He's a friend."

"Terrific," said the cop, weary and disgusted. "Another one."

"Jonas? What happened?"

"Domestic disturbance," the woman cop said, very drily.

"Domestic disturbance?" Could that mean Jonas had given Brian that face? Christ.

"Just shut up, okay?" said the male cop. He turned to Brian. "So what's it gonna be, pal? You want to press charges, we'll haul you both in, you can make a statement. Otherwise, we'll take you to an emergency room, get you fixed up. Your choice."

"The thing to bear in mind," said the woman, "is, you file a complaint, it's public record. It'll be in *The Chron*. Probably local TV as well. And social media, of course." Her face suddenly brightened. "Won't just be you with the black eye. The opera'll have one too."

Brian had his head in his hands. "Just get me to a doctor," he mumbled. And then, to Jonas, with a snarl, "Don't be here when I get back."

"I wasn't planning to," said Jonas. He still had the half-smile on his face. "Your stuff too."

"That I can't promise. Might have to come back for it."

"Fuck you."

"All right," said the woman roughly, rapping her hand on the table, "that's enough." Another sudden incongruous smile. "I don't think you want to get him riled, Mr. Hughes. You should know that by now. He can take you."

The male cop looked over at Toby. "You wanna make yourself useful, Shirley? Get this guy outta here."

"Shirley?" Toby could have been affronted, knew he should be, but laughed instead.

"You'll have to forgive Denny," the woman said. "He sometimes forgets his sensitivity training." She was laughing too.

"This isn't funny," Jonas said. Plaintively, but he wasn't immune to the humor. Maybe it was the hour, or the sheer weirdness of what was happening, but a kind of hysteria was gathering steam; the cops were laughing, and Toby, and, after a moment, however reluctantly, Jonas. Only Brian seemed unaffected by the mounting hilarity, staring down at his kitchen table without moving, shoulders slumped, while the others dissolved in giddy laughter.

Less than a half hour later, Toby and Jonas were in a Lyft heading toward Cow Hollow. Jonas had a large suitcase and his viola with him. They hadn't spoken much, but now Jonas said, "For a minute there, I thought the *chica* was gonna ask Brian for an autograph."

"Nah, she was being smart. She let him know he was recognized. It was strategic. To keep him from pressing charges, to nip this thing in the bud." After Jonas nodded his acceptance of the point, Toby went on, "You want to tell me what happened? Was it Jeremy?"

"You knew?"

"Just a guess. But it seemed obvious all of a sudden."

"It does, doesn't it? On some level I must've known for months. Without knowing. I could smell it, but I wouldn't acknowledge it."

"And something happened tonight?"

"Something happened, right. Don't make me go into it, okay?" He sighed. "It isn't that we expect fidelity. It doesn't work like that. We mess around. Sometimes together. But this breaks all rules. "

Toby nodded. He got the gist.

Jonas went on, "There's a very narrow silver lining: It happened before the wedding."

"Oh Jesus, I forgot all about that."

"Three weeks away." He snorted. "Brian came out to his mother for nothing. Unless that was the real point all along, and I was just a means to an end."

"You sure it won't still happen? Maybe you can work it out. People do."

"Not this time."

His tone was so final, Toby changed the subject. "You did quite a job on him, I'll give you that. I think you broke his nose."

"Never underestimate the fury of a viola-playing Jew fairy."

"I've seen you play racquetball, I knew you had a vindictive streak. He didn't lay a glove on you, did he?"

"You should have seen him." Jonas, with exaggerated effeminacy, put his hands over his face and pretended to cower. "Don't hurt me, please don't hurt me!" And then he laughed bitterly, one short harsh burst. "Hope I didn't damage my hands." He held them out and flexed his fingers. "I was just getting started. If a neighbor hadn't heard the commotion and called the cops, Brian would be known forever after as 'Maestro Gummy.'"

"You probably shouldn't enjoy this too much."

"Believe me," Jonas said, and turned away to look out the window. After a minute or two, he said, "I gave up my fucking apartment." He didn't sound self-pitying, he sounded irate. "Had it ten years. Walking distance to the Opera House. Affordable. *His* fucking idea. 'Let's make a real commitment,' he says. Meanwhile, Mr. Real Commitment's blowing Jeremy Metcalf every chance he gets. Which is plenty because of their goddamned opera. And now I'm totally fucked. The miserable bastard."

"You can stay with Cathy and me as long as you need."

"That's good of you, Shirley."

"We have a guest room. Small, but not horrible."

There was another silence. Jonas must have been considering for the first time the ramifications of what he'd done. He muttered, "It'll be weird going to work tomorrow."

"Weirder for Brian, with the face you gave him. Getting up in front of everybody."

"Oh man," agreed Jonas. And then, "I guess I should have thought things through before wailing on him."

"Well, yes, acts of impulsive mayhem really ought to be preceded by careful planning."

"This could get messy."

"Can he fire you?"

"The union protects me, thank God. Otherwise, he might be vindictive enough to do it. He *could* try to demote me from first chair. Needs the consent of the players' committee, so it depends how they feel. Pissed at Brian for trying to shape the orchestra to fit his love life, or at me for getting involved with him. They never liked that. No one said anything, not to me at least, and we were pretty discreet. But you can't keep shit like that totally secret, and there's a kind of unwritten rule we broke. So they might decide Brian's a crapulous bastard, or they might think I'm getting my comeuppance."

It was tempting to pile on, to express one's longstanding mistrust and even dislike of Brian, to feel free, finally, to give vent to all the complaints held in check for so long. But it was a bad idea. For one thing, Jonas and Brian might reconcile. No matter what Jonas said now and how definitively he said it, he might reconsider after a while. The blow-up was only an hour old; there were still many emotional stages in store. Should that happen, Toby would very much regret having shared his misgivings. Besides, no matter how angry he was, Jonas was unlikely to enjoy hearing anyone else abuse Brian. Jonas's rage belonged to himself.

"God," said Jonas, "now that I think about the wedding, and how he pushed for it, and the hassles we went through…what could he have been thinking?"

"He likes drama," Toby suggested.

"Goes without saying. He's an opera conductor. But that hardly begins to cover it." He turned away again, directing his attention out the window. A moment later, he began to cry. He made no sound, but the way his shoulders were shaking was unmistakable. After a few seconds, he said in a choked whisper, "My taste in guys is abominable."

Toby reminded himself how patient and sympathetic Jonas had been when he and Jessica split. These were the moments that tested a friendship, and also the moments that justified it. Fail to be worthy now and you've failed the only test that matters.

"You once told me love is self-hypnosis. Remember?"

"I did, didn't I?"

"You were fairly persuasive on the subject."

"Did I convince you?"

"No."

"There you go."

"Are you disavowing the notion now?"

Jonas took out a handkerchief and blew his nose. Then he said, "Haven't decided." A sigh. "Look, I know I'll get past this. It's just… before I get past it, I have to get through it. I'm going to be hurting a while. Like that Linda Ronstadt song."

"You seem to be doing okay."

"I'm in shock. The bad stuff is still around the corner." He turned his head and met Toby's glance. His eyes were red, and he looked very tired, but he managed a wan smile.

Love is such a mystery, was Toby's uninspired thought. How could Jonas, so skeptical, so shrewd, have fallen for Brian Hughes, whose personal failings were so ineptly camouflaged? Did something happen when they were alone that no one else could guess at? It didn't have to be sexual; given Jonas's technicolor sexual history, it probably wasn't. But still, Jonas, no cockeyed romantic, no blushing ingénue, must have found something in Brian that answered to something deep within himself, the future absence of which rendered him inconsolable.

Maybe it was Toby who had a blind spot where Brian was concerned. After all, Brian was the only person Toby knew who had an actual fan club. True, it consisted almost entirely of people who'd never met him, old ladies and lonely gay guys. Nevertheless, Jonas had company.

"Tell me something," Toby said now. He pressed ahead with the question before he had the chance to think better of it. "You're so angry at him that you beat the crap out of him. Do you...do you still love him?"

Jonas nodded and started to cry again.

~

TOBY DIDN'T KNOW WHAT to expect when he strode into Brian's office the next morning. An existential moment. But he had a job to do.

Brian was seated at his desk, looking down at some papers. When he glanced up, Toby almost gasped. His right eye was badly discolored, there were cuts on his cheek, his lower lip was swollen with a jagged black line perpendicular to the lip itself, and there was a big white bandage covering his nose.

"*Ecce homo*," he said grandly as Toby ventured further into the room. "That's Latin for 'behold the homo.'"

Toby smiled uncertainly. He'd been unsure what reception to expect, and this joke—showing considerable panache under the awkward circumstance—provided no enlightenment.

"Look, before anything else, there's something I need to say—"

"Just don't make it funny, okay? It's my lip. If I laugh, the cut'll open." He spoke as if he had a speech impediment, moving his mouth with evident care, his words thick, his consonants muddy. But he sounded perfectly cordial.

"It won't be funny, Brian. I just wanted to say...look, you and I are professionals, we're associates, we have a job to do, and what happened between you and Jonas has no bearing on that. I hope that's your feeling too."

Brian looked surprised. "Of course," he said. "To hell with Jonas."

Toby bridled. "That *isn't* what I'm saying. Jonas is my best friend. He's living in my house right now, as a matter of fact. I want to be clear: I'm not casting my lot with you against him. I'm simply prepared to do my job, and I hope you and I can leave the other stuff aside."

Brian began to frown, but sudden pain stopped the process. "He tried to kill me," he said.

"See, that's a perfect example of the kind of conversation I don't want to have."

Brian's brow furrowed, which, given the state of his right eye, probably hurt as well. "I needed nine stitches. He broke my nose. How can you defend him?"

"I'm not defending him. I'm just not discussing him."

Much more curtly, Brian said, "All right, is that all you came to say?"

"No, it isn't. I also came to tell you Doris wants a copy of the libretto."

"Yeah, fine, I—"

"Today."

"That may not be possible."

"I think you have to make it possible. She has a right to see it." Doris had told him to play rough if necessary. She'd been dicked around enough, she said. Corner the bastard if need be. "A contractual right, not just a moral claim."

"Too bad. What's she going to do, call the sheriff?"

"Do you plan to push it that far?"

"I'm not pushing anything. I'm saying she may have to wait. I don't have it here."

First sign of weakness. Conceding the general point, at least implicitly, by falling back on a practical excuse. "It isn't on your computer?"

"No."

"Can't you get somebody to fetch it from your house?"

"You telling me what to do?" Brian looked at Toby levelly. He deployed a good stare, more intimidating than Toby might have guessed. Especially considering that eye and the bandage over his nose. This must be how he skewered players who fluffed their entrances.

"No, Brian, I wouldn't dream of telling you what to do. I'm conveying a request from the general manager. And trying to convey some of the urgency she expressed. It's in the form of a request as a courtesy, but you should probably regard it as an order."

Brian abruptly stood up. "Let me tell you something, friend." It was almost comical, the tough-guy demeanor he was affecting in combination with the muzzy pronunciation. He leaned across his desk toward Toby, gesturing with his index finger. "You're backing the wrong horse. If it comes to a face-off, I'm not the one who'll lose."

"Why is everything a conflict with you?"

Brian shook his head, disgusted. What a nerve. "Tell Doris she'll have her libretto soon. I don't know when exactly, but soon."

"There's no reason she can't have it tomorrow. Even taking everything you say at face value, you can bring a copy when you come to work. If you don't, she'll probably consult counsel. I hope it doesn't come to that."

He waited to see if Brian had anything to say. It wouldn't do simply to walk out on him. It would make this seem personal, which was precisely what Toby hoped to avoid.

Brian said nothing. Toby waited a few extra seconds, and then, without saying goodbye, turned and strode out of the office. Maybe it *was* personal. Maybe that was unavoidable.

∾

TOBY WAS LYING NAKED in Amy's king-size bed, waiting for her with the familiar eagerness that hadn't lessened even slightly over the last six months. She was in the bathroom, making the mysterious preparations she sometimes made before lovemaking. Six months of pretty frequent sexual contact and he still felt like an adolescent, except he was now adult enough to savor the anticipation along with the sex. She broke into his reverie by calling from behind the closed door, "You should know, Brad's antennae have been quivering lately."

"Is it something to worry about?"

"It's something to be aware of," she said. A moment later, the bathroom door opened, and Amy stepped into the darkened bedroom. Backlit by the light from the bathroom, she was a study in chiaroscuro. Her small shapely breasts, her lithe tomboy figure, were contoured and textured by the light spilling over her body.

She flicked off the bathroom light—everything went black—and approached the bed. "He was asking about you," she said. Toby could barely see her; she was little more than an approaching region of deeper darkness. "Whether we'd seen each other between that Republican thing and the Raskov party. And whether I think, gay or not, you're attractive."

She'd climbed on the bed. He pulled her on top of him. "Yeah? What's the verdict?"

"Meh."

His palms shaped themselves over her buttocks. "I have never, ever, in my entire life, wanted to fuck someone as much as I want to fuck you right now," he said.

"Smooth talker," she said. "Keep it up, you just might persuade me."

She rolled off of him, to his left. He kicked the covers off himself impatiently and moved face first across the bed toward her, toward the vague shape in the darkness that was her body. The first flesh he encountered was her pubic ridge. He wrapped his right arm under her thighs and the left under the small of her back, lowered his head toward her, and slowly licked down along the gentle declivity toward her lower abdomen. She sighed.

The phone rang.

"Goddamn," she said. Then, "I'm sorry, Toby. I have to."

"Him?"

"That would be my guess."

"Tell him you're otherwise engaged. Or that I was about to perform an earth-shattering act of virtuoso cunnilingus."

"Shh!" She reached for the phone. "Hello?" she said, her voice bright and conversational. Toby rolled away from her onto his back and tried to stay as quiet as he could. Amy went on, "Oh, hi...Yeah, I am, as a matter of fact. You could tell?" And then, "No, I planned to get to sleep early." And then, "No, I'm...I'm much too tired."

She reached for Toby's hand and grasped it. He squeezed back; he felt no inclination to be punitive. Lying quietly, he listened as the conversation went on.

"It's been a tough day...I know, but let's take a rain check...Yeah, almost..." She laughed uncomfortably. "Why do you want to know?... Okay, panties..."

She squeezed Toby's hand again. She hadn't forgotten him.

"What in the world has gotten into you?" She snorted. "Of course, but...I am not..." She laughed again. "Bradley Solomon, I am hanging up this phone...Yes I am...Because I'm tired and you're acting very peculiar...Okay, me too...'Night."

She hung up. Toby remained stock-still.

"That was Brad," she finally said. Toby waited. "He was acting weird. Asked if I was naked. Started saying all these sort of...like he wanted to

284

have phone sex or something. Believe me, that's never happened before. It's completely unlike him."

"Hmm."

"You're not saying anything."

"I grunted."

"It's not the same thing."

"There isn't much *to* say."

"Don't you think it's weird?"

"What do you want from me?"

"You're upset?"

"I guess. Yeah. Very."

"Does that mean...that earth-shattering thing you mentioned before...?"

Toby didn't laugh. For close to a minute, he didn't make any noise at all. Then he abruptly swung his legs off the bed and stood.

"What are you doing?" she asked. Then, when he didn't answer, she said, in an unfamiliar, timid voice, "You're not going?"

It was the first time he'd heard her sound even slightly timid. "Yep."

"Where?"

"I don't know. Somewhere. Home. I think we've reached the end of the line."

"What? What does that mean? Are you giving me some kind of ultimatum?"

"No, no. Well, yeah, maybe I am. We've been in this limbo for so long now, can you tell me what we're waiting for?"

"It's easy for you, you're a free agent. I'm in an ongoing relationship. Ongoing for ten years. It's a preexisting condition. And he's someone I'm indebted to and care about."

"And who there's no possible future with." She didn't offer an argument to this, so he went on, "I hate sharing you and I hate the secrecy. Jesus, Amy, you seem to want to have it both ways. This is too big a deal to be cavalier about."

She suddenly flicked on the bedside lamp. The look on her face wasn't so much troubled as deeply serious. She stared at him for a second. "Okay," she finally said.

"'Okay?' What does 'okay' mean?"

"It means you're right. It means I agree.

"Does it mean you'll tell him?"

"Yes, it means I'll tell him."

"Really?" He felt an internal flutter. It seemed momentous. But also almost anticlimactic: Too quick, too easy.

"I've been putting it off because it's so much easier to put off than to do. Like a trip to the dentist when you have a toothache."

"You want me to do it?"

"Uh-uh. I understand you're not intimidated by him, and please don't think I'm unimpressed by that—hell, even *he's* impressed by that— but this is my responsibility."

"You can face it?"

"Just let me pick the moment, okay? Brad's off to LA tomorrow. I'm not going to drop a bomb on him by phone or email. He deserves better." She added, and it almost sounded like she was talking to herself, "It's not like things with him have been going anywhere. We've been in a rut a long time." She looked up again and met Toby's gaze. "It's probably a good thing he called when he did. Got you pissed, and that gave me the push I needed."

"You're sure?"

"Take yes for an answer, why don't you?"

He smiled. She was right, but he still felt leery, cautious. "Shouldn't there be champagne? Cake? *Pomp and Circumstance*? Something befitting the occasion."

"You don't like champagne."

"Personal taste is irrelevant. A guy who becomes president may not like 'Hail to the Chief,' but that's beside the point on Inauguration Day."

"Come here," she said.

He took a couple of steps toward her. She was sitting on the bed, facing him, her feet on the floor. She extended her arms. He waded in, and she pulled his head down and kissed him.

They separated. She took a breath, and said, "Now...seriously...that earth-shattering business...?"

This time he did laugh.

3

WHEN TOBY WENT DOWNSTAIRS the next morning, he found a small crowd in the kitchen. Cathy, Hank, and Jonas were all at the table, eating breakfast. Cathy and Hank were reading *The Chron*, Jonas was slouched over his iPad. It was like living in a *pension*.

Cathy noticed him and noticed too that he seemed nonplussed. "Come join the fun!"

"This does take me back," Toby said. "Senior year, I lived in a house with three guys."

"Sounds dreamy," said Jonas.

"It wasn't."

Toby began to assemble a small breakfast for himself. Grape Nuts, yogurt, fruit, coffee. While he did so, Cathy asked, "Have fun last night?"

"Full of mischief, aren't you?"

"The three of us had a quiet evening," Cathy said. "Hank brought over a couple of pizzas, we watched *Imitation of Life*. It was very homey."

"Just one big happy family," Toby suggested.

"Except one of my daddies is always with his girlfriend."

"To be fair," said Jonas, looking up from his tablet, "Cathy's got a squeeze along with two daddies. Her bases are covered."

"Can I ask something?" put in Hank. "I'm new to this scene, so it's hard to tell...is all this good-natured, or—?"

"Good-natured," Toby said, carrying his food to the table. "Joshing is our *lingua franca*."

After Toby seated himself, Jonas said, "By the way, Tobe, to set your mind at ease..." He held up his iPad. "I'm on Craigslist."

"Checking out hookups?"

"I'm apartment-hunting, fuck-head."

"Finding anything? Not that there's any rush."

"No? Then I'll check the hookups." And then, "Truth is, I've got a few leads."

"Take your time. All joshing aside." Trying not to be too obvious, he gave Jonas a quick once-over. It wasn't easy to tell how bad he was hurting. Hank's presence—maybe even Cathy's—encouraged him to camouflage his distress.

Cathy quickly chimed in, "It's great you're here. You don't have to move out ever."

"It doesn't hurt to see what's available." Jonas couldn't suppress a sigh.

"It'll seem less immense in a few weeks," Toby said.

"Anyway," Cathy said brightly, "I'm off to a dorm soon." And then to Hank, "I wonder if they have rules about overnight guests."

Toby grimaced but said nothing.

～

"HAVE YOU READ IT?" Doris demanded. She was standing near her desk as Toby entered her office. She had a thick pile of pages in her right hand.

"That's the libretto? Brian finally yielded it up?"

"Oh yes, the suspense is over. So…have you read it?"

Toby had expected praise for having pried it loose. But Doris was too upset to bother with such niceties. He answered, "Haven't seen a word of it."

Her reading glasses were hanging by a cord around her neck. She put them on. They made her eyes look huge. "There's a problem," she said, her voice taut.

"It isn't any good?"

"It isn't, as it happens. In fact, it's downright bad, taken simply as a piece of writing. But that's not the problem. Lots of stage-worthy pieces have weak books."

"And besides, we haven't heard the music yet."

Without warning or preparation, in a startling explosion of frustration and rage, she flung the script across the room, shouting, "Damn it, you're not listening! That isn't the point!"

He had never heard her shout before or seen such a naked display of anger on her part. The violence of the gesture and the volume and raw vehemence of her voice startled both of them. Toby noticed her hands were shaking. He knelt down and picked up the script. "All right, Doris," he said gently, "okay." He extended the pages to her.

She took the pages from him with manifest distaste. "Read it," she said.

"I will. But give me a hint."

"It's...there's no way we can put this thing on."

"I need more information."

"Please, just read it. Then by all means tell me I'm wrong. I'd be thrilled. You won't, though. If we put this on, we'd lose half our subscriber base, and...and I'd have to quit. I'd leave rather than stay with an organization that didn't fire me for permitting it."

"Will you tell me the problem?"

"You know, I disliked *The Death of Klinghoffer*. I found it offensive. But I defended it. Regardless of my feelings, the thing was defensible, and therefore deserved to be defended as a serious work by serious people. I'm not averse to controversy, and I'm not a commissar."

"Uh-huh."

"And God knows I'm not homophobic. Christ, virtually every man I deal with in this building is gay. Except you."

"I'm sure no one's accusing you of homophobia, Doris."

"But this libretto...there's no way. It's indefensible. Vulgar, jejune, vile. And *libelous*."

Her telephone rang. She turned to it furiously, grabbed it, and growled, "Not now, damn it, I said to—" She stopped abruptly, and then, after listening a few seconds, said quietly, "Oh my God." As she sank back into her chair, she said, "Have you sent flowers? Good, good. I'm sorry I barked like that, you did the right thing, of course." She hung up, looking ashen.

"Is something wrong?" Toby asked, fatuously.

She nodded, and took a second to catch her breath. "Judy Solomon." She removed her glasses, letting them drop down against her chest, and rubbed her eyes. "Massive stroke. Last night. Died instantly." A deep sigh. "Poor, poor woman. But her life was such a misery, maybe it's a blessing. For *everyone*."

~

TOBY SAT AT HIS desk. Brian and Jeremy's libretto was in front of him, but he hadn't tried to read it, had barely glanced at it.

He'd phoned Amy the moment he got back to his office. Some byplay with Priscilla was unavoidable—her chirpy tone suggested she hadn't heard the news—but he eventually ascertained Amy was out. Phoning her on her cell would be reckless, since there was no telling where she was. Which was precisely the problem.

More than an hour had gone by since. No word from her.

What difference would Judy Solomon's death make to him and Amy? That was the crucial question. It was a selfish concern in the wake of such a tragedy, he knew that, but he couldn't bring himself to feel guilty. He didn't know the woman. He hadn't wished her dead and couldn't wish her back to life.

He reached for the phone to call Amy's office again, but after the first three digits, hung up. Pointless. Priscilla was reliable. Either Amy wasn't back or was choosing not to call.

He glanced down at the libretto on the desk before him. Another fine mess. Concern about his love life had been diverting his attention from this other problem. The title page read:

The Castro
Opera Libretto by
Brian Hughes & Jeremy Metcalf

Could Doris be right? Was it really so awful? Toby wasn't sure he could trust his own judgment any more than Doris's. Who knew what was acceptable anymore? *Porgy and Bess*, for example, surely wouldn't be, not as a new piece. The barely disguised subtexts of *Parsifal*, *Siegfried*, and *Die Meistersinger* would render those operas dubious at best. Would audiences put up with *Così fan Tutte* if it were newly written? The title alone was toxic.

What if Doris is right, and the opera can't be produced? Brad gave money specifically to fund this project. Who would be delegated to explain the situation to him? Who would try to dissuade him from demanding a refund? He knew the answer: Hey, Mr. Widower, this is your ol' pal Toby. I've got some more bad news for you. And a big favor to ask. Would this conversation occur before or after Brad learned he was being dumped? Being dumped *for Toby*?

Toby groaned. Welcome to my perfect storm.

He glanced at the telephone again. It looked malevolent, grimly smug in its persistent refusal to ring. Why hadn't she called? Where was she?

He shook his head, disgusted with himself, as well as the situation. It was time to focus. He turned over the title page of the script, leaned down onto his desk with his weight on his elbows, and began to read. With mounting dismay.

~

TOBY WENT HOME EARLY. "Hello!" he called out loudly as he stepped through the front door. "Anybody home?" A little warning in case either Cathy or Jonas might be taking amorous advantage of an empty house. There was no answer, but he heard the sound of the TV coming from the living room, so he headed in that direction. And found Jonas curled up on the sofa, a duvet over him despite the summer weather, staring at some daytime talk show. Obese people accusing each other loudly of various moral transgressions, the audience whooping its disapprobation. There was a half-empty glass of red wine on the coffee table in front of him. He barely looked up when Toby entered the room.

"Ah," said Toby, "an inspiring vision."

Jonas managed a half-smile. "I was planning to go apartment hunting this afternoon," he mumbled. "But I couldn't face it."

"Feeling low?"

"Never lower." He laboriously righted himself on the couch. "You know that feeling that you'll never be happy again? Forget happy. You'll never not be miserable?"

"It's called depression."

"Naming it doesn't help." He reached for the remote and switched off the TV. "Nor does knowing other poor sods have it worse." He kicked off the duvet. "It's such a bore, too. Might be romantic when Sinatra sings about it, but..." He trailed off. "You're home early."

"I'm a little low myself."

291

"Pour yourself some wine." So saying, Jonas made a grab for his glass and took a swig. "See Brian today?"

"Uh-uh."

Jonas shut his eyes. "I need to stop thinking about him. I'm an expert on heartbreak, I know the drill. Not thinking about the person is step one. The hardest step. Brian may be a total shit, but…" His face clouded over with a thought or memory to which he didn't give voice.

"He *is* a total shit," Toby said.

Jonas, sensing a fresh area of anguish, looked alert. "What do you mean?" he asked, his tone almost eager. Amazing what we do to ourselves. "Another man? A *woman*? I wouldn't put it past him."

"Nothing like that. The libretto. It's nuts. No way it could ever be done. Opening with an orgy in a steam bath? Moscone with underage prostitutes? Gavin Newsom snorting coke? DiFi…Dan White…Even poor Harvey Milk gets pummeled. Full-frontal in what seems like every scene, blow-jobs and buggery galore. Does Brian think he's the reincarnation of Joe Orton? Jesus, we aren't some underground cabaret, we're the San Francisco Opera! Not that an underground cabaret would touch it either."

Jonas's eyes had widened. But he responded quietly. "There are precedents, no? Nudity in *Salome*. The orgy in *Moses und Aron*. Lesbianism in *Lulu*. Twentieth century masterpieces all."

"Care to read it and tell me what you think?"

"Sure don't."

"Just as well." Toby didn't need confirmation. The libretto was as poisonous as Doris said. Badly written, designed to offend, impossible to stage. "It's a rancid piece of work. I don't get why they bothered."

Jonas shrugged. "Brian sometimes gets his jollies by seeing what he can get away with. Peck's bad boy. He used to embarrass me in public. Soul-kisses in restaurants, saying rude things too loud, shit like that. It could be funny, but I was never comfortable with it."

"And Jeremy?"

"This would have been Brian. Not that I'm defending Jeremy, I hate his guts. He may not be evil or malicious, I don't know him well enough to say, but Brian and him, they act like the music director and the composer-slash-rock-star are above ordinary human obligations. They treated me like I didn't count. And I resent it, even if it's true."

"Of course you count."

"People count only if you decide they do. Especially when they aren't able to retaliate. Then the choice is yours." He looked at Toby. "Anyway, this has Brian's DNA all over it. Is it fixable?"

"I can't imagine Doris would want to fix it."

"So you've got a problem."

"I've got *lots* of problems."

❧

BY THE END OF the next day, Toby still hadn't heard from Amy. She wasn't answering her cell. He'd phoned her office twice more, and was it his imagination, or did Priscilla sound a tad impatient? He left a studiously impersonal message on her home answering machine— that anomalous piece of retro equipment—a message so impersonal that if Solomon heard it, he wouldn't blink. And he'd written several emails, trying hard to suppress the wheedling, whining tone that kept threatening to break through. Just a word. Tell me you're okay. Tell me *we're* okay. Why haven't you called? When can I see you?

The following morning, when he checked his phone, he found a short text from her. "Still can't call. Lots happening. Miss you." Hardly enough to put his mind at ease.

And now it was mid-afternoon on an unusually hot day, the hottest of the year, and he was sitting in the back of a cab with Doris. It was stifling, but she wouldn't let him open the window, presumably to protect her hair, although she didn't say so. "Do not mention the opera," Doris was instructing him. "If he asks—I'm sure he won't—be evasive. This is neither the time nor place. It isn't even permissible. Discussing business when you're sitting shiva is forbidden. Luckily for us."

"Do you really think I should be here?" He had tried to get out of this visit once already, when she'd first suggested it. She was insistent.

"Gestures like this mean a lot. He's suffered a loss. It's one of those times when you err on the side of caring. And look…we're in a situation, we're going to need his good will."

Toby nodded. From her point of view, she was a hundred percent right. From any point of view, really, except that of Amy's secret lover. "Is he grieving, do you think?"

293

"God, who knows? Who understands other people's marriages? He loved her once. Sure he was a player, but he loved her. I assume he went on loving her. Of course it changed, he became a caretaker more than a husband. But marriages change over time even when people are healthy. I certainly don't blame him for fooling around. He was a mensch where it counted."

Another thought occurred to him. "Should I be wearing a yarmulke?"

Doris looked over at him and smiled, amused perhaps by the notion of Toby in a skullcap. She hadn't seen him at his wedding, or Cathy's bat mitzvah, or Jessica's memorial; she didn't know he was an old hand with a kippah. "This isn't really a religious event. Brad isn't observant."

Brad might not be religious, but in Toby's experience he could be pretty observant.

Doris went on, "I doubt he'll be serving ham and cheese sandwiches, but...well, according to the Talmud, he's not supposed to have sex during the mourning period. How do you rate the odds of that? Especially now that he and what's-her-name are free to run amok."

"Her name's Amy," Toby said tightly.

Doris seemed surprised, either by his tone or his having the information so readily to hand. "Amy. Of course." And continued, "It's an interesting moment for the two of them, isn't it? They'll find out now whether it was the impediments that kept the relationship going."

Amy and Solomon *would* find that out, yes. Toby felt himself starting to sweat. "How long do we need to stay?"

She answered sharply. "As long as seems appropriate. I had Sherry cancel my afternoon appointments." She relented slightly. "Probably not more than an hour, but you never know. This isn't about *us*."

The door to Solomon's house was open when they arrived. Toby wasn't sure what to expect as he and Doris crossed the threshold into the magnificent foyer. Marble floors, antiques, an immense Henry Moore reclining nude. What appeared to be several greenhouses' worth of flowers. It made even the Raskovs' place seem like a hovel. A red-haired woman dressed in black greeted them very quietly at the door, and led them along a short corridor and then down two steps into a sunken living room. There were about thirty people there, standing and sitting. Considering the number of people, the noise level was remarkably muted. Conversations were being conducted in whispers. Solomon was sitting on a sofa, an elderly man on one side of him, an elderly woman on the other. He had a drink in his hand.

Doris led the way over to him, Toby following a pace behind. "I'm so sorry, Brad," she said when she reached him. "You know how fond I was of Judy."

He looked up at her for a moment, and then put down his drink and stood. He was dry-eyed, and it would be more accurate to describe his appearance as solemn rather than grief-stricken. He took Doris's proffered hand in both of his, and then, a moment later, pulled her to him and embraced her. "Thank you, Doris. She was fond of you too. Thank you so much for coming." He kissed her cheek, then released her. "We knew something like this could happen any time, but you can't prepare yourself for it." He turned to Toby. His impassivity seemed, in some ineffable way, to deepen. "Toby. It's thoughtful of you to come."

"I wanted to express my condolences. This must be a painful time."

Solomon gestured across the room. "Help yourself to some food."

Toby hesitated. It struck him it might be a little greedy to race straight to the buffet table after such brief commiserations. Solomon noticed his hesitation. "Go ahead," he said. "There's nothing to be shy about. Jews eat at times like this. We regard chopped liver as a sacrament."

It was hard to tell whether Solomon was being a good host or dismissing him. But either way, Toby didn't feel he had a choice. He nodded and crossed the room to the buffet table. A big catered spread, handsomely presented. Spirits, wines, club soda, soft drinks, herring in sour cream, lox, egg salad, chopped liver, matzos. Toby had had lunch less than an hour before; he wasn't hungry. And it was too early to consider drinking anything potent. He put some ice in a glass and poured the contents of a small bottle of club soda into it.

As he was pouring, taking care not to let the bubbles overspill the rim of the glass, someone glided up beside him. He turned and saw a man a few years younger than himself, short, stocky, heavy-featured, with thinning hair. Wire-rim glasses, somber charcoal suit, monochrome gray tie. Toby said hello.

"Yeah, hi," the man said, at the same time pouring himself a glass of red wine. After he had completed the operation, he said, "You and

I seem to be the only people here under a hundred and seventy-five years old. Are you a friend of my dad's?"

"I'm Toby Lindeman." Toby offered his hand.

The man shook it. "I think I've heard your name. I'm Mark Solomon."

"I'm very sorry about your mother."

"Thanks." He began spreading chopped liver on a piece of matzo. "Did you know her?"

"Uh-uh."

"To be honest, it's impossible to regard it as a tragedy. Her death, I mean. By itself. The whole last ten years or so, that's a different story."

It wasn't easy to respond. Toby made some sort of sympathetic noise.

"Dad's mentioned you. You're like, what? Something with the opera?"

"That's right."

"He seems to like you, is my impression."

"How's he bearing up?"

"He's being very brave." This was accompanied by the suggestion of a sneer. "But hey, I give him credit for observing the proprieties. He's not keening and ululating, but he's not declaiming the peroration of 'I have a dream' either. You know. 'Free at last, free at last, thank God Almighty I'm free at last.'"

This was so sour, so cynical, Toby was shocked. And the look on his face must have said as much, because the man went on hastily, "I don't mean he's overjoyed. But he's a tough guy. The kind of businessman who knows when to cut his losses. These last few years were hell for my mom, but they were no picnic for Dad either. He's got to be relieved they're over."

Toby, still unsure what to say, took a sip of water. Meanwhile, Mark had pivoted around, surveying the room. "He's keeping the hypocrisy-level to a minimum. You gotta respect that. No crocodile tears."

"Everybody deals with these things differently," Toby said, his tone neutral.

Mark glanced over at him, raising an eyebrow slightly. "I'm sure." And then, "It's in character, I'll say that. He was always correct with my mom while she was sick. Handled the situation decently. Without letting it stop him from getting on with his own life, God forbid."

Toby was suddenly aware of Mark's barely contained rage. Despite the fellow's subdued tone, this wasn't idle chat, this was venting. Why had he chosen Toby as a confidant? The similarity in their ages? Had his anger been clamoring for an outlet for days, or even years?

"It's hard to condemn him for that," Toby offered.

"I'm not condemning him."

"I wasn't suggesting you were. All I meant was, as a culture, we don't expect surviving spouses to commit suttee."

"He's got a girlfriend. He isn't exactly bereft."

Mark was looking directly at Toby as if seeking some specific reaction. "Did your mother know?" Toby finally asked. It was none of his business, but hell, he hadn't introduced the topic.

"Oh, probably," Mark said. "She never said anything, at least not to me, but..." Suddenly, distressingly, his eyes filled with tears. He made an effort to pull himself together, took a gulp of wine. Then he said, "She felt *guilty* about her stroke. Isn't that fucked up? Like she'd let Dad down. Maybe she didn't think she could begrudge him." He dabbed at his eyes with a napkin.

Toby had many reasons to want to extricate himself from this conversation. But the guy was hurting, he'd just lost his mother, he needed to talk. There was no way to terminate the conversation without appearing callous. But for the third or fourth time in the last few minutes, he didn't have a clue how to respond. He took a sip of water and contrived to keep the look on his face judicious and sympathetic.

"You haven't met the girlfriend?" Mark asked.

Fortunately, it proved to be a rhetorical question. Before Toby could devise an answer, Mark went on, "She isn't what you'd expect. You know, some tart. Which is good, since she's probably gonna be my new mom." He snorted with mordant amusement. Toby turned away, afraid his face betrayed him. Mark, oblivious, plunged on: "She's my age, so that's already weird. The question..." He glanced across the room at his father again. "The question for me is, what does she see in *him*? She's doesn't seem the fortune-hunter type. And it's not like...I mean, except for the money, is Dad such a prize?"

At that moment a heavily made-up elderly woman appeared at the buffet table, gripped Mark's arms, and kissed him, leaving traces of powder on his face. Her arrival came several minutes later than Toby would have liked, but the interruption was welcome all the same. "Your mama's ordeal is finally over," the woman murmured, in a sententious tone suggesting she was offering something both profound and consolatory. Toby quickly patted Mark's shoulder, a small but he hoped adequate gesture of commiseration—both for the loss of his mother and for having to deal with this comfort-giver—and stepped away without waiting to hear more.

He carried his fizzy water across the room to a straight-back chair and sat down. Time to try for a Zen-like state: Serene, patient, insensible to the passage of time, free of personal desire. Thinking this reminded him of Amy's joke from some months back about achieving sartorial splendor, and the memory made him smile. But he realized almost instantaneously how inappropriate a smile was in this house of mourning and at the same time felt a sudden painful spasm of anxiety. By now the absence of communication could only be viewed as ominous. Did Mark Solomon have it right?

Zen-like serenity was no longer an option. He'd have to fake it, just sit quietly with an expression of sorrow and concern on his face. That last part, at least, was a piece of cake.

Over the next forty minutes or so, simultaneously deeply agitated and bored to distraction, he barely stirred. Twice he got up and refilled his glass with seltzer, but otherwise he remained virtually immobile. Doris caught his eye once or twice and gave him a quick, surreptitious nod, to let him know she was aware of and appreciated his patience. That was about all the thanks he could reasonably expect.

The liquid he'd drunk finally announced its presence to his bladder. He made his way toward the entrance foyer, assuming there must be a guest bathroom in that direction. The red-haired woman who had greeted him and Doris when they'd arrived saw him coming and wordlessly pointed down a corridor. He nodded his thanks, found the bathroom, used it, washed his hands with the fancy perfumed soap provided, and stepped back out into the foyer. And encountered Solomon, waiting right outside the door.

"Oh," he said, "sorry. Were you waiting for…?" He gestured back toward the room.

"I was waiting for *you*," Solomon said. "We need to talk."

"Okay."

Solomon put an arm around Toby's shoulder and guided him along the corridor, away from the direction of the living room. Toby felt a shiver of apprehension, but what Solomon said next assuaged some of his anxiety. "I saw you talking to Mark before."

"Briefly."

"This thing has hit him hard. He and his mother were very close."

"It must be tough."

"I think he blames me in some irrational way. There's a lot of anger in the boy." He sighed. "It's been a tough few years for all of us. But he's almost forty, it's time he came to terms with it. Maybe Judy's death... after he's had a chance to mourn..."

They had come to a narrow back staircase; probably once upon a time it had led to servants' quarters. Solomon gestured for Toby to precede him up the stairs. Puzzled and more than a little reluctant, Toby hesitated. "Go on," Solomon said. Refusing seemed impossible. He climbed the stairs, Solomon behind him. "It's a pisser, though," Solomon was saying in an ill-humored growl. "Sometimes I get the idea the kid basically hates me. Which doesn't stop him from working for me. His principles take him only so far. Unless doing a crappy job is his idea of principled protest." This was enough for Toby to guess at a whole world of dysfunction. But he withheld judgment, both of Solomon *pere* and Solomon *fils*; all families are dysfunctional to some degree, and outsiders have no right to apportion blame. Not unless they're Tolstoy.

When they reached the upper level, Solomon led Toby toward a door at the end of a short corridor, opened it, ushered Toby through, and followed after. The door led to a spacious sort of roof garden boasting a breathtaking view of the Golden Gate Bridge and the Marin Headlands. Along one side was red-stained wooden garden furniture: two chaises longues padded with some sort of weather-resistant material and a few easy chairs. In the center was a glass table, sheltered by a large parasol in a cement stand, with four chairs around it.

"This is lovely," Toby said. It was hot, though, the air sticky and thick.

"Sit down," Solomon said. A command.

Toby pulled one of the chairs away from the table and sat down, taking care to position himself in the parasol's shade. Solomon remained standing, staring down at Toby fixedly. Toby felt a return of that apprehension he'd experienced a few minutes before. Something wasn't right, and it had nothing to do with Brad's relationship with Mark.

"I want you to explain something," Solomon said quietly.

"I'm willing to try."

"Why'd you tell me you were gay?"

Uh-oh. "Huh?"

"You're deaf all of a sudden? I said, why did you tell me you were gay?"

"I didn't. You assumed it."

Solomon shrugged, unimpressed. "You didn't correct me. All that banter, all that back-and-forthing. You're no more a fruit than I am."

"That's true." Toby tried to camouflage his mounting alarm. "Not that it's a contest."

"Magda Szerly let me know you've been screwing her for years. Her and, according to her, approximately half the attractive women in town."

"Did she?" Toby was reeling, although he hoped it didn't show. And thinking, Perfidious bitch. He couldn't imagine how such a conversation had taken place, but there was no way her role was innocent. She'd intended harm. Grievous harm. What had he done to provoke that level of malice?

With another tight, nasty smile, a smile that was almost a sneer, Solomon was saying, "Which leads me to wonder, as I said, why you didn't correct me."

Every signal his body had evolved to register alarm was going off at once: A violent, thought-obliterating explosion of cranial static, an accelerated heartbeat, a hollow whooshing in his ears, and sweating in profuse rivulets down his back, his armpits, and his forehead into his eyes. Under this sort of duress, quick thought was almost impossible. But he struggled to master himself and said as levelly as he could, "I didn't think my sex life was any of your business, frankly. And…to be honest, I found it funny. I enjoyed the banter. I didn't see any harm in it."

Brad gave him a hard, searching stare, and then, his voice so low it was almost a growl, said, "You didn't think it showed disrespect?"

Toby's response was quick. "Maybe the reverse, if anything. I admired the way you dealt with a situation some people might have found awkward."

Solomon narrowed his eyes. "Do you know who I am, Lindeman? Do you have any idea who you're dealing with?"

"Of course."

300

"The fact that I've been pleasant...indulgent, even...putting up with your crap...do you think I don't have a choice? Don't you know I could squash you like a bug if I felt like it?"

"I don't think in those terms."

"Maybe it's time you started."

Toby stood up. This had gone far enough. "Look," he said, "I'm very sorry about your wife, and I'm sure this must be a very painful time, but—"

"Sit down," Solomon said curtly.

"I don't think so."

"I'm not done with you." For a moment, it seemed as if Solomon was going to push Toby back into the chair. But instead, after what seemed a brief internal tussle, he stepped back, away from him, and turned his back on him, looking out toward the bay. "It's easy to be contemptuous of power and money when you don't have any," he said. "To pretend you're above all that vulgar stuff. Trust me, no one's above it. If you don't have power over people, they have power over you. You may not be confronted with it on a daily basis, you may think you've managed to opt out of the system, but sooner or later...push comes to shove."

He paced toward the parapet, then wheeled around again, facing Toby. "I'm sure you think you're a very clever fellow, but you don't have the slightest idea what you're up against. I don't like being played for a fool, and I'm not someone you should even *dream* of fucking with."

Even with his heart beating like mad and his brain beclouded with alarm, Toby suddenly realized Solomon wasn't sure of his ground. In this long menacing rant, he hadn't made any direct accusations, hadn't mentioned Amy, hadn't even alluded to her. The speech was clearly designed to intimidate, but it was a fishing expedition too. Brad had his suspicions, but he didn't *know*. The stupidest thing Toby could do was cave. So he said, "I'm confused. This bluster, these veiled threats, this Ayn Rand soliloquy...all because I didn't tell you I like girls?"

"Just don't try to put something over on me."

"I'm not trying anything of the kind. I came here to pay my respects. It was apparently a mistake, although I'm not sure why. If my presence offends you, I apologize." Toby wiped his forehead with the back of his hand. It did no good. He was sweating too heavily.

Solomon hesitated, his forehead bunched, and then something in him gave way. His posture slumped. He reached out and gripped the back of a chair, steadying himself. After a few seconds, he said, "Have you ever lost a loved one, Toby?" It didn't quite sound like an apology, but his tone was gentler. The frontal assault had been repelled.

"My ex-wife," Toby said.

"You were married?" When Toby nodded, Solomon shook his head with a mixture of amusement and irritation; it wasn't enough that Toby was heterosexual, he'd even had a wife! "How long ago?"

"A few months."

"Aw shit, I had no idea."

"No reason you should."

"I guess that wasn't my business either."

"I try to keep my private life separate from my professional life." Even in the heat of the moment, Toby wasn't oblivious to the ironies in this assertion.

"Kids?"

"One. A daughter."

"So you're a single parent now?"

"Right."

"That's rough."

"At least she doesn't work for me."

Solomon saw the point and smiled. Then he shook his head and said, "I don't know, kid. I brought you up here to ream you out. But…it's hard to stay mad at you, for some reason."

Toby wasn't sure what to say to that. He counseled himself he wasn't out of the woods yet. Whatever had provoked this scene hadn't disappeared.

"I can see why you've been successful with women," Solomon continued. "You're a winning guy."

"Magda's inclined to exaggerate that success," Toby said. "Exaggerate it a lot. She likes her personal drama lurid."

Solomon's voice turned hard again. "I'm maybe too punch-drunk to focus right now, but I strongly urge you to remember this conversation. Plenty of people will tell you I'm not a forgiving person."

"I believe it."

"You should. Now go in there and eat some lox or something. And I need to hear what's happening with my opera sometime soon. I'm starting to think something isn't kosher."

Another thing to look forward to. Toby's relief at being dismissed was equaled by a sense of foreboding.

∽

IN THE UBER BACK to the Civic Center, Doris talked about the gathering, about Brad's deportment (she felt he had managed a difficult balancing act gracefully), about the long-standing problems in Brad's relationship with Mark. She finally noticed Toby was barely participating and asked him why he was so quiet. He mumbled a few words about mortality and melancholy. She knew about Jessica, enough to assume a connection and let the matter drop.

When he got back to his office, Daniel handed him several pink slips. He glanced through them anxiously while still standing in the anteroom area. One was from Amy. At last.

He called as soon as he reached his desk. Priscilla, without any banter, switched him through. "I need to see you," he declared when Amy came on the line. He could hear the edge in his voice, although he was struggling to keep it neutral. "I mean immediately."

"All right. Hold on a sec…" He could hear her breathing, her mouth close to the receiver. She was evidently weighing alternatives. She said, "There are a few things I need to take care of. Shouldn't take long."

"I can grab a cab to your office."

Another few seconds, then, "Uh-uh. I doubt Brad's around—there's some Jewish memorial thing, they apparently don't conduct business during that—but you never know, he might pop in just to get away from…everything. I'd feel safer at my place. In an hour?"

He was able, with an effort, to busy himself. He made a few phone calls, checked in with a number of people in his department, and reviewed the text of a mail solicitation campaign they were preparing. But his mind kept drifting uneasily to Amy, and he kept having to yank it back.

The time finally passed. Feeling a disquiet so pronounced it was almost dread, he arranged his desk, put on his jacket, and left the building. He forced himself to proceed deliberately, resisting every instinct to hurry. As if the fates, in their limitless malevolence, shouldn't be alerted to how much he had riding on the next few hours.

He hailed a taxi on Van Ness, took it to Amy's, got out, paid. And then experienced another quandary. Lately, whether Amy was home or not, he simply let himself in. Today, though, he felt unsure of his territorial status. He rang her buzzer.

"Yes?" came her voice.

"It's me."

"Lose your key?"

"No, I—" But she buzzed him in without waiting to hear the rest.

She was waiting for him in the foyer, a fiercely resistant Feeney in her arms. She was wearing a business suit, navy with chalk stripes. Smiling, but her expression looked serious.

"Well, hi there," she said. "I beat you by a couple of minutes."

He had reached the door. He now put his hands on her shoulders, feeling an unfamiliar awkwardness, and leaned in and kissed her. Because she was holding Feeney, her forearms made a sort of barrier against his chest. It wasn't any kind of statement, but still, it felt to him as if he were somehow being warded off. He kept the kiss brief and chaste.

"Come in," she said. He followed her inside. As soon as he shut the door, she set Feeney down. The cat scampered off. Then she righted herself, and they faced each other for a moment.

"Let's try that again," she said, and held her arms out to him.

He reached for her and pulled her close. Feeling her against him was like the completion of a perfect cadence. Maybe things weren't as black as he feared. He said, "Hope I'm not too funky. I was out in the heat today. And *feeling* the heat."

Uncharacteristically, she didn't seize on the hint. "I like it when you sweat," she said. They separated. "I've been missing you," she added. Matter-of-factly, but at least she said it. "And speaking of funky, I just got home, I could use a shower. Join me?"

"I don't have anything to change into. Getting back into these clothes after a shower is not an attractive proposition." This was true, but not the whole truth. If they showered together, they'd make love. He was determined not to be detoured by sex.

"Well, keep me company, then."

She took his hand and led him into her bedroom. Once there, to cool off, he removed his jacket and tie, tossing them onto her bed, and rolled his shirt cuffs up his forearms; the AC felt delicious against his skin. Amy stripped quickly, without a show, hanging her suit in the walk-in closet, tossing her underclothes into a hamper. The absence of any deliberate provocation didn't stop Toby from finding the operation provocative. Her trim little body retained its power.

Naked, she proceeded into the bathroom. When he entered after her, she was already leaning into the shower stall, a fancy glass-and-granite unit, turning on the water. He couldn't stop himself from reaching over and fondling her butt. She wiggled it humorously, and then turned to face him. "Sit down." She gestured toward the closed toilet. "I'll only be a minute."

He sat down as instructed, and she tested the water temperature with her right hand, and then, satisfied, stepped inside, pulling the glass door closed. He watched her stand under the water for a moment, slowly turning around once, and then begin to soap herself. She wasn't self-conscious about being observed. A moment later, the familiar sandalwood aroma reached his nostrils. There followed a few moments when neither of them said anything. Then Toby broke the silence. "I saw Brad today, Amy. We're in his sights."

"I can't hear you over the water, sweetie."

He repeated what he had said at a higher volume.

She said, "Yeah, I know."

"You do?"

"He's been asking about you a lot lately. And he's been very prickly. Of course, with Judy dying...I mean, he was already curious, but it seems worse. I don't know why."

"I do. Magda told him I'm straight. Told him she and I had been lovers."

Her eyes widened. Her chagrin was palpable. "This is bad." She sounded scared. "He's been suspicious anyway. Not about you necessarily, just...he could tell something was different." They looked at each other through the glass. Her upper body—including those tricky breasts—was coated in lather. "Why'd she do it? That isn't something you mention casually."

"To make trouble. Malice aforethought."

"She knows about us?"

"She figured it out."

"You didn't tell her?"

"Christ, Amy, no."

"Fuck." And then, "How do you know about this?"

"From Brad. Today. At the shiva thing."

"You went?"

"Doris made me. It was grim. And Brad took me aside and kind of... it wouldn't be an exaggeration to say he threatened me. I didn't get the impression he's sure of anything, but there's no doubt he's on high alert."

She turned off the water. A second later, dripping copiously, she stepped out of the shower, reaching for a towel hanging from the rack nearby. Her hair was flat against her head. She started to dry herself.

"Who else was there?" she asked. "Anyone you know?"

"Oh God, it was like the bridge party in *Sunset Boulevard*. Except for his son. Mark."

"Holy hell."

"I guess you've met." He was tempted to tell her about Mark's puzzlement at what she saw in Brad, but this wasn't the time to score cheap points.

"Couple of times. He and Brad...it's pretty tense. This must have hit him hard. He and his mom were close."

"He seemed angry."

"He *is* angry." Her attention was suddenly caught by something on the big toe of her left foot, a callus or a blister, and she held it up, in her right hand, for a moment, peering at it, steadying herself with her left hand against the wall. Toby found her unaffected ease with her own body adorable, a precious vestige of the Michigan tomboy she'd once been. But hell, everything about her was adorable. Better to find her a little less damned adorable.

Her foot was back on the floor, forgotten. She probably wasn't even aware she'd been examining it. As she went about the business of drying her thighs and legs with the towel, she went on, "Brad thinks Mark's anger's 'cause of *me*. Not as a person, but as the one his father betrayed his mother with. And I'm sure that didn't help, but Brad believes that's how it started, and he's *so* fucking kidding himself. He was just a lousy awful father. Mark's been angry since he was a kid. Years of therapy, he finally figured out his anger's justified. Brad's one of those guys with no talent for parenthood. And Mark was a disappointment to him. Not as smart as he expected, not as aggressive, not...all those things a certain kind of man wants his son to be. An athlete, a go-getter. A second him."

"Have you ever told him that?"

"It isn't really my business, is it?"

"I don't know. Is it?" She glanced up at him, hearing the new significance in his tone. He went on, "Mark said something—it was offhand, a sort of joke—about your becoming his stepmother."

"Oh, that's just—"

"No it isn't. Two days ago, you were ready to end things with Brad. Now the whole situation's changed. I need to know where we stand."

She folded the towel carefully, squaring the edges, and put it back on the rack. She was so damned appealing. That little frown of concentration, those perky boobs. "There's no point in pressuring me. The man's hurting. I wouldn't tell him anything now anyway."

It was the word "anyway" that felt like a nail in the coffin. "Meaning, you wouldn't tell him anything even if you had something to tell him?"

She reached for a fluffy terry bathrobe hanging from a hook on the bathroom door, and wrapped it around herself. It was a perfectly natural thing to do, but Toby found it ominously symbolic. Covering up, hiding, putting a barrier between herself and him.

He said, "You're reconsidering."

She put a hand on his arm. "You have to understand—"

He pulled away. It felt childish, but he couldn't bear her touching him.

"Toby. Please, hear me out. Try to listen like someone without a stake in the outcome. I've been with Brad for ten years. For all but the last few months, we both assumed we'd be together. Eventually. Judy was the only obstacle. If she hadn't gotten sick, he would have divorced her. Happens all the time. Even after the stroke, most guys in Brad's position would have done it. Seen to it she was taken care of—maybe—and left. Brad wouldn't do that. He's an honorable man, no matter what you think. And I never once asked him to. I would have been offended if he'd offered. We just...managed. As best we could."

307

She opened the bathroom door and exited. Toby followed her. The bedroom was much cooler than the steamed-up bathroom. Toby felt goose bumps rise on his arms. Amy climbed onto her bed and arranged herself on top of the duvet, leaning back on the bolster resting against the bed's headboard. Toby sat down on the edge of the bed.

"So anyway," she said, "things with Brad were just kind of going along, and then, bang, you showed up. I don't think you were prepared for me, and I sure as hell wasn't prepared for you. I liked you right away, of course, but I had no idea it would turn into...*this*. I was blindsided. It messed up everything. I had to back off. You know the rest. I couldn't do it. It still amazes me. I didn't know these feelings existed outside of pop songs."

"So what is there to think about?" Toby suddenly demanded, rising from the bed. He began to pace, continuing earnestly, "There's nothing to think about. Except timing, maybe. If you feel it would be insensitive to say anything while Brad's in mourning, I won't argue. But other than that...You love me, I love you. Extravagantly. Epochally. Case closed."

She smiled at him with great tenderness, following him with her eyes as he walked up and down the floor. And then she suddenly frowned. After another second, she said quietly, "Except it isn't that simple. He expects me to move in with him. After, you know, a decent interval, for appearances. I've temporized, I haven't given him an answer, but—"

"So tell him no." Toby stopped pacing and faced her.

"On some level, I've been waiting for this moment for years."

"So what?" Toby was almost bellowing. He couldn't believe he was still being balked. "Things have changed! Everything's different!"

"But I love him too." Toby started to say something, but she rode over him. "You want to disregard that because it's inconvenient, but it's a fact."

"Not the way you love me."

"No," she admitted, "that's true. He's...oh, I'm not going to try to characterize it. I feel safe with him. Cared for and protected. I learn from him. I find his foibles—and I don't deny he's got his share—I find them endearing. He's a fascinating man. Don't look at me like that! I'm trying to be honest!"

"Just listen to yourself!"

"I *don't* love him the way I love you. I'm not minimizing that, it's huge. But I have to ask myself, how important is it *really*? In the long run? Will the loss of it count for more than the loss of what Brad offers? I've been with him ten years. Will I love *you* the same way in ten years? Can you honestly say I will? I'm trying to be practical. Rigorous and objective." She risked a small smile. "The way they taught us at Stanford." The smile faded quickly. "Based on everything I've seen, based on all the people I know, I have to believe things between you and me will change over time. So I have to put that in the mix. A year of these feelings? Two years? Three seems optimistic. And what would we have afterward? It's true I don't love Brad the way I love you, but in ten years I doubt I'll love *you* the way I love you."

Toby collapsed onto the bed. "You're doing a cost-benefit analysis," he said in a monotone. "You're doing a cost-benefit analysis of our life together."

"In a way. If you like. But it isn't as cold-blooded as you make it sound. It's awful."

"It's the money, isn't it?" He said it tightly, but also angrily, an undisguised accusation.

She wasn't insulted, and she wasn't defensive. "Not really. I mean, the money's there, you can't ignore it. And it enables a lot of other stuff that makes life easier. But I have enough of my own. At first his money put me off more than it appealed to me, it distorted everything. He's spoiled; he can be like a petulant child. If money was the only thing he had going for him, the choice would be easy. But there's more. Solidity. Comfort. Security. And also…Brad as a person. What he has to offer. Experience, wisdom, seriousness. As he'd say, he's a mensch."

"And I'm not?" Her honesty was one of the things he adored. Right now, though, he would have appreciated a little less of it.

"Not in the same way, no. Which—don't get huffy—is part of *your* appeal. You're different. You're a stand-up guy, and you've got qualities Brad *doesn't* have. Qualities he doesn't even know exist. He wants to be a master of the universe, he has to dominate every room he enters. You couldn't care less. I like that. At least, I like it most of the time. You scorn the bullshit that's all around us that most people accept without noticing. It's uncanny how you and I understand each other. And also…you know…the earth moves.

But you're…there's something a little lost about you. Incomplete. Here you are, in your forties, a widower with a grown daughter, and you're still kind of *questing*. So when I draw up the balance sheet—"

"I lose?"

"It doesn't work that way, damn it!" For the first time, she revealed some agitation. "I wish it did. Everything would be simpler. I don't know what to do. I honestly don't. It's eating me up. If I lose you, I'll feel like I'm dying inside. Every day. I've been there, this isn't idle speculation. I'll wonder what you're doing, I'll try to imagine how you'd react to this or that. I'll think about you with another woman and my stomach will start to clench. And every night, in the dark, I'll think about the way you touch me."

"Well then—"

"But it won't last!" she interrupted. "It'll last a long time, I'm sure. Some vestige of it may even last a lifetime…There'll always be a pang when I hear your name, a scrunch when I remember something we did. If anything interesting happens, my impulse will be to call and tell you. I'll always wonder if I would have been happier if…if…But the really intense stuff…it'll pass. We're made that way. We recover, we go on. People have gotten over much worse catastrophes than heartbreak."

"This is chilling," he said, almost admiringly.

"I'm disciplining myself to be dispassionate. It's how I was trained to solve problems. I don't know what else to do. It's too overwhelming otherwise." She started to cry, without preparation or warning. She didn't put her hands up to her face, she made no effort to protect herself or hide what was happening. Her shoulders started to shake, she lowered her head slightly, and the tears started.

Toby held out as long as he could, all of ten seconds or so. Then he reached over for her, took her by the shoulders, pulled her to him. She wasn't resisting, but she was almost dead weight. Still, her body went where he pulled.

He murmured, "You wouldn't be crying if you picked me. You know that, right?"

She buried her head into his shoulder and wrapped her arms around him.

"Okay, here's what I think," he said. "Are you listening? You have to pay attention."

She nodded.

He hesitated, feeling like an attorney making his final summation to the jury. But it was his own life, not a client's, on the line. "Some things are too precious to weigh in a balance," he said. "They exist beyond cost-benefit. They're unique, they're incomparable. What's *Las Meninas* worth? The Taj Mahal? This is like that. This is magic. Sometimes you have to put your faith in magic. It compels a certain respect."

"They don't teach magic at Stanford."

"I'm sure."

"Listen." She looked up at him. Her eyes were red, but the tears were no longer flowing. "I hear you. And maybe…isn't there some kind of compromise? Can't we just go on the way we were? It won't be exactly the same, but…I mean, even if I move in with Brad, even if he and I get married, I can keep this house. We could get together here."

Toby felt something lurch inside himself. She might not know it herself yet, but her mind was made up. "No," he said, "that's not possible." He couldn't go on arguing. She understood what was at stake. If she decided against him, it wasn't because she failed to grasp the argument, it was because that was who she was.

"Why not?"

"Because this isn't something you bargain with." He stood up and reached for his tie and jacket. "This is…pardon my pomposity, but it's something you accept with gratitude and humility." He slipped his jacket on, overcome with an immense sense of weariness. He thought of Jonas on the night of his break-up with Brian, a burn victim before the pain set in, calmly aware of what was coming, able to describe lucidly the horror in store. Toby had no doubt this break-up would be much more devastating than the first. This time he knew what he was losing.

He slipped his tie into his pocket—the idea of putting it around his neck seemed too symbolically apposite to be borne—and started out of the room.

"Sweetie, wait."

He didn't wait. He kept walking, right out the bedroom door. Feeney was on the other side, eavesdropping. He stooped down and petted her. "'Bye, puss," he said. "I'll probably miss you too. Who would've thought?"

Feeney purred. Insensitive cunt. He kept walking, with Feeney mewing and purring underfoot. When he came to the front door, he picked Feeney up, opened the door, turned, tossed the cat back into the house as gently as he could manage, and then hurried out the door, shutting it firmly behind him.

He was beginning to feel awful. Ahead of schedule.

Behind him, the door to the house opened. He turned. Amy was standing in the doorway in her fluffy white robe, Feeney in her arms. Her eyes were redder than before. "Please, Mr. Toby," she said huskily, "I don't want things to end this way."

"How do you want them to end?"

"I don't. You know that."

"You made your choice."

"You forced me to make a choice."

A noise behind him. Toby turned around and saw a limousine at the curb. The rear door opened, and Toby was suddenly face-to-face with Brad Solomon. A moment of consternation. Then Solomon rasped, "You!" in a voice of harsh gravel. He broke the stare and noticed Amy. He blinked once, slowly. He had evidently taken in her reddened eyes and the anguish written on her face. Also her nakedness under her robe. He looked back at Toby. "Cocksucker," he said levelly.

"Don't worry about it," Toby said. "You've won."

Still not raising his voice, Solomon said, "You're dead meat, Lindeman. You're finished. You hear me?"

"Fuck you," Toby said through a thick wad of misery situated somewhere in his esophagus. He turned away and proceeded down the walkway to the street.

4

IT WOULDN'T BE ACCURATE to say most of September was a blur. In retrospect, the days might seem to have run together in a miserable undifferentiated slough, but while living through them, Toby experienced each as a distinct (and interminable) test of emotional endurance, possessing a specific, dreadful character of its own.

There was, for example, the day immediately following the day he walked out of Amy's house and out of her life. A doozy by any yardstick. He'd arrived at work late, with a monster hangover. The full complement of standard symptoms: headache, sore eyes, dry mouth, sour stomach, nausea, fatigue, stupidity. Easily his worst hangover in a decade. But the previous night he and Jonas ignored the protests their bodies were registering and didn't pace themselves at all. They'd first got roaring drunk, then maudlin drunk. Two soldiers wounded in the love wars on a bender. They had nothing new to say on the topic, but that didn't stop them from saying it, repeatedly and at length. Toby barely remembered dragging himself off to bed.

Which explains why it took him a few extra seconds to understand Doris when she called him into her office in the late morning, and announced almost immediately, with no preparation beyond commanding him to take a seat, "I want your resignation on my desk this afternoon."

He was sitting on her sofa, as instructed, and she was standing by the window, her back to him, peering down into the street below. Looking at her, which required looking into the bands of sunlight pouring through open slatted window blinds, exacerbated his headache almost intolerably. The pain came in pulsations. When she turned to face him, her hands clasped behind her back, all he could say was, "What?"

"You're being terminated. Effective immediately would be my preference. The board has been consulted and concurs. Fight it, and things'll get ugly. You'll lose. Go quietly, and we'll make it as painless as possible, at least from a financial point of view."

He understood her this time all right and was surprised to discover he had no emotional reaction. The business with Amy must have numbed him to anything else; the heart's capacity for pain apparently has an upper limit. But in some distant way, he *was* stunned. There was no warning at all, and Doris always seemed so happy with him.

"May I ask why? I've exceeded my projections every year I've been here."

"Have you read the *Castro* libretto?"

"Yes."

"Do you agree with me about it?"

"Yes."

"Brian agrees as well, or says he does. I talked to him last week. He offered to make changes. We're not going to accept…the thing's too tainted. We'll just write off the advance. He and Metcalf might be able to peddle it somewhere else. Some European house might take it. For all the wrong reasons. They'll laugh at us for being philistines. Brian and Metcalf will be seen as political martyrs or queer heroes or something. Frankly, I couldn't care less."

"But what does this have to do with firing me?"

"Brian claims you pushed them to write the libretto the way they did."

"What? That's nonsense." It was too absurd to merit a cogent refutation.

"It's what he says. He claims you told him to ruffle feathers, take risks, violate taboos, offend people, create a scandal."

"Doris! You know that's bullshit. I didn't tell him anything. Even if I said what he says I said, which I absolutely didn't, why would he pay attention? I'm just the money man."

"It's your word against his. If there's a face-off between the music director and the director of development, who do you think will come out on top?"

If it hadn't been for the hangover, he would have made the connection sooner. "This is Solomon's doing." Not a question. Nothing else made sense.

Crossing the room back toward her desk, avoiding eye contact, she said, "The point is, you're finished here. There'll be a severance package I trust you'll regard as generous. I urge you to accept it without a fuss. Best for all concerned. Clear out your desk this afternoon."

"I thought we were allies."

She was now facing him again, leaning—half-sitting—back against her desk. She regarded him for a moment. Her look was almost blank, but there was something implacable about it. "It's over, Toby."

The odd thing was, even though he was too numb to have an emotional reaction to being fired, he felt tearful. It wasn't that he was hurting, not yet. It was more that he felt singled out by fate, as if, Job-like, he was being kicked when, or because, he was down. But he pulled himself together quickly. "All right," he said. There was no point arguing. You couldn't mistake the note of finality in her voice.

He stood up. It was going to take time for this to sink in. He'd been raising money for the opera for a good long time now. It was his identity: The Money Man. He thought, I'm unemployed, I don't have a profession, and I need to find a job. It was like jabbing the back of his hand with a pin to test his susceptibility to pain. But he didn't feel much, and the words didn't carry a lot of meaning. He started for the door without uttering a word.

"Toby?" she suddenly said. He turned to face her. "Just between us? This totally stinks. You're getting shafted. But I don't have any choice. I wasn't going to say anything like that, but…Come here."

She held her open arms out to him. Without much volition, he approached and accepted her embrace. "Try to forgive me. You've been a great colleague and fun company, and I'll write you a glowing recommendation. You'll be okay. I'm going to miss the hell out of you, though."

"Okay, Doris. Thank you."

"Which isn't to suggest you've been blameless. You were playing a very risky game."

So she knew the situation. "I accept that," he said.

She kissed his cheek. "Love's a bitch. Without it, there wouldn't be many operas, and let's face it, most of the good ones are tragedies." She held him close for another moment. "I guess there's not much left to say except goodbye. Maybe we'll see each other around."

"I doubt it," he answered. "We don't really move in the same circles." And then, "Watch out for Brian. He's got you in his crosshairs. You could be next."

"I'm aware of that."

He was out of her office in seconds, out of the building in under half an hour. Daniel was away from his desk, probably having lunch, so Toby didn't get a chance to say goodbye. No great loss. They'd never established a close relationship, and in any case, he was bound to ask what had happened. The sequence of events leading to Toby's dismissal was impossible to explain without exposing the whole of his personal life.

He was confident, though, there would be a lot of gossip and speculation in local arts circles over the next few days. He found some comfort in the knowledge it would certainly be erroneous. Keep 'em guessing had always been his motto. Even in ignominious defeat.

TOBY DIDN'T START LOOKING for work right away. The severance package was generous, as Doris promised, and he had some money saved. But Cathy's tuition at Cal wasn't negligible; he'd have to find something eventually. He didn't have the stomach for it yet, though. During that miserable September, just getting out of bed in the morning and getting showered and dressed (and occasionally shaved) used up all the energy he had for any given day. Afterward, following a trail blazed by Jonas before him, he planted himself in front of the TV and watched game shows, talk shows, and an occasional movie. Sometimes he read a book or a magazine or put a CD on the stereo, although never anything operatic.

After the first week or so, he couldn't even count on Jonas's company. Jonas wasn't looking appreciably improved, he still had an aura of defeat, but he'd rallied sufficiently to find an apartment. He hadn't moved in yet, but he was there a lot, fixing it up, painting, moving furniture, trying to establish some proprietary command over his newly acquired space.

One day, when he came back to Toby's house in the early evening, he said something strange: "Don't think me callous, Tobe, but in one way your situation has done me a favor."

Toby looked up from the couch, puzzled rather than offended. "How's that?"

Jonas plopped himself down next to Toby. "Scooch over. I was at Brian's today, picking up some of my stuff. It was fairly cordial. We've reached a tacit truce. Seemed necessary, since I'm still in the orchestra."

"It's okay. You don't owe me an explanation."

"Right. I know. But anyway, he sort of casually mentioned we ought to consider giving things another shot. And I realize this makes me look like a putz, but damn it, I was tempted. A personal failing, I admit it, but what can I say, I miss him all the time. You of all people must know how that works. So I might have done it, or at least wavered, except I remembered how he got you blamed for the libretto. And I thought, 'Uh-uh, count your blessings, this guy's poison.'"

"Yes, he is. I'm not arguing." And then, "Feel like getting drunk?"

"Tempting offer, but I'm gonna say no. I'm trying to pull myself together."

"Jeez, you're no fun." But it was a useful reminder you can't wallow in misery forever. Even Jonas had figured that one out.

One afternoon a few days later, Magda called. A complete and completely unwelcome surprise. "Darling, I just phoned your office. They said you're no longer with the organization."

Toby could hear the worry in her voice. "That's right," he answered coldly.

"What happened? I was under the impression you were there for life."

"Go to hell, Magda."

She didn't waste his time claiming ignorance or innocence. "You're angry," she said.

"Angry enough not to want to talk to you."

The ensuing silence went on so long that Toby considered just hanging up. Magda broke it in the nick of time. "I suppose you have the right," she conceded.

"I suppose so too."

"Toby...what I did...when I did it, it felt mischievous rather than evil. But looking back, I don't know what I was thinking. I'm mortified at myself."

"Spare me."

Another long pause. "But your job...you don't think...?"

"Let's just say goodbye, okay? I'd really rather not hear your voice again."

"Toby, I'm so sorry—"

This time he didn't wait. He hung up mid-apology. It wasn't as satisfying as he might have hoped. Like putting a check mark by an item on a to-do list, nothing more.

She'd offered him emotional support when he'd been flailing, and now, several years later, she'd sabotaged both his job and the love of his life. Could these things be equilibrated? He felt no obligation to make the effort.

~

WITH SEPTEMBER UNDERWAY, CATHY was out of the house all week, coming home on weekends and occasional sudden mid-week whims. She loved Cal, she loved Berkeley, she loved undergraduate life. Knowing Cathy, Toby expected her to change her mind about all these things several hundred times over the next four years, but for now she was happy. Good on 'er.

Of course, Cathy knew he and Amy were kaput. He told her right away; there was no point not to, and she would have figured it out anyway. She asked him what had happened, but only once; when he answered noncommittally, she dropped it. Apparently, along with all the other adult traits she'd been displaying lately, she'd acquired tact.

He also told her about his firing, although once again he didn't go into details. "Office politics," was all he offered. "I got caught in the wrong revolving door."

"I thought you were good at office politics," she said.

"Pretty good, yeah. But sometimes even experts forget to duck."

"Are we in trouble? Mom left me money, you know. We can dip into that."

"No, honey, it's nice of you to offer, but we're okay."

"Should I be looking for a job?"

"Oh, probably," he said. "But because work is good, not because we're in financial trouble."

He was a fine one to talk, invoking the work ethic when he was lolling around the house all day.

"You all right?" she sometimes asked when she caught him staring moodily into space.

Once he answered, "Oh sure. I mean, not really. But I'll survive."

Another time, after observing Toby for a few minutes one hot Saturday afternoon, Cathy said, "I didn't realize this happens to grown-ups."

"Believe me, I'm more surprised than you."

"How long do you think you're going to be like this?"

"Hard to say," he answered.

She looked troubled. "I'm sure it's obnoxious for me to lecture you, but Toby...you do need to shake yourself out of it."

Toby nodded and switched off the television. He never knew how frank to be with his daughter, this semi-grown-up, quasi-stranger who was an integral part of his life. "The thing is, if you're forty-four years old the first time you fall head-over-heels, you worry it won't happen again until you're eighty-eight."

"It didn't happen with Mom?"

This frankness business was a slippery slope. "I loved Jessie, but, in all honesty, it wasn't like this."

"You're saying Amy Baldwin is the only woman in the world for you?"

"It felt like it." He looked away. "Still does."

"That doesn't mean it's true."

"That's what Jonas says. Or used to say. 'Love is just self-hypnosis.' But he and I are different. *He* falls in love all the time."

"It's not true for him either. He's hurting bad. But he's rallied, he's gone out and found an apartment and so on. If you had a job, at least you'd have something else to think about."

Where had she acquired this maturity? God forbid it might have come, even indirectly, from Hank. "I need a little more time, okay? I'll get there."

She nodded uncertainly.

319

He still wasn't moved to go beat the pavement, but a few days later he got a surprise call from Doris, one of several people he never expected to hear from again. "How are you, Toby?"

"Never better," he answered dully. "How's that old gang of mine?"

"You're missed, dear, I can tell you that. The job isn't half as much fun without you. But that's not why I'm calling. Listen up. Do you have a pen handy? I've been keeping my ear to the ground, and there's a position coming online at SF-MOMA. The title isn't quite as grand as the one you had here, but the salary's close and the job isn't an embarrassing climb-down. They won't be officially announcing the search for over a month, work doesn't start till the end of the year, so act fast and you can preempt the whole process. They knew your name and reputation, and I talked you up, told them you're the best, said losing you was like cutting off an arm. That got their attention. Write this name down—Peggy Letelier—" She spelled the second name for him. "And write down this number." She told him the number. "Now don't waste time, call her immediately while the conversation's fresh in her memory."

Toby's head was spinning. He didn't know how he felt about this. But he knew what the situation required. "This is awfully good of you, Doris."

He got a snorting noise in response, followed by, "Oh crap, I owe you more than a stupid job lead. You got royally buggered. But it's the best I can do, so make the call."

"Okay, Doris, thanks."

"And I want to see you sometime. I'll have Sherry call and set something up."

"Great."

"This isn't some let's-have-lunch bullshit. I mean it. Now make the call."

Peggy Letelier, the SF-MOMA director of development, was a fashionably turned-out, slender, attractive Black woman a couple of years younger than Toby. Her first gambit after they'd greeted each other and sat down was, "Okay, now tell me what *really* happened."

"Happened where? Happened when?"

"Come on, work with me here."

"At the opera, you mean?"

"Of course that's what I mean. You're the company golden boy and suddenly you're out the door? Something isn't right, I can smell it."

"You're a very suspicious person."

"There's a story there."

"Didn't you ask Doris?"

"Of course. She gave me the runaround. Blah-blah-blah politics, blah-blah-blah personality clash, blah-blah-blah bullshit bullshit."

"Sounds like she pretty much spilled the beans."

"Oh yes, it was like a session in the confessional." She grimaced. "Doris assures me you're the greatest thing to come down the pike since Saran Wrap, and I'm familiar with your reputation, people in the community have always spoken highly of you. So I have to ask myself, what's the catch? You're suddenly available. It seems too good to be true. You don't have to tell me every dirty detail, but…are you being sought for questioning by police in some other state? Have you developed psychotic symptoms? Suffered an alien abduction, say? Gotten messages from the Freemasons through the fillings in your teeth? I have a right to know."

"I'm sound in mind and body, and I don't even have any outstanding parking tickets."

She regarded him with frank curiosity, but she also seemed amused. "How about, when you've been here a year, you tell me the full story over a drunken lunch?"

"I won't promise, but the scenario you describe is well within the range of possibility. Does your question imply I have the job?"

"Not so fast." Her eyes were sparkling. She was enjoying herself. "More seriously, I'd better ask you this: You were head of the whole shebang over there. Will you have any problem being an underling? Answerable to someone with your former title?"

"No problem. I never cared about pecking order. If I had, I might still have my job. Whoops, did I let slip a hint?"

"Tease," she said. And then, "How about…look, will it be a problem for you that I'm a woman? Being under my authority, I mean?"

"I was under Doris's authority," he pointed out.

"That's true."

"Way under."

"How about that I'm younger than you, and Black, and Canadian, and a lesbian? Will any of that make a difference?"

"You're Canadian?" He waited for her smile, which arrived on cue, and then said, "Nope. We're okay."

"You know anything about art?"

"Just what any dilettante might pick up on the fly. But I'm a quick study."

"Okay, that's fine. We're not making you a curator." She clasped her hands on her desk in front of her. "Here's the deal. We need to be seen to go through a search process. Place an ad in a few venues, interview candidates. Then, barring something unexpected, we'll hire you." After telling him about compensation, less than he'd been making but not by much, she went on, "You'll begin officially in December, but it would be useful if you started hanging around before that to familiarize yourself with the place. The incumbent won't mind. Unlike some people I could mention, she's leaving on her own terms. Any objections to spending unpaid time here before you start?"

"None."

She stood up and offered her hand. "I have a feeling you'll be fun to work with."

"The feeling's mutual," he said, taking her hand and shaking it.

"In the meantime, don't do whatever it was that got you fired, okay?"

"Okay, fine," he said. "It's a sacrifice, but...no more sex with chickens."

He left the building feeling better than he had in several weeks. Having something else to think about took his mind off his misery, if only temporarily.

Of course, he wouldn't have to think about it again until the end of the year. But it was a relief to know the job was there. It was also a relief to know he had a couple of months' grace before he began. Perhaps by then the very sharpest of the pain would have begun to subside.

Except a couple of days later, he had reason to wonder whether he might in fact be down for the count. He was puttering around in the kitchen, and Cathy, Hank, and Jonas were in the living room playing three-handed hearts when the phone rang. Toby picked it up, said hello, and heard Amy's voice. "Toby?"

He caught his breath. "Amy." He kept his voice as bland as he could. It was so odd; a few weeks ago, she was the one person from whom he kept nothing, but now he was trying desperately, and probably vainly, to camouflage all trace of emotion.

"I…I wanted to say hello. And find out how you are. It's been a while, and…"

"I'm okay." He fought an urge to blurt out what Brad had done, tell her that her boyfriend had gotten him fired. There was no point. It would be like tattling.

"I miss you, Toby." Her voice was a little quavery; she sounded short of breath. "I don't want to lose touch with you."

"But the thing is, I need to lose touch with you."

"We can still—"

"No," he interrupted, "no we can't. I don't want you to call. Please don't call."

"But sweetie…"

Hearing her call him "sweetie," he almost lost it. He swallowed hard and said, "Leave me alone, Amy." He hung up abruptly, went to the kitchen table, and sat with his head in his hands until he felt able to deal with the other people in the house without humiliating himself.

The following weekend, he, Cathy, and Jonas had an early dinner in North Beach to celebrate Jonas's new apartment and Toby's new job. A subdued occasion. Cathy was sad to see Jonas go and Toby was starting to worry what it might be like, living alone again. After dinner, once they were out on the street, Jonas gave them both a warm hug, then hailed a cab and went directly to his new apartment. He'd moved the last of his stuff earlier that day. Toby and Cathy watched the car move up the street, and then hailed a passing cab of their own.

When they got back to the house, Cathy strode into the kitchen, and almost immediately came out again, a Post-It in her hand. Proffering it, she said, "Hank was here earlier. He left a note. Someone named Bradley Solomon called."

Toby started, visibly enough so that Cathy asked, "The real one? The billionaire guy?"

Waving the Post-It away, he said, "Just toss it."

"You're not going to call him back?"

"Uh-uh."

"You know what it's about?"

"No. But I don't care."

Which wasn't strictly true. It was impossible not to be curious: What could Solomon want with him now? But not curious enough to find out. He was determined not to think about Brad or Amy. Fat chance but worth a try.

He noticed Cathy was regarding him curiously. Almost suspiciously. She said, "This is weird, Daddy. A call from that guy. Could it have something to do with Amy, maybe?"

How had she figured that out? Was it the way he'd recoiled? "Probably not," he said.

"But maybe?"

"Let's drop it, okay?"

She shrugged, unhappy with him but effectively thwarted.

The next morning, after Cathy had left for Berkeley, the phone rang. Toby, sitting at the kitchen table nursing a cup of coffee, rose, crossed to the counter, and picked up the receiver on the third ring. "Hello?"

A female voice said, "I have Bradley Solomon on the line for Toby Lindeman."

"Wrong number," said Toby, and hung up.

Persistent cuss. Was he calling to gloat? Abuse and upbraid? Warn he wasn't finished yet, had only begun to exact revenge? Whatever. Toby didn't need to hear it.

When the phone rang again ten minutes later, he didn't answer. Instead, he grabbed his keys and slammed out of the house, making sure to leave his cell phone at home. It was a beautiful day, and there was a beautiful city to wander in. He'd been a shut-in for too long.

For the next several hours, mostly walking but resorting twice to public transportation, he roamed San Francisco, taking in the sights at touristy venues like Ghirardelli Square and PIER 39, checking out the shops on Clement St., stopping for a bite at Perry's on Union Street, and generally glorying in the sunny day and the fact that he was actually moving again. He finally made his maundering way home on foot, stopping en route at his neighborhood Italian delicatessen for gnocchi and pesto and at the neighborhood liquor store for a bottle of Chianti.

When he turned into his street a little after four o'clock, he was startled to see a familiar black Lincoln town car double-parked about half-way up the block, the same car that had greeted him the last time he'd left Amy's house. A few steps nearer, he was unsurprised to recognize Solomon leaning back against the rear of the car, his glen plaid suit jacket open, his red tie gleaming, his hands in his pockets. A compact hand grenade of a man. Toby braced himself, and approached with a firm tread.

"I'm guessing this isn't just a bizarre coincidence," he said when he'd reached him.

Solomon looked Toby up and down and produced the ghost of a smile. "Well," he said. And then, "Hop into the car, let's take a ride."

"Is this where you drive me to Fort Miley and break my legs? Or dump my body somewhere where it'll never be found?"

"Don't be a child. Get in the car."

"I don't think so."

Solomon laughed. "You really think I'm here to offer violence?"

"I have no idea. I know you're a mean and spiteful person and there aren't many practical restrictions on you."

The words had an effect. It wasn't dramatic, but something combative, something feisty, seemed to disappear from Solomon's stance. "All right," he said quietly, as if conceding that a fierce crosscourt volley had landed inside the baseline. Followed by, "How about we just take a little walk? Around the block. In full view of passersby."

Seemed safe enough. Toby shrugged.

"I'd appreciate it," Brad said. "Please."

Shrugging again—he hoped it looked as rude as it felt—Toby, bag of purchases in hand, began walking up the street. Brad fell into step beside him. After they'd gone a few paces, Toby noticed that the Lincoln was following half a length behind.

"So," Brad said. Although he was glancing in Toby's general direction, he wasn't meeting his eye. "Your job. I see you're pissed. Did you figure it out for yourself, or did Doris tell you?"

Toby stopped walking. "We bump into each other at Amy's and a day later I'm fired for transparently bullshit reasons? I didn't need Doris to bone that particular fish."

"Yeah. Well. It wasn't like you weren't supposed to figure it out."

"Message received. Is that what you wanted to know? You could have sent an email, saved yourself a trek."

Toby turned away and resumed walking, and Solomon double-timed to catch up, matching his pace again. "Okay, look, I got pretty hot under the collar back there. I'm a guy, you know what we're like. But I've had a few weeks to cool off. I admit I was being vindictive. It was mainly an ego thing. What did I gain by punishing you? I was just lashing out."

"Is this an apology?"

Solomon didn't answer. After a moment, he demanded, "Was it about me? Is that why you were banging her? To get at me? Or get *back* at me, for some injury you felt I'd done you?"

Toby regarded Solomon incredulously. "No, Brad, sorry, but it had nothing to do with you at all except you happened to be in the way. It was about Amy, solely and completely. You were never more than an inconvenience."

"Yeah, okay. It's just…"

"I know. You've got a resentful son. Well, I'm not him."

Solomon snorted. It was another concession. Then he said, "You want your job back?"

Toby was too startled to answer. Of course this was within Brad's power to offer. How had he gotten Toby fired in the first place? Presumably by telling Doris that was the price for keeping his contribution, which he had every right, after the *Castro* debacle, to demand back. And maybe by suggesting he could persuade some of his friends to withhold their contributions, or, alternately, increase them, depending on how Doris proceeded. He'd have the same leverage if he wanted Toby reinstated. No biggie.

"Well, do you?" Solomon pressed.

"I don't know," Toby said. Followed almost immediately by, "I've lined up something else." He was thinking, I never want to feel beholden to Brad Solomon in any way. And, I never want to work in the same organization as Brian Hughes. But also, God, it would be fun to see Brian's face the day I showed up for work.

"Already?"

Toby didn't even consider mentioning Doris's role. He didn't trust Solomon's change of heart and didn't want to compromise her. "The fates were kind."

"You're a lucky guy, Lindeman."

"That's me all right."

Solomon cleared his throat. "There's a third possibility, of course. You never gave me a definitive answer about joining my outfit."

For the second time within two or three minutes, Toby stopped dead in his tracks. When Solomon stopped too, Toby turned on him. "Are you actually out of your mind? Is that what's going on here? Did you forget to take your Clozapine?"

"Don't be hasty."

"Hasty? I'd live in the desert and subsist on locusts and honey before I'd work for you. Christ. What do you take me for?"

"The kind of guy who'd say something like that to me. It's one of the reasons I'd like to have you on my team."

"*Your team*? You want me on *your team*?" Toby rolled his eyes, even though it made him feel like Cathy. "No, Brad, 'fraid I'm not going to join *your team*. You know, I never thought I'd have a chance to say this a second time, but my ship must have come in: *Fuck you*."

Solomon laughed. "I've gotta say, for a charming guy you have a bit of an attitude problem."

"Get off my street."

"We're not on your street anymore," Solomon pointed out. They had in fact turned the corner. The Lincoln had come to a halt beside them. "Just get into the car, okay? You must realize by now I'm not here to abduct you."

Solomon reached over, opened the car's rear door, and waved Toby in. Toby shrugged, placed his bag of pasta, pesto, and wine onto the center of the seat, and then climbed in himself. Solomon followed. A second after they were seated, the car pulled out into the street.

"Circle the block," Solomon told the driver, and then closed the partition separating the rear seat from the front. Turning to Toby, he said, "See? Air-conditioned comfort. Leather upholstery, rosewood paneling. Just a hint of what could be yours if you worked for me."

"Shove it."

"Would you like a drink?"

"Sure."

"You're a bourbon drinker, right?"

"Usually."

"Maker's Mark okay?"

"Good enough."

Solomon reached forward and opened the bar. There were crystal glasses, assorted bottles of spirits, and an ice bucket. "Just help yourself," Solomon said.

While Toby was pouring, Solomon continued, "So let me sum up what's occurred so far, insofar as I understand it. You don't want to return to the opera even if I get you your old job back, and you won't accept a position with Solomon Enterprises. Is that correct?"

Toby took a sip of bourbon—it was just what the doctor ordered—and said, "Why are you here, Brad? What's this about? Seriously. You want me not to hate you, is that it? 'Cause if it is, what do you care? There must be thousands of people in this town who hate you. Tens of thousands. Most of the people who ever met you. What's one more or less?"

"Aw, cut me some slack, kid. I'm cutting *you* slack, and you were shtupping my girl."

"But that wasn't aimed at you," Toby said.

"But it wasn't a problem for you."

"No, that's true, it wasn't. Except, like I said, you were an impediment. I was in love with her."

Solomon nodded. Then, a moment later, he said, "'*Was*?'"

"The verb tense I choose is none of your damned business."

Solomon laughed again. After a few seconds, he said, "I'm not your enemy, Toby."

"When somebody goes out of his way to get me fired, he isn't my friend." Toby put his glass down on the little ledge by his seat. "What is this really? Remorse? Too bad. I don't forgive you. Okay? *I do not forgive you.* You're a bully, and you have too much money. And you're a fucking sore winner. There's nothing lower. So stop the car, and I'll get out and that'll be that. I can't believe you care, but regardless, I don't give a flying fuck about your fucking remorse."

"No? What if it's *buyer's* remorse?" Solomon leaned back against the leather upholstery and met Toby's eye. "Just listen, okay? Just shut up for a change and listen to me. The Baldwin gal...Amy..." He sighed deeply, turned to look out the window, and started over. "Let me tell you how I do business. I thought I had a deal in LA. Been working on it for months. Huge piece of real estate. Gazillion square feet of office space. Hundreds of units. Downtown location. I invested a lot of time negotiating. Hand-to-hand combat. We reached an agreement, a good deal for all concerned. But lately I'm getting hints the other side ain't happy, thinks I've suckered 'em in some way. So you know what I plan to do?"

He waited for Toby to answer. Toby, perplexed, shook his head. "Walk away, that's what. Eat the costs and take a powder. I'm pissed, but sticking around with people who think they're getting screwed won't do anybody any good. They'd find a way to take it out on me somehow. Life's too short for that shit. If somebody signs a contract and then starts to have second thoughts...if it happens before things have gone too far, I do not enforce the goddamn contract. I don't give a shit what my lawyers say. Doing business with unhappy people is a mug's game, everybody loses in the end. You see what I'm saying?"

"I don't have a clue."

Solomon reached for his mobile phone. "The kid's miserable, that's what I'm saying. She cries. Not when I'm there. When she thinks I don't see. And this is not a girl who cries. Plus, she says snotty things to me all the time for no reason. She can't stand for me to touch her." He jabbed a speed dial button. "We've been waiting to be together for, I don't know, ten years? More. And maybe it just took too damned long, the moment's passed. Or maybe you're the reason; it's just she fell for you. I don't have a clue. Life's a fucking mystery, that's all I know."

Toby felt a prickling in his scalp behind his ears. "What are you saying?"

"You deaf? *She can't stand for me to touch her!* I reach over, I can practically see her flesh crawl. Know what that's like? Ever been in that situation?" He shook his head. "Ruins everything. She must think she's obligated. You know, after all those years. Especially with me being a widower. Like she's fulfilling some onerous duty. Ruining her life 'cause of a promise. Sure, she cheated on me once before, but there was something kind of bratty about that episode, like she was trying to get my goat. This is different. Oh, wait."

While Toby was considering the pluses and minuses of informing Solomon there had been more than one cheating episode—and regretfully concluded the minuses outweighed the pluses—Solomon leaned away from him and muttered into his cell phone, "Hold on a sec."

He put his large, hairy hand over the mouthpiece and turned back to Toby. "I may be a bully with too much money, like you say, but being with Amy under these circumstances, it's no fun. I feel like her jailer. Who needs that? It's like that building in LA. Only worse. I don't care if the *building's* happy. So we had a long talk, me and her, and…well, she started bawling, and she couldn't stop, she couldn't even talk, and Jesus Christ there's nothing worse…I don't mind a good fight, but when they start crying like that, you can't even get mad, it's game, set, and match. And then she said—between sobs—she said you told her to never call you again, which I have to say was pretty shitty of you…and then she cried some more…So I don't know, Toby…like Moses Maimonides says, you gotta know when to fold 'em."

He held up a finger, to indicate he was shifting his attention away from Toby for a moment, and spoke into the phone. "You still there, baby? No, I'm in the car. He's here. Hold on." Solomon swiveled toward Toby and proffered the phone. "Here you go, pal," he said. "Take it. It's for you."

Acknowledgments

WITH SINCERE THANKS TO Mimi Haas, Susan Braddock, Pamela Rosenberg, Christopher Hest, Jake Heggie, and the late Lotfi Mansouri for their insights into arts fundraising generally and opera development in particular. While in some cases, acceding to its own narrative requirements, this novel has included situations that contradict what these knowledgeable guides told me—they bear no responsibility for such deviations—their advice and experience were never less than indispensable.